"Would you mind if I kissed you?"

Hutch leaned in slightly, testing her intent, but giving her enough room to skitter away in case she had second thoughts.

"Don't hold back," she said, reading his mind. "I'm not a doll. I'm a real live woman."

Yes you are.

"I want to be kissed by a good man with a kind heart."

Oh baby, why did you have to say that? I'm pretty damn far from good.

Her pupils widened, darkened to midnight blue, the color of misty twilight. Tentatively, he dipped his head, kept his eyes trained on those beautiful lips.

He stopped, waited for her to make the first move.

"I changed my mind," she said.

That's okay, that's okay. His muscles were corded so tight a cannon-ball would have bounced off them. Delta Force operators were nothing if not highly controlled.

"I want you to kiss me."

By Lori Wilde

Available from Avon Impulse

*Now available in print as

*This book is dedicated to my sister-in-law,
Melanie Derrick Blalock. You've been through so
much darkness, but you've managed to come out of it
as a bright and shining light. You are an inspiration.*

ACKNOWLEDGMENTS

A personal crisis led me to the writing of this book. Like many of us, I have lived with, and loved, family members afflicted with mental illness. Psychological disorders take a terrible toll on the sufferers, their families, friends, neighbors, coworkers and society at large. The emotional pain is often unbearable, and the sufferers feel helpless, alone or discarded and don't know how to reach out for help. The effects of untreated mental health issues ripple throughout families for generations. There's such a stigma attached to mental illness that people are often reluctant to talk about it, or admit that they, or someone they love, needs help.

According to the National Alliance on Mental Illness one in four Americans suffer symptoms of mental illness in a given year and one in seventeen lives with a serious mental illness such as schizophrenia, major depression or bipolar disorder. Suicide is the tenth leading cause of death in the US, more common than homicide, and it's the third leading cause of death for those aged 15-24. More than 90% of people who commit suicide had one or more mental disorders. Alarmingly, although military members comprise less than 1% of the US population, veterans represent 20% of suicides nationally. Each day about twenty-two veterans die from suicide.

But there is hope. Treatments have improved drastically, resources exist, and early intervention is key. If you or someone you love is struggling with mental or emotional issues, start with visiting the National Alliance on Mental Illness www.nami.org/.

I owe a debt of gratitude to Dr. Brandi Buckner PhD LPCS, who showed me that I needed to heal myself first before I could help others. She guided me in understanding bipolar and borderline personality disorders, gave me books to read, and enlightened me about emotional self-care.

And to Sandra Vanatko, owner of the yoga studio Indra's Grace, who is teaching me how to live mindfully in the moment, let go of attachment with love, and find peace and balance in a chaotic world.

Chapter 1

Walter Reed National Military Medical Center,
Bethesda, Maryland
November 22

Delta Force Operator Captain Brian "Hutch" Hutchinson hated group therapy almost as much as he hated the mind-warping meds.

He slumped in the hard wooden folding chair that was part of a circle of ragtag military burnouts, watched the clock over the door, and counted off the seconds until this charade was over. His legs, encased in desert camo fatigues, were sprawled out in front of him. Muscular arms, crisscrossed with scars, lay clamped across his chest, a don't-fucking-look-at-me scowl digging a trench between his eyebrows. All the damn benzos they pumped into him left the inside of his head feeling as jagged as glass shards, and conversely as foggy as a hot breath on an icy winter morning.

You sure it's the benzos and not brain damage?

To keep from thinking about that too much, Hutch studied the olive drab wall behind a legless GI in a wheelchair who was detailing his fantasies of eating a bullet.

Someone had taken a pathetic stab at decorating for the holiday. A cardboard rendition of a live turkey had been taped to the wall along with a cherubic boy in a Pilgrim costume carrying a big black musket. Brightly colored leaves, gathered from the hospital grounds had been stuck underneath the cartoon boy's feet, strung out like a path, leading him right to his target. The opposite wall depicted a Thanksgiving feast, complete with a golden roasted bird, foretelling what was in store for the hapless turkey.

The room fell silent. The legless GI had stopped talking, his eyes filled with so much damn pain that Hutch felt it in his own gut.

"We all understand what you're going through," said the group leader, Major Jenner, a skinny-assed psychologist with a bad comb-over.

Hutch tightened his arms and snorted. Jenner had never been within sniffing distance of a battlefield. He knew shit about life. Or death.

The major pivoted to face him.

Aw, hell. Why had he snorted? So far, he'd managed to stay off the shrink's radar.

"Captain Hutchinson, you've been here for three weeks and you've yet to share in group. It's time."

What the hell? Hutch glowered and slapped the raw scar at the base of his throat.

Jenner dipped his head, and shot Hutch a this-is-for-your-own-good glance over the top of his glasses. "Yes, yes, you suffered an injury to your throat, but have you even tried to speak?"

What did the son of a bitch think he did all day when he wasn't stuck in this claustrophobic room with five other guys just as screwed up as he was?

Anger flashed through him, hot and quick. He bolted upright in the chair, and clenched his hands into fists against his thighs. Once upon a time he'd been the easiest going operator on his team. Always ready with a smile. A cracker of jokes. More friends than he could count. He'd been the one to break up fights, calm hotheads, smooth choppy waters. The skill had earned him the moniker Igloo in a group that was already known for their cool heads, because he was so unflappable.

But those days were gone.

Just like everything else.

He stared down at his left hand that was missing the index finger. A lost finger, a damaged trachea, a pinch of PTSD. He was lucky, damn lucky, and he knew it. All he had to do was look across at the legless GI for confirmation. He'd made it back, relatively in one piece. Not so the rest of his squad.

Lone survivor.

He'd never understood before how truly terrible those two words were. The names of his lost team members were indelibly etched into his brain—Joe Prince, Lincoln Johnson, Rick Gutierrez, Kwan Lee, and Michael Keller. Known affectionately in The Unit as Razor, Axe, Hurricane, Wolf, Killer. To think he would never see them again whittled his insides to shavings.

Deciding to take the high road, Hutch picked up the

Magic Slate that his speech therapist had given him. It was a peel-back, dry-erase drawing board most commonly found in children's Christmas stockings back in the sixties and seventies. The speech therapist insisted he use it to strengthen hand-eye-brain coordination through old-fashioned handwriting as opposed to using modern technology to communicate in face-to-face conversations.

Feeling like a jackass using a kid's toy, he grasped the red plastic stylus attached to the drawing board with a string, wrote F-OFF, and held it up for Jenner to see.

"Ah, anger, the most vocal stage of grief. See, even without your voice you can still express yourself. You're making progress, Captain Hutchinson."

Hutch added X'S 2 to the F-OFF.

"I realize you've been through great emotional trauma." Jenner spoke slowly, deliberately, as if Hutch was stupid instead of simply incapable of speech. "But it's time. You need to speak."

Hutch narrowed his eyes, shook his head.

"I know it's not easy, but you're Special Forces. This is nothing compared to what you've faced in training, and on the battlefield, not to mention the troubled past that drove you to the army in the first place."

The blood in Hutch's body chilled, slowed. Why was the bastard talking about his childhood?

Jenner smiled as if he wasn't courting a fist to the face. "A mother with a personality disorder. She kept a revolving door of men coming and going through her life that threatened you and your little sister too. You've fought a lot. Fought hard. Fight this."

Hutch's anger flared from vibrant red to gas-flame blue. His mother had been no saint, but she'd done the best she could, and she'd loved him the only way she knew how. He hadn't doubted her love for a second, not even when she'd screamed that she hated him. Where did this jerkwad get off badmouthing his mother?

"You want to tell me off, don't you?" Jenner taunted. "Do it then."

The psychologist was baiting him, trying to provoke a reaction. Hutch wasn't going to give him the satisfaction. Difficult as it was, he uncurled his fists and hauled in a deep breath all the way to the bottom of his lungs.

Held it.

"Bravery is feeling the fear and doing it anyway, right?" Jenner's tone softened.

Everyone in the room was watching them, bodies tuned for hair-trigger response, nerves tensed, waiting for an explosion.

Hutch exhaled, felt his muscles loosen, but his anger darkened, lingered, smelled of brimstone.

"Speak," Jenner commanded, as if it were just that easy.

Hutch's throat spasmed the same way it did every time the speech therapists worked with him. He clenched his teeth to keep from wincing. No one seemed to get it. He *could not* speak. His trachea was too damaged.

Apparently, they'd all decided he wasn't talking because he didn't want to speak. More than anything in the world, he wanted to get his voice back so he could visit the families of the men who'd fought beside him. Face them. Tell them how brave their sons and fathers, brothers and uncles had been. How much heart, will, and iron control they possessed.

The pilgrimage would be filled with unthinkable pain both for him and for the families, but his pain did not matter. Hutch knew the families could never really begin the healing process until he made that journey. It was his sworn duty.

But right now, he wanted his voice back so he could yell, rant, curse God, tell everyone to go to hell. A soldier couldn't debrief without talking. Everything he'd experienced out there in that goddamn Afghan desert was still locked down deep inside him. Without a voice to shout, how did a man resolve his pain?

The five other members of the support group—the exact same number of soldiers who'd lost their lives because of Hutch—stared at him, waiting for him to speak. He could see it in their faces. They were aligned with Jenner.

He was as alone as when he staggered down the streets of Aliabad, unaware that he'd even been hit, but vaguely realizing his helmet was gone because the relentless sun burned his scalp. The bodies of his team were strewn around him—dead, dying, screaming in agony, calling his name, begging for his help.

Talking.

He'd been talking when they were ambushed. Trying to lighten the dark mood after the top Al-Qaida operative they'd been sent to extract from Abas Ghar turned out to be long gone. He'd been running his mouth about something stupid. Who was hotter, Olivia Wilde or Emma Stone?

Poetic justice that a piece of shrapnel lodged in his throat during the ambush, silencing him forever. Muteness was his cross to bear. His life sentence. He could not speak. He didn't deserve to speak.

Jenner advanced, claiming ground until he stood directly in front of Hutch. "Tell me about your mother."

Fury was a noose, strangling him. Hutch knotted his fists, shot to his feet. The folding chair collapsed backward behind him. The smack of impact vibrated the air.

Instantly, the soldiers reacted. Leaping to their feet, going for guns they did not have, ready to battle unseen enemies. Even the legless GI, who apparently had forgotten he had no legs, was now on the floor cussing a blue streak.

Hutch moved to help the guy back into his chair, but he got off only one step.

Jenner nodded at the two soldiers who had been sitting on either side of Hutch, and they took him to the ground.

He had violated Cardinal Rule #1 in dealing with a roomful of PTSD sufferers. *No loud sudden noises.* He lay there struggling to breathe against a GI's knee jammed into his lungs, and a hammy palm pressing his face into the concrete floor, getting a whiff of Jenner's boots that smelled of dog turd.

Yep, he fucking hated group therapy.

Hot Legs Spa, Twilight, Texas
December 1

The spice aroma of gingerbread scented the darkened massage room with holiday memories. The single source of illumination came from the flame of a tea light candle in a pumpkin-pie-colored holder, squatting atop a black lacquer shelf. It flicked light blue at the core, cupped by a dancing white-yellow that lowered to deep orange-red at the base. Lulling spa music slipped softly through sound system speakers, a solo flute holding a long, mournful note. The silky feel of warm oil heated bare skin.

Normally, masseuse Meredith Sommers immersed herself in movement, focusing on making her clients feel better, and in turn that practice created a Zen-like calmness inside her.

But not today.

Today, she could not quell the inner voice that whispered, *Something's wrong.*

She'd learned not to ignore that voice. Over the course of the last five years, it had saved her life more than once.

This time, however, it wasn't her own well-being she was worried about, but rather that of her landlady and housemate, Ashley Hutchinson. Last night, Ashley had gone on a date with a new man, leaving Meredith to watch Ashley's four-year-old daughter, Kimmie. Meredith hadn't minded a bit. She adored the little girl, who was the same age as her son, Ben.

"Don't wait up," Ashley had said as she headed out the door. "If everything goes well, no telling when I'll be home." Then she gave a big wink and took off.

Meredith hadn't known what to make of that. It wasn't her place to tell Ashley how to live her life, but the thought that her roommate was planning on having sex on the first date with a man she barely knew didn't sit right. She understood why Ashley was meeting her date at a club in Fort Worth—until you knew you could trust a man, you didn't want him anywhere near your home and your child—but Meredith wished she could have met the guy first, sized him up, and gotten a read on him.

And do what? Warn Ashley off if her gut told her

the guy was no good? Ashley was a grown woman. She was allowed to make her own mistakes.

Still, Meredith couldn't help wishing that someone had warned her five years ago before she'd—

That was all water under the bridge, wasn't it? No changing the past. And besides, no matter how horrific the last few years had been, if she hadn't lived the life she'd lived, she wouldn't have her son, Ben.

And he was worth any price.

This morning, when Ashley's car was not in the driveway and her bed had not been slept in, Meredith told herself not to worry. Apparently, her housemate had made a love connection and spent the night with her date. Meredith got Kimmie ready for preschool right along with Ben, and made excuses to the child for her mother's absence. She hoped Ashley was not going to make a habit of overnight, out-of-town trysts.

Meredith had been living on the second floor of Ashley's house for the last six weeks, and so far the arrangement was working out great, but if Ashley was one of those single mothers who neglected her kid once she had a man in her life, Meredith wouldn't sit still for that. She would have to move again, no matter how broke she was.

Before coming to work, she'd texted Ashley, asking when she could expect her home. So far, she hadn't heard back from her housemate and it was almost noon.

"Jane?" said Raylene Pringle, the older woman on her massage table. Someone had told her that Raylene used to be a former Dallas Cowboys cheerleader, but even if she hadn't known, Meredith could tell from the woman's muscle tone that she'd been athletic most of her life.

"Jane?"

"Yes?" Meredith blinked. Oh no, in her worry over Ashley, she'd forgotten her latest alias.

"I've called your name three times. Are you all right?"

"I'm sorry, I must have been woolgathering."

"So I assumed. You keep rubbing the same spot on my calf."

"I do apologize."

"Don't worry," Raylene said. "Happens to the best of us. That reminds me of a dog I once owned. Her name was Elspeth and we got her from the pound. She was part Australian shepherd, and she was the prettiest color of silver-blue you've ever seen. Her original owner was going into an assisted living facility and had to give her up."

"That's must have been hard for the owner."

"I tried to rename her Tequila, seeing as how Earl and I still owned the Horny Toad Tavern at the time. But that dog would have none of it. I'd call her by the new name, but she flat-out refused to come. It got to where it was a joke around the neighborhood. 'There's Raylene hollering for tequila. Somebody give Ray some tequila.' Finally, I just gave up and went back to calling her Elspeth."

"Please lie on your back now, Mrs. Pringle, and scoot down off the headrest," Meredith said as she raised the sheet and glanced away to give Raylene privacy while she turned over.

Raylene scooted down, and Meredith brought her rolling stool to the head of the massage table and sat down to massage the older woman's scalp.

"You have such gentle hands." Raylene closed her eyes.

"Thank you."

Raylene opened one eye, peered up at her. "You really don't look like a Jane to me."

For one panicked moment, Meredith thought, *She suspects!* Her lungs tightened and her pulse quickened and her skin prickled. *Calm down. Breathe deep. How could Mrs. Pringle know?* "What do I look like?"

"Jane is such a girl-next-door name. You know tomboyish, freckles, jeans and T-shirt, chatty, cute as a bug, like your neighbor Flynn Calloway. You on the other hand…" Raylene paused. "You've got a regal air about you. Quiet. Reserved. Those high cheekbones and that alabaster skin. You need a name that fits. Cassandra or Alexandria or—"

"Cleopatra?"

Raylene lifted a hand from underneath the covers, and pointed a finger at Meredith. "You've got a wry sense of humor too."

"Janes don't have wry senses of humor?"

"Hell, no. Janes lean toward self-deprecating humor."

"What kind of humor do Raylenes have?"

"Why, bawdy of course." Raylene chuckled.

"You've given the topic of names and humor a lot of thought. I had no idea the topic was so complex," she teased.

"It's something to do with the time while I'm lying here with nothing to do."

"You're supposed to be relaxing."

"Easy to say, hard to do. I only started getting massages because my cardiologist suggested it."

"Breathe deep and just let go." Meredith's pulse slowed. Raylene was just making small talk because Meredith hadn't answered when she called to her. But she was going to have to be more careful. Jane. Jane. Her name was Jane.

A few minutes later, Meredith completed the massage. "I'll let you get dressed now. Come out when you're ready."

She stepped into the hallway, pulled her cell phone from her pocket, took it off airplane mode, and waited for the server to update to see if Ashley had texted or tried to call her while she was in the massage room.

Nothing.

Her heart dropped into her stomach, heavy as an iron anchor. She thumbed a text to her housemate. U OK?

Raylene came out of the massage room and Meredith handed her a bottle of chilled water. "Be sure to drink lots of water to flush out your system."

"Thanks, sweetie." Raylene leaned over to tuck a hundred-dollar bill into the pocket of Meredith's uniform. "You have a merry Christmas."

"Wait, wait, Mrs. Pringle, this is too much," Meredith protested, and fished the bill from her pocket. *Shut up and take it. You can get Ben's presents out of layaway with this.*

Raylene folded her hand around Meredith's. "Accept it, please. I know what it's like to be broke at Christmas."

"You?" It was Meredith's understanding that Raylene and Earl Pringle were among the richest people in Twilight.

"Honey, I was raised on the wrong side of the tracks. It wasn't until Earl's family struck oil on their land that we had a pot to piss in. Go on. Take it."

"What makes you think I need the money?"

"You're a single mom renting a room from Ashley

Hutchinson. 'Nuff said. Now let's not hear any more about it."

Meredith straightened. "While I do appreciate the gesture, please donate the money to the Christmas Angel charity that you're a part of. Plenty of people need this money much more than I do. In fact, hold on a minute."

She darted into the employees' lounge, got her purse from her locker, and opened the worn brown wallet to find a twenty-dollar bill and sixteen ones. She gulped. She never kept a bank account—not since, well, never mind that—and this was all the money she had. But there had been times when she didn't have a quarter to her name, and Friday was payday. She had groceries in the house, gas in the minivan, and probably six or seven dollars' worth of coins on top of her dresser. She'd get by. Not so the mothers of children whose names were on the Angel Tree.

Resolutely, she plucked the twenty from her wallet and took it back to Mrs. Pringle. "Here, please add this to the fund."

Raylene wrinkled her forehead. "Are you sure?"

"Absolutely. I just wish I had more money to give."

"That's so kind of you." Raylene touched Meredith's shoulder and looked at her with a mixture of sympathy and you-got-guts-girl admiration. "Are you planning on coming to our annual Christmas cookie swap this Friday evening? We'd love to have you join us. The party is at my house. I'll e-mail you directions."

Raylene was the fifth person to invite her to the party. She couldn't go. That meant money for cookie ingredients and a babysitter for Ben. "Thank you for the invitation, but I'm a bit of a homebody."

"The Christmas cookie swap has only five rules," Raylene said in a cajoling tone.

"I wasn't aware cookie swaps had rules."

"Oh yes. No men. No kids. No store-bought. No chocolate chip. And no gossip."

"Why no chocolate chip? Aren't they everyone's favorite?"

"The rule exists precisely because they are everyone's favorite. The upstagers. Christmas is the time for other cookies to get their due."

"I see."

"Don't be alarmed by the rules. Someone always breaks the no gossip rule, usually it's me." She gave a saucy wink. The woman was a firecracker. "Ye Olde Book Nook holds a pajama party for the kids during our cookie swap. They serve cookies and hot chocolate and read Christmas stories aloud. Your boy would have a ball."

"We'll see."

"You need to get out more," Raylene urged. "You'll love Twilight once you get to know everyone. We're an easy bunch to fall for."

Truth was, Meredith already loved the quaint little lakeside community she'd had the good fortune to land in when her minivan broke down on the outskirts of town the week before Halloween. With its interesting boutiques, great restaurants, colorful local history, and quirky townsfolk, if she allowed herself, this place could so easily feel like home.

But she couldn't do that. She would never have a permanent home. Not as long as—

The ringing of her cell phone cut off that thought.

"I'll let you take your call," Raylene said as she

headed toward the reception area. "But please come to the party. It won't be the same without you."

Meredith lifted a hand in good-bye and immediately glanced at her phone's caller ID. Ashley. Thank God. Relief thrust her breath from her lungs in a long sigh and she leaned one shoulder against the wall to help hold her up.

"Where are you?" she asked. "Are you all right?"

"Oh Jane! I am so much more than all right!" Ashley exclaimed. "I've been swept off my feet."

The hairs on Meredith's arms raised, an internal alarm system backing up the sick feeling in her gut. "That's not a good sign. It sounds good, it sounds romantic, but when it comes to men, you need to keep your feet firmly planted on the ground. No sweeping allowed. Do not be swept."

"Pfft. don't be such a spoilsport."

"Listen to me on this," Meredith cautioned, her throat constricting around the words. "You can't trust what you're feeling right now. It's lust and hormones, nothing more."

"Is that what happened with you and Ben's father?"

A cold chill blew through Meredith's body like February wind across the Siberian tundra. She tightened her grip on the phone. Ashley's warm, airy laugh was in sharp contrast to the polar ice cap of fear freezing her bones.

"Yes," she said. "Ben's father swept me off my feet and it ended badly. Come home. We'll talk it through."

"Don't worry, I'm not you and Eric isn't your exhusband."

"You're idealizing the guy."

"And you sound jealous." Ashley voice turned petulant.

"I'm not jealous, honest—"

"Then be happy for me. I've found my Prince Charming. He's headed to Acapulco on a business trip and he's taking me with him."

"When?"

"Right now."

"What?"

"We're at DFW Airport about to board the plane."

"You barely know this man!"

"One look in his eyes and I knew everything there was to know. He's my soul mate."

"Ashley, do not get on that plane!"

Another masseuse, who was passing in the hallway, paused. "Is everything okay, Jane?"

Meredith forced a smile, mouthed, *Fine.*

"After last night, I know him better than you might imagine." Ashley's chuckle turned sultry. "Anyway, could you please watch Kimmie until I get back? I'll pay you, of course. I know you need the money."

"No, I won't enable you—"

"Thanks so much," Ashley said breathlessly. "You're the best."

Clearly, scolding her housemate wasn't going to work. "Wait, wait. Don't hang up. When will you be back?"

"I'm not sure."

"Before Christmas?"

"Oh sure. I wouldn't miss Christmas for the world."

"Where will you be staying?"

"A private villa owned by Eric's company."

"What company is that?"

"How would I know?"

"Ashley—" Meredith was about to scold her again, but stopped. She'd learned in counseling that you couldn't control what other people did. But knowing something intellectually and accepting it emotionally were two different things.

On Ashley's end, a feminine voice announced the boarding of an American Airlines flight to Acapulco, interrupting their conversation.

"I gotta go. Tell Kimmie Mommy loves her bunches."

"Please don't do this."

"You worry too much, Jane. You've got to trust your instincts more."

"My instincts are what's telling that this is a terrible idea."

"I'll try to call you when I get there, but Eric says the cell reception is really spotty."

"Stop and think. What if this guy is a serial killer?"

"You watch too many movies. I'm fine. Eric is fabulous. The best lover, so kind and attentive and utterly charming."

"Sociopaths *are* utterly charming. That's how they lure you in, and then once you're caught they show their true colors."

"You really do have some serious trust issues, Jane. Chill out. Everything is going to be just fine."

"But what if it's not and you never come home? What will happen to Kimmie?" Meredith asked.

"I'll be fine, but just to indulge you Miss Worrywart, if something happens to me, my brother will take care of Kimmie."

Disoriented by this information, Meredith shook her

head. "You have a brother? You never told me you had a brother."

"We don't get along. He's too bossy, but he loves Kimmie more than anything else in the world."

"What's his name? Where is he? How do I contact him?"

"Oops, final boarding call. I really do have to go now."

"Don't get on that plane!" Meredith beseeched.

But Ashley had already hung up.

Chapter 2

Three of them came at him at once.

Hutch's surgeon, Dr. Yani Gupta; his squadron commander, Colonel John Finetti; and the shrink, Major Thomas Jenner. Hutch had just returned to his room on the rehab wing, following an intensive round of speech therapy, when a knock sounded on the door and the three men scudded in.

The second Hutch saw the men, he knew something serious was afoot. This wasn't a social call. He stood up, put steel into his spine.

"Take your seat, Captain." Colonel Finetti waved at the chair Hutch had just vacated. Finetti was a hatchet-faced Iowan, and everything about him was sharp—

his tone of voice, his oversized nose, his elbows, and the pointy incisors that caused the guys in The Unit to dub him Colculetti (a creative morphing of "colonel,"

"Dracula," and his real name) behind his back. From just looking at the man, no one would suspect he was a damn good dad to six kids, raised labradoodles, and home-canned the heirloom tomatoes he raised in his backyard garden.

Hutch shook his head.

The three men exchanged glances.

There were three chairs in the room and four men, but there was an empty bed as well; Hutch's roommate had been dismissed that morning.

"This will be easier if we're sitting down," Finetti said.

Easier for whom? Aw shit, this was gonna be bad. Hutch tried for a smile, but it fell off his face, broke.

Dr. Gupta and Colonel Finetti sat on the chairs while Jenner perched on the foot of the vacant bed. Hutch kept standing.

"Please." Gupta waved him down into the remaining seat like he was one of Finetti's rambunctious labradoodles. Gupta was a brilliant surgeon with a forehead like a mad scientist, oversized and shiny. He wore break-apart magnetic-clip reading glasses around his neck, and he had a purple stethoscope sticking from the pocket of his white lab coat.

Warily, Hutch joined the other men, sinking down into the drab gray chair positioned beside his bunk, muscles coiled tight, ready to spring up at the first hint of trouble. He didn't like being ganged up on.

No one said anything.

Gupta met Hutch's challenging stare. Finetti was actively avoiding looking at him.

And Jenner? That asshole was smiling.

Normally, Hutch wasn't a contentious guy. He started off assuming everyone deserved his respect until they proved otherwise. Not only had Jenner proven otherwise, but ever since the ambush, Hutch had not been himself. Resistance had become his default mode. He didn't like it, but there it was. Negative personality change. Ugly aftermath of war.

Gupta tugged at a fleshy earlobe.

Uneasiness rippled over Hutch like a professional piano player tickling the ivories. He picked up the Magic Slate. Penciled: WHAT'S UP?

"We're dismissing you," Gupta said.

Hutch relaxed. He lifted the top sheet of the Magic Slate, causing the words to disappear, and then wrote: GOOD. READY TO GET BACK TO WORK.

The three superior officers exchanged those looks again.

Colonel Finetti cleared his throat. "Not just from the hospital, Captain. You're being dismissed from the Army."

He stared. Surely he'd misheard. He was being kicked out of the military?

This can't be easy for them, whispered a glimmer of the old, naïve, rally-round-the-flag-boys Hutch. *Cutting a guy loose who's done so much for his country.* But the new, cynical, war-in-Afghanistan-makes-hell-look-like-a-Sunday-tailgate-barbecue Hutch, who had lost everything, wasn't buying into it.

"The medical board has reviewed your case. You'll receive an honorable discharge for medical reasons and retain your full benefits," Gupta went on. "We thank you for your service."

Hutch's ears started ringing the way they did whenever he'd been too near an explosion. The only thing he'd ever wanted to do was serve his country and he never did anything half-assed. Best of the best. That had been his goal, and he'd achieved it. If he wasn't part of The Unit, who in the hell was he?

Furiously, Hutch scribbled on the Magic Slate. PTSD IS TREATABLE. FULL RECOVERY POSSIBLE. YOU CAN'T DISCHARGE ME FOR THAT. He shoved the drawing board at Gupta.

Gupta slid a glance at Jenner and then returned the Magic Slate to Hutch. "If it were just PTSD we wouldn't be having this conversation."

Finetti's eyes were full of pity. Jenner's face was unreadable.

Hutch wrote: MISSING FINGER.

"It's not the finger," Gupta said, not unkindly. "It's your inability to speak."

Hutch held up the tablet for them all to see what he'd written. SHRAPNEL TO THE THROAT. LINE OF DUTY.

"I know. I removed the shrapnel. But it missed your larynx. I thought by the time the swelling went down, you'd have your voice back." Gupta's head moved back and forth like windshield wiper blades set on slow.

ONLY BEEN TWO MONTHS, Hutch wrote.

"The last tests we did showed there is absolutely no reason why you're incapable of speaking. The speech therapist concurs. Your problem isn't physical," Gupta continued.

"It's mental." Jenner piggybacked on the physician's statement. "You've got selective mutism."

Mental? How could it be mental? Whenever he opened his mouth, no words came out. He *wanted* to talk. Tried his best to speak. Didn't they get that?

They let him stew on that for a minute. No one said a thing. All right. He thought they were wrong, but just in case they were right, he'd consider it. Losing his team might have turned him into an irritable prick, but he'd stay open-minded. He picked up the stylus. PART OF PTSD?

"After extensively reviewing your medical and family history, we"—Gupta's windshield-wiper head swiveled from Finetti to Jenner and back to him—"don't believe that to be the case."

A strange sensation pulled at the center of Hutch's solar plexus, as if he were belted into a centrifuge just starting to spin and he couldn't reach the brake to stop the damn thing.

"You have a family history of borderline personality disorder." Jenner picked up the conversation. "Your mother, your sister. BPD does have a genetic component. Although in men, the malady usually manifests as antisocial personality disorder, and those are the behaviors you've been presenting."

Hutch stared at Jenner, unable to believe what he was saying. Before the ambush, he'd been Mr. Effing Congeniality. He had more friends than he could keep up with. He got along with everyone. A team player, they'd called him in basic training, an asset to the military. Ah, but now...now he was broken and they weren't interested in spending the time, money, and effort necessary to put him back together again for combat.

Legally, they couldn't kick him out of the army for having PTSD, but they could boot him for a personality disorder. That's what this frame-up was really about. It was easier to break into Fort Knox than it was get into Delta Force. The military had known about his family history when they'd allowed him in. It hadn't been a deal breaker then. It shouldn't be one now.

Not wanting to give weight to their accusations, but not willing to take this lying down either, he calmly wrote: BULLSHIT!

Gupta studied his shoes. Finetti's mouth pulled flat in a sorry-about-this expression. Jenner's gaze remained steady, but his nose twitched. They *knew* it was bullshit and they didn't care.

He had survived the ambush, but now he was an embarrassment and they were grasping at anything they could use to get rid of him. Everyone in the room knew it would have been so much better if he'd died up there on the ridge that day with his team.

But he hadn't and they wanted him gone.

"We put a rush on the paperwork so that your family can have you home for Christmas," Finetti said, like they were doing him a big favor.

Railroaded. He was being railroaded, slamming him on the caboose and blasting coal to the engine.

"As of oh-eight hundred hours tomorrow, Captain Hutchinson," Jenner finished, "you're a civilian."

Twilight, Texas
December 3

"When's Mommy coming home?" Kimmie asked as she did every day when Meredith picked up the little girl and her son, Ben, from their pre-K classroom at Twilight Elementary. Kimmie also asked the same question every morning when she woke up and every evening when she was tucked into bed.

"I'm not sure," Meredith answered, because she didn't know what else to say.

"I bet she's at the North Pole visiting Santa." Kimmie's eyes sparkled. She looked so adorable in a red pinafore and patent leather Mary Janes, honey-colored curls tangling down her back. This North Pole thing was the latest fantasy that Kimmie had dreamed up to explain her mother's absence. "Like in *The Magic Christmas Cookie*."

The Magic Christmas Cookie was a popular children's novel written by local author Sadie Cool, the pseudonym for Sarah Walker, a young woman Meredith had met at the local book club she'd joined a couple of weeks ago. The same group that was hosting the Christmas cookie swap that Raylene Pringle had invited her to. Meredith had been reading the story to Kimmie and Ben every night before they went to sleep.

"I bet she brings me back lotsa toys." Kimmie sighed hopefully.

"Do you think she'll bring a toy for me too?" Ben asked.

"I think you both will have plenty of toys for Christmas," Meredith said, helping the children into the back of her minivan.

She had spent the last few days stewing on what to do about Ashley. She was furious at the woman for abandoning her daughter to run off to Acapulco with a stranger. But ultimately, she couldn't bring herself to tell anyone about it. Not yet. If she got the authorities involved it would turn into a big mess, and she didn't want to get Ashley into trouble with Child Protective Services unnecessarily.

Of course, if she did report her, she would have to call anonymously. And then say what?

From what Meredith had seen of Ashley in the six weeks she had lived in the house with the woman, she was a good mother. She had simply allowed this guy's attention to go to her head and she had made an error in judgment. Kimmie was safe and well fed, and Ashley *had* made arrangements—albeit last-minute and inconsiderate—for Meredith to watch her.

Still, was that just a rationalization?

Ashley had called when she reached Acapulco, but the telephone reception had been pitiful and the service dropped the call after a couple of minutes. Meredith had tried several times to phone her back, but she'd never been able to get through and she hadn't heard from the woman since then.

Today, Kimmie and Ben's teacher, Flynn Calloway, had asked about Ashley.

"She's on vacation," Meredith said.

"Ah." A knowing look came into Flynn's hazel eyes. "Another guy?"

"She's had a lot of boyfriends?"

Flynn held up both hands, curled her fingers into her palms, then flashed them open and closed several more times, indicating Ashley had had many boyfriends.

That had alarmed her. If Ashley did this all the time, maybe she *should* mention her disappearance to someone. But to whom?

The brother Ashley had spoken of?

Except Meredith had no idea how to contact him or

even what his name was. She was respectful of other people's privacy and would never dream of snooping, but she might be forced to go into Ashley's bedroom and search for the brother's contact information.

She thought about expressing her concerns to Flynn, but then some other mother wandered over and struck up a conversation about the upcoming Christmas play, and the opportunity was lost. But Flynn lived across the street from Ashley's house. Maybe she would invite Flynn over tonight after the children were in bed and feel her out.

Meredith loaded up the children in the minivan and drove around the town square, where volunteers were setting up for the annual Dickens on the Square event she'd been hearing so much about. She wished she could volunteer, but life on the run meant keeping a low profile. Back in Albuquerque, before her grandmother got sick, they'd loved volunteering for holiday events together. Meredith heaved a sigh. So much had been stolen from her.

Quickly, she shrugged off the sadness and regret. No point in getting depressed over something she could not change. And made a mental note to gather up some canned goods for the local food bank that had been asking for donations. It wasn't much, but it was all she dared. Going to the book club was risky enough, and she was already wondering if she should drop it. The members seemed far too interested in luring her to their party.

Workmen constructed stages on all quadrants of the courthouse lawn. Carolers, bundled in warm clothing, practiced their vocal range. Vendors stocked kiosks. A UPS man unloaded boxes. People waved. Nodded.

Tooted their car horns at one another in greeting. The busy little tourist town buzzed with enthusiastic holiday activity.

Built in the late 1800s, the three-story courthouse was constructed of limestone in the elegant style of French Second Empire. It provided a queenly contrast to the surrounding buildings of Old West architecture. The entire town square was listed in the National Register of Historic Places.

The square was picture-postcard perfect. Longing for something she could never have burned Meredith's nose. How she wished she could make this adorable town her permanent home.

It's not real, she told herself. *It's just a fantasy.* Dark secrets hid behind happy façades. She should know. She had a doozy of her own.

"Mommy!" Ben exclaimed. "Look, look there's Santa Claus!"

Meredith braked at the stop sign as Santa, and an entourage of elves handing out candy to the passersby, crossed the street in front of them. From the rearview mirror, she saw Ben undo the buckle on his car seat, pressed his face to the window and holler, "Santa! Santa! Come over, come over. We want candy too."

"Ben, sit back down and put your seat belt on," she cautioned. "Mommy's driving."

But her son had already summoned Santa and he wasn't sitting down for anything. Resigned, Meredith put down the window so he could talk to Santa.

"Ho! Ho! Ho!" Santa exclaimed, holding his plump belly and strolling up to Ben's side of the minivan. "And who do we have here?"

"It's me, Santa." Ben's voice wobbled. "Dontcha

'member me? We moveded again." He leaned over the seat to pat Meredith's shoulder. "Mommy, you said Santa would still remember me when we moveded."

"Of course I remember you," Santa recovered quickly. "But you've grown so big I almost didn't recognize you."

Ben wriggled like a happy puppy. "Santa, pwease, pwease, pwease bring me a real Thomas the Train. The kind you ride on. Pwease, pwease, pwease."

Meredith winced, prayed that Santa didn't make any promises she couldn't back up. The Thomas the Train riding toy Ben wanted cost a hundred dollars. Money she simply didn't have to spend.

"Have you been a good boy?" Santa asked.

Ben's head bobbed.

Kimmie undid the buckle of her car seat so that she could lean across Ben. "Where's my mommy? My mommy is suppossta to be with you. Where is she?"

Santa shot Meredith a helpless look.

"Kimmie, sweetie, you and Ben both get back in your car seats," Meredith said, hoping to derail her.

"Canna have some candy?" Ben held out a hand.

"What do you say?" Meredith prompted.

"Pwease canna have some candy?" Ben pressed palms together like he was praying.

"Santa, where's my mommy?" Kimmie wailed.

"Isn't that your mommy driving the car?" Santa asked.

"No," Ben said. "It's *my* mommy."

"You two aren't brother and sister?" Santa teased. "You look so much alike."

"No," Ben said proudly, and hugged Kimmie around the neck. "But we're twins."

Meredith smiled. Lately, they had taken to calling themselves twins and even asked to be dressed alike.

"Twins, huh?" Santa winked at Meredith. "Well, I think that calls for two pieces of candy apiece." He produced four fun-sized chocolate bars from his pocket. "But let's give them to Mommy to keep them until after you've had supper."

"She's not my mommy." Kimmie sighed.

"But she's taking care of you, right?" Santa smiled.

Kimmie nodded.

"Thank you," Meredith told Santa, and accepted the candy. The other drivers behind her had been very patient, but she was holding up traffic. "Get back in your car seats, kids. The sooner we get home, the sooner we can have dinner and the sooner you can have the chocolates for desserts."

The kids climbed back into their car seats and they waved good-bye to Santa, and Meredith took off.

"He never did tell me where my mommy is," Kimmie murmured sadly.

She studied the forlorn child in the rearview mirror. Her sweet blue eyes misted with tears, yanking Meredith's heart right out of her chest. This couldn't go on for much longer. She was going to have to do something about Ashley's disappearing act.

"Don't worry," Ben told Kimmie. "I'll share my mommy with you."

The children strained against their seat belts to hug each other.

Meredith made a fist and laid it across her chest. As soon as she got the kids to bed, she was going looking for Ashley's brother's contact information. She'd call

Flynn first and ask what his name was and if she knew how to get in touch with him.

She took Highway 51 and drove north out of town. They lived in a middle-class community snuggled on the banks of the Brazos River. Stately oaks lined the streets, bare of leaves this time of year. The majority of houses were decked out for Christmas. Peppermint candy canes graced walkways. Nativity scenes sprawled across lawns. Painted plywood cutouts of gingerbread houses, snowmen, and Santa Clauses topped roofs

Ashley's home was the last house on a street that ended the development. Beyond the neighborhood's confines, fenced ranchland stretched to the right and the river to the left.

When Meredith first moved in, she'd been nervous about living on the waterfront with a four-year-old, especially since she had never learned to swim. But it was cold weather and Ben hadn't shown the slightest interest in the river. They would be gone before summer anyway. In the meantime, she'd lectured him on staying away from the water, and never allowed him to go outside without her.

The kids were chattering about Santa, and her thoughts wandered back to her dilemma. How would she explain the situation to Ashley's brother? Obviously, he wasn't very close to his sister. Ashley had never once mentioned him.

Preoccupied, she was almost to the house before she spotted the pickup truck parked in the driveway.

A pickup she did not recognize. It was big and black and shiny new, an aggressive Dodge Ram tandem axle. The silver ram's head emblem on the tailgate glared at her.

Meredith gasped and turned quickly, taking the circular road that led her back to the entrance of the housing development, blood sprinting through her veins.

Was it *him*?

She hated to even think *his* name for fear it would conjure him up, like Beetlejuice. She had been so careful. Moving every six months. Changing her hairstyle and color with every move. How had he found them again?

Meredith thought about the .40-caliber Colt Defender she kept stashed underneath her bed in a lockbox. Fat lot of good it did now.

Damn her. She thought she'd finally lost him in the move to Texas. How had she allowed herself to become so complacent? The son of a bitch was as persistent as Michael Myers and twice as mean. She should have killed him when she had the chance.

Ben whipped his head around. "Hey, Mommy, you passted our house."

"We're taking a little detour, honey." She struggled to keep the panic from her voice, gripping the steering wheel so tightly that her knuckles numbed.

Calm down. She had to calm down. After everything they'd been through, Ben easily picked up on her distress. Thankfully, her son didn't question her, and he settled back in his car seat.

What now? Where was she going to go? Not the police. She couldn't go to the police. There was a warrant out for her arrest.

Maybe she was overreacting. She'd be the first to admit that her danger receptors were tuned high. What if it wasn't *him*? What if it was Ashley back from Acapulco and her boyfriend had given her a ride home? Or what if it was someone else entirely?

"Mommy, Mom, I'm hungry," Ben whined.

"I have to tinkle," Kimmie said in an urgent tone that meant, *Right now*.

Her mind spun in circles, going down the drain. Fight it. She had to fight the panic.

Mrs. Densmore was standing on the curb taking mail from her letterbox. Dotty Mae was at least eighty, but Meredith knew her from the book club, and she had to get the kids to safety. Now. She pulled up to the elderly woman, and rolled down her window.

"Good afternoon," Dotty Mae said brightly.

"I hate to trouble you, Mrs. Densmore," Meredith said, peering into the side-view mirrors to make sure the driver of the black Dodge Ram hadn't come after her. "But I've locked myself out of the house and Kimmie needs to go to the bathroom."

"Why of course, sweetie, you come on in." Dotty Mae beamed.

"Could I also trouble you to keep an eye on them while I wait for the locksmith?" she lied. Almost five years on the run had turned her into a pretty good liar.

"Absolutely."

"Thank you, thank you so much."

Meredith killed the engine and helped the kids out, all the while tossing furtive glances over her shoulder. "Go with Mrs. Densmore. She'll take you to the restroom."

"But I'm hungry," Ben protested.

Dotty Mae laid a comforting hand on Meredith's shoulder. "Don't you worry one bit about these little ones. I know what it's like to be a harried young mother. I'll give them a snack. Can they have peanut butter?"

"Peanut butter is fine, yes. Thank you again."

Kimmie was hopping around with her knees pressed together. "Tinkle, tinkle!"

"Right this way." Putting a palm to each small back, Dotty Mae ushered the children up the walkway into her house.

Meredith jumped into the minivan and drove around the neighborhood again. Her heart was pushing her blood through her ears so hot and fast she could barely hear. As she neared the house again, she slowed the van to a crawl.

The black pickup was still there.

An icy chill licked the back of her neck and her stomach pitched like a skiff in a squall. *License number. Memorize the license number.*

And do what with the information?

She didn't know, but she had to do something proactive. Just as she passed the house a second time, the front door opened and her heart literally stopped for a full second.

Omigod, omigod. Same height. Same muscular build. Same dark brown hair.

But the man coming out onto the porch was not *him*.

Instantly, spent adrenaline flooded her body, leaving her shaking so hard she wondered if she was having a seizure. Vaguely, she realized she was still in motion, her front tires had left the pavement, and a white, split-rail wooden fence lay directly in front of her.

She jammed on the brake just as she hit the fence.

The man looked startled, and came running toward her.

Desperately, Meredith slammed the minivan into

reverse, but he was standing directly behind her. If she backed up, she'd run over him.

What if he was a hired gun? He looked as if he could be a hired gun. She had to get out of here.

Back over him if you have to.

But what if he wasn't a hired killer? Odds were that he wasn't.

She could keep driving forward and crash through the fence, but then she'd end up in the river.

He was coming up fast on her side of the minivan. Self-preservation warred with common sense. What to do? What to do?

Meredith slung the van into park, grabbed her purse from the passenger seat, dug through it, and found the canister of pepper spray at the same time he opened her car door.

She was so jacked up on adrenaline that she couldn't think straight and there he was, big and looming and dangerous, not saying a single word.

Without hesitating, she pointed the nozzle in his face and sprayed.

Chapter 3

For a fraction of a second, Hutch took the pepper spray in the face like the Delta Force operator he was. He grunted mildly, blinked, and planted his feet. After all, he had been through the Confidence Chamber in basic training, where a solider went into the chamber with his classmates and they put on gas masks, and then the drill instructor unleashed a tear-gas tablet. In order to pass the drill, he'd been required to rip off his mask, throw it in a trash can, and recite his full name, rank, and service number.

But that was tear gas. Compared to this, tear gas was easy as a hot shower. This was something else entirely.

The inflammatory agent hit him full bore.

Brilliant pain exploded in his nostrils, singeing his mucous membranes. Vivid red agony stabbed his eyes, instantly swelling them shut. His throat—which he only thought was pretty damn useless lately—seized up. His skin burned as if a million fire ants were stinging him in unison. An overwhelming urge to rub his face gripped him, but he knew that doing so would only make things worse.

He dropped to his knees, and through the pain was barely aware of voices, and people surrounding him. They were talking, but his ears rang so loudly he couldn't understand what they were saying.

First mute, now blind and deaf. Move over, Helen Keller.

His chest heaved and he made a noise like a wounded wildebeest. Tears poured from his puffed-up eyes, a torrent of liquid streamed down his cheeks. He coughed, gagged, and inhaled a big mouthful of pepper-tainted air that triggered more coughing.

"Water," a man said. "We need to get him inside and get his eyes rinsed out with water, immediately."

Hands went around him, helping him up. His muscles twitched and quivered, marshalling to fight the potent chemicals flaming through his nerve endings. He staggered, stumbled, slumped heavily against someone.

A female someone. Soft and pliant.

"I'm sorry," she whispered in his right ear. "I thought you were trying to harm me."

Aw, this must be the driver of the minivan that had crashed into his fence. He wanted to ask her if she was okay, but he couldn't speak, and even if he could, he was too busy trying to catch his breath to forgive her for pepper-spraying him.

"This way." Her slender arm went around his waist.

Someone else had hold of Hutch's left hand—the hand missing an index finger—and was guiding him forward. Was it the man who'd suggested washing his eyes out with water? The ringing in his ears lessened and he could hear other voices. He recognized some of them. Friends and neighbors he hadn't spoken to since he'd left on his last deployment.

His final deployment, as it turned out.

"Lift your feet up if you can," the woman said, one of her hands on his right elbow, the other still pressed against his lower back. "We're going over the curb."

Blindly, he lifted his leg, pawing at the ground like a high-stepping pony until he made contact with the curb. The trip to the house seemed like a thousand miles, each step jarring painfully.

How long did this shit last? He felt as if a heavy-weight-boxing champ fist-clutching Morgua Scorpions had beat the hell out of him in a back alley.

The woman guided him up onto the porch and he heard the door creak open. She had the softest voice and a gentle touch that conflicted with the aggressive way she pepper-sprayed him.

No shrinking violet. This gal was tough.

The aching in his lungs lessened and he was finally able to suck in a full breath of air. Bad idea. A fresh burn seared all the way down.

"I'll help you get him into the bathroom," the man said.

Hutch tried to pry his eyes open to see who was talking, but nothing doing. The second he opened his eyes, the stinging intensified and his eyelids involuntarily shuttered back down.

A bumping noise, the scrape of chair legs against hardwood.

He was weaker than he should be. That damn two-month hospital stay had sucked the wind right out of his sails. Maybe it was the medication. He'd stopped the benzos cold turkey even though Gupta had told him to taper off slowly. He wanted that crap out of his system.

Hutch reached out a hand, touched the wall, the wainscoting. He wanted to sit, but the woman put her knee against the back of his leg and nudged him forward. "Bathroom," she explained.

Another door hinge creaked, the scuffling of feet. His. Hers. Theirs.

"How you doin', buddy?" the man asked, and clamped a hand on his shoulder. "You okay?"

Hell, no. He nodded.

The woman released him.

Aw, where did she go?

Hutch heard the shower come on and he slumped against the wall, concentrated on pulling air into his lungs and tasted the oily heat of pepper.

"Bathroom isn't big enough for all three of us," the man said.

"I've got it from here, Jesse. Thank you." The woman's voice sounded as shaky as Hutch's kneecaps.

The man must be Jesse Calloway. Jesse had been released from Huntsville penitentiary four years ago, after serving ten years for a crime he had not committed, and had married Hutch's next-door neighbor, Flynn MacGregor. Hutch had even attended their wedding. When he was on leave last Christmas, Jesse and Flynn had been renting a small house in downtown Twilight, and they'd been expecting their first child. They must have moved into Flynn's family home across the street.

But Hutch was too knotted up with misery to give his neighbors more than a fleeting thought.

"You sure?" Jesse asked the woman. "Can you handle him?"

"I've got him, if you could just check on Ben and Kimmie for me. I left them with Dotty Mae and I know two four-year-olds can be a handful for me, much less a senior citizen."

"Sure thing," Jesse said. "I'll get the kids and bring them over to our house. Flynn is picking Grace up from day care, but she'll be home any minute."

Kimmie. His niece.

But who was Ben? And who was this woman? And where in the devil was Ashley?

The door clicked shut and Hutch could only assume that Jesse had closed it, leaving him alone in the small front bathroom with the woman he did not know and could not communicate with.

He forced his eyes open, blinked hard against the zinging sting. Everything was blurry, fuzzy. She was moving around, opening drawers, digging around underneath the cabinet for something. He could barely make out her silhouette before pain forced him to snap his eyes closed again. Underneath his boots the floor tiles seemed to shift.

Shit. Don't faint. You're Delta Force.

Was. He *was* Delta Force. Emphasis on past tense.

Still, that was no call to faint like a girl.

The woman came closer. He could feel her body heat. Feel her nervousness too.

She touched his left forearm with a gloved hand. But of course, she had to protect herself. That's what she'd been looking for in the cabinet. Medical gloves.

Through the blistering stench of peppery chemicals, his nose finally caught her scent. It was a lovely smell, talcum powder and sugar cookies and raspberry shampoo, and her sweet fragrance instantly soothed his excoriated senses.

She took him by the shoulders, maneuvered him around until his back was flat against the wall. He hated being backed into a corner, but he was in no position to protest or resist. One blast of that canister and she'd effectively rendered him helpless.

Dammit. He hated being helpless.

It had come to this. Would he ever be whole again?

He felt her hands at his chest. Unbuttoning. She was unbuttoning his shirt. He stiffened, pulled away from her.

"I don't like this any more than you do," she said in the no-nonsense tone of voice that reminded him of military nurses. "But we have to get this contaminated clothing off you."

He wanted to tell her that he could do it, but hey, he couldn't talk. And for another thing, it was all he could do not to topple over.

"I'm sorry I sprayed you," she said. "But you did come storming out of my house."

Your house? Lady, this is my house. Who was she and what was she doing laying claim to his home?

"How was I to know you were Ashley's brother? For all I knew you were a burglar."

She was just trying to justify her edgy trigger finger. Why did she have such an edgy trigger finger?

"To tell you the truth, I didn't even know Ashley had a brother until a few days ago." She had already undone his second button, was working on to the third. "It's Brian, right? That's what Jesse told me your name was when you were out of it."

Not since he was a kid. Hutch. Everyone called him Hutch.

"Jesse also said you're a captain in the Army and a war hero. Is that what happened to your finger and your…" Her voice hitched. "Throat? The wounds still look fresh."

Yakety-yak. Was that all people in Twilight ever did? Talk. Gossip. Chat. Tittle-tattle. Chew the fat. Shoot the breeze. Open their gobs and spew?

"Jesse also said you were the nicest guy he ever met."

Sorry, sweet cheeks, things change. Hutch's shirt gaped open and he welcomed the hit of air against his chest.

She inhaled sharply, and her hand tensed on his arm before she dropped it to her side.

Ah. That was why she was gabbing. She was nervous. He scared her.

Scared maybe, but apparently undaunted. She reached underneath the waistband of his jeans to pluck out his shirttail, and in the process her fingers brushed against his skin.

Holy shit.

Despite that just a couple of minutes ago, he'd taken pepper spray to the face. Despite that he'd been through hell and back these last few months, losing his finger, his voice, his career, and his entire team. Despite that he had no idea what the woman looked like other than that split-second glimpse of a short, black, wavy hair and a startled, wide-eyed face when he'd peered into the window of her minivan before she'd brought the hammer down on him. The ludicrous happened.

Hutch got hard.

* * *

Meredith tried not to look at him. For one thing, it hurt clean to her bones to see how badly she'd messed him up. His face was violent crimson, his eyes swollen, his breathing shallow and jagged.

For another thing, he was more magnificently built than any man she'd ever seen, and she'd seen a lot of people naked. There was no softness to him. Not a morsel of fat. He was rock sinew, hard bone. Every muscle was honed and delineated. Where was he when she was in nursing school learning the musculoskeletal system? What a gorgeous teaching aid he would have made.

No time for admiration. She had to get these clothes off, get him in the shower and that pepper spray washed off him. Immediately.

Besides, she had zero desire to check him out. She'd written off sex five years ago and hadn't been the slightest bit interested in rekindling those primitive and unwanted urges.

Her body, however, disagreed. When she peeled off his shirt and got a good look at his hard, masculine form, something stupidly feminine inside her whispered, *Woo-whew.*

Alarmed by her response, she dropped her hand and her gaze.

He had an erection.

For a fraction of a second pure panic swept through her, and her mind, alert and trained for danger, thought of the pepper spray and the gun underneath her bed. But then the inner calmness she'd spent the last five years cultivating through yoga and meditation and time spent in nature, the inner calmness that had escaped her when this man had lumbered up to her minivan, whispered in her ear.

Listen to your instincts. Hear your intuition. Ignore the chattering monkey mind.

She took a deep breath and slowly let it out, felt her muscles loosen.

Instinct told her that he was not going to harm her. She knew it in her core. If she hadn't, she would never have come in here with him. It surprised her, this knowing, because he was rather frightening to look at. But if the past had taught her anything it was that looks could be deceiving.

But the brain was hard to ignore or defy, even if she had learned that intellectual reasoning could lead her astray when her heart and gut never had. Unfortunately, she didn't always know how to listen.

Meredith swallowed and stepped back.

Honestly, his hard-on wasn't the real issue. She understood that men couldn't always control their erections. She had been undressing him. It was a normal biological response. She got that. It might even be some kind of bizarre physiological reaction to the pepper spray.

No, it wasn't the involuntary erection that shocked her as much as it was his potent virility and her unexpected attraction to him. Five years. She hadn't wanted a man in five years.

Vulnerable. She was so damn vulnerable right now.

Then again, so was he. Debilitated not only by her pepper spray, but by combat as well. The index finger of his left hand was missing and his neck was puckered with dark pink scars.

Guilt took hold of her. He was in pain because she

was hypervigilant, consumed by fear, and had overreacted. But what else could she have done? She'd seen a stranger coming out of the place where she lived.

Overkill.

Blasting him with the pepper spray had been overkill. She'd seen it on the wary faces of her neighbors as they'd gathered around identifying and vouching for him. She'd worked herself into a panic when she'd seen the black pickup truck, imagining that her stalker had found them again, and primal fear had eclipsed everything else.

He didn't apologize for the erection, but he did place a strategic hand over his crotch and turn his face from her, clearly embarrassed.

"Most of the pepper spray went on your shirt," she said. "You can probably leave your pants on for the shower. Can you get out of your shoes?"

He nodded, bent over to untie his shoelaces, but immediately lost his balance and crashed heavily against the wall.

"Hang on. I'll get those laces for you." She squatted in front of him, but kept her head ducked so that she wouldn't be eye-to-eye with his crotch.

She untied his shoelaces, rocked back on her heels, and stood up.

He toed off his shoes and, using his palms, felt his way into the shower. The water hit his chest first. He fumbled for the nozzle, found it, and tilted it up to catch him squarely in the face.

With her gloved hands, she picked up his shirt, redolent with the stench of pepper spray, and stuffed it in a trash bag she retrieved from the bathroom cabinet. Smelling the stuff secondhand in the closed space made her eyes and her nose sting. She coughed against the fumes, stripped off her gloves, and tossed them in the trash basket.

"I'll wait outside," she told him. "Holler if you need anything."

He simply grunted.

She sneaked a peek over at him. Water splashed his face, sluiced down his bare chest. His wet jeans were plastered against his body, and thankfully his erection was gone.

Meredith closed the door behind her, paced the hall, and wrung her hands. He was going to need something to put on. The last thing she wanted was for him to come strutting out of there wrapped in nothing but a towel.

Strut? Considering the shape he was in, Captain Brian Hutchinson wasn't going to be strutting anywhere anytime soon. And it was her fault.

Cringing, she thought about going across the street to ask Jesse if he could lend Brian jeans and a T-shirt, but the captain was a lot bigger than Jesse.

What about the spare upstairs bedroom on the second floor where she and Ben lived? Maybe there was something in that room that he could wear. She wasn't a snoop. She'd never been in that spare bedroom, but perhaps that's where he stayed when he came to visit his sister.

Torn between waiting by the door to see if he needed anything and the need to find him clothing, Meredith hesitated.

She knocked. "You okay?"

He didn't answer.

She knocked again, raised her voice. "Brian?"

Nothing.

Oh no. What if he had passed out in there?

She wrenched open the door.

He was standing there in front of her, wet and naked as the day he was born, glaring at her with bloodshot devil eyes.

She yelped.

He snorted like an angry bull.

She peeked down.

He was no longer erect, but even so, he was still frighteningly large.

She slammed the door, raced into the living room, her heart pumping so fast it set her head spinning.

It wasn't his fault. She had gone charging in there.

But he hadn't answered her. Surely he'd known she would come in there if he didn't answer her. Why hadn't he answered her?

From the top of her scalp to the bottom of her toes, every nerve ending in her body tingled. Her cheeks burned. She plastered her palms on either side of her face. Her arms quivered. Her knees buckled. What *was* this feeling?

Not fear.

Why *wasn't* it fear?

Instead, she felt bizarrely ultra-alive, the way she did as a kid when she and her playmates had played tag between the chase-crew vehicles and hot air balloons being inflated across flat grassy fields. The rhythmic whoosh of the gas burners, the damp scent of morning dew, the freedom, the thrilling pleasure of running to reach base ahead of the tagger just as dawn broke brilliant over the horizon.

A crazy smile yanked at her mouth and for a moment, she thought she might be losing her mind. Finally, she identified the feeling.

Giddy. She was giddy.

But why?

Maybe it wasn't giddiness as much as delayed relief that the intruder was not her stalker and the grateful realization that now Brian was here, he could figure out what to do about Ashley.

Hutch's eyes still burned like flamethrowers. The cool shower had helped and the swelling was slowly going down, although his blister-hot lungs cried out for cold fresh air.

With a towel wrapped around his waist, he stepped from the bathroom. He glanced left, then right, searching for the woman. No sign of her.

Maybe she'd hightailed it out of here. Who was she anyway? One of the strays Ashley inevitably took in?

Great. He'd have to be the one to send her packing.

He lumbered down the hallway, still unsteady on his feet. That was some potent pepper spray, as heavy-duty as the variety that riot cops used. He paused at the foot of the stairs, wished he could call out and warn her in case she was quivering in some corner somewhere armed with more pepper spray.

Ouch. He winced at the mere idea of being sprayed again. Cocking his head, he listened for sounds of her.

Silence.

Coast clear.

He went up to his bedroom, retrieved the duffel bag he'd dropped on the floor when he arrived. Dressed in cargo pants, a green T-shirt, and a pair of deck shoes and no socks. He felt naked without his dog tags. After more than a decade in the military, he missed the tags almost as much as he missed his ability to speak.

Forget it. Move on. Somehow, he'd muscle his way through this confounded PTSD and get his voice back if it killed him.

Hutch started to go back down the stairs, but on impulse stopped outside the bedroom across the hall. He turned the knob, booted the door open.

It wasn't the empty bedroom he'd left behind on his final deployment.

Girly lotions and potions were lined up on the dresser. A pair of pink bedroom slippers were tucked under one corner of the bed, and a matching bathrobe with frayed sleeves hung from the hook outside the en suite bathroom door. A slightly wrinkled brown and gold uniform, the pocket embroidered with "Hot Legs Spa," lay draped over the foot of the bed. The uniform rang a bell and he remembered the woman had been wearing it when he sidled up to the window of her minivan.

On the side table was a picture of a young boy about the same age as his niece, Kimmie. Nestled in the nook of the bay window was a trundle bed covered with a Thomas the Train bedspread.

Hutch veered over to finger the bedding. Was the boy in the photograph the one who was sleeping in this bed? Was this the Ben the woman had spoken of?

From the look of things, Ashley had not only picked up another stray, but this one had a pup as well.

Ah hell. He knew he should not have allowed Ashley to move in here last Christmas, but she'd had nowhere else to go and the house would be standing empty while he was overseas. How could he refuse his sister a place to live when she had Kimmie to look after?

Hutch exhaled cautiously, rested his head against the wall, and closed his eyes.

"What are you doing in my bedroom?" came an indignant bark from behind him.

He pivoted, opened his mouth to enlighten her on just whose bedroom it was, forgetting for a second that he could not speak, and a harsh garbled noise scraped up his throat. He sounded like a wounded animal caught in snare trap. Instantly, he slammed his jaw shut.

"Out." She pointed a trembling finger toward the door. "Get out of my room."

He held up both palms. Surrendering. Getting out of her space. Possession was nine-tenths of the law, or so they said. Never mind that he owned the place, Miss Pepper Spray was in charge and she knew it.

Hutch wished his vision was better so he could adequately size up his opponent. She wasn't big. No taller than five-six and no heavier than a hundred and ten pounds. She needed some meat on those bones. But she was brave and she wasn't going to take any guff off him.

That coal black pixie haircut made her look all of fourteen years old. She wore holey jeans that bagged on lean hips. Not trendy jeans made to look worn out for an exorbitant price, these were plain old Wranglers she'd probably had since she *was* fourteen. The light blue sweater, which hugged high, pert breasts, was only slightly less worn out than her jeans. He noticed a moth hole in the right cuff, also noticed her pull the sleeves down over her petite hands until all he could see were delicate fingertips, the nails painted a shimmering pale pink the color of dawn.

Her pupils widened and she nibbled on her bottom lip. The column of her slender throat moved visibly when she swallowed. A gulp? Was she still scared of him?

He was making her uncomfortable and that was not his intention. He nodded, turned, and trekked past her.

"Wait," she said, her voicing lifting at the end.

He paused, glanced back at her over his shoulder.

"We need to talk."

He raised his right eyebrow. Letting his face ask the question that his mouth could not.

"But not right now. Your face…" She swallowed, lowered her gaze. "Let's wait until your…" She waved her hands in front of her eyes.

He got it. She was having troubling looking at him. Too bad. If she was tough enough to pepper-spray him, she was just going to have to deal with the aftermath of her handiwork.

"Do you want something to drink?" she asked.

His parched throat cried yes, but he was afraid drinking something would reactivate the burning. He shook his head.

She sank her hands on her hips. "This strong, silent-type routine isn't working for me. Say something."

He put three fingers to the base of his throat, and then to his lips, shook his head again.

"You're deaf?" She pressed a palm up her forehead, distress pulling her mouth into a grim line as if she was the one who had caused his pain. "And here I've been nattering on. You must read lips though, right?"

He scowled, shook his head sharply, cupped his palms around both ears and nodded.

She frowned for a moment, but her lips parted on a

quick uptake of breath as she caught on. "You can hear but you can't talk?"

Yes. Yes. He pumped his head up and down.

"Oh dear. You and I need to have a serious conversation. How is this going to work?"

Serious conversation? About what?

He held up a finger, indicating that she should give him a minute and he stepped back across the hall for the Magic Slate. She tagged along after him, not waiting, and when he turned, she was so close to his elbow that he almost ran into her.

The urge to step back away from her was strong, but he wasn't going to let her see how much she ruffled him. He grabbed the stylus attached to the Magic Slate. SO TALK.

"Not here," she said. "Let's go out on the deck and watch the Brazos roll by."

WHY? Hutch wrote.

"You need fresh air and I'm afraid I've got bad news to deliver about your sister."

Chapter 4

The Brazos River was a sight for pepper-sprayed eyes, soothing Hutch all the way down to the marrow of his bones. The water held a magnetic pull over him. When he'd been in those dry desert mountains of Afghanistan, he dreamed almost nightly of this liquid beauty. He could read the river like an engrossing mystery series authored by Mother Nature. Her sly twists and turns evolving over time, continually surprising and delighting him with unexpected secrets.

He thought of his boat parked in the boathouse and securely covered with a tarp, the pull of the water whispering at him to ignore winter weather and get his ass out there.

The house had started out as nothing more than a simple fishing cottage that he'd bought right out of high school with his half of the money their mother had left them. When he was on leave from the army, he slowly added on to the house when time and money permitted, building the second story and the backyard deck with his own two hands, learning as he went. It had taken him four years to complete, but when he was finished, the worth of the house had doubled and he held the title free and clear.

He meant the place to serve as a waterside getaway between deployments and nothing more, figuring that when he met the right woman, they would buy a place together. Now, he was simply grateful he had a place to call home.

But this stranger was also calling his house home, a cute stranger that he couldn't seem to stop staring at.

When he arrived that afternoon, the temperature had been a balmy sixty degrees, not at all uncommon in early December in North Central Texas. But with the approaching twilight and damp wisp rising up off the water, it was at least fifteen degrees colder.

He dragged in a deep breath, inhaling the scent he would eternally associate with homecoming—the earthiness of wild mushrooms, the tinny odor of minnow buckets, the sluggish tug of ore-rich soil. The woman was right. The cold air was helping.

She had grabbed a faded jean jacket from a hook at the back door and she stood on the opposite side of the deck from him, hugging herself tightly.

He tilted his face to the graying sky and took another long, deep breath, his chest aching against the pepper spray residual.

"I apologize again for—"

He held up a palm and shot her a let-it-go look. No sense making her feel bad. It was over with, done. In the grand scheme of things it was nothing worse than a case of hiccups.

She turned up the collar of her denim jacket and lifted her shoulders to her ears at the same time she tucked those shy hands up inside her sleeves again.

He inclined his head in the direction of the house, raised an eyebrow.

"No," she said, picking up on his sign language. "This is helping you and I'm okay."

She joined him at the railing, but stayed several feet away, and stared down at the Brazos churning below. The higher water level and rapid current told him that it had recently rained. The orange rays of dying sunlight caught her hair, gave a bluish tinge to the coal black locks. The color didn't suit her pale skin or match her light brown eyebrows. Why did she dye it that dark?

A sand crane swooped gracefully over the water, looking for a safe place to bed down for the night. Somewhere downriver came the sound of a johnboat engine. A fisherman was headed home for dinner. From the loblolly pine tree that sheltered the right side of the deck, a squirrel scolded and swished its tail as it scampered higher into the branches.

"It's weird," she said. "I can't swim, but I'm not afraid of water. I love the water, in fact. It's so peaceful. Of course, whenever I go in, I always wear a life jacket, and I do worry about Ben. But I started putting him in swim lessons every summer after he turned two. I don't want him to end up like me. Twenty-seven years old and not knowing how to swim."

She was nervous, babbling. He wanted to ask her why she'd never learned to swim, but they had more pressing matters to discuss.

Her eyes glued to him. Kind blue eyes full of sympathy and remorse. Her inner goodness was almost touchable, a purity as white as fresh snowfall, and for a moment, all he wanted to do was make snow angels.

But that was stupid. Dirty as his soul was, if he touched her, he would stain her for life.

He scribbled on the Magic Slate. WHAT'S YOUR NAME?

She hesitated for a second—just long enough for Hutch to wonder why—and then she murmured, "Jane. Jane Brown."

Funny, she didn't seem like a Jane. PLAIN NAME.

She shrugged.

He lifted the top sheet of the Magic Slate, making the words disappear, and jotted, SOUNDS LIKE AN ALIAS.

Her eyes widened and the muscle at her temple jumped. "My parents were unimaginative. Deal with it."

Prickly. Her calm was gone. What was that all about? He was the one entitled to the bad mood.

He didn't write anything else. Just waited.

She rubbed her hands up and down her arms, and cleared her throat. "I didn't know until two days ago that Ashley had an older brother. I thought she owned this place."

He shook his head. MINE.

"So I've gathered. I've also gathered you didn't know she was renting the upstairs bedroom to me and my son."

He shook his head.

Jane drummed two fingers against her chin. "So Ashley has been keeping us a secret from each other."

That did not surprise him. His sister was full of secrets.

Hutch fumbled the Magic Slate. It hit the deck. He
leaned to pick it up, but because of his missing finger, misjudged the distance and had to swipe at the
ground twice before he managed to scoop it up. How
long would it take him to get used to his loss? Trying
to look unflustered, he straightened and scratched his
message: WHERE IS SHE?

The woman sank her hands on her hips. "Well, you
see, that's the thing. I don't know. Not for sure. She
took off on us."

Hutch closed his eyes. He had suspected as much
when Ashley had not answered his texts or returned
his phone calls. She'd taken off without notice before.
More than once. Opening his eyes, he penciled on the
slate. SHE LEFT KIMMIE WITH YOU?

"Yes. Your niece is safe. I've been looking out for
her. Ashley is the one I'm worried about." The Jane-
who-didn't-look-like-a-Jane proceeded to tell him a
story about his sister running off to Acapulco with a
man she barely knew.

Yes, it wasn't the first time something like this had
happened. But since she'd had Kimmie and started seeing the counselor he paid for, Ashley had been some-
what less impulsive. Stupidly, he'd been lulled into
thinking that becoming a mother had tempered his
sister's emotional instability. Friends and neighbors in
their tight-knit community kept tabs on her for him and
no one had raised a red flag. He should have known
better. Parenthood hadn't stemmed his own mother's
recklessness. Why would it work for Ashley?

Denial packed a humdinger of a sucker punch, seducing him into believing that everything was going to be all right. He had traveled this same road with his mother, but still he'd let himself hope that things could be different for Ashley.

Borderline personality disorder was so tricky. People who suffered from BPD looked so normal from the outside, and then, boom, their emotions would overwhelm them and their behavior would turn irrational and they would do anything—even push you away and threaten suicide—to avoid abandonment, as paradoxical as that seemed. He'd spent his life trying to understand his mother and sister's erratic and illogical thought processes, and he was no closer to figuring it out than he'd ever been.

He wrote: MY SISTER HAS BORDERLINE PERSONALITY DISORDER.

Jane's mouth opened into an innocent O, her eyelashes fluttered, and a why-didn't-I-figure-that-out expression pulled her lips back over her teeth. "I didn't know. That explains a lot. Is she on medication?"

He shook his head, silently mouthed the words he could not speak. *Medication doesn't work.*

"Therapy?"

He nodded.

"I've never seen her go."

He ran his tongue over his upper teeth, got a lingering taste of pepper spray. Dammit. He should have paid the therapist directly instead of sending Ashley the check. But he wanted to show her that he trusted her. That idiotic denial again.

The porch light came on against the encroaching darkness. On the water, a fish slapped its tail against the surface. Hutch's vision was slowly improving and he could make out Jane's features more clearly. Her jaw-line was soft, ultra-feminine, in contrast to her nose. Size-wise, the nose fit her face, but it was crooked at the bridge, as if it had been broken, maybe more than once.

His fingers worked the stylus. HOW LONG HAVE YOU BEEN LIVING HERE?

"Six weeks."

About the same time he had been trying to come to grips with the fact his entire team had died. HOW DID YOU MEET ASHLEY?

"The transmission in my minivan conked out on me. I was standing on the side of the road, my son on my hip, with no one to call." She gave a little laugh that was filled with anxiety instead of humor. There was nothing remotely funny about what she'd just said.

Hutch wrote: NO MAN IN YOUR LIFE?

Her chin hardened and for the flash of a second, he saw in her eyes the same expression he'd seen on the faces of Afghan villagers—distrust, distaste, disgust. Some son of a bitch had treated her badly.

"No."

His fingers ached from all the writing. YOUR SON'S FATHER?

"Dead," she said flatly, cleanly, as if she was glad for it. "Ashley drove by, gave us a ride, and the rest is history. Your sister has a very generous heart."

IMPULSIVE, he wrote, and a cramp spasmed through his hand. He flexed his fingers, shook it out.

"I suppose you could look at it that way. She was a great housemate, though. That is, until three days ago."

The sun slipped below the horizon, the twilight sky deepening from cool purple to deep blue. The scent of someone's dinner, spaghetti and meatballs from the smell it, surfed the breeze.

"What are you going to do about your sister?" she asked.

He shrugged. There was nothing he could do. It had taken him some time to come to the realization that Ashley was responsible for herself. She was an adult and he could not fix her. Kimmie, however, was another matter.

Kimmie.

Ah, hell. What was he going to do with his niece? He was in no shape, either mentally or physically, to take care of a four-year-old girl by himself.

"You're not going to do anything about her?" She sounded horrified.

He shook his head.

"But what if this guy she's gone off with is a rapist or worse?"

BEYOND MY CONTROL.

"Well," she said, sounding pissed off. "You're certainly no help."

A stiff silence stretched between them. Finally, to ease the tension, he wrote on the slate. YOU'RE NOT RESPONSIBLE FOR HER EITHER.

"Ashley took me in when I had nothing. She got a friend of hers to fix my minivan and he's letting me pay him out. She gave me a place to live. Helped me find a job as a masseuse at Hot Legs Spa. I owe her."

He curled his finger around the stylus. YOU'RE TAKING CARE OF KIMMIE. CONSIDER YOURSELF EVEN.

"I don't turn my back on friends." There was that

stubborn chin, hardening again. Extreme loyalty had caused her problems in her life, Hutch could just tell.

ASHLEY TURNED HER BACK ON YOU.

She squinted into the darkness, trying to read what he'd written. He stepped closer so she could see.

She puffed out her cheeks with air, ran a hand over her short cap of curls, and then let out a defeated sigh. "Ben and I will be out of here tomorrow."

He penned, WHERE WILL YOU GO?

"I'll find something."

TAKE YOUR TIME.

"No. I can't stay here with you. This is your home. Tomorrow. We'll be out of here tomorrow."

He didn't know why, but her words brought a sting of rejection. He was happy to be rid of her. I'LL GIVE YOU MONEY FOR A MOTEL UNTIL YOU CAN FIND A PLACE TO LIVE.

"No," she said sharply. "I do not take money from men."

REFUND ON YOUR RENT.

"I paid that money to Ashley, not you." She stepped back, almost disappearing into the thickening shadows.

Jane Brown was a complicated woman and she piqued his interest. Who was she exactly and how had she come to end up broken down on the side of the road in Twilight, Texas? He wasn't in any shape for this pro-longed conversation. He was bone-deep exhausted and wanted nothing more than to collapse into his bed and sleep for a week. He told himself to let her go. He had enough troubles of his own without taking on hers.

"I've got to pick up the children. It's time for their supper."

He touched his chest with a quick flick of his hand,

pointed at her and then at the door to indicate he wanted to go with her.

She nodded, but moved quickly to get ahead—or away—from him.

They passed through the sliding glass door, through the kitchen, and out the front of the house, Jane several feet ahead of him.

He left the Magic Slate on the foyer table and hurried after her, anxious to see Kimmie again. During the course of the past year, whenever his job allowed, he chatted with his sister and niece over Skype conversations on the computer, but he hadn't had contact with Ashley since August when The Unit was sent on a counter-terrorism black ops mission.

After the ambush, he'd asked the military not to tell Ashley that he'd been wounded. They wouldn't have told her about the operation anyway and he hadn't wanted to worry her. Little things could throw her world out of kilter. The more routine her life was, the better she did.

He wondered what had thrown her out of whack this time, but the woman striding up the sidewalk to the Calloways' home was answer enough. Having new people in the house couldn't help upsetting Ashley's routine.

The closer they got to the front door, adorned with a cheery candy cane wreath and twinkle lights, the tighter the knot in Hutch's chest grew as it all fully sank in. What if his sister never returned? On the other hand, what if she did? Could he really ever trust her with Kimmie's welfare again?

Jane rang the doorbell.

Hutch lagged behind, fear slowing his steps. What if his niece didn't remember him?

He'd been there the night Kimmie was born. No dad

around. Ashley claimed not to know who the father was. As wild as she'd been, that was probably the truth. Back in those days, he'd been so optimistic, so full of that damn hope. He'd passed out pink bubble gum cigars as if he were the father, bought pizza for the entire maternity ward, and flirted with the nurses. Even though he'd known it was not going to be an easy road for either Ashley or her new daughter, he believed he could make a difference.

Kimmie's birth had been one of the happiest days of Hutch's life.

What a dumbass he'd been.

The door opened and there was Flynn Calloway, a baby on her hip, Jesse standing behind her. They looked so happy.

The storm in Hutch's stomach moved to his throat, spun there like a tornado.

A little blond-haired boy—the same boy in the photograph in Jane's room—came bursting in between Jesse and Flynn and hurled himself at his mother. She swept him up in her arms and dropped kisses on his face.

The boy giggled, and snuggled his head against his mother's long, slender neck.

In the glow of the twinkle lights, love shone in Jane's eyes as she held her son. She was the epitome of Christmas, of a mother's love. It was so pure, so perfect, the two of them together in that moment, Madonna and child. It might just very well be the most beautiful thing he'd ever seen.

Hutch felt like an intruder. He didn't belong anymore. He was scarred, his soul soiled black with the soot of war, and if it weren't for Kimmie, he might well have turned and walked away for good.

And then there was Kimmie, coming out of the house, a sweet smile on her angelic face.

"There's someone here to see you, Kimmie," Jane said, put a palm to the little girl's head, and guided her to the sidewalk, Ben still on her hip.

After that, Hutch couldn't retreat.

Overwhelming love for his niece shoved Hutch forward, and in his eagerness he forgot about the lingering effects of pepper spray. Forgot about his inflamed features and bloodshot eyes. Forgot about the scars on his neck and his missing index finger. All he wanted was to hold her again. Hug her hard and tell her how much he loved her.

Pulse thumping hard, chest tightening with emotion, Hutch held out his hand, waited for her to recognize him and fling herself into his arms.

Kimmie took one look at him and let out a terrified scream.

The little girl's scream echoed throughout the quiet neighborhood.

Jesse, Flynn, and Grace Calloway startled. Porch lights came on. Curtains swished at windows. A dog barked, setting off a chain reaction of barks down the block.

Meredith put Ben down on the sidewalk beside Kimmie, leaned over, and whispered into the little girl's ear. "It's okay, sweetheart. That's your Uncle Brian."

"Hutch," Jesse murmured. "Everyone calls him Hutch."

"That's your Uncle Hutch," Meredith corrected. "Do you want to say hi?"

Kimmie buried her face against Meredith's hip, shook her head.

"He's come a long way to be with you."

The child fisted a wad of Meredith's jeans in her little hand, but would not raise her head.

Hutch stood on the Calloways' lawn looking forlorn and broken, loneliness rolling off him in waves.

Meredith's heart wrenched for the poor veteran, for all the veterans who came back irrevocably changed and for all the servicemen and women who would never return home. War was awful.

Although it wasn't the same thing, she had been through her own version of combat. Could relate to the hell of violence and how it twisted you up inside, making it hard to trust another human being.

And then Ben, bless his little heart, moved toward Hutch, lifted his hand. "Hi."

Part of Meredith was proud of her son's bravery and empathy, but another part of her, that part that had been running scared for almost five years, wanted to grab him by the collar of his shirt and drag him back.

Hutch raised a left palm in greeting.

"Kimmie's Uncle Hutch can't talk," Meredith told Ben.

Ben angled his head, considered this. "You can't talk?"

Hutch shook his head.

Ben turned back to her. "How come he can't talk-eded, Mommy?"

"He got hurt in the war." She bent to explain. "See those scars on his neck?"

Hutch sank to the ground on his knees, eye-level with her son.

Ben stepped forward, studied Hutch's scarred throat with honest, little-boy curiosity. "Cool."

Hutch let out a short, abbreviated laugh that sounded more like a snort.

Ben inched closer, reached out a finger to trace the scars at Hutch's neck. "Bad guys hurt you?"

Hutch nodded.

"That's mean," Ben proclaimed.

Meredith couldn't see her son's face but she could tell from the set of his little shoulders that he was frowning. Kimmie had unglued her face from Meredith's hip and was peeping around at her uncle.

"I hate bad guys," Ben said staunchly, as if it were always easy to tell the bad guys from the good ones. He turned back to where Meredith and Kimmie were still standing on the porch with Jesse, Flynn, and their baby daughter, Grace.

"Honey, don't say hate," Meredith corrected gently. "Hatred isn't a good thing."

"But I do hate 'em. They hurteded Kimmie's Unca Hutch."

Curiosity drew Kimmie down the walkway to join Ben in front of her uncle.

Hutch smiled softly at his niece, but he didn't make a move.

"I 'member you now." Slowly, Kimmie reached out to touch Hutch's face with her palm. "You tooked me for i-scream."

He nodded once more.

It was hard to tell in the darkness, but Meredith thought she saw a sheen of tears mist Hutch's lashes, but it could have been nothing more than the reflection of Christmas lights in his eyes.

"I hate bad guys too," Kimmie said, just as fiercely as Ben. Then she wrapped her little arms around Hutch's neck and planted a kiss on his cheek.

There might not be tears in Hutch's eyes, but there certainly were in hers. Meredith pressed the back of her palm against her nose and sniffled. She blinked, turned to Jesse and Flynn. Their eyes were none too dry either.

Jesse plucked the keys from his pocket and put them in her upturned palm. "I moved the minivan to your driveway. You left the keys inside. You've got a crunched fender, but the fence took the brunt of it."

Meredith glanced over her shoulder at the fence. It was split right in two and leaning over. No one mentioned the pepper spray. "Thank you. I do so appreciate you keeping the kids."

"No problem," Jesse said.

"Anytime." Flynn smiled. "The children were so good. Ben's an utter joy."

"He has his moments." Meredith ruffled her son's hair,

"Are you coming to the cookie club swap party on Friday night?" Flynn asked. "We'd love to have you."

She didn't want to get too close to the people in this town. If she made friends, it would only hurt that much more when she had to leave. "I don't know."

Flynn touched her shoulder. "Please come."

"Maybe. Right now I have to get these two home to their supper. Thanks again for everything."

Hutch got to his feet, loomed tall over the children now, but he looked uncertain as to how to proceed.

The Calloways said good night and shut their door, leaving the four of them alone in the darkness.

A momentary awkwardness fell over them. Ben and Kimmie held hands, looked from Meredith to Hutch and back again.

"C'mon," Meredith said, acting as if this was a totally normal day. "Let's go eat. We're having macaroni and cheese for dinner. Last one to wash their hands is a rotten egg."

Chapter 5

Now that he could see clearly, Hutch noticed how much things had changed.

The cabinets and drawers, which had been a sloppy mess when Ashley and Kimmie lived here alone, were neatly organized. Bowls stacked according to size and construction, plastic bowls on one side, earthenware on the other. Silverware was separated by type in a drawer divider instead of being thrown into a heap. Oatmeal and a variety of nuts and dried fruit filled the pantry instead of the Pop-Tarts, sugary cereals, crackers, and cookies that Ashley usually bought. Fresh apples, oranges, and bananas sat in a wicker basket on the island. Yellow smiley face magnets pinned the children's artwork to the refrigerator. A waist-high wire shelf was parked against the north wall, and on it rested a Christmas cactus in full bloom, two poinsettias, several seedlings in small black plastic containers that had just started to sprout.

This woman was good for his sister. She brought peace, tranquillity, and a sense of order to the house.

He stood in the doorway of the kitchen, arms folded over his chest, shoulder braced against the wall, watching Jane microwave macaroni and cheese—homemade leftovers from the looks of it—and then put green beans on the stove to heat. She moved with such grace, her body loose and fluid, as if she had dance training. The woman was a cut above most people Ashley associated with, and he was fascinated.

Who was she really? He had so many questions, but he was simply too weary to bother with a Magic Slate conversation. Was this how his life was going to be from now on? Full of things he wanted to say but couldn't?

"You're unnerving me," she called over her shoulder. "Staring at me like that."

Yeah? Well, whether she knew it or not, she unnerved him plenty too.

She turned her head to peek at him, an unexpected smile on her face that made his chest swell. *She likes me.* But then he realized she was actually looking at Ben, who was holding out his wet hands for her inspection.

A sheepish heat burned his gut.

"Those are pretty clean hands. A little wet though," she said, and gave the boy a cup towel to dry his hands on.

"Mine too?" Kimmie thrust her hands out.

"Perfect," Jane approved.

"Who's the rotten egg?" Ben asked.

"Hmm. Is it you?" Jane leaned down to sniff her boy.

"No, you smell squeaky clean." Flaring her nostrils in exaggeration, she moved to Kimmie. "Is it you?"

Kimmie lifted her shoulders up to her ears as Jane sniffed her and giggled sweetly. "It's not me."

Jane raised her own arm and sniffed there. Both kids giggled. "It's not me."

Hutch could tell this was a game they'd played before, a funny ritual between them as if they were all family. His niece was totally comfortable with Jane, and it occurred to him that she had been taking care of Kimmie a lot.

"Where's that rotten egg smell coming from?" Jane tipped her nose up, sniffed the air like Smokey Bear sniffing out a forest fire.

That drew a fresh round of giggles from the children.

"I know!" Kimmie cried. "Unca Hutch is the stinky one."

The three of them descended on him, laughing and sniffing, and in that moment, the anger, resentment, loneliness, and grief that dogged him evaporated. In that sweet second, the rage at losing his team that had simmered inside him nonstop from the moment he'd awakened at Walter Reed was gone, and for one sweet moment, he was his old self again.

Amazingly, Hutch was laughing too. He hadn't laughed since before the ambush. And it felt like an utter betrayal of the men who'd fought beside him and died. They would never again laugh with their families.

His gaze met Jane's and his laughter vanished.

Happiness leached from her dark blue eyes. Eyes that said she couldn't believe she was cavorting with him any more than he could believe she was doing it. She sucked in a deep breath, and stepped back. The wall came up. Her face tightened and her lips thinned and she was once again the terrified woman who'd pepper-sprayed him.

She lifted a shaky hand, brushed her fingers across her temple as if she were pushing an errant strand back over her ear, but the close-cropped style was too short for flyaway locks, making him wonder if this haircut was something new that she couldn't get used to.

For the first time, he spotted a jagged, silver scar behind her left ear that staggered up into her hairline as if someone had broken a bottle over her head. Aware of where his gaze had gone, she dropped her hand, and her eyes turned flat, empty.

What on God's green earth had happened to her?

The microwave dinged and Jane exhaled audibly. She bustled around the kitchen serving up the food.

"Dinner's ready, kids," she sang out, but the sound was forced, fake, devoid of her earlier joy as she carried the plates to the table.

The children, not picking up on the shift in mood between the adults, were still giggling and sniffing.

"Join us, Hutch," she invited, waving toward the seat at the head of the table.

Feeling like a guest in his own house, Hutch sat.

Jane herded the children to the table, taking extra care not to look at him. She had no more than settled the kids in their chairs when Ben leaped up from his seat and moved to throw his arms around Kimmie.

"We're twins," he announced to Hutch.

"Twins!" Kimmie cried, and hugged Ben back.

"They share the same birthday," Jane explained as she sat down, her tone letting him know that she was ignoring everything that had just passed between them, the laughter, that brief moment of connection, his recognition that far more lay below the surface than she could or would reveal. "They've gotten it into their heads that means they're twins."

"We are," Ben said firmly, brooking no argument.

"Twins," Kimmie confirmed. "They've been inseparable ever since they met," Jane said in that plain, not-giving-anything-away tone, her gaze fixed firmly on the cheesy elbow noodle on the end of her fork as if it held the key to the secret of the universe. "It's the main reason I moved in here with Ashley. It's been hard for—"

She broke off. Put her fork down. Her breathing had quickened. She kept her head down, refusing to let him see her face.

Hutch wished he could speak. He wanted to press her and find out what was so hard that it had led her here. She seemed like a proud woman, but she hid an ugly secret. It practically oozed from her pores.

That scar…

Maybe it was better that he couldn't ask her questions without tracking down his Magic Slate. Maybe it was better not to know. He didn't like people prying around in his head. What business did he have to dig around in hers?

Finally, she shot him a quick glance, but there was nothing in it. She'd mastered whatever emotion it was that had momentarily choked her up. "Don't you like mac and cheese?"

He nodded. He'd been so busy trying to read her body language that he hadn't taken a bite.

"I could make something else."

He shook his head, silently mouthed, *It's fine*.

"Do you…" She motioned at her throat. "Have trouble swallowing?"

In answer, he took a bite, swallowed, made an exaggerated "mmm" face that had the kids giggling again. He and Jane ate in silence while the children chattered about Christmas. He'd never seen two kids of the same age get along so well.

"Mommy, can me and Kimmie have the candy Santa gave us?" Ben asked.

"First, eat your green beans."

Ben looked like he might argue, but after a stern look from his mother, he popped a green bean in his mouth and chewed as he idly kicked the rungs of his chair. Kimmie eyed him, nudged the green beans off her plate, and then looked over at Jane, challenging her.

"You too, Kimmie," she said mildly.

Kimmie wrinkled her nose, rested her elbow on the table, let her shoulders drop into a sag. "I don't wike green beans."

"You ate green beans last week and said you loved them," Jane said in a kind, affectionate tone.

"That was before." Kimmie poked at a green bean with a chubby little finger.

Jane set her fork down, gave Kimmie her full attention. "Before what, sweetheart?"

"You know." Kimmie shrugged and her eyelashes misted with tears. "Before my mommy went to visit Santa."

Jane reached across the table to pat Kimmie's hand. She didn't make false promises or excuses for Ashley. A tear rolled down his niece's face and she ducked her head.

It hit Hutch exactly what he was up against. Until

Ashley decided to come home, Kimmie was his total responsibility. He thought of everything involved in taking care of a kid, meals and baths and taking her to and from school. Regular bedtimes and doctor appointments and making sure she brushed her teeth. It was hard work and he was in no shape to take on the task. It was the stuff of Hollywood comedies, a maimed soldier with PTSD in charge of an active four-year-old girl. Might be cute on the screen, but in reality there was so much that could go wrong.

No clue. He had no clue what to do.

Better damn well get a clue. And fast. Kimmie was here and her mother was not and he wasn't about to turn his niece over to Child Protective Services. He knew firsthand what happened when they took you away from your mother. He couldn't allow that to happen to his niece.

"Kimmie, you better hurry and eat your green beans," Jane teased. "Ben is going to beat you."

"What?" Kimmie straightened, swiped the tears away.

"He's almost done with his green beans. I bet you can beat him if you hurry and you'll get your candy first," Jane coaxed, gently shifting Kimmie's attention off her missing mother.

"No way, Jose!" Ben exclaimed and gobbled his beans.

"I gonna beat you," Kimmie cried in a singsong voice, and stuffed green beans into her mouth.

Jane looked at Hutch. "Maybe it's not the optimal way to get kids to eat their veggies, but…"

He got it and thought she was doing an amazing job.

"I win!" Kimmie mumbled past a cheek full of food,

bits of green bean sticking to her lips, and raised her arms over her head.

"Nuh-unh." Ben protested.

"It was a tie," Jane said diplomatically. "The candy is in the pocket of my uniform on the bed—"

Before she could finish, the kids were out of their chairs and tearing up the stairs. Jane dropped a small smile and turned in her seat to watch them.

"Ben and I are really going to miss Kimmie," she said.

Hutch tried not to hear her wistful note, but while he might be Delta Force–trained, he wasn't made of stone. She cared about Kimmie and he needed help. Hard as it was for him to ask, it was time to choke down the pride. He levered himself up from the table, and left the kitchen.

"Hey, I know I'm no gourmet cook, but my mac and cheese isn't really that bad, is it?" Jane called after him, her tease barely hiding the anxiety slathered underneath.

Hutch went to the foyer, closed his hand over the Magic Slate. Did he really want to get tangled up with a woman he knew nothing about?

But Kimmie liked her and, really, how many options did he have?

He caught a glimpse of himself in the oval wall mirror mounted above the foyer table. The mirror, decorated with fake plastic mistletoe, reflected unkempt black eyebrows standing out starkly on his forehead, bleary bloodshot eyes, a bristle of beard dusting his jaw, angry scars puckering the skin of his throat.

Yeah. Not a prize. Slice it any way you like. He was not on anyone's list of most desirable roommates.

He wouldn't blame her if she refused his proposition. Most likely she would refuse it. Any sensible woman would. She would never understand how much it cost him to do this, to grovel. This was for Kimmie.

If there was any other way, he'd take it, but his bag of tricks was empty. She was all he had.

Surprised to see that his hand was trembling slightly, Hutch picked up the stylus, wrote I NEED YOU on the Magic Slate, and took it back to her.

I NEED YOU.

Meredith stared at the words scribbled on the pad, and for one startled second thought he meant sexually. Worse, her body instantly lit up. Nerve endings tingling, stomach tightening. She got warm down *there*.

Oh no. She looked up at him, blinked, and as soon as she met his harried eyes, she realized he was talking about Kimmie. He needed her help with his niece.

I NEED YOU.

Looking at those words unnerved her. She lifted the filmy top sheet of the slate, making the writing disappear, and handed it back to him. She could hear her heart thumping in her ears.

His hands were clenched, his jaw tight; a muscle at his eye twitched. Asking for help didn't come naturally to this man. He was used to being in control, in charge, and he hated being in this inferior position.

It had taken a lot for him to write those three little words.

He didn't return to his seat at the head of the table, but instead remained standing, forcing her to crane her neck up at him. The children came charging back into the room, unwrapping their mini chocolate bars and talking so fast she could barely make out that they were discussing Santa, oblivious to the tug-of-war tension pulling between her and Hutch.

Meredith got to her feet. "Let me get the kids ready for bed. Then we can talk. You take it easy. Watch TV or something."

Honestly, it was a little soon to put the children to bed, but she needed to get away from him in order to process his proposal and how she felt about it.

It took her over an hour to get the kids bathed and settled down for their nightly bedtime story. Kimmie insisted on *The Magic Christmas Cookie*, but Ben begged for *The Polar Express*. Meredith compromised and read both.

Yes, it was an avoidance technique, she knew it, but for that lovely space of time, it felt good to snuggle in bed, a child tucked on either side of her as she read. Kimmie fingering her blankie, Ben sucking his thumb.

Ever since Ashley had taken off, Meredith had allowed both children to sleep in her bed. It was probably not a great habit to get started, but how could she leave little Kimmie alone in her room on the first floor? And how could she let Kimmie share the queen-sized bed with her and not Ben?

Just before eight o'clock, both children fell asleep and Meredith tiptoed downstairs. She wished she was wearing something more flattering than ragged jeans and a worn-out sweater, but what else would she have put on? It wasn't like she had a fashionista wardrobe. And why would she change for him anyway?

The living room was empty. The TV turned off.

Where was Hutch?

She went into the kitchen to find the dishes washed

from his back pocket, ran it through his damp air, slicking it off his forehead.

She moistened her lips.

He picked up the tablet, wrote for a long moment, and then leaned forward to pass it across the coffee table to her.

She caught the smell of him, rich and manly mixed with the scent of outdoors. She peered down at the tablet. To get his words on the small page, he'd crammed the letters up small and she had trouble reading his handwriting. She squinted. He turned on the lamp beside the recliner.

Ah, illumination. She read the first line.

I NEED HELP.

Great first step, right? Admitting that you need help. She eyed him through the fringe of her lashes. He was staring at her. She dropped her gaze, kept reading.

I HAVEN'T SEEN KIMMIE IN A YEAR. SHE HARDLY KNOWS ME. BONDED WITH YOU AND YOUR SON. COULD YOU STAY HERE UNTIL ASHLEY COMES HOME? I'LL PAY YOU & FREE ROOM AND BOARD.

While she gathered her thoughts, she kept her head down so he couldn't see what she was thinking. Honestly, she had nowhere to go and no money to float a move even if she did.

But the notion of staying in this house with him was a bit terrifying. Not because she was wary of him, but precisely because she wasn't. She *should* be wary of him. She'd learned to distrust all men. You never really knew what they were capable of. One look at Hutch—all silent and burly and battle-scarred—and any ordinary woman would be at least a little wary of being alone with him. After all she'd been through, why wasn't she wary of him?

Maybe it was because he'd looked so brokenhearted when Kimmie had screamed at her first sight of him. Maybe it was because her son had so readily accepted him. Maybe it was because he'd washed the dishes while she put the kids to bed.

Maybe it was because she had finally healed enough to take a few tentative steps toward trusting again.

Or maybe it was the two words that had flashed through her head when she'd caught him standing in her bedroom after his shower—hair damp, T-shirt stretched across those broad, powerful shoulders, relaxed stance. Those two words, startling in their impact, lit up her brain.

True North.

Beyond the effects of pepper spray, she could see the underlying symmetry in his face, an appealing balance of eyes, nose, lips, and chin. He was a handsome man, but the feelings churning inside her were about much more than good looks.

Strength of character emanated from him. There was a genuineness about him that said, *I am credible. You can believe in me.* An honesty that was almost palpable.

When she was a little girl, she loved hearing the story of how her mother met Meredith's father. How her mother had known he was the one she wanted to spend the rest of her life with.

Her mother would pull Meredith into her lap, and run her fingers through Meredith's hair in a soothing gesture, a beatific smile on her face. "We met when he came to the Albuquerque balloon festival. I was piloting my first balloon. It was a simple balloon because it was all I could afford. I've shown you pictures of Old Blue. Your father, however, was flying the motorcycle-shaped balloon and it made me think he was a cocky hotshot. Which he was." Her mother would always laugh at that.

"What happened next?" Meredith would clasp her hands underneath her chin and lean against her mother's chest.

"We got caught in the box on the same current," she said, referring to the wind phenomenon that made Albuquerque so excellent for ballooning. If conditions were right, balloonist could take off at a low altitude and the wind current would take them south, then as they gained altitude, they caught the northerly current that would take them back in the direction they'd come. In this situation, a balloonist could go up and down, back and forth for two hours. "As luck would have it, our balloons stayed together the entire time. We stared at each other, flirting with our eyes. When we landed, your father came up to me and said, 'You're my True North.' While I was thinking the exact same thing about him."

Meredith would sigh happily, safe and secure in the romantic story of her parents' love.

"True North," her mother would say as she wound up the story. "Never settle for less than your True North."

In spite of the great story, she hadn't really understood what that meant and she'd been led astray by what she thought was her True North.

But this feeling was unlike anything she'd ever experienced. She had been so thrown by it, she'd snapped at him for being in her room.

And that True North sensation was back again, urging her to trust him.

Don't, don't, don't, chanted the part of her that knew just how disastrous trusting the wrong man could be.

But this wasn't just about her. She had Ben to consider. In just a handful of weeks, Ben had come to love Kimmie like a sister.

It was all the more reason to get out of here. The longer she stayed, the more attached her son would become to the little girl. Meredith closed her eyes, inhaled deeply. Daily yoga practice for the last five years had taught her to quiet her thoughts and listen to her body. She exhaled slowly. Took another deep breath and then another.

There was no tension in her body. Her muscles were relaxed, her lungs full, her heart warm, and her stomach settled.

The same sense of panic that had overtaken her that afternoon, when she first spied his truck in the driveway, crawled across the back of her brain like a black widow spider. Was it gut instinct or intellectual reasoning driving the fear? Would saying yes to his proposal bring her closer to the emotional healing she so desperately wanted? Or could it place both her and her son in a dangerous situation?

She raised her head, opened her eyes.

He hadn't moved.

She lifted the top sheet of the Magic Slate, erasing his plea, set the tablet on the coffee table, and cleared her throat.

Hutch leaned forward in the chair, elbows on his knees, hands clasped, the index finger of his right hand rubbing the seam of the healing scar where his left index finger used to be.

"Phantom pain?" She nodded at his finger.

Chagrin passed over his face, but quickly disappeared like the words from the Magic Slate, but the emotions were still buried below, the same as the words trapped in the wax blackboard beneath the filmy gray top sheet. Unseen, but etched deep. Embarrassment. Shame. Resignation. Defeat.

I need help.

I need you.

Once upon a time, she'd been so trusting, so eager to help. Generous to a fault, her friends described her. "Meredith will not only give you the shirt off her back, but her pants and shoes too." But when you gave someone else your clothes, that left you naked and exposed.

"Boundaries," said Dr. Lily Gardner, the counselor Meredith had first started seeing three days after her honeymoon, when she realized she'd made a horrible mistake. "You keep giving away pieces of yourself and there will be nothing left of you. You need to learn to set healthy boundaries in order to have healthy relationships."

At the time, Meredith hadn't really understood what that meant. How could she set boundaries and still be intimate with someone?

It was only later that she came to fully understand that she could not truly be intimate with someone until she *had* established boundaries. Set up the ground rules. Made it clear what lines she would not cross. Hold strong to which behaviors she would and would not accept from loved ones. Loving unconditionally did not mean surrendering herself to someone else's will.

Unfortunately, those lessons had come far too late.

Hutch wiped a palm over his mouth. A slight sheen of sweat pearled on his forehead. His eyes were steady, but the pulse at the hollow of his scarred neck jumped rhythmically. He was nervous. Afraid she'd say no.

She cleared her throat.

He straightened, his spine military-stiff.

"I have conditions," she said.

He sank back against the seat, let out a long-held breath, his lips lifting in a relieved twitch.

"This isn't a yes." She injected steel into her voice and pointed a strict finger at him. "Not until you agree to my conditions. I have ground rules."

His right eyebrow shot up, and he cocked his head, giving his face an oh-yeah-Little-Red-Riding-Hood mien in the spill of lamplight.

"One." She pulled her left index finger back with her right. "You'll need to move downstairs to the first floor. Kimmie's bedroom is down here and she doesn't need to be on the first floor alone. Plus, Ashley and I already have an agreement. The top floor is mine, and other than the kitchen and living room, which we deemed as communal areas, the bottom floor and garage are hers. Although to ease your mind, in case you were wondering if I've been snooping, I have not been in your room. I respect other people's privacy. I expect nothing less from you."

He gave an accepting nod.

"Two." She ticked off her second finger. "No swearing. As a soldier your life has been rough and hard and I'm sure it's natural for an alpha he-man to use every cussword in the book, but do all that away from me and the children."

He touched his mouth, held up his hands, shrugged, smiled.

Her face heated. "I'm sorry, I keep forgetting you

can't talk, but cursing is part and parcel of angry impulses. Even if you can't swear, you'll still be mad over whatever it was that made you want to curse. So if you're having anger control issues, please see a counselor. And while it's human to get angry, it's not acceptable to act aggressively because of it."

He shot her a you-have-no-idea-what-I've-seen-and-done expression.

Meredith pressed her lips together. "I really do hate that bad things happened to you over there, but the children and I shouldn't have to be punished for what you went through and I won't tolerate violence of any kind. No throwing things. No punching a wall. Nothing. Got it?"

His jaw tightened, but his nod was firm, his eyes agreeable.

"Three." Down she pulled her third finger. "We work together to give the children a good holiday. There's a lot going on in their lives. Kimmie's mother has disappeared and you've shown up unexpectedly. There's going to be an adjustment period, but it's Christmas and we should do all the traditional Christmas things for them. Put up a tree. Watch the kids perform in their school play. Take them to Dickens on the Square this weekend and to see Santa Claus. Caroling. Even though you can't sing, you can lip sync. The whole nine yards."

He raised both thumbs.

Meredith paused a moment. Her final condition was not going to be an easy topic to bring up, but she had to say it.

"Four." She waved all four fingers at him. "I don't want anyone to get any wrong ideas. Not you, not the kids, not the neighbors…" *Not me.* "This arrangement is one hundred percent employer/employee, landlord/renter relationship. You need someone to help you care for Kimmie until her mother returns, and I need a place to live through the holidays. However, living in close quarters can stir physical urges and you've been at war."

This time his expression said, *What do you take me for? A pervert?*

"We have a dicey living situation. In the interest of avoiding trouble, you don't touch me. I don't touch you. Ever."

His eyes narrowed teasingly and she could see his mental wheels turning.

"Not ever," she reiterated. "If I have a heart attack, go next door and get someone else to do CPR on me."

Amusement plucked the corners of his mouth.

"Boundaries. I'm just setting solid boundaries." She drew her spine up tall. "If there are any boundaries issues that you want to bring up in regards to this situation, this is the time to do it. Although if you think of something you'd like to add or change later, we can certainly renegotiate the terms if needed."

He waved a hand in an I'm-good-for-now gesture.

"Do you agree to the conditions I've outlined?"

A slow, friendly nod.

"Violate my rules and I throw you out on the spot."

He stabbed her with a hard-edged stare and settled the tips of two fingers to the center of his chest.

"Yes, you. I throw you out. The children need a roof over their heads, and right now, Kimmie needs a mother figure more than she needs a surrogate father. You'll have to find somewhere else to live until Ashley returns. At that point, my son and I will move on. Is this acceptable? If it's not, the arrangement is off."

His mouth tightened in a grimace. He wanted so badly to say something. He needed his tablet.

She reached for the Magic Slate on the coffee table at the same time he did.

Their hands touched.

An instant tingle of hot awareness shot up her arm. Meredith sucked in a startled breath, lungs swelling, causing her breasts to rise sharply and attract Hutch's masculine gaze.

She held her breath. His gaze shifted from her chest to her face, and there was no denying his hungry eyes.

He wanted her sexually.

A shiver ran through her and she did her best to suppress it so he wouldn't see the goose bumps dotting her skin, wouldn't figure out that her treacherous body wanted him too.

"Just so you know," she said as casually as she could muster. "I own a .40-caliber Colt Defender, and don't doubt for a second that I know how to use it."

He looked dutifully impressed.

"Do you agree?" she asked.

He picked up the tablet, settled back in the recliner, jotted something down, and then looked at her with half-lidded eyes before he turned the Magic Slate around so she could see what he'd written.

WHEN DO WE OFFICIALLY START? BECAUSE I THINK I ALREADY VIOLATED RULE #4.

Chapter 6

Talk about a tough cookie. Jane was a lot feistier than Hutch originally thought. Still wide awake at two a.m., he lay in bed replaying everything that had happened that afternoon.

It wasn't all bad. For the first time since the ambush, his mind was not consumed by the loss of his team, but in the span of a few short hours, his life had changed yet again. Apparently, turmoil was the name of the game. Who up there kept shuffling all the cards on him?

Stop feeling sorry for yourself, Hutchinson. There's a four-year-old kid in there whose mother took off on her.

Kimmie. What was he going to do with her? Yeah, he'd hired Jane to take up the slack, at least through the Christmas holidays, but what was he going to do after that if Ashley decided to make her wild adventure permanent? He gritted his teeth. Who was the son of a bitch she'd run off with?

He closed his eyes, tried to will himself to sleep, but his mind was racing with dark thoughts and horrible what-ifs. Maybe he shouldn't have gone off the benzos cold turkey, not with all this shit getting dumped into his lap. Gupta had warned him to taper the drugs. He should have gotten that prescription filled.

He was not going to think about Ashley. That led him down some ugly rabbit holes. Think about something else.

His mind complied and produced the image of how Jane had looked when their hands brushed and their eyes made sizzling contact.

Man, what was that all about?

Even now, he could still feel the power of that single touch, and he shook his head in amazement. Whatever it was had triggered primal cravings in him, and he found himself ensnared in a swift current of stark electricity.

She had sucked in her breath and those glorious tits had risen under that faded, worn sweater. God help him, he'd tried not to stare, but he could not fight off the impulse. Could not stop thinking about what color of bra sheathed those boobs, and that had set off a whole fantasy of just how quickly he could unhook the bra and get his bare hands on her soft, pillowy flesh.

In that moment, his brain figured out what his dick had already known in the bathroom when she'd undressed him.

He wanted her.

A lot.

And even though he knew she would rather die than admit it, she wanted him too. He'd seen it her eyes, in the way she'd licked her lips and leaned in toward him. Why else make up rule #4? She needed the rule to keep her own desires at bay.

The temptation to kiss her had been ass-kicking strong. Every cell in his body hollered at him to kiss her. In the old days, he *would* have done it. Shown her exactly what she was missing by holding herself back.

But she was scared.

Underneath that sassy bravado, she'd been through some serious shit. He wasn't forgetting the pepper spray and how frightened she'd looked when he'd come up to the window of her minivan. She was broke and living with his sister when she was a mom who should have a place of her own. There was a story there, and his gut told him it was anything but pretty.

So what? You've got enough problems of your own. Last thing you need is to shoulder her baggage.

He thought about her, lying in the bed across the hall, and his dick hardened.

She was right, of course. Being in close quarters together, especially with this underlying sexual chemistry, was bound to stir up trouble. Keeping their distance was the safe choice, the right choice.

But could he keep his promise?

He had to keep it. For Kimmie's sake. His niece had had enough disruption in her life. It was his job to make her feel safe and loved and cared for, and that was a tall order for a soldier who could barely take care of himself. He simply couldn't do it on his own.

Not yet. Not until he got his voice back.

If what Gupta and Jenner said was true and his loss of speech was strictly psychological, he was pretty screwed up.

Before he could fully function as Kimmie's guardian, he had to deal with his issues, and the last thing he needed was the attraction between him and Jane muddying the water. He vowed to stick to Jane's rules.

Every last one of them.

The bed was empty.

Meredith blinked fully awake.

The bed was empty and the children were gone.

Adrenaline shot her off the mattress. Panic flared. She'd let down her guard. Slept too soundly, and now the kids weren't here. What if *he* had come into the house and kidnapped them?

She was on her feet, knees quivering, body reacting before her mind could reason out the situation. From downstairs came the sound of children's voices.

It was okay. Ben and Kimmie were here. They were safe.

He hadn't found her again. *He* hadn't snuck into the house as she slept. *He* hadn't stolen the children.

Instead, Captain Brian Hutchinson had come home. That's why the kids weren't here. It was why they hadn't awakened her with requests for breakfast. Why she'd gotten the best sleep she'd had in five years.

Hutch had returned.

This was a good thing.

Why couldn't she accept that? Relax a little?

Because Hutch or no Hutch, the sociopathic stalker who'd sworn to kill her in a million horrible ways was still out there. And in spite of the frequent moves and the job changes and the hair dye and the weight loss to change her appearance and the gun in the locked box underneath her bed, she believed him. She knew what that monster was capable of.

Breathe.

She took several deep, cleansing breaths, did some yoga stretches to quell her quaking muscles, but her mind couldn't fully focus until she was one hundred percent certain that the children were okay.

It was six-forty-five. Normally, she never slept past six, even on the weekends. How and why had she slept so soundly? Not even rousing when the children got out of bed.

Quickly, she dressed in a clean uniform, and not bothering with makeup or combing her hair, hurried downstairs.

She heard their laughter before she saw them, Kimmie's high-pitched girly giggle, Ben's boyish chuckle, and Hutch.

Hutch was laughing too. A deeply masculine sound that rolled around throughout the house and immediately lifted Meredith's spirits. He might not be able to talk, but he could laugh.

They didn't see Meredith as she drifted into the kitchen. Hutch was at the stove with two kitchen chairs at either elbow, complete with a four-year-old standing on the seat of each chair. On the noses of all three cooks was a smear of yellow pancake batter, along with twin slashes of batter decorating their cheeks like war paint. All three wore aprons. The aprons were oversized and baggy on the kids. She'd never seen the aprons before and wondered where he'd gotten them.

Kimmie's apron read: "Life Is Short. Eat Dessert First." Ben's proclaimed: "Real Men Cook." Red rubber spatula in hand, Hutch dwarfed the navy blue apron tied around his neck. It announced in gold lettering: "My Job Is to Cook, Yours to Eat."

Underneath the apron, Hutch wore jeans and a blue plaid flannel shirt that gave him a lumberjack appearance. His face was clean-shaven. His eyes bright and clear. Fresh day. Fresh start.

A platter of crispy bacon cooked to perfection rested on the counter. On a buttered grill, poured in the shape of Mickey Mouse's head, pancakes browned. How had he managed that? It was a mystery on par with the aprons.

Meredith's worrywart impulse was to tell the children to get off the chairs and scold Hutch for allowing them to get so close to a hot stove. But they were having so much fun that she bit her tongue, pressed her palms together behind her back in reverse prayer pose, and watched.

A minute later, Hutch glanced up and met her eyes.

The way he looked at her singed her panties. She felt like she was bowling pins and he was the bowling ball, ripping down a shiny waxed lane for the perfect strike.

A vision that was completely unwanted, but there nonetheless, popped into her head. She saw herself taking him by the hand, leading him upstairs to his bedroom, yanking off his clothes to see if he really could cook up something she was eager to eat.

This was craziness.

Why wasn't she afraid of him? After everything she'd been through, she should be terrified of him. She didn't know exactly what had happened to him, but the fresh scars were clear. He was in a bad place and so was she. Why couldn't she stop thinking about sex whenever she looked at him? Why did she keep wondering what he tasted like?

This feeling had nothing to do with his steely jaw, chiseled cheekbones, prominent brow, and big, muscular body. Okay, that wasn't quite the truth. It had something to do with his handsome masculine attributes. Most women would fall at his feet. That was a given. But why was *she* doing it? She'd fallen for that testosterone-soaked, alpha male, he-man stuff once and it had turned out to be the biggest mistake of her life.

Was she that stupid?

Or had she honed her inner emotional radar enough to pick up on and decipher the small things that spoke volumes?

The innate kindness that softened his eyes whenever he looked at the children, and the sound of his laughter, hearty and honest and open, that belied the rigid set to his shoulder. His sense of humor that cropped up unexpectedly as it had last night with his joke about violating rule #4. It was in the way that Jesse had spoken about him, when he told her who Hutch was after she'd pepper-sprayed him, his voice top heavy and sincere with admiration.

In spite of his gruffness and rough edges, Brian Hutchinson was a good man.

But it didn't matter.

Meredith could not act on the attraction. She had nothing to offer him. Nothing to give. She lived on the run. Did her best to take care of her son and stay one step ahead of the dangerous man who dogged her. That was all she had the time and energy for.

"Mom!" Ben exclaimed. "Look what we made."

She stepped over to the stove to admire the Mickey

Mouse pancakes, tried not to notice that Hutch was barefooted and had the sexiest feet she'd ever seen— not too big, not too small, not too narrow, not too broad, long straight toes, trimmed nails. Perfect feet.

Eyes on Mickey.

Meredith pressed a palm to her son's back to center her thoughts. "You made these?"

"He helpeded me." Ben threw an enthusiastic arm around Hutch's waist.

Her son was touching Hutch and she was touching Ben, creating a physical link between the three of them. Even though she wasn't physically touching Hutch herself it was too close, too much like violating rule #4. Meredith dropped her hand, moved back.

"Unca Hutch." Kimmie hopped down off her chair, almost tripping over her apron. "His name is Unca Hutch."

"Unca Hutch," Ben repeated, and beamed up at Hutch.

"Hold on, kids, let me get those aprons off you before you hang yourselves." Meredith moved to untie the aprons from around the children's necks. "And be careful not to touch the stove. It's hot."

"I know that," Ben said in an exasperated, I'm-growing-up-let-me-do-things-on-my-own tone he had started using lately.

She was overprotective. She realized that, but she had good reason to smother. Disaster could very well lie around the next corner. All she had to do was let her guard slip for a second and Ben could be taken from her in the snap of a finger.

One of these days her son was going to demand independence, and then what?

Meredith pulled down her shirtsleeves over her hands. She'd worry about that when the time came. Until then, he was still within her control.

Hutch brought the food to the table and they sat down to eat breakfast together like a real family.

The atmosphere was different from last night's meal. She and Hutch had come to an understanding. Everything was going to be all right, at least through the Christmas holiday, and that was all the certainty she needed.

While it sounded good on the surface, Meredith couldn't help feeling wistful. Would a day ever come when she and Ben would have this for themselves—a strong family unit, a welcoming community, a permanent home and everything it represented?

It was a pointless question because she already knew the answer.

There would be no safety for her. No security. No freedom from fear. Not ever.

Not as long as her ex-husband, LAPD Detective Vick Sloane, lived.

After Jane took the children to school before heading on to work, Hutch washed the dishes, tidied up, and then moved his things out of his bedroom and into his sister's bedroom as Jane's rules demanded. The bedroom had actually been his to begin with before Ashley moved in, but all signs of him had vanished amid the mess of her scattered possessions—clothes, makeup, jewelry. No telling when she would be back, but he didn't want to displace her things because she could pop up tomorrow, so he'd made a path through the clutter, changed the sheets, and called it good.

Once he finished those chores, he was at loose ends, prowling the house looking for something else to do and it wasn't even ten a.m. For most of his adult life he'd been a soldier. Every day was regimented, and the last couple of months had been consumed with his recovery.

Now here he was with time on his hands.

He could take his boat out, but it was drizzling. Not that he'd melt or anything, he just couldn't seem to rally the enthusiasm.

He could try to track down Ashley. Snoop around on her computer and see if he could unearth anything about this asshole she'd run off. But he'd been down that road before. If not this asshole, it would be someone else. The path always led to over-the-top drama and crazy, left-field accusations, in which he always came out the villain. That was the most frustrating thing in dealing with someone who suffered from BPD.

The more he tried to help her, the more it backfired on him. The same had been true of his mother before she finally succumbed to her demons and took her own life. After many years and many false steps, eventually he came to understand that he didn't have the power to fix his sister, and by continuing to try, he was actually making things worse. Growing up, she'd been his responsibility. Letting go of that mindset was almost impossible, but he had to do it for his own sanity. Joining the military had been his salvation in that regard, but now that was gone.

Ashley was a grown woman. If she wanted to take off with some sketchy character, he couldn't stop or change her. As long as Kimmie was safe and well cared for, that's what mattered.

He could do some digging and find out exactly who

Jane Brown was. On the surface, she appeared to be everything she said she was, but underneath she was hiding something. He felt it in his bones. Still, did he really want to stir that hornet's nest? They'd agreed to stay in the house and put on a nice Christmas for the kids. If he started poking around, he had to expect blowback. Was he ready for that?

Or he could fix the fence Jane had knocked down with her minivan and then put up Christmas lights as a surprise for the children when they got home. He imagined their happy expressions, and he smiled a smile that felt rusty, but good.

Yeah. He liked that idea. Christmas lights.

He headed for the garage where he stored the decorations, but before he got there, the doorbell rang. Who could that be? Most likely it was some overly helpful neighbor. For better or worse, Twilight was full of 'em.

His initial impulse was not to answer the door. He couldn't talk and he didn't want to get into explaining the whole mess via Magic Slate.

Yeah, but the sane thing to do was open the door, even if he didn't feel like it. If he didn't have Kimmie to consider, he wouldn't give a damn, but he had to get his head on straight for her.

Suck it up, Hutchinson. Do the right thing.

The doorbell rang again.

He looked around for the Magic Slate, forgot where he'd stashed it. He'd had it at the breakfast table. Not there. Not on the bar. He was helpless without the damn thing. Had he left it upstairs?

A knock sounded on the door this time, a strong, masculine knock.

Where was that Magic Slate? Stalling. He was stalling. Just grab a pen and paper.

He snatched a pen and paper from beside the phone
charging station in the kitchen and strode toward the
door. Through the blinds covering the window beside
the front door, he could see the shadow of three men
standing on the front porch.

Hutch faltered. Stopped.

"Maybe he's not home," one of the men said, and
Hutch recognized the voice as belonging to Sheriff
Hondo Crouch.

Hondo had been wounded in Vietnam and had come
home with a heroin addiction. He'd been one of the
lucky ones, who with therapy and community support
had turned his life around. Last Christmas Eve, he'd
married his high school sweetheart, Patsy Cross, forty
years after they'd first fallen in love. Hutch had been a
groomsman at the wedding.

"His pickup is in the driveway," said the second man.

"He could be out fishing, Nate," Hondo speculated.

The second man must be Nate Deavers. Nate was a
former Navy SEAL who'd moved to Twilight the previous year. Nate was six or seven years older than Hutch
and they'd formed a good-natured SEAL/Delta Force
rivalry. Trash talking each other's branch of the service
in jest, getting competitive at pool and darts down at
the Horny Toad Tavern whenever Hutch was on leave.

When he first met Nate, Hutch sort of hoped Ashley would hook up with him. His sister needed a strong
older man who could handle her mood swings, and Nate
would have made a great father for Kimmie. But the
SEAL had fallen head-over-heels for Raylene Pringle's
daughter, Shannon Dugan. In hindsight it was prob-

ably the best thing, for Nate's sake anyway. Nate and Shannon made a cute couple, and he'd heard through the grapevine that Shannon was pregnant with their first baby.

"Boat's on the side of the house," the third man said. "I saw it when we drove up."

Hutch recognized his voice too. Former Green Beret Gideon Garza.

He and Gideon had gone to high school together, played varsity football together, bonded over the fact they both had fathers who would not claim them and mothers with mental health issues. If there was one person in Twilight who knew exactly what Hutch was going through, it was Gideon. For eight years, everyone in town thought Gideon had been killed in Iraq. He'd lost a hand in a bombing, lost his memory for a while too, and turned soldier of fortune in Afghanistan. Gideon had come back to Twilight after his biological father died and left him a ranch a few years ago. Life had been tough for Gideon, but he'd reconnected with his high school sweetheart, Caitlyn Marsh, and discovered her son, Danny, was his child. Gideon and Caitlyn had gotten married and now they'd had another baby boy.

It seemed as if all the wounded veterans from Twilight had gotten their happy ending except for him.

"Maybe he's just not ready," Nate said. "You men know what it's like when you first get back. You feel like you don't fit in, like no one knows what you're going through."

"Which is why we're here," Gideon said. "To let him know he's not alone."

Pity visit. That's what this was. Hutch dropped the pen and paper onto the foyer table.

"If his doc hadn't called me and told me he hadn't gotten his meds refilled, I wouldn't be so damn worried. But he's heading down a dark road, and the sooner we nip this in the bud, the better."

Shit. This was worse than a pity visit. It was an intervention. And screw Gupta. Who did he think he was interfering in Hutch's life after he'd had the gall to kick Hutch out of the Army? He wished like hell he hadn't put Gideon's name down as a second emergency contact in his files.

One of the shadows on the front porch shifted and Hondo came into his line of sight.

"Hell," Hondo said, his voice louder than it had been before. "I'm here because I want to hear Igloo's tall tales. He's the funniest son of a bitch I know, and he can talk the hind leg off a dog when he's in a storytelling mood."

That's when Hutch realized Hondo had seen him too and he was making out like this wasn't an intervention. So Hondo wanted to hear his stories. That wasn't happening. He wouldn't be entertaining them. He wouldn't be cracking wise or pulling practical jokes.

Because the man they'd come to see no longer existed.

"Let's give him some space," Nate suggested.

"Wallowing in self-pity isn't the answer," Gideon said. "I know. I tried it. He's hurting and can't see a way out of his pain."

We might have played on the gridiron, buddy, and knocked back a few beers, but that don't mean you know me. Hutch knotted his fists, ran his thumb over the stump of his index finger.

"Nate's right," Hondo said, and started walking away.

"Hold on. I can't just leave him hanging. Anybody got some paper? I'll write him a note."

There was silence for a minute, presumably while Gideon wrote the note. Hutch felt stupid just standing there in the hallway waiting from them to leave, but he didn't really know what else he could do at this point. Hondo had already seen him, and knew he was hiding out. And it wasn't as if he could open the door, grin, call them all assholes, pound them on the back, and go off to have a beer like everything was normal.

Finally they left, and he waited a good two minutes before he opened the door and retrieved the note tucked under the doorknocker.

Igloo,

If you need to talk, we're here. And if you feel like getting out of your own head, we could use some help with the Angel Tree toy drive.

Below the note, Gideon had listed his, Nate's, and Hondo's names and phone numbers.

The message was simple and to the point. Reaching out. Trying to help.

Without really knowing why, Hutch doubled up his fist, hauled back, and punched the metal front door with so much force it rattled his teeth.

Chapter 7

Hutch's pickup wasn't in the driveway when Meredith got back with the kids on Thursday afternoon, but the fence had been repaired, Christmas lights strung from the eaves of the house and down the sidewalk. In the middle of the lawn, Santa's sleigh had been set up.

What a sweet surprise.

Enchanted, Kimmie and Ben insisted that she turn the lights on, even though she told them it wasn't dark enough yet. She helped the children remove their coats and hang them in the front hall closet.

The Magic Slate lay on the foyer table. Hutch had gone off without it. Her curious son toyed with it, lifting the top sheet.

"Leave it alone, Ben. That's not yours."

The empty house was spotless, and she had to admit she was a little relieved that he was not home. All day at work, she had caught herself thinking about him in the middle of a massage. How mysterious he'd looked stepping out of the mist last night. How sexy his feet were. How he prepared breakfast for her and the kids, cooking pancakes far more delicious than the ones she made, and he'd offered to make dinner as well.

She found herself charmed, and that was a terrifying thing. The last time someone had charmed her, she'd ended up with a sociopath.

Shivering, she closed her eyes. Hutch wasn't Sloane. He was real, genuine, nothing slick or sly about him. Still, that terrible choice she'd made five years ago haunted her. How could she ever trust her estimation of anyone?

Dr. Lily had told her that she couldn't blame herself, that sociopaths could fool trained professionals. They were skilled manipulators, adept at presenting the face society wanted to see, at least until after they'd conned you.

Meredith shoved thoughts of Sloane aside. He'd dominated too much of her life. She'd learned to seize peace, happiness, and contentment in minute slices. The past couldn't be fixed, the future uncertain. All that mattered was right this moment, and she refused to allow him to ruin that.

True to his word, Hutch had left a pot roast simmering in the slow cooker and a bowl of salad, covered with plastic wrap, in the refrigerator.

She sent the kids to change their clothes, and put on a *Rudolph the Red-Nosed Reindeer* DVD. As a child, it had been one of her favorites, and she made watching it every year a family tradition. She popped some popcorn and went to sit on the couch to share it with the children.

By the time Rudolph triumphantly rescued the misfit toys and saved Christmas, Hutch still hadn't returned. She didn't know his cell phone number so she couldn't text and ask if he was going to be home for supper.

Why was she worried about what he did? They were housemates, sharing child-rearing duties. Nothing more. He'd made the food. She would serve it. If he chose to stay out late, it was none of her business. Although it was a little inconsiderate that he hadn't left her a note. That was just common courtesy, right? He should have left her a note. She might have to add that to her list of rules. Let her know if he was going to be out of pocket.

"Who wants to make candy cane reindeers?" she asked after the show was over.

"Me! Me!" the kids chorused in unison, crawling over Meredith and bringing a smile to her face.

"Okay. Wash your hands and I'll meet you at the kitchen table."

They made reindeers with candy canes, using red pipe cleaners for antlers, gluing small red pompoms for a nose and black googly eyes she'd picked up at the craft store for eyeballs. The kids giggled nonstop. Ben had blossomed since coming to live here. Kimmie had too.

Such a shame she and her son would be moving on after the holidays.

A cloak of melancholia fell over her, but she gave herself a mental shake and shrugged off the emotion. She enlisted the children's help in cleaning up their craft project and hanging the reindeer over the sides of coffee cups on the bar for Hutch to see when he came home, and set the table for supper.

"Where's Unca Hutch?" Kimmie asked.

"He's out." Meredith didn't know what else to say.

Ben tugged on the hem of her shirt. "When's he comin' back?"

"I'm not sure. We'll go ahead and eat without him."

"Did he go to visit Santa like my mommy?" Kimmie worried her bottom lip with her teeth.

"No, sweetie. Who wants to help me make iced tea?" Meredith asked. The kids loved putting the cartridges in the single cup brewer, and that got them off the topic of Hutch.

They ate dinner. She sent the kids into the living room to play while she washed the dishes and put away the food. Then she loaded Ben and Kimmie up in the car and they drove around the neighborhood looking at Christmas lights for half an hour. After that, she put them to bed.

The phone rang as she was brushing her teeth, and she thought, *Hutch!* But when she got to the phone Flynn Calloway's name was on the caller ID. "Hello?"

"Jane?"

Meredith paused for a second, thinking, *Who's Jane?* before remembering the alias she'd chosen to go by in Twilight. In the last five years she'd lived in eleven cities and towns. The false names were getting harder and harder to recall. She tried to keep them plain—Mary, Sue, Ann, Sally, Dee—and for the last three moves, she'd kept the last name of Brown just to make things easier, but that was risky. In the next town maybe she would keep Jane, but change her last name. Now that Ben was getting older the name changes were trickier. For his preschool enrollment in Twilight, she'd used his real birth certificate; getting fake documents was complicated and expensive. When Ben was born she'd put down the father as unknown and given him her maiden name of Sommers. She was terrified that Sloane—with his omnipotent power as a police detective—would trace Ben through school records. Although she'd left Sloane before he knew that she was pregnant, he'd learned about their son when he'd tracked her down the first time.

"Jane? Hello? Are you there?"

"Yes."

"I didn't wake you, did I?"

"No, I was up."

"Oh that's good. I saw the Christmas lights were on and hoped you were still up."

"Wide awake. What's happening?"

"Nothing really. I just wanted to encourage you to attend the cookie swap party. I know you're something of an introvert…"

Not really. Not by nature. Not by choice. But Sloane had made her that way. She couldn't afford to get too chummy with people, give too much away. She'd only started attending the local book club because they held it on the same day Ashley hosted a weekly girls-night-in party with her friends, and Meredith hadn't wanted to intrude. Plus, Ye Olde Book Nook where the group met had story time for the kids. While the moms held their discussion, she could take Ben and Kimmie with her. It felt good to get out of the house, and with the topic of conversation centering on books, no one had asked anything too personal.

"I don't want to be pushy," Flynn continued, "but we really do like you, and the group would love to get to know you better. You'll have fun, I promise."

"I appreciate the invitation, Flynn. Honestly—"

"Let me just interrupt you right there." Flynn's voice took on a Mary-Poppins-efficient cheerfulness. "This is where I dispense with all your buts."

It was flattering to hear that everyone liked her and wanted her to be part of the group. The old desires for love and belonging stirred inside her. The desires she'd put aside in order to achieve the most basic of needs— food, water, a roof over her head, safety, security. She *wanted* to go. Not only for her own mental health, but also to find out everything she could about Hutch.

"I told you Ye Olde Book Nook is our built-in baby-sitter for tomorrow night, and we're having the cookie swap at Raylene's house not half a mile from the bookstore. So what else is making you hesitate?" Flynn asked.

"Ms. Pringle told me the rules of cookie club and she made it clear 'no store-bought cookies.' I simply don't have time to whip up a batch of homemade."

"Oh, is that all?" Flynn laughed. "Pay that rule no mind. People break it all the time. What it really means is no packaged cookies from the grocery store. You can head on over to the Twilight Bakery and pick up a couple of dozen from Christine Noble. She makes the best cookies in town. Half the people at the party will totally be bringing cookies from Christine's bakery."

"Thanks for the tip."

"So you'll come?" Flynn wheedled.

"Sure. Why not?"

"Great." Flynn chuckled as if she'd won a bet with someone who'd told her there was no way she could get Meredith to show up. "We're looking forward to getting to know you better."

"Me too," Meredith said, although she planned to divert all their questions with questions of her own. Questions about Hutch. "See you then."

Flynn said good-bye and hung up, leaving Meredith to the quiet house.

When Hutch wasn't home by ten o'clock, she locked up and went to bed. Boundaries. She was going to have to add rule #5. For the sake of the children, if Hutch wasn't coming home, he had to let her know. Personally, she didn't care what he did.

Was he out getting drunk? Or maybe picking up a woman? He was a soldier, after all, and she had no idea how long he'd been over there. She should expect it. No one could deny his potent virility. Jesse told her Hutch was Delta Force. Only the best of the best made it into that elite, testosterone-driven group, and they all shared certain characteristics—extreme machismo, keen intelligence, highly driven.

For almost five years, she had slept lightly, one ear always tuned for the sounds of something abnormal, her eyes ready to pop open at the slightest hint of trouble. This was the first time she'd lived on the second floor, and that bothered her too. If an intruder was downstairs, she and Ben would have to go out the window to get away. After she moved in, she bought a rope ladder and stashed it in the compartment underneath the window seat just in case.

Twenty minutes after ten, she heard the front door open. Quietly, she eased from the bed so as not to awaken the children, slipped a housecoat on over her sleep shirt, and padded downstairs, ready to read him the riot act.

From the top of the stairs, she could see a pile of

shopping bags in the middle of the living room floor, and Hutch was coming through the door with a fresh armful. He had been Christmas shopping, not drinking or whoring.

Chagrinned, she started down the stairs toward him.

He looked up at her and a convivial smile lightened his craggy face—no, the smile was much more than convivial. It was one of those priceless, spontaneous smiles that bubbled up from deep inside, completely heartfelt and guileless. It landed on her like a caress, locking on her as if she was the only woman in the world that he'd ever gifted with such an irresistible smile. It was a smile that said, *Hi, honey. I'm home, look what your conquering hero brought back for you.* It was a smile that left her completely exposed.

Meredith tightened her belt and her resolve. She wasn't falling for it. "I was worried," she said. "Why didn't you leave a note?"

His smile ebbed, but hung on. *I did,* he mouthed the words.

"Where? I looked all over and didn't see one."

He left the pile of packages, returned with the Magic Slate, and held it up for her to read.

She moved forward and noticed his right hand. It was black and blue, the knuckles busted open and swollen. He'd been in a fight.

"What happened?"

He looked down at his hand like it was nothing, shrugged casually, and handed her the slate.

"Who did you punch?"

No one, he said silently.

She put a hand to her mouth. Should she make a big deal of this? Even though it look like the results of a fistfight, the rest of him looked fine. No black eye. No busted lip. This other hand was fine. She decided not to push the issue. "Let me take care of that injury."

He shook his head, and mouthed, *I'm fine*. She could tell from the look on his face that in his mind the wound was nothing more than a minor annoyance, no bigger than a gnat on his banana.

Still nervously eyeing his fist, she quickly glanced down at the Magic Slate. The filmy top sheet was empty, but she could still make out trace images of the words he'd written.

GONE XMAS SHOPPING IN FORT WORTH. BE BACK LATE.

"Ben," she said, feeling embarrassed for having rushed to judgment. "He was playing with the slate and must have erased it. I'm sorry I jumped to conclusions. I was worried." Why had she admitted that? She didn't want him thinking she'd lost sleep over him.

He wrote slowly, the busted skin on his knuckles pulling open and dotting with blood. MY FAULT. SHOULD HAVE WRITTEN NOTE WITH PEN AND PAPER.

"We need to exchange cell phone numbers. So we can text each other. And stop writing. It's making your hand bleed."

He nodded, beckoning her closer, that never-ending smile back on his face and turning Christmas cryptic.

She moved toward him, her breath slipping quicker over her lips. What was it about him she found so compelling?

Hutched fished around in an extra large Toys "R" Us bag, and peeled the paper to reveal a Thomas the Train ride-on toy. His face split into radiant pride, as if he just summitted Mount Everest without a Sherpa or oxygen.

"How did you know Ben wants one of those more than anything in the world?" she asked.

He cupped a hand behind his ear, meaning, she supposed, *I listen.* Her son did have a mad crush on Thomas the Train and talked about the train engine all the time.

"It's too much, it's too expensive," she said, her heart doing a herky-jerky little dance in her chest.

He lifted a casual shoulder, still flashing that amazing smile that said, *Your boy deserves a good Christmas.*

Meredith had no idea what compelled her. Her heart or her gut. It certainly wasn't her intellect, because her brain screamed, *Do not break rule #4.* But Hutch's face was aglow and he looked so happy, so proud of his purchases that she went up on her toes and kissed him.

She kissed his cheek as if she were a princess and he a knight who had just slain a hundred dragons for her. He had an irresistible impulse to kneel down at her feet. His skin burned sweetly where her lips had branded him, and he reached up a palm to touch the spot.

From all appearances, she was just as stunned as he. Her eyes widened and she stepped back. "I… I…"

Despite the fact that his bruised fingers didn't want to cooperate, he wrote on the tablet. RULE #4 IS A BITCH TO KEEP.

She fingered lips that were forming into a shy, I-can't-believe-I-just-did-that smile. "I'm grateful to you for buying Ben the toy that he wants so badly and I could never afford."

He lifted one corner of his mouth and the opposing

eyebrow, trying not to show how much she bedazzled him. This wasn't an ordinary situation and she was not an ordinary woman.

"I don't want you to think this means anything else, because it doesn't." There was something unexpected and wild in her voice, as if she didn't believe a word she was saying.

Hell, he didn't know what to think.

"This doesn't negate rule #4."

He nodded. *No, princess, it doesn't.*

Her hands went to her hips. "You're not going to argue?"

He sent her a look that said, *Do you want me to?* Struggled, and failed, not to glance at her breasts.

"No, of course not," she said, getting damn good at reading his body language. She folded her arms over her chest, but she was nodding. Did she realize she was nodding?

A year ago if this had happened to him, he would have taken her into his arms and given her a kiss that erased all doubts about what he wanted. But now, things were so different.

He was different.

Also, he had a feeling that if he reached for her, even though she was sending mixed signals, she'd resist. She was like an orchid blooming in the desert, brave as hell, but so damn vulnerable. Sooner or later the sun was going to burn her up.

CONSIDER US EVEN ON RULE #4 VIOLA-TIONS. He let her see what he'd written, and then lifted the top sheet to erase the words so he could add more. LET'S CALL A MULLIGAN AND START FROM SCRATCH.

Relief flooded her face and she gave him a strained thank-you smile.

Good. Great. The applecart had been righted, so why the distinct feeling that he'd lost something important?

Afraid she would read the disappointment in his face, Hutch wheeled around to the packages and started taking out the gifts he'd bought to show to her—a doll for Kimmie, a football for Ben, a Snow White costume, a Hot Wheels track, LEGOs and talking books and Leap-Frog computers, one in pink and one in blue. He showed her everything except for the little blue box that he kept tucked in the bottom of the bag, out of sight.

"You're spoiling those kids rotten." She said it as if spoiling them was a bad thing, but her tone was light.

She looked amazed, her pupils widening as he stared into those gorgeous blue eyes. If he had known eyes this gorgeous had been at his house just waiting on him, he would have come home a whole lot sooner.

After Gideon had left him that note, Hutch had started thinking about why he hadn't answered the door. Why he'd rammed his fist into it. He flexed his hand, savored the sting. He was accustomed to being in charge. He took care of other people. He used to be the mentally healthy one. At least he had been until the ambush. But the bombs and bullets had taken away his control. To accept help from his buddies meant that he couldn't take care of himself. That he couldn't be counted on to take care of the people he cared about.

So he'd gone shopping. Modern-day version of bringing home the bacon.

Was that pathetic?

Maybe. The only thing he knew for sure was that right now, Jane was gazing at him like he'd just hitched the world up on his shoulders, Atlas-style and she was certain that everything would be okay because of it. She made him feel honored and honorable, capable and competent. In that kickass moment he'd felt like his old self.

"Are you hungry?" she murmured.

He nodded.

"C'mon," she said. "Let's hide those toys and I'll heat up the leftover pot roast."

Just like that, the balance between them that she'd upended when she kissed him was restored. Rule #4 was firmly back in place.

But the daring Delta Force operator in him couldn't help wondering what it would take for her to break it again.

The following morning, Meredith got up before dawn, dressed in leggings and a loose T-shirt, and went out onto the second floor landing to practice yoga. She'd skipped it yesterday when she slept in, and a day without yoga left her feeling antsy.

Then again, maybe she was antsy about something else.

Maybe it was the kiss she'd planted on Hutch's cheek last night. What on earth had she been thinking?

Clearly, she had not been thinking. That was the problem. Whenever she was around him, logic did a double gainer out the window.

Why? What was it about Hutch that dismantled her finely honed defenses? She was getting too close to him. She knew it.

Move. She should move.

With less than three weeks until Christmas?

She breathed, slow and deep, fully expanding her

lungs. After several minutes, she struck triangle pose. Enya played through the earbuds of the mp3 player clipped to her waistband: "Only Time." She closed her eyes and allowed the hopeful music to spirit her to tranquillity.

Between the breathing, the poses, and the music, Meredith found the calm center that had carried her through the darkest of days. It would carry her through this too. Her muscles softened, her heart rate slowed, and for those blissful few minutes, she was transformed.

Hutch stood halfway up the staircase, his heart in his throat. He'd heard Meredith moving around on the second floor and he came up to ask her how she liked her eggs. He never intended to spy on her.

But that was exactly what he was doing.

Captivated by the sight of her practicing yoga, his feet welded to the floor and he couldn't seem to make himself go either up or down.

She was seated on the floor, her legs crossed in lotus style, elbows out, palms pressed together in prayer pose. Her breathing was steady, controlled. Her chest rising and falling slowly as she fully expanded her lungs with air. Her hair lay in soft waves, framing her radiant face. Her eyes were closed and an otherworldly smile tipped her lush, pink lips, as if she'd just gotten a glimpse into heaven.

Simply watching her calmed him. He drank her in, storing the sight of her deep within his memory banks. When she was gone, he wanted to be able to remember this moment so he could take it out and touch it whenever he felt harried or stressed.

Thinking about her and Ben leaving chipped a hollow place in the dead center of his breastbone, as if a skilled whittler had taken out a pocketknife and carved a hole. How had he managed to get so attached to her and the boy in just a couple of days?

Not good.

Never mind that whenever he was around her he felt more like his old self. Ignore the fact that her presence kept him from dwelling on his handicaps. Overlook that her smile humbled him, made him ache to be a better man. He barely knew her. This was nothing more than a fantasy he was building up in his head.

But last night when she'd kissed him…

She'd immediately regretted it. He couldn't forget that.

Her fluid movements as she shifted from one pose to the next, with her eyes still closed, carried along by instinct and practice, mesmerized him. What talent, what skill! Her soft face was so kind, so at ease even in the midst of exertion.

He wanted what she had. Peace. Calm. Contentment. If yoga would do the trick, sign him up.

For another few minutes, he watched as long as he dared. He'd better get back down the stairs before she opened her eyes and caught him staring at her. Reluctantly, Hutch sheered away, dragging his spirits behind him.

Yeah, it wasn't so much his fantasy that was the problem. Rather it was the realization that he had no idea what was going to happen to him and Kimmie when she was gone.

Expelling her long-held breath, Meredith opened her eyes all the way and studied Hutch's retreating back.

She'd known the second he'd come up the stairs. Even though she hadn't heard his footsteps over the gentle music whispering through the earbuds, she had felt floorboards vibrate.

She lifted her lashes just enough to see him standing on the stairs if she kept her head tilted slightly back, and debated whether to acknowledge him. She loathed being spied on—five years of being stalked by a maniac would do that to a person—but there was something in the way he looked at her, an expression full of reverence and respect, that kept her silent. It hadn't been creepy or voyeuristic. Instead it was as if she'd bewitched him, ensnaring him in a feminine spell, and he was helpless to glance away.

His awe made her feel powerful.

You put on a show for that man.

She had. She couldn't deny it. Showing off her yoga skills. When had she gotten so audacious?

Why had she gotten so audacious?

And she'd been watching him as intently as he watched her. She read his face like a navigator studying a map, seeking signs of the road up ahead, understanding that forewarned was forearmed. Were there things to avoid? A washed-out bridge? A pothole-riddled stretch of highway? A ten-car pileup?

But the scenery distracted her from those questions. She studied the firm lines of his shoulders, the hard muscles of his broad chest, the clean lines of his narrow waist, the fall of his dark hair across his forehead.

Delicious. This detour.

Nothing wrong with looking, just as long as it didn't lead to touching as it had last night.

Her cheeks burned and her mind would have started

women inside—joke and tease and eat cookies and sip wine to her heart's content. She longed to be normal, to fit in, to recapture that wonderfully beautiful feeling of being loved and cherished that she had experienced as a child. She wanted the same thing for her son.

Inside, she would find goodwill and Christmas cheer and a community eager to welcome her into the fold. It would be so easy to fall into friendly arms and allow herself to be accepted.

But if she did that, leaving Twilight was going to hurt much more than it already did. And she *would* have to leave. There could be no long-term home for her. Eventually, Sloane would find her again. He always did. Constantly moving around and changing her identity was the only way to stay one step ahead of him.

"He's not The Terminator," Dr. Lily had said, two days before Sloane had murdered her. "He's not all knowing and all powerful."

But he was and her psychologist had paid the price for not realizing just how relentlessly ruthless he was.

The LAPD ruled Dr. Lily's plunge off Mulholland Drive an accident. Of course, Sloane had been one of the investigating officers. No matter what the police said, she knew in her heart that the brakes of her doctor's vintage Porsche had been tampered with. That was one of the many fates Sloane used to threaten her with on a daily basis.

She imagined the same thing or worse happening to the people she met in Twilight. Ashley, Kimmie, Hutch, Raylene, Flynn, Jesse. She couldn't bear it.

It wasn't too late to leave.

She spun on her heel, only to come face-to-face with two women from the book club headed up the walkway behind her. Sarah Walker, the author of *The Magic Christmas Cookie*, who wrote under the pen name Sadie Cool, and Emma Cheek, a Hollywood actress turned director and the owner of the Twilight Playhouse Theatre. Sarah was a tall, quiet brunette, Emma a petite, bubbly redhead.

"You came!" Emma exclaimed, and threw an arm around Meredith's waist. In the crook of her other arm, she carried a red wicker basket filled with cookies. Wearing a red and green plaid skirt, and a green sweater with jingle bells sewn on the front, she looked just like one of Santa's elves. Over her shoulder Emma called to Sarah, "And you said she wouldn't come."

Sarah lowered long, thick eyelashes. "I just remember how difficult it was for me at my first cookie swap party. You guys can be overwhelming."

"But in a good way," Emma told Meredith. "Sarah's shy, but she's getting over it. Ooh! You brought Christine's lemon squares. I'm sitting next to you."

Before she could back out, Emma looped her free arm around Meredith's and dragged her through the front door, Sarah trailing behind them.

"We're not going to knock?" Meredith balked.

"We Twilightites don't stand on formalities and Raylene is expecting us," Emma explained. "Keeps her from running to the door every time someone shows up."

From the foyer, as they took off their coats and hung them on the coatrack, Meredith could see a roaring fire in the fireplace that warmed the house. A flocked tree, decorated exclusively with Dallas Cowboys ornaments. Women peered at them from the living room, calling out greetings. Some of them Meredith knew from the book club group, and some were massage clients.

Emma passed off her basket of cookies to Raylene, who handed Meredith a cup of eggnog. "This is virgin," Raylene said. "The good stuff is in the kitchen with an assortment of wines if you want that."

"Thank you."

"C'mon," Emma said, still latched on to Meredith's arm. "Let me introduce you to everyone."

There were at least thirty women in the room. No way could she remember everyone. She shook hands and smiled and made small talk and for the first time in a very long time, she felt like a normal part of society again. Oh, this was dangerous. She could grow so accustomed to having friends again.

After all the guests arrived, the older women migrated to the kitchen, leaving the younger ones seated around the living room. Meredith found herself tucked into the corner of an oversized leather sectional with Emma on her left side, Flynn on her right. Sarah sat next to Flynn. On the other side of Emma was florist Caitlyn Garza. At one point, Emma had whispered to her that Caitlyn was married to Hutch's best friend, and he was a former Iraq war veteran who'd lost his left hand to an IED.

Emma tracked down a corkscrew and opened several bottles of wine—Chardonnay, Cabernet, Riesling, and Pinot Noir.

"What do you want to drink?" Emma asked Meredith.

"I'm a lightweight in the wine department," she admitted.

"You'll love the Riesling then. It's light and sweet." Emma passed her a glass half filled with white wine.

The women loaded down red plastic plates with

goodies—a variety of cheeses, specialty crackers, sliced fruits, crudités, chips, dips, and cookies. Acres and acres of them. Spice cookies and peppermint cookies. Thumbprint cookies topped with maraschino cherries. Pecan sandies and red velvet cheesecake cookies. Butterscotch haystacks and Russian tea cookies. Gingerbread people and lime angel wings. Shortbread cookies and walnut crescents and the quintessential sugar cookies topped with butter cream frosting. Kimmie and Ben were going to love the leftovers she brought home.

Although she tried not to overindulge in sweets, Meredith was something of a cookie-aholic and she couldn't make up her mind about which ones to choose. So she got one of each. She might regret the hangover in the morning, but for tonight, she was going to enjoy this small oasis of community, neighborliness, and kinship in the desert of life as a fugitive.

Thin ice. Where you're skating the ice is thin as tissue paper.

Livewire Emma leaned in close once everyone had filled her plate and found a place to perch. "We're dying to know what's going on over at the Hutchinson house. You and Hutch are living together?"

She hadn't expected the diminutive redhead to be so direct. "No," Meredith denied. "Well, yes. But it's not like that. I'm just renting the upper floor."

"Oh, I didn't mean you were sleeping with him." Emma laughed. "I mean he's only been home, what, a couple of days? Unless you're a fast mover. Are you a fast mover, Jane? But Hutch is one of the most eligible bachelors in Twilight. All the single gals in town are going to want to know if you have designs on him."

"Certainly not." Meredith put a little bristle in her

voice. Boundaries. Boundaries were important. Especially when she was caught up in a group, Meredith tended to go along with the flow. She'd never been a boat rocker. Well, until Sloane had forced her into the role. He'd toughened her up, she had to give him that, the sociopathic bastard.

"Why not?" Emma asked. "Hutch is hot as a firecracker and such a wonderful guy. The best of the best. Top of the heap with our husbands." She winked at her friends. "Right, girls?"

A murmur of confirmation rippled around the room.

"Hutch is so much fun, but at the same time he's so practical and down-to-earth," Flynn said. "It's a rare combination."

Meredith shifted on the couch, put the Russian tea cookie she had in her hand back on her plate. Powdered sugar dusted her fingers and she sat there rubbing her fingertips together, trying to get it all off. "I have a son."

"A son who needs a daddy."

"Emma," Sarah cautioned. "You're making Jane uncomfortable."

Emma looked crestfallen. "Goodness. I didn't mean to pry. It's just that we all love Hutch so much and want to see him happy."

Every head bobbed in agreement.

"When the building on the square that housed Jesse's motorcycle shop and my Yarn Barn burned down, Hutch started the grassroots fund-raiser that helped us rebuild," Flynn said.

"Get this." Emma laid a hand on Meredith's shoulder. "When my husband Sam's younger brother, Joe—he and Hutch were best friends in grade school—got

diagnosed with Hodgkins and lost his hair from chemo-
therapy, Hutch shaved his head in solidarity."

"He once saved a young boy from drowning in the
marina," Sarah said. "*Good Morning Texas* did a story
on him."

One by one, they told their Hutch stories. Whenever
a buddy got his heart broken, Hutch was the first to
take him out for a night on the town. He attended the
weddings, funerals, and birthdays of family, friends,
and neighbors. He loved pulling good-natured practical
jokes. He was the go-to guy if you needed help moving
or painting your new crib.

Meredith was surprised by some of their descrip-
tions of him. Not the brave and noble parts of Hutch,
but the carefree, fun-loving parts. What they described
as a playful nature must be buried underneath pain and
grief, although she had seen glimpses of it in his inter-
actions with the children. The war had clearly changed
him. The fact that he could not speak amplified the dif-
ferences.

"What happened to him in the Middle East?" she
asked.

Everyone got quiet.

"His entire team lost their life in a black ops mission," Flynn said. "That's really all we know. Their mission was highly classified and the military managed to
keep the media in the dark."

"We wouldn't even know that much if my husband
hadn't heard about it through secret sources." Caitlyn
Garza spoke for the first time. She smelled faintly of
roses, and there was a quiet tranquillity to the florist
that appealed to Meredith. It wasn't shyness, as with
Sarah, who quickly turned talkative when she felt com-

fortable. Rather Caitlyn seemed to be a woman who saved up her words and used them only when she felt she had something to contribute to the conversation. "Gideon still has contacts over there."

Meredith couldn't wrap her head around the horrors he'd been through. Losing his entire team like that. The poor guy.

"Anyone for more wine?" Emma chirped, but her voice was falsely cheerful.

A few women had their wineglasses topped off.

"If he's such a great catch, why isn't Hutch married?" Meredith asked.

"He proposed to a woman once," Caitlyn said. "But she rejected him because of Ashley. Whenever Ashley felt like Hutch was ignoring her in favor of spending time with his girl, she'd fly into jealous rages. Once Ashley broke into his girlfriend's apartment and cut up all her clothes. It was too much for the woman, and of course Hutch wouldn't turn his back on his sister."

"Hutch has had such a rough time of it with his mother and sister. The man is a saint to put up with all he's put up with," Flynn said.

Intrigued, Meredith leaned forward. "What's he put up with?"

"He didn't tell you?" Emma popped a cookie into her mouth.

"He told me that Ashley has an emotional disorder.

"His mother had it too. She hung herself when Hutch was sixteen, and he was the one who found her." Emma looked stricken. "He and Ashley ended up in separate foster homes and that boy moved heaven and earth to get himself declared an emancipated minor so he could be allowed to take care of her."

Meredith put a hand to her throat. "That's horrible. What about Hutch's father?"

Flynn shook her head. "His father was never in the picture. Just like Kimmie's father."

"It's sad." Sarah sighed. "How the family dynamics can play out from one generation to the next."

"Hutch didn't have a childhood," Flynn continued. "Despite being one of the most handsome guys in town, he never had a girlfriend in high school. He had too much responsibility heaped on him way too soon."

"It's not fair," Sarah said. "The poor man can't even throw a penny into the Sweetheart Fountain and wish to be reunited with his high school sweetheart because he didn't have one."

Puzzled Meredith frowned. "What are you talking about?"

Sarah blinked, wide eyes incredulous. "You haven't heard about the sweetheart legend?"

"No."

Flynn bit the head off a gingerbread man, chewed thoughtfully, and then said, "We've been remiss."

"I can't believe no one told you about the sweetheart legend." Sarah seemed troubled by this. "Didn't you notice the Sweetheart Fountain in Sweetheart Park?"

"I haven't been to the park." She'd been too busy working and trying to lie low.

Emma glanced around at the other women. "Who wants to do the honors and tell Jane about the legend?"

"Let Flynn tell it," Sarah said. "She was the first of our generation to be reunited with her high school sweetheart."

Flynn set her plate down and eagerly rubbed her palms together, her eyes aglow as she launched into the story. "It started with Jon Grant and Rebekka Nash, who were teenagers torn apart by the Civil War. Jon was a Union soldier, Rebekka a Southern belle. Although their love appeared forever doomed, they never stopped thinking about each other. Fifteen years later, they met on the banks of the Brazos River where the town of Twilight now stands. This was before they dammed up the river and transformed it into Lake Twilight. Neither had married, nor did they know that the other had moved to Texas. With that one look, they rekindled their romance. The Sweetheart Fountain was erected as a tribute to their undying love."

"And so," Emma interjected, "the legend was born that if you throw a coin into the fountain, you'll be reunited with your teenage love."

Meredith glanced around at the roomful of women, and they all looked so serious that she burst out laughing.

No one else did.

"You guys are pulling my leg. You all can't seriously believe this legend."

"Scoff if you want," Flynn said, "but every single one of us in this room ended up marrying our high school sweethearts after years of separation, and all of us threw coins in the fountains and made the wish."

"You're joking. Every single one of you?"

The dozen women in the room raised their hands.

"It's the same in there." Flynn jerked a thumb in the direction of the kitchen, where the older women had gathered.

"But legends aren't real," Meredith insisted. "Or they are a gross exaggeration of an actual event."

Sarah held up her palms as if presenting Meredith

with the Ten Commandments stone tablet. "Tell Jon and Rebekka that."

"It must be a self-fulfilling prophecy. You believe and you go looking to make things happen with your high school sweetheart and it does."

Flynn shrugged. "Maybe. Maybe not. But we believe."

This was just wacky, but she was a guest, so she didn't point that out. "What happens to people like me and Hutch who didn't have high school sweethearts?"

"Aww." Emma pressed her palms together and rested them against her cheek in a gesture that said, *That's the saddest thing I've ever heard.* "You didn't have a sweetheart in high school either?"

"No."

"How come? You're so pretty with that pale skin and those intriguing dark blue eyes." Emma slapped a palm over her mouth. "I'm being too nosy. Ignore that."

"I was homeschooled. My parents were hot air balloonists. That's how they made their living, and we traveled around the country, attending festivals and fairs."

Emma's eyes lit up. "How fun!"

"It was different and fun, yes, at times, but life on the road has its drawbacks. It can get weary and you have to be pretty independent. No family and friends to rely on." While leading the gypsy lifestyle had been a challenge, ultimately it had prepared her for life on the run.

"Wow," Flynn said. "I can't imagine growing up without a strong community of friends and family."

"Well, balloonists are their own community, even if we are often on opposite sides of the country from our friends. It's the only life I knew until my parents were killed in a ballooning accident when I was sixteen, and I went to live with my grandmother. Then she got sick and I nursed her until she died." Meredith rushed through the story to get it over with. Why was she telling them all this? They were sucking her into their world.

Sarah leaned over to pat Meredith's hand. "You and Hutch have so much in common."

Yes, no high school sweethearts, dead parents at a young age, too much responsibility on their shoulders too soon. Meredith took another sip of wine to keep from thinking about it.

"Is Ben's father still in the picture?" A matchmaker gleam came into Flynn's eyes.

"Ben's father is dead," Meredith said flatly. It was what she told everyone, and she didn't consider it a lie. Because the man she thought she'd married was not the man she believed him to be. The charming guy who'd swept her off her feet just weeks after her grandmother's death was a monster. She couldn't bring herself to tell anyone about him. After all, Sloane had killed the only person who knew her secret, and he would kill again if it served his twisted purposes.

"You know." Sarah's eyes twinkled. "There's another Twilight legend that works for people who didn't have a high school sweetheart."

Meredith laughed again. The legend might be nutty, but it had drawn a laugh out of her twice tonight. That was something. "I'm good. I don't need a sweetheart, high school or otherwise."

"Everyone needs love," Emma said.

"I've got love. I have the most awesome four-year-old son."

"Ben is an amazing kid," Flynn agreed. "But a woman has other needs."

"You don't have to believe it," Sarah interjected, "but can I at least tell you my story?"

"You guys are incorrigible." What the heck. Maybe she'd get a laugh out of this legend too. "But go ahead."

"Technically, I wasn't Travis's high school sweetheart." Sarah said it like she'd broken some kind of cardinal sweetheart rule. "I had a crush on him, but he treated me like a kid sister."

"What worked for you?" Meredith asked, playing along.

"The legend of the kismet cookie."

"Let's hear it."

Sarah wriggled in her seat. "If you sleep with a kismet cookie under your pillow on Christmas Eve, you'll dream of your one true love. It works. Every year that I slept with a kismet cookie under my pillow from the time I was a teenager to the year Travis and I got together, I dreamed of him. I've got the recipe on me if you'd like to try it."

"Are there any kismet cookies here?" Meredith asked to humor her. "I'd like to try one."

"Oh, you'll need to make a fresh batch for Christmas Eve. You don't want a stale cookie for this, but yes." She plucked a cookie off Meredith's plate. "This is the kismet cookie."

"Mmm. Okay. What happens if you dream of someone you don't like?"

"You won't," Sarah said with the assured zeal of a true believer.

Meredith nibbled the kismet cookie, tasted oatmeal, coconut, cranberries, white chocolate, and macadamia nuts. It was one of the kitchen-sink-style cookies, but it was delicious, and she said so.

"My grandmother's recipe." Sarah's chest puffed with pride and she reached into the pocket of her sweater, extracted a stack of laminated index cards with the recipe for kismet cookies printed on them, and passed a card to Meredith. "Try it. If nothing else, you'll get a batch of cookies everyone will rave about."

"Thanks." Meredith tucked the card in her purse. Kimmie and Ben would have fun making the cookies on Christmas Eve. "I really do want to thank you all for a lovely evening. It was good to get out of the house."

"Aww," Emma said. "Do you have to go already?"

"It's eight-thirty." Meredith nodded to the clock over the mantel.

"Oh my, it is," one of the other women said, and jumped up from her chair.

That broke up the party. Meredith went to find Raylene and thank her for inviting her. When she threaded her way back through the living room, most of the younger women were gathering up cookie tins, putting on coats, hugging each other, and saying good night.

All except for Caitlyn Garza, who was still seated on the sectional. But as soon as she spied Meredith, she got up and came over.

"Could I speak to you a moment?" Caitlyn murmured.

Meredith hesitated. "Mmm, I really need to be getting back."

"This is something you should hear." Caitlyn's tone was serious.

"Okay." Heart thumping, Meredith followed Caitlyn to an out-of-the-way corner of the room.

Caitlyn pressed her lips together, drummed her fingertips on her chin. "Listen, everyone loves Hutch and he was a great guy and if you're romantically inclined in his direction, I don't want to scare you off but—"

"I'm not." Meredith shook her head rapidly. "Romantically inclined."

"Are you sure? Twilight has a way of romanticizing love and this whole bunch is matchmaker crazy. It would be so easy to get caught up in their enthusiasm."

"You said Hutch *was* a good guy instead of *is* a good guy. What do you mean by that?"

"Here's the thing. He's not going to be the same guy that he used to be. The guy we knew is gone. And it remains to be seen if this new Hutch is better or worse than the old Hutch."

Meredith gulped, thought of Hutch's busted knuckles and how she'd let it go without demanding an explanation. "Are you telling me he could be violent?"

"He was in special ops, but those guys are known for their self-control, so even if he has changed, I don't think he could ever harm you."

"You don't think he could, but the possibility exists." Icicles of fear froze her blood.

Caitlyn blew out her breath. "Let me tell you what happened to me. My husband, Gideon, was in the Middle East for a long time and it changed him. We had a rough go of it when he first came back. Even if you're not interested in Hutch romantically, if you're going to live in the same house with him, there's some things you need to know about the veterans coming back from over there, particularly the ones who were wounded."

The happy glow from the wine, food, and good company evaporated completely. Her knees went loose, and a hot, sick sensation slicked her stomach in the inevitable pattern—the eerie crawling sensation at the base of her neck, an invisible black widow spider spinning through Meredith's brain. Prickles of dread plucked at her skin and the scar behind her ear burned.

"What's that?" she whispered.

"The majority of them have some form of PTSD. In Hutch's case it could be very mild, but I would be very surprised if he wasn't dealing with some kind of fallout from what happened over there."

"I see." Nausea swept over her. Dear God, don't let her throw up.

"I don't mean to alarm you. Before he went into special ops, Hutch was the most honest, open man I ever met, and that's a miracle considering how he grew up. He's a resilient guy and I don't mean to speak ill of him, but I feel I'd be remiss if I didn't tell you what I know about the effects of PTSD."

"Please." Meredith licked her lips nervously. "I want to know."

Quietly, Caitlyn told her how Gideon had pulled a gun on her when she'd awakened him from a deep sleep. "It was an automatic response. He was Green Beret and trained to always be on alert, but the incident scared us both and we almost didn't make it over that hump. Gideon was so full of remorse and self-loathing."

Meredith was almost afraid to ask the next question, but she had to know. "How is Gideon now?"

A sunshine-bright smile broke over Caitlyn's face and her voice lightened. "He's made a complete recovery. PTSD is curable, but it doesn't happen overnight. And Hutch's case is more complicated because he can't talk. It's hard to debrief when you can't speak."

"What did you do to help Gideon through it?" Meredith couldn't believe she was asking this. She needed to pack up her son and leave, not try to help Hutch get over his PTSD.

"We went to counseling together, but there again, Gideon was able to express himself more freely. Traditional therapy might not work for Hutch. Anything that reduces stress and anxiety will help. Exercise. Biofeedback. Deep breathing techniques."

"Yoga?"

"Ooh, yes, yoga would be good. Mostly vets carry a great deal of guilt and self-blame, and with Hutch, losing his whole team like he did…" She shook her head. "He's got to be feeling isolated and alone, but loathes showing it."

So many mixed emotions churned through her. The caring nurturer inside her wanted desperately to help him, but the part of her who'd been a victim of domestic abuse was screaming at her to open her eyes and smell the coffee. It wasn't her place to heal him.

"Hanging out with other veterans, someone who knows exactly what he's going through, helps too," Caitlyn went on. "Gideon and some of the other local vets went over to see Hutch the other day but he wouldn't come to the door."

"Maybe he wasn't home."

Caitlyn shook her head. "They could see him through the blinds, standing in the hallway like he wanted to answer the door, but just couldn't make himself do it."

"Thank you so much for telling me this." Meredith tried a smile, felt it falter on her lips before it reached her eyes. "I do appreciate your concern."

"Listen, if you ever need to talk—" Caitlyn broke

off to dig a pen and piece of paper from her purse. She wrote down her phone number and passed it to Meredith. "If you ever need to talk, you can call me anytime."

"That's very sweet of you."

"Cheer up. There is hope for Hutch. Don't give up on him. I'm certain he'll pull through this, but there's a lot of bumps in the road ahead. I'm just glad he has you."

He doesn't have me, Meredith wanted to say, but the truth was that as long as she was staying in his house, she did have to deal with him.

If it wasn't Christmas, if she wasn't broke, she would load Ben in the minivan and take off.

Leaving Kimmie all alone with no mother and a wounded uncle? And that was the kicker, wasn't it? How could she, in good conscience, walk away from that little girl?

Chapter 9

After Jane attended the cookie swap, Hutch noticed a change in her.

He caught her throwing him wary glances the way you'd eye a tame circus tiger, wondering if the day would come when the wild beast would grow tired of the game and start slaughtering the audience.

What had she heard about him at that party?

He might have lost his ability to speak, he might have PTSD, but he would never, ever harm her or the children. Still, he could not blame her for being cautious. She did not know him. He could reassure her until the cows came clopping home, but actions always trumped words, and she was watching his every move.

On Saturday morning, he got up before dawn, as was his custom, to find Jane downstairs, dressed in yoga clothes and standing on a purple yoga mat, instead of on the upstairs landing where she usually practiced.

Damn. Sweat broke out on his forehead. If she was going to do all that downward-dogging stuff in front of him, wearing those stretchy black leggings and looking all sexy and bed-rumpled, he was going to have to go back into his room and take care of his lusty impulses in the most basic way possible.

That's when he saw the second yoga mat. This one was blue.

She sat cross-legged, patted the blue mat with the heel of her hand, and crooked a finger at him.

He held up both palms, shook them and his head.

She nodded, keeping crooking that cute little finger. "C'mon."

He continued to shake his head, but he walked over. Why was he walking over?

She hit play on the boom box that sat on the floor beside her, and new agey, girly spa music curled into the room with some chick singing something about only time will tell.

"Nothing difficult this morning," Jane said. "Just breath work. It will help you relax. We'll progress to poses later. Breath work is called pranayama."

As if he gave a crap. But he found himself sitting beside her.

She gifted him with a soft smile that melted all his resistance. The woman was like the ocean, beautiful, calming, and forceful as hell.

For the next half hour, she led him through a series of breathing exercises that left him tingling from his scalp to his toes and his lungs feeling clearer than he'd felt in years. Hey, maybe there was something to this yoga mumbo-jumbo.

"You did so well." Her eyes lit up. "I'm proud of you. We'll do this again tomorrow."

He bobbed his head. *Christ, Hutchinson, knock it off. You look like a freaking bobble head.*

"If you keep practicing, yoga will work miracles in your life, I promise."

He didn't know about that, but he did know that her addictive smile hooked him, and he wanted more. Had to have more. And hey, maybe she was right. Maybe this breathing stuff would calm his mind, and calming his mind would release tension, and releasing tension would get him speaking again.

"I have two massages to give this morning," she said. "But when I get back, we'll take the kids to Dickens on the Square."

She returned at noon. He had the kids dressed warmly and he braced himself for battling the town square thronged with tourists and townsfolk alike. They had to park in overflow parking half a mile away from the square and walk.

Hutch's stomach tightened every time someone greeted him. A lot of people wanted to talk to him, thank him for his service, ask how things were. Whenever he could, he tried to get away with forced smiling and nodding. The task of telling dozens of people that he could not speak was exhausting, and it made him feel like a shadow of his former self. He saw the pity-filled glances and that's-such-a-shame shake of heads, and he hated it.

After a while, sweet little Ben started doing the job for him, saving him from pulling out that damnable

Magic Slate each time by automatically telling everyone who approached, "Unca Hutch can't talkeded."

The kid was quickly headed up near the top of the list of Hutch's favorite people.

After about an hour, Hutch started to loosen up and enjoy the event as he saw it through the children's eyes. He'd long forgotten what it was like to possess such an openhearted sense of wonder.

They took the kids on pony rides, Kimmie screaming with frightened delight as the pony moved beneath her. They ate street food—roasted turkey legs, corndogs, sausage on a stick, soft doughy pretzels, and hot roasted nuts. They drank lemonade and hot apple cider and finished off the meal with the best fudge he'd ever eaten. Local merchants were dressed in Dickensian clothing. Beefeaters and London bobbies strolled the sidewalks. They shook hands with Scrooge and Marley, Tiny Tim, Miss Havisham, and Oliver Twist. Kimmie and Ben had their faces painted and then they all participated in the Scrooge Scavenger Hunt, where everyone received a prize. The kids won coloring books and crayons.

It was a perfect day, and by the end of it, the mood between him and Jane shifted again.

On the way back to the minivan, they took a shortcut through Sweetheart Park. The children raced ahead of them, playing tag, the sound of their running footsteps and high-pitched giggles echoing throughout the park.

Twilight sewed up the sun, and quaint, faux glass lanterns came on as they wandered down the path side by side. The urge to take her hand was so great that he had to stuff his hands into the front pockets of his jeans.

While keeping the kids in their line of sight, they crossed the wooden footbridge spanning a fingerling tributary of the Brazos River. As they neared the end of the bridge, Jane's shoe caught on a rough section of planking, and she lost her balance. Before Hutch could grab for her, she tumbled over the railing to the water below.

Instead of a splash, he heard a soft thump, and Jane cried, "Oh!"

He peered over the edge of the bridge to see she had landed on a wheeled wooden platform covered in red carnations. Someone must have parked it under the bridge after the morning's parade.

Laughing, she peered up at him, wide-eyed. The impact of her sudden weight caused the back of the float to tilt forward sharply and carnations rained down in flush cascades, blooming the front of the platform with red, fluttering petals, the flowers dripping into puddles at the corners, kissing her body with crimson blooms, coloring her ebony hair and pale skin with dark cherry froth until only her eyes and cheeks peeked out at him.

What were the chances? What were the odds that a cart of foliage would be there to catch her when she fell? In that moment, the float embodied the spirit of Christmas and everything it represented—generosity, kindness, love—and she was at the heart of it, the creative fount from where all goodness sprang.

It was a romantic thought. Poetic. And totally out of character for a man who spent his life steeped in war, struggle, and strife, but something came over him like an out-of-body experience. It was she. Jane was the one who lifted him to heavenly heights, the one who raised him from the mire of base human behavior. He had no name for what he was feeling because he'd never experienced an emotion like this.

Transfixed, he cocked his head, studied her, saw radiant delight in her eyes, saw the flowers move up and down on her in waves as she breathed, and it took every morsel of willpower he had not to race down to the water's edge, haul her from the cart, and kiss her.

"Mommy!" Ben called, breaking the sweet silence of the simple now. "Where are you?"

"I'm taking Ben to church tomorrow," she said after the children fell exhausted into bed that night. "Would you like me to take Kimmie with us?"

Hutch had no idea what possessed him. He'd never been a religious man, but he picked up the Magic Slate and posed a question that seemed to surprise her as much as it did him. MAY I COME TOO?

Jane gifted him with a smile that sucked the air right out of his lungs. "Yes," she replied, her eyes softening at the corners. "We'd love that."

So Hutch went to church. He sat in the pew beside Jane, Kimmie to his left, Ben on Jane's right, acutely aware of how close they were. Almost touching. During the service, he sneaked a sidelong glance over at her.

The morning sun through the stained glass window backlit her profile and he'd be damned if she didn't look exactly like an angel, all soft and ethereal. Happy. She looked happy.

Her scent, a homey smell of soap and sugar cookies and raspberry shampoo, cuddled up in his nose, driving a dangerous impulse to move his right leg over half an inch and rest it against her outer thigh.

Hutch savored the moment like fine aged whiskey, comparing where he was now to where he'd been a few short months ago. He'd lost a lot, sure, but look what he'd gained.

She's not yours. You're fooling yourself.

What was he doing here? What fantasy was he playing with? He was too messed up to do anything about his impulses. He had nothing to offer her. Not as long as he could not talk. Not until he got his speech back. Not until he made his pilgrimage to visit the families of the brave men who'd fought beside him and died. Until then, he was too broken, fragmented, and she deserved better than that.

Yeah? So you want her? Then start talking. For Kimmie's sake if not your own.

If Gupta and Jenner were right, if his loss of speech was due to psychological mutism and it was not rooted in something physical, then he did have the power to speak again. What would it take to get there?

Jane dampened two fingers with her tongue and smoothed down Ben's recalcitrant cowlick, such a deep expression of love for her son on her face that Hutch felt compelled to touch her. But he had promised not to do that. Instead, he slipped the comb from his back pocket and passed it to her to use on Ben's tuft of hair.

She took the comb from him, transferring that loving smile to him, and for one split second, they were both touching the comb, joined briefly by a slim piece of plastic.

The minster was talking about faith. How it could move mountains. How all it took to change your life was faith the size of a mustard seed.

"But true faith," said the minister, "is not about control. It's about release, the turning loose of those mistaken beliefs that do not serve us. To find peace, we have to trust that peace is possible. To find love, we have to trust that it's within our reach."

Hutch turned to look at Jane just as she turned to look at him.

Their eyes met and he could almost hear the sharp snap of lightning hitting the ground, sizzling and hot. Her eyes widened and her lips parted and he could see her straight pearly teeth. Her breathing was fast and shallow, but so was his.

"Trust," crooned the minister. "Trust that everything will be all right. Trust that your life is working out the way it's supposed to."

The choir stood and started singing "Trust in Me Now." Everyone around them stood up, eyeing the words to the hymn that were projected on the screen at the front of the church.

Call him blasphemous, but he had eyes only for Jane. She looked at him and he looked at her and it was as if his entire life finally made sense. Everything he'd done had led him here with her, and nothing had ever felt so right. If Hutch lived to be two hundred years old, he would never forget this moment of stunned wonder.

Jane did not speak to him on the way home. Was her silence out of respect for the fact that he could not hold a conversation while driving? Public service announcement: Don't Magic Slate and Drive? Or was she as staggered as he was by what had passed between them in church?

Either way, it wasn't an uncomfortable silence. In fact, he was really starting to like silence. In comparison to the noises of war, silence truly was golden.

But he couldn't get too used to silence or like it too much. He refused to allow his handicap to weaken him.

He *was* going to speak. He couldn't get better until he did. If he wanted to lay claim to his growing feelings for Jane, he had to find a way to say—not write—the words. *I like you. I want you. Let's throw those damn rules out the window and see where this thing leads.*

For the first time since leaving the hospital, Hutch's focus was clear, his goal front and center again. No matter how long it took, no matter what he had to go through, he was going to speak. He was going to keep his sworn duty and make that sojourn to the families of his team members.

And when he returned, he was going to restart his life. Clean slate. That's what he craved most—a sound mind, a clear voice, a strong body, and a clean slate.

For the next three days, Hutch practiced yoga with Jane. After she went to work and the children were at school, he did his morning routine. One hundred push-ups, fifty pull-ups. Light exercise, just enough to get the blood pumping. Then he practiced trying to speak. He stood in front of the bathroom mirror, glowering darkly at himself. All he needed was one syllable to start with, just one sound. The speech therapist at Walter Reed had told him that the easiest sound to make was *baa.*

He inhaled deeply—already his lung capacity was improving with pranayama—and pushed out from his diaphragm, expelling air through his lungs and up his trachea, where it stalled. It was as if his own throat muscles were battling against him, shutting down, seizing up, refusing to cooperate. He could feel his larynx vibrate, trying to do what he asked, but there was a disconnection between his voice box and his mouth, as if an electrical plug had been yanked from a socket.

One, two, three, four times he attempted it. A pitiful strangling noise emerged, more choke than real speech, and then his throat convulsed and he couldn't shove another sound through it. He snorted air through his nose, felt it shiver on the way down.

Three days it was always the same. More. He needed to push himself harder.

On the fourth day, he tried a dozen times. When he saw no improvement, Hutch tried a dozen times more. The next day, he added a session at night, before he went to bed. Never mind that his throat was raw and his neck muscles achy. He'd survived Delta Force training. In comparison this was like being fanned and fed grapes by a dozen harem girls.

Another day passed and then another. Nothing changed.

He forged ahead, upping his game with more practice. Nada.

Frustration built. Why couldn't he do this? Why couldn't he speak? He considered going to a therapist, but what good would that do when he couldn't say a word?

To deal with his frustration, he spent the days cutting down overgrown trees on the property and chopping them into fireplace logs. He took a load of wood over to Dotty Mae Densmore. His neighbor was in her eighties and lived alone and he worried about her.

Dotty Mae thanked him profusely, and then just as he turned to leave, she said, "I remember who you used to be."

Hutch paused and raised a quizzical eyebrow.

"When you were a kid. Before you joined the military. Before your mama truly went crazy."

Why was she bringing all that up?

He should have let it go, waved, left. Instead, when she offered him a cup of coffee, he nodded and sat down at her kitchen table. Not many people spoke about his mother these days. Not many people left who'd really known her. Not many who were comfortable talking about death.

But at her advanced age, Dotty Mae was staring death in the face. She understood, as Hutch did, as all soldiers with boots on the ground in foreign lands did, that death was an inevitable part of life and the Grim Reaper could be lounging around the next corner, whistling a while-away-the-hours tune, just waiting for you to show up.

"A shot of peppermint schnapps?" she asked after she'd poured the coffee and set a steaming cup in front of him. "To celebrate the holiday."

Hutch wasn't a big fan of peppermint much less schnapps, but he hadn't had a drop of liquor since the ambush. He edged his cup toward her and she tipped in a hefty dollop of schnapps from the silver flask she produced from the pocket of her apron. She added an equal helping to her coffee as well.

"Some people can't be saved." Dotty Mae capped the flask. "But you can." She took a long sip of schnapps-laced coffee, sighed happily, and settled back in her chair. "And Jane. She can be saved too."

Saved from what? What did Dotty Mae know about Jane that he did not? Christ, he wished he could talk. Hutch speared his fingers through his hair. He was getting shaggy, even for men in The Unit who did not have to abide by military dress code.

"Now Ashley?" Dotty Mae said and shook her head. "That girl…"

She didn't finish her thought.

Hutch drained his coffee, gave the elderly lady a tight smile, and scooted out of there. Once in a while, not being able to speak was a blessing.

When Jane got home from work, he had a fire in the fireplace and food on the stove. She gave him a grateful look and told him he didn't have to keep preparing supper. But what else did he have to do? Besides, he liked taking care of her and the kids. It made him feel useful.

In the days leading up to Christmas, they settled into a nice routine that revolved around taking care of the children. Occasionally, he'd catch her looking at him in lusty bewilderment, as if she couldn't believe she was attracted to him. Once, a glimpse of the old Hutch roused and he'd winked at her. She turned away with red cheeks and an oh-gosh-this-can't-be-happening smile on her face, and for a couple of minutes there he forgot everything else but her and the happiness in his belly.

Ashley never called, and when Hutch tried to text her, she never replied. According to Jane, she'd been gone almost two weeks.

Kimmie had stopped asking about her mother, and Hutch didn't know which was worse: the sadness that bit a chunk out of him whenever she asked, or the sadness that sank bone-deep when she didn't.

He was worried. Yes, Ashley had impulsively taken off before without warning or explanation, but she'd never been gone this long. He recalled one time when he was twelve and Ashley was eight that their mother had gone off with some random guy she'd met at a bar and hadn't come back for three weeks. Leaving him to take care of Ashley with no food in the house. He'd stolen vegetables from the neighbor's garden. They must have seen him, because after that, a basket full of food showed up on the doorstep. At least Ashley had left her daughter with a responsible person like Jane.

Saturday was the Christmas play at Kimmie's and Ben's preschool. Both children were playing wise men and Jane was trying to get them to settle down enough to put their costumes on, but they were wound up, chattering and hopping around.

"You guys wanna hop around, let's hop." Jane turned on the boom box in the kitchen, selected a playlist, and Michael Franti & Spearhead bounced into the room with "I'm Alive." The second the song started, the kids and Jane sprang into wild dancing, utter bliss on their faces.

Hutch stood in the doorway arms folded over his chest, watching.

"Dance, Unca Hutch, dance!" Kimmie cried.

Jane smiled and crooked her finger, inviting him closer, into their little madcap circle of wriggling and giggling.

Ben darted over, took his hand, led him to the middle of the kitchen floor just as the song changed to "Best Day of My Life" by American Authors.

Jane did an innocent bump and grind around him, swinging those luscious hips, her eyes sparkling bright. "C'mon, big man, let's see your moves."

Knock her socks off, thought Old Hutch. Forgetting all about rule #4, he grabbed her by the hand and swept her off her feet, spinning her around the room. An old girlfriend had made him take ballroom dancing with her, and Hutch knew his way around a dance floor. *Here we go, sweetheart.* Hutch dipped her deep.

Jane's eyes flew wide and her mouth formed a happy, startled O. Apparently, she'd forgotten about rule #4 as well.

For one brilliant second, they were frozen in a picture-postcard moment.

The kids wanted in on the joy. They hopped up and down, begging to be included, and then there were four of them, laughing and dancing in a circle, hands joined. A unit. Whole.

Just like a family.

Except not.

The music changed tempo, slowing into a wistful but hopeful "Everything's Okay" by Lenka. The musical shift had Jane dropping her hand, stepping back, looking away from him.

"Okay, kids, energy burned off. Let's get into those costumes." She clapped her hands. "Chop, chop. The show must go on."

All the way up to the school, excitement tingeing her little voice, Kimmie kept saying, "My mommy's comin' to see me. Mommy's comin' to my play."

He glanced over at Jane and she met his gaze, her dark blue eyes worried as she nibbled off her lipstick. He shook his head, hoped his eyes didn't show the tears he couldn't allow himself to shed.

They sat together in the audience as adorable four-year-olds acted out the birth of Jesus. They took lots of pictures and applauded like mad people when the fifteen-minute skit was over.

The woman seated next to Hutch leaned over to ask, "You and your wife look so happy. It's so sweet of you to come with her to a children's play. I can't blast my husband out of bed until noon on Saturdays. How long have you two been married?"

Hutch shook his head, pointed to his bare ring finger.

The woman nudged Hutch in the ribs. "What are you waiting for to make an honest woman of her? You'd be hard-pressed to find someone else you're so compatible with."

Hutch just smiled.

"Men." The woman muttered under her breath and as she was leaving, leaned over to tap Jane on the shoulder. "Honey, he's not going to buy the cow as long as the milk is free."

Jane gave Hutch a what-the-heck-was-that-all-about look. He shrugged, winked.

Her cheeks pinked.

Kimmie came running off stage toward them, a long beard glued to her chin, a wooden crook clutched in her pudgy little hand, swiveling her head from side to side, going up on tiptoes to survey the crowd of adults getting to their feet. "Where is she? Where's my mommy?"

"Who's up for hot chocolate when we get home?" Jane asked as Ben joined them.

"Unca Hutch?" That white beard trembled and a tear trickled down Kimmie's cheek. "Where's Mommy?"

He couldn't answer. Couldn't even speak to comfort his niece. Dammit! He had to conquer this muteness shit. Hutch curled his fingernails into his palms, anger, frustration, and guilt punching him with a hard upper cut.

Jane crouched, eye level with Kimmie, and took her hand. "Sweetie, your mother couldn't be here, but I took lots of pictures to show her what a wonderful wise man you were."

His niece flung herself into Jane's arms, buried her head against Jane's breast, and sobbed her little heart out. Jane stood up and carried Kimmie to the minivan, Hutch and Ben bringing up the rear.

The ride home was somber, filled with the sound of Kimmie's soft cries. Jane sat in the backseat with the kids, gently rubbing Kimmie's back and kissing the top of her head.

"I sorry, Kimmie," Ben said. "I sorry 'bout yo mommy."

When they got home, Jane sent the kids to their rooms to change out of their costumes and they went into the kitchen to prepare lunch, the solemn mood in sharp contrast to the earlier joy they'd shared in this same room an hour ago. From the refrigerator, Hutch pulled the brisket he'd cooked in the outdoor smoker earlier in the week, and started slicing it. Jane stood beside him at the counter, slathering mustard on thick slices of rustic Italian bread.

She stopped in mid stroke, laid the mustard-covered knife down on a paper towel. "This can't keep up. What are we going to do about Ashley? It's horrible what she's putting her own daughter through. I can't understand why she hasn't called. What if something's happened to her? Shouldn't we report her missing?"

Hutch didn't like the situation any better than she did, but she didn't understand that this was how Ashley operated. She would do something impulsive and/or irrational, get into an undesirable situation, but was loath to admit she messed up. Once, when he caught Ashley stealing money from his wallet, she begged his forgiveness, saying, "I'm pond scum carpet. I don't deserve to breathe air."

There was so much pain in her eyes he knew it wasn't simple melodrama. She truly believed she was not worthy of forgiveness. She truly believed that if she made a mistake she didn't deserve to live. She truly believed that if he was mad at her in the moment, he would be mad at her forever.

He tried to soothe her. Tell her everyone made mistakes. But unable to tolerate the misery of her distorted belief system, she got angry and lashed out at Hutch, saying that if he gave her a bigger allowance, she wouldn't be forced to steal from him.

"You've humiliated me," she declared, her face burning the color of cinnamon jellybeans. "It's all your fault."

Hutch had blinked, confused, caught in the whiplash backdraft of his sister's emotional illness. It was the first time he truly understood that he could never win. The best way to handle her was simply to disengage his emotions and refused to be pulled into her delusion. It might look cold to others, but it was a basic survival technique. He only wished he had learned the art of detachment years ago. It would have made life with his mother so much easier.

But Jane had a point. What if Ashley had gotten in over her head? What if it was a case that she couldn't call or come home if she wanted to? Then again, what was he going to do? He had no clue where to start looking for her and it wasn't as if he could pick up the phone and have a chat with the airline or hotels, much less fly to Mexico and start asking questions, scrawling on that stupid Magic Slate in English.

Goddammit. The time when his niece needed him the most he was completely useless.

"I can't believe a mother would do this to her child." Jane sank her hands on her hips, glared at him.

He knew she was mad at Ashley, not him, but guilt, dark and heavy, crawled up inside him.

"You need to do something."

Hutch made a fierce slashing motion across his neck, glowered back at Jane. He was just as pissed off about this as she was. More so. It was his family, not hers. He was so steamed that he opened his mouth to tell her precisely that, and then snapped his lips together.

Do it. Talk.

Inhaling deeply, he propelled the air up through his lungs, into his throat, felt the familiar tightening. Keep going. He pressed on, and the sound exploded from his mouth in a soft, raspy pop. "Baa."

Baa.

The noise he'd been practicing for the last week, over and over. The simple syllable he'd been unable to make. He should be thrilled he managed that much. Instead, he was pissed off. He sounded like a damn sheep.

Baa.

He gritted his teeth. Months of anger, guilt, despair, turmoil, and depression had come to this.

Baa.

Jane went for the Magic Slate lying on the table, trotted back over, and shoved it into his left hand, her eyes sparking flint. She was pissed off too.

They weren't mad at each other. He knew that. They were frustrated with Ashley and worried for Kimmie and they were taking it out on each other. But he couldn't seem to stop himself from reacting out of hurt.

Hutch hardened his jaw. He took the tablet, intending to toss it back on the table. Writing on that stupid children's toy couldn't begin to communicate what he was feeling, but his second finger hadn't yet learned how to act as an effective index finger. He misjudged how much pressure it took to toss the tablet over the cooktop and onto the kitchen table beyond.

The slate flew off the tip of his second finger, bulleted over the cooktop, rocketed past the table, slammed into the wall, and with the peculiarities of force and geometry, spun off the wall and came boomeranging back, whizzing over the top of Jane's head as she ducked, and smacking the center of Hutch's chest.

Fear flooded Meredith's body and she was jettisoned back five years ago to a time just days after her honeymoon, when Sloane had knocked her across the room for slightly singeing his steak, and broke her nose for the first time.

Her face drained of blood, going ice-cold in an instant, and reflexively her hand flew to cup her nose, protecting herself. Caitlyn had tried to warn her, but she'd been lulled into a sense of complacency by how easy things had become between her and Hutch.

Idiot.

She wasn't going back to that dark place, to the foolish young woman she'd been who'd believed love could conquer all. She'd warned Hutch she wouldn't put up with any displays of anger and she meant it.

"Out!" she cried, pointing a finger toward the front door. "Get out of here!"

The look in Hutch's eyes was bone-deep remorse. Anguish carved deep the hollows of his cheeks. This man was sorry, but it was too late. At least he couldn't speak, couldn't talk back and try to wheedle his way out of banishment.

"Out," she said again, her voice a stark whisper, her entire body quivering. "I mean it. Don't make me call the police." That was a bluff. She couldn't afford to call the police and this was his house, but she had to make him believe that she would do it.

He nodded, picked up the Magic Slate that had fallen to the floor between them, and straightened, his face now devoid of any emotion. He held the tablet to his chest, lumbered away from her.

The children were standing in the doorway, eyes wide. Kimmie was sucking her thumb. Ben was crying.

"Where you goin', Unca Hutch?" Ben's voice was shrill.

Hutch did not look at her son, just skirted the children, headed toward the front door.

"Unca Hutch," Kimmie shrieked, attaching herself to his leg. "Don't leave! Don't leave."

Meredith's stomach pitched. Why did this have to happen in front of the children? As much as it hurt her to put the kids through this, she could not back down. After that fit of pique with the Magic Slate, she had no idea what Hutch was capable of, and she wasn't going to wait around to find out.

"Kimmie," she said sternly. "Let go of your uncle. He needs to leave. He's not going away forever. He will be back to see you, but for right now, he needs to leave."

Hutch stopped, detached Kimmie from his leg. Tears streamed down the little girl's face. He squatted in front of her, gently wiped the tears from her face with his thumbs. Nodded, smiled, kissed her forehead.

"You need to talk to someone," Meredith said. "You can't do this on your own. You need professional help."

His eyes said he wanted to challenge her. To tell her, she imagined, that it was damn hypocritical of her to point mental health fingers when she obviously had issues of her own.

He straightened. Dark shadows shrank his eyes into his head as if he were wasting away right in front of her. Meredith's stomach spasmed and she thought she might throw up. He turned to go.

The children trailed after him. He stopped once more. Shook his head sternly. Both kids were sobbing.

Moving stiff and slow, as if he were stricken with severe arthritis, Hutch took his coat and cap from the coatrack and trudged out the door.

Chapter 10

Jane had been completely right to kick him out of the house. It hurt, of course, leaving the children behind, but what if one of them had been standing in the way when he'd thrown the Magic Slate? Never mind that he hadn't meant to turn the writing tablet into a projectile, he'd done it.

And Jane had the courage to stick to her guns, even when Kimmie and Ben had become so distraught. He respected and admired her strength.

Aimlessly, he drove around town, berating himself for what he'd done. People smiled and waved as he passed, forcing him to smile and wave back. Twilight was too damn friendly for its own good.

Why had he slung that tablet? The way Jane had looked at him, terrified as a bunny rabbit in a den of snakes, slaughtered his soul. Someone had hurt her.

Hurt her badly. No, not someone. A man. A man had hurt her. Beaten her.

A blind red hatred burned through him. He wanted to find the son of a bitch who'd hurt her and beat *him* until he begged for death.

Violence.

It had been part of his daily life for years. Killing. Bloodshed. He'd done it to protect his country. To keep Americans safe. But he wasn't living that life anymore. He had a new life, and now he was the threat to the ones he loved.

The enemy.

His stomach roiled and he had to pull over the truck and empty his stomach. He bent double, an animal moan rolling from his throat. He leaned against the truck, wiped his mouth, wiped his eyes with a sleeve.

This anguish he felt was about much more than the tablet incident. It was about the men who'd lost their lives on that desert ridge amid sheets of gunfire and rocket propelled grenades. It was about the finger that had been blown from his hand. The shrapnel that had embedded in his throat. It was about his sister and her madness and his inability to change any of it.

Hutch stared down at his hands. They were the hands of a killer. This was in his nature. The way he'd been trained. The Unit believed there were very few world problems that couldn't be solved with a well-placed bullet or a high explosive, and he'd bought into that mindset. He had no choice. It was part and parcel of being a counter-terrorist operative.

No wonder Jane had been terrified of him. He was capable of terrible things. But he would never ever intentionally hurt her or the kids. He'd take himself off the face of the earth first.

The scars on the backs of his knuckles were healing, but they were reminders of the anger he did not fully have under control. He'd been trying to stem his emotions on his own, but it wasn't working. Teamwork had been instilled into him from his first days at boot camp, all through Ranger training, to his schooling in The Unit. Instilled? Hardly. The concept that he was part of a team, and no longer an "I," had been drilled home with the impact of a pile driver. Teamwork. Every other word he heard. Teamwork. Teamwork. Teamwork. Never go it alone.

He'd been trying to tackle this alone. That's where he'd been stumbling. That's why he'd failed. Teamwork. He'd lost his team, and with that loss, he'd forgotten the most basic military tenet. Teamwork.

He needed help.

Suddenly, he looked over and saw the Twilight Fire Department across the street from where he'd parked. His gaze traveled to the men loading toys into an enclosed trailer. Men he recognized. Hondo. Nate. Gideon.

The men who'd reached out to him.

Had his subconscious mind, desperately in need, driven him here?

They were loading the truck with toys that people had brought to the fire station for the annual Angel Tree distribution for needy families in Hood County.

Hondo stopped, met his eye. Nate stopped beside him. Then Gideon. They all raised a hand in greeting.

Gathering up his Magic Slate, his truck keys, and his shattered pride, Hutch crossed over to his salvation.

* * *

The children were inconsolable over Hutch's absence. For the entire weekend, they moped around the house, not even tempted by the game console when she told them they could play video games for thirty minutes.

Honestly, Meredith missed him too. She'd grown accustomed to having him there, not just for helping her take care of the children, but for the comfortable camaraderie they shared over household chores. She missed knowing there was a man in the house who could protect them. She missed the masculine smell of him and the way he looked at her as if she were something truly special.

Hutch was only human. He'd made a mistake, but she was leery. She'd been through too much to take chances. She'd set boundaries. Made it clear from the beginning what her rules were. He'd broken them, and she was well within her rights to throw him out.

He broke a rule when he touched you, danced with you, and that didn't bother you.

Okay, call her two-faced for enforcing the rules with negative consequences while letting rule violations with pleasant results slide.

How much of an anger issue did Hutch have? Could she in good conscience let him back into the house?

Was she painting him with a dark brush because of her experiences with Sloane? Was she being unfair or smart? Her mind, the useless thing, waffled.

"First Mommy goes away and now Unca Hutch." Kimmie sighed mournfully as Meredith tucked her into bed beside her on Sunday night. "You won't go away too, will you, Auntie Jane?"

"Her name's Mommy," Ben said from the other side of the bed.

"Can I call you Mommy too?" Kimmie asked. "At least till my mommy comes back."

"Yes." Meredith kissed the top of Kimmie's head. *Oh, Ashley, where in the hell are you?*

After the children fell asleep, Meredith couldn't sleep. She got out of bed and tried to call Ashley, as she had several times a day since Ashley had taken off to Mexico. And as it had every time, the call went to voice mail.

"Hi, if you're someone good, leave a message," said Ashley's gleeful recorded voice. "If not, you can go to hell."

Meredith had heard that message a hundred times over the course of the last two weeks, and while she'd found it off-putting, it hadn't really dawned on her that this message showcased Ashley's personality disorder and the way that sufferers of the malady divided the world into good or bad, black or white, angel or devil. She couldn't help wondering if she had somehow crossed over Ashley's internal delineation from good to evil.

When the woman finally did decide to come home, she was going to talk to Hutch about staging an intervention. Clearly, his sister needed professional help, and Kimmie deserved to grow up with a mentally stable mother. Since Hutch had told her about Ashley's diagnosis, she'd done some research, and while therapy was expensive and intensive, if someone with the disorder was fully devoted to recovery, there *was* a chance she could beat it.

"Ashley," she said. "This is Meredith. If you get this message, please, please, please call me."

She hung up, feeling worse than she did before she called. Pacing the house, she wondered where Hutch was spending the night. She had overreacted. Making him pay for her troubled past.

Gnawing her thumbnail, she picked up her phone again and called Caitlyn Garza. Caitlyn answered on the third ring, just about the time Meredith had decided she was intruding and almost hung up.

"This is Mer—Jane Brown," she finished quickly. "Did I wake you?"

"We have a toddler in the house." Caitlyn laughed. "I'm rarely asleep. I was just putting a clean diaper on the baby and Gideon is at a veterans' support group meeting."

"He still goes after all this time?"

"Oh, he's a group leader now. Helping other GIs in the same shape as he once was. Like your Hutch."

He's not my Hutch, Meredith started to protest, but let it go. "I wish Hutch would go to Gideon's support group."

"He's there right now." The other woman sounded surprised. "You didn't know?"

"No."

"Oops. I hope I didn't give away something Hutch wanted to keep quiet. I just assumed he'd told you."

Meredith said nothing for a long moment. How frank should she be?

"Are you still there?"

"I threw him out of the house," Meredith confessed.

"Hutch? What did he do?"

"It's nothing like what happened with Gideon. In

fact, I worried that I made a mountain out of a molehill."
Slowly, she told Caitlyn what had happened.

"You've had a bad experience with an abusive man before, haven't you?" Caitlyn ventured.

"How did you know?"

"I just got that vibe from you."

She was giving off vibes? Meredith pulled her bottom lip up between her teeth. "So, was I out of line?"

"Did you feel threatened?"

Had she? "I didn't think Hutch was going to physically harm me. It was more like I had flashbacks to before, you know?"

"You could have some PTSD yourself."

Yes. Dr. Lily had treated her for PTSD and she thought she'd gotten past it, but when Hutch had lost his temper, she'd been jettisoned right back to that day when Sloane hit her the first time.

"I didn't stay with him long," Meredith said. "I want you to know I'm not a doormat."

"I'm not judging." Caitlyn's voice was gentle.

"I was naïve. I thought I could change him. I thought—"

"You don't have to justify yourself to me. Does Hutch know about this other man who hurt you?" Caitlyn asked.

"No," Meredith admitted. "I can't believe I'm telling you all this."

"It's okay," Caitlyn assured her. "What you tell me goes no farther. I won't even bring it up with Gideon. Thank you for trusting me with this."

"I had to talk to someone."

It was true. She'd had no one to confide in since Sloane had murdered Dr. Lily. She'd been terrified to drag anyone else into her torment for fear they would suffer the same fate. But Caitlyn had been so sympathetic and she understood what was happening with Hutch.

"I'm flattered you chose me."

They made a date to meet for coffee the following week and hung up.

So Hutch was attending a support group. That was good news. A step in the right direction. Meredith smiled, and hope filled her heart. He was getting help. She was happy for him. And Kimmie.

Her cell phone dinged as a new text message came through. Could it be from Ashley?

No, the text came from Hutch's phone.

It was a long text, meant to be a letter, but the server had broken it down into four text bubbles.

Dear Jane,

I can't begin to tell you how sorry I am for flinging the slate at the wall. I never intended to throw it that hard. I'm still adjusting to life without an index finger and having trouble gauging distance and how much force to use. But I won't make excuses. I was angry when I tossed that slate. Not at you. But at Ashley and at myself and I took it out on you. It was wrong, stupid, and immature, and you didn't deserve any of that grief. My anger hurt you, and for that I am deeply sorry.

It kills me to see you and the children unhappy because of my actions. When our arrangement began I promised I would not display anger in front of you and the children, and I failed to live up to that promise. I failed both of us.

I know an apology is not enough. Anyone can say they are sorry, but I want to make amends. I've taken the first steps to getting my anger under control. I've joined a support group of local veterans and even though I can't verbally share with them what I'm going through, I'm getting a lot out of the meetings.

I understand the gravity of the situation and I hope, for the sake of the children, that you can find it in your heart to forgive me and allow me to come back home. If you can't bring yourself to do that, I understand completely. You deserve to live in a peaceful, harmonious house. Please text me if you're willing to see me.

Hutch

She read the letter through twice. Sank down on the couch. Should she say no and keep him at arm's length? Or should she give him another chance? It was his house, after all. Legally, he could have her thrown out if he wanted.

For a long time, she just sat there, practicing a variety of controlled yoga breathing and getting in touch with her inner voice.

Finally, she picked up her cell phone and texted Hutch.

I'm taking the kids to see Santa on the square tomorrow at three. You can come along if you want.

Nervous to the core, Hutch paced the town square, waiting for Jane to show up with the kids. To keep himself occupied, he got change for a ten-dollar bill at Ye

Olde Book Nook and, pockets jingling, prowled the surrounding parking lots, feeding meters to benefit holiday shoppers, hoping to bring a smile to a few faces for the holidays.

By now, most everyone in town had heard that he'd lost his voice, so whenever someone stopped to say hello, the women would invariably touch him on the arm, while the men favored a light punch to his shoulder. The first thing out of their mouths was some version of "We heard what happened to your voice, we're so sorry for what happened to you over there. Thank you for your service. You're a true American hero."

That last comment got him every time. He was no hero. In fact, he was the opposite of that. He was a killer. When he joined the military, he believed in shiny ideals of bravery, honor, and protecting his country from foreign invaders. It was only when his boots were on the ground in someone else's country he realized that *he* was the foreign invader. In the heat of battle, philosophical arguments vanished, and it was all about survival. Heroism didn't enter into it. Neither did honor or bravery. It was simply kill or be killed. Fact of life for anyone living in a war zone, no matter what side he was fighting for.

It was only later, when a fighter tried to integrate back into society, that the implications of his actions came back to haunt him. In Gideon's support group, he'd learned everyone felt the same way he did. That they weren't heroes, because they'd done bad things in order to survive. It was the psychological disconnect between how others saw them and how warriors saw themselves.

Forgiveness, Gideon told him, was his only hope.

Gideon had also given him an assignment. Go out among people wearing fatigues. Accept their praise. Accept his feelings about it. Don't judge either as bad or good. Experience the feelings and let them go.

The minivan pulled into a parallel parking space at the curb on the north side of the courthouse. Hutch was standing on the west side of the square, having anticipated she would come into town off Highway 51. She must not have come straight from home.

He hustled around the square, hurrying to greet them. It wasn't until Jane—wearing leggings, boots, short denim skirt, and gray faux fur jacket—got out of the vehicle, met his gaze, and smiled that Hutch realized he'd been holding his breath.

The kids got out of the vehicle on the curbside of the street and ran toward him.

He crouched to catch one kid in each arm and accepted the dual kisses they rained on his cheeks. In that moment, hell if he didn't feel like a hero. Three days he'd been gone from the house. It felt like three years.

"Aww," said one passerby to another. "Isn't that sweet. A daddy coming home from the war to see his twins for Christmas."

Even if he could speak, he wouldn't have corrected their assumptions.

Jane stepped up onto the sidewalk. The smile stayed on her face, simmering like hot soup on a cold winter evening. "Hello."

He stood, both kids slipping their mittened hands through his. He smiled back, hoping he didn't look as shy and awkward as he felt.

She led the way across the street to Santa's Workshop set up on the courthouse lawn. A long line of children, waiting with their parents, snaked up the walkway. Nearby kiosks sold hot chocolate and roasted nuts. The smell of pine, and peppermint filled the air. An outdoor speaker played "Jingle Bell Rock."

The children clung to his hands, chattering nonstop. Kimmie told Hutch about a picture she'd drawn for him, while Ben talked about the coolness of Thomas the Train.

Jane stopped at the end of the line. Hutch and the children came to stand behind her. She smelled of yeast and vanilla, as if she'd spent the morning baking.

Seemingly reading his thoughts, she said, "No one booked a massage for today. At the beginning of December, my schedule is jam-packed, everyone wants to de-stress before the holidays, but things are slowing down the closer we get to Christmas. So we've been baking stollen. My grandmother used to bake it every year."

It was the first time he'd ever heard her mention anything personal about her family. He wanted to ask a million questions. Was her grandmother still alive? How about her parents? If so, what did they do for a living? Was she going to visit them for the holidays? Would they come here to visit her?

He wanted to tell her things too. Like one of the few things he remembered about his mother's mother, who'd died when he was eight, was that she made fruitcakes every year and he loved to steal the candied citron from the ingredients she stacked on the kitchen counter. She never scolded him for it, and in fact, she was the one who first showed him how to cook. How much he missed her when she died because there was no longer anyone to shield him and Ashley from their mother.

Hutch wanted to tell Jane how pretty she was, how he appreciated her help with Kimmie. And he wanted to ask her what she most wanted for Christmas and where she saw herself ending up a year from now.

But even if he could speak, Hutch wouldn't have asked her these things. He was on shaky ground with her and he didn't want to do anything that might tilt the balance out of his favor.

"I'm worried," she whispered, leaning in so close that her breath warmed his ear, "that Kimmie is going to ask Santa to bring her mommy home for Christmas. She's stopped asking about Ashley, but I know she's still longing for her mother."

Hutch shook his head. He hated what his sister was doing to her daughter. When Ashley got home, he was going to lay down the law. Either she agreed to treatment for her personality disorder or he was going to take her to court to get custody of Kimmie. On his own, he had little chance of gaining custody of his niece, but with Jane's testimony, he stood a fighting chance.

Would Jane agree to testify in his behalf if he did go for custody?

It was a battle he wasn't really ready to think about yet.

Kimmie sneezed. Jane dug a small package of tissues from her purse and passed one to her.

"Thank you, Mommy," Kimmie said.

Jane shot him a meaningful look over his niece's head.

The sky was overcast with temperatures in the mid-forties, nippy with a slight breeze coming in off Lake Twilight, but not uncomfortably so. Jesse and Flynn stood ahead of them in line with their daughter, Grace.

They waved and the women called out to each other, having a conversation about something called Kismet cookies.

"Are you comin' back home, Unca Hutch?" Kimmie asked.

He didn't know what to tell her, so he took the easy way out and flagged down a passing vendor pushing a popcorn chart and bought two small bags of caramel popcorn for the kids.

Jane gave him a chiding look. "It'll spoil their dinner."

Sheepishly, he shrugged.

At the entrance to Santa's Workshop, half a dozen elves greeted them, putting plastic candy cane garlands around their necks and ushering them inside the plywood building painted to look like the North Pole. Inside was Santa's sleigh being pulled by nine animated, talking reindeer, Rudolph in the lead with his shiny red nose.

Kimmie sneezed again and Jane automatically handed her another tissue.

"I wonder if she's allergic to something," Jane fretted. "Mountain cedar is high this time of year."

Finally, they reached Santa and their turn came. Kimmie and Ben insisted on going up together, one on each knee. Elves shot professional photographs, but Jane had her cell phone out, snapping pictures like mad.

Ben predictably asked Santa to bring him a Thomas the Train that he could ride on, and when Santa turned his attention to Kimmie, Hutch held his breath. Would she ask him to bring her mother home?

"And what would you like, little girl?" Santa asked with a jolly laugh.

Kimmie looked right in Santa's eyes and said, "I'd wike Auntie Jane to be my new mommy and Unca Hutch to be my daddy."

Santa looked startled. "Is there a toy I could bring you from my workshop?"

Kimmie's little face fell along with Hutch's stomach. She ducked her head and mumbled, "I guess I wike a princess doll."

If Ashley had been there, Hutch would have a hard time not grabbing her by the shoulders and shaking some sense into her, but if his sister had been there, Kimmie wouldn't be aching for a good mother.

Santa gave each child a candy cane and sent them on their way, extracting promises that they would be good children.

Jane took Ben's hand and he took Kimmie's. An elf escorted them to the exit. The courthouse clock chimed four as they stepped out onto the south side of the town square.

Hutch wasn't sure what to do now. He glanced over at Jane.

She had stopped in the middle of the walkway, and she was staring off into the crowd, her eyes fixed, her face the color of flour.

"Mommy," Ben said. "Your hand is cold."

Jane did not respond.

Hutch followed her gaze, spied a man about his height and build turning the corner on the east side of the square. He glanced back at Jane. The same kind of sheer, hopeless fear he'd seen on the faces of Afghan women and children after their villages had been dev-astated by warfare. Her entire body shook from head to feet.

Was she having a seizure? Alarmed, Hutch moved closer.

"Mommy?" Ben tugged on her arm.

Jane snapped to, blinked, and met his gaze with utterly desperate eyes. Worry lines curved around her mouth like parentheses.

Who was that man? What was he, that just the sight of him could turn her into a terrified zombie?

More than anything in the world, he wanted to reach out and touch her, but he didn't know where he stood, and touching her would violate the fragile lifeline of forgiveness she'd tossed him when she offered to allow him to come with them this afternoon. And he couldn't ask her what was wrong, or offer verbal reassurance.

So he stood there sending her a look that he hoped showed his concern for her and said what he could not say—*I care, I'm worried, please tell me what's wrong.*

"Hutch," she said, her voice as shaky as her body. "Would you please come home?"

Chapter 11

Dear Lord, Meredith prayed, *please don't let it be Sloane*.

Many times over the last five years she thought she'd seen him in a crowd. The sightings had been more common in the beginning, and had gradually dissipated until he caught up with her in Denver two years ago. After that, she saw him everywhere.

But since her move to Twilight, she'd started to feel safer and she hadn't once had a Sloane sighting.

She didn't know if it was the welcoming community that had lulled her or Hutch's appearance in her life, or both, but she had stupidly let down her guard. She hadn't even realized she was doing it—trusting more, being more open—but bit by bit she had started to feel safe here.

And until this moment, when she spotted the man

who looked eerily like her ex-husband, she hadn't realized what a huge mistake she'd made.

The man had been too far away for her to know if
it was a false alarm or not, but she wasn't taking any
chances. She had to either leave or get Hutch back in the
house at once. Even then, she should probably just pack
up and go. If it wasn't for Kimmie and Hutch, she would
immediately flee home and start packing her things.

Maybe she would do that anyway as soon as Hutch
was asleep.

Hutch was staring at her strangely.

She forced a smile. "We miss you."

He neither nodded nor shook his head. Just stood there
silent and strong as an old oak, his eyes tender and filled
with concern. She had such an overwhelming urge to
bury her head against his chest and confess everything.

A few days ago, she'd been worried about his capacity for violence. Now, weighed against the idea that
Sloane might have found her again, she wished that she
could tell him and unleash every bit of warrior that he
had in him on her ex-husband.

"Yah!" Kimmie exclaimed. "Unca Hutch is comin'
home with us."

"Hutch?" Meredith asked, her voice unnaturally
high. "Are you coming home with us?"

He smiled a smile that belied the wariness on his face
and the tension in his body. She wasn't fooling him. He
knew something was up. He made her wait one beat,
two. Then slowly, he bobbed his head up and down.

Relief expelled the air from her body in an exaggerated sigh. "Thank you," she said, her gratitude as heavy
as the cold humidity. Snow was on the way. She could
feel it. "Thank you."

Kimmie sneezed.

"Come on, sweetie. Let's get you home and get some warm soup into you." Meredith picked up the little girl, and Hutch hefted Ben on his shoulders. They hiked back to their vehicles together, Meredith frantically searching the crowd for signs of Sloane. She didn't spot him again, but just the fact that she *thought* she'd seen him was enough to send her into panic mode.

"Could you take the kids home in the minivan?" she asked Hutch when they reached the vehicles.

She hated to have Ben out of her sight for even a second, but she had to start covering her tracks. If she couldn't have him with her, Hutch was the only other person she truly trusted to take care of her son right now. The man was a Delta Force operative. If he couldn't best Sloane, then neither could Satan himself.

His eyes were suspicious, but he nodded and they swapped vehicles.

She climbed into his truck, watched him help the kids into their car seats. The cab smelled of him, manly and comforting. Her pulse thudded erratically and her hands shook against the steering wheel.

Inhaling deeply, she practiced a series of yoga breathing techniques to calm herself. Acting out of panic would only cause her to make mistakes, as she'd done the day she had pepper-sprayed Hutch. She had to be cautious. She could not afford a single misstep.

Her very life, and that of her son, depended on her keeping a cool head.

That night, Hutch's bedroom door creaked open, jolting him awake from a dead sleep. Automatically, he rammed a hand under his pillow going for the gun he'd forgotten wasn't there. He'd put away his weapons when he'd gotten home, locking them in a gun safe to keep the children protected. Fat lot of good that did him now against an intruder.

But his midnight invader wasn't some unknown threat.

Instead, it was his niece padding over the threshold. The moon shining through the part in the curtains, bathed her in a creamy yellow light. Behind her, she dragged a baby blanket, and she was whimpering softly.

Christ! Good thing he had locked up those guns.

Hutch swung his legs off the bed, reached for his blue jeans thrown over the footboard. Normally, he slept in the buff, but with kids in the house, he'd taken to sleeping in boxer shorts.

Kimmie rubbed her eyes. "I don't feel berry good, Unca Hutch."

He wrestled on a T-shirt, knelt in front of her, and tucked her against his chest. She crumpled into the crook of his elbow, pressing her head against his shoulder.

The kid was burning up!

With Kimmie clutched tightly in his arms, he rose to his feet and reached over to turn on the bedside lamp. Her face was red, perspiration beaded in that spot between her button nose and Cupid's bow mouth, and her lips were cracked and dry.

She had a fever and she was dehydrated.

How had this happened so fast? She'd been fine this afternoon. Sitting on Santa's lap, making unrealistic wishes for a family of her own. Her blue eyes, normally so clear and bright, turned murky and her gaze locked on him for a moment, her lashes dusted with a fine mist of tears. She rubbed the back of her hand over her lips, but dropped her arm halfway through the movement. She was too weak to hold her arm up even long enough to wipe her mouth.

Poor kid.

Her eyes shuttered closed and his chest carried the full weight of her little body. Her breathing was quick and hot. Too quick and too hot. Her hair, damp from sweat, was plastered against her head.

Hutch's pulse took off at a gallop, chasing a chill through his bloodstream in freezing contrast to Kimmie's thermal heat. Gooseflesh blanketed his skin. Acid bile burned his gut and a taste like oxidized pennies flooded his mouth. Fear, as strong as any he'd ever felt, grabbed him by the scruff of the neck and shook him like a baby cottontail in a pit bull's mouth.

He staggered from the bedroom, one arm cupped around Kimmie's pajama-clad bottom, the other pressed firmly against her back, her little legs dangling around his waist. Wrenched open the door to the downstairs bathroom, flipped on the light.

Kimmie grunted against the brightness, buried her face against his chest.

Sorry, baby, sorry.

Frantically, he did a one-handed search, pawing through drawers, yanking open cabinets, tossing around the contents. No thermometer. Damn his sister anyway. She had a four-year-old. How could she not have a thermometer in the house?

He had medical training. Everyone in The Unit knew more than just basic first aid and CPR, but he'd only used it on burly grown men. He'd applied tourniquets, stitched up wounds, given injections. But this was a kid here. He couldn't mess around. He wished he could ask her what else was wrong. Did she have a stomachache? A headache? Did she hurt anywhere?

His mind felt liquid, scattered, like it had turned to mercury, and he was trying to pick it up with his bare hands and it kept rolling through his fingers, shiny, bright, and hopelessly out of reach.

Don't lose it, man. This kid is depending on you.

Jane. She was a mother. A good mother. She would have a thermometer.

Relief poured through him. Jane would know what to do.

Hefting Kimmie up higher on his hip, Hutch scaled the stairs two at a time. He saw a light on under her door. Thank God, Jane was already awake.

He didn't knock. He was that upset, just turned the knob and bolted into her bedroom.

Her bed was still made up and a suitcase, stuffed with clothes, lay open on the bedspread. What was this? She was packing? Leaving?

The packed suitcase disoriented him and for a moment he thought he was dreaming. But he could feel the braided rug beneath his bare feet and the burn of Kimmie's fever against his skin. Dreams weren't this tactile. Unless this was a nightmare. He'd been having a lot of those lately, but they always revolved around combat.

From the trundle bed, Ben roused and sat up, yawning. His hair stuck up in the air like a woodpecker's topknot. He blinked and called out, "Mommy."

Jane opened the adjoining bathroom door and peeked out; she was toweling her hair dry. Hair that had once been coal black, but was now the color of burnished copper.

Her eyes widened at the sight of Hutch.

He rushed toward Jane, grabbed her startled hand. She dropped the towel stained with hair dye and it fell to the floor. Still holding her by the wrist, he pressed Jane's palm to Kimmie's forehead.

"She's burning up."

He nodded.

"Put her on the bed. Here wait, let me move the suitcase." She grabbed the suitcase without zipping it closed and tossed it in the corner. It hit the ground with a loud smack, slipping clothes all over the floor.

Hutch set Kimmie on the bed. She drooped against the mattress, moaned softly, and then her eyes rolled back in her head and her body stiffened. Ah shit! Hutch clutched at the sides of his head with both hands. What was happening to his niece?

Instantly, Jane turned Kimmie on her side and gently propped pillows around her while the tremors ran through her little body. "She's having a febrile seizure."

Kimmie's body shook, twitched.

Someone made the keening sound of a wounded animal caught in a trap and he realized it was he. Kimmie was having seizures. He wasn't messing around. He was calling 9–1–1. He leaped to grab Jane's cell phone lying on the table beside the bed, turned it on, and realized he couldn't tell the 9–1–1 dispatcher a damn thing.

"It's okay, Hutch," Jane said calmly. "She's coming out of it."

Kimmie's eyes fluttered opened. They looked glassy and confused.

Jane stroked Kimmie's hair. "There, there, sweetheart, you're all right," she cooed.

"Is Kimmie okay?" Ben asked, looking worried.

"She's got a little fever, honey, that's all. Try to go back to sleep," she told her son.

Ben settled back under the covers, but kept an eye on Kimmie.

Hutch sank against the wall, his legs no longer strong enough to hold him up.

Jane glanced over at him. "While febrile seizures are scary to watch, in children they don't usually require any treatment. I'll take her temperature and give her some children's ibuprofen to lower the fever, and then we'll take her to the doctor tomorrow. There's no need for an expensive and traumatic ER visit in the middle of the night."

Hutch's chest heaved, his throat tightening like a noose. His head spun and he slid down the wall until his butt hit the floor.

"You're hyperventilating." Jane got up and went over to put a hand on his shoulder. "I don't need two patients. Remember the yoga breathing I taught you. I'm going to let you deal with that while I go get the ibuprofen and a cool cloth for Kimmie's head."

Hutch nodded. What the hell kind of Delta Force operator was he? Going to pieces like that? Yeah, well, bullets and stab wounds were one thing. But a sick kid? Jesus. He pressed the heel of his palm to his forehead.

Jane went into the bathroom and he sat there, breathing deeply, trying to wrest back some shred of dignity and self-control. A minute later, Jane returned with an electronic thermometer, a damp washcloth, a bottle of ibuprofen, and a plastic one-ounce Dixie cup. She took Kimmie's temperature, pressed the cool cloth to the child's forehead. Her movements were so practiced. As if she'd done this many times before.

"A hundred and three," she told Hutch.

That sounded awfully high to him.

"Does she have a history of febrile seizures?"

Hutch lifted his shoulders in a helpless gesture. He had no idea.

"Do you have a headache?" Jane asked Kimmie.

Kimmie shook her head.

Jane bathed her face with the cloth. "Does your neck hurt?"

"No," Kimmie mumbled in a tiny voice.

"Can you do this?" Jane tilted her head from one shoulder to the next.

Kimmie imitated her movements.

"Good girl." Jane stroked Kimmie's cheek with a finger. "That's an encouraging sign," she called over her shoulder to Hutch. "If spinal meningitis were causing her fever, she'd have a splitting headache and/or neck stiffness and pain."

Hutch hoisted himself off the floor, came over to stand beside the bed.

"I'm going to sit you up now," Jane told Kimmie. "So you can take some medicine to bring down that fever. Can you swallow?"

Kimmie nodded mutely, her cheeks as red as Santa's suit. Jane measured out the medication into the plastic cup, and lifted up Kimmie's shoulders. "Swallow it fast to get it down."

His niece gulped the medicine down and Jane went back to the bathroom to get Kimmie a cup of water to wash it down with.

"Good girl." Jane patted Kimmie's back. "You're going to sleep right here with me tonight." She peeled back the covers and helped Kimmie scoot underneath them. To Hutch, she said. "I'll let her sleep here so I can keep a close eye on her."

Hutch wanted to argue. To tell her it was his job to take care of his niece, but he had no voice, and the Magic Slate was all the way downstairs.

Jane turned out the bedroom light, but kept the one in the bathroom on. Kimmie's eyes closed and her breathing slowed and within five minutes she was asleep.

"I've got it from here if you want to go back to bed." She stood there, her new red hair shining in the slant of light from the bathroom, looking like a professional nurse, the upended suitcase on the floor behind her, clothing strewn all around.

He remembered how she'd changed after they came out of Santa's Workshop. How her gaze had been fixed on a man disappearing in the crowd, how her face had paled, how she'd trembled all over. How she'd sent him on home with the children ahead of her. He'd known all along that she was hiding something. He couldn't play ignorant anymore.

Hutch turned toward the door, heard her deep sigh of relief. If she thought he was just going to walk away and leave things as they were, the woman had another think coming.

Meredith had been packing to leave town, her gut screaming at her to go, go, go. Yelling at her that it had been Sloane whom she'd seen in town, even though she had no proof.

But her brain had been reluctant to pull that trigger. Ben was happy here. Christmas was upon them, and poor little Kimmie would be left alone with a man who could not talk to her and was not her parent.

She'd eaten three candy bars to start putting on weight for her physical transformation and dyed her hair red. She hadn't been a redhead since three years ago in Kansas City.

She sat beside Kimmie for half an hour, then checked her temperature again. It was down to 101. Thank heavens. Feeling shaky with relief, she stepped into the bathroom to splash cold water on her face, and ran a comb through her damp, short hair. Time to grow it out again. God, they'd been here only about two months, and she was starting all over again so soon. When she'd first escaped, her only thoughts had been of survival, but as time went on, it got harder and harder to stay in place on constant red alert.

Life on the run was affecting Ben, even more so the older he got. How could it not? She wanted so much more for him than this ghost life. She wanted him to grow up feeling safe and secure. But she could not give him those things.

Tears sprang to her eyes as she stared at herself in the mirror—so many towns, so many appearance changes. She didn't even know who she was anymore. If it weren't for yoga, she wouldn't be able to hold it together.

She grabbed the empty box of hair dye to toss into the wicker trash basket beside the commode. A door hinge creaked. Her anxiety hollered, *Sloane!* She jumped, spun around, her heart rate instantly scraping the ceiling, and stuck her head out of the bathroom again.

Hutch stood in front of her, his gaze dark and intense, his neck muscles bunching tight, and rounding his shoulders. The bathroom light fell over his face but could not breach his locked-up eyes. He held the Magic

Slate, framed on either side by his big hands, the red stylus dangling from its string.

Her gaze dropped from his inscrutable face to the tablet. WHO ARE YOU?

She froze, her hand curled around the Clairol Nice 'n Easy Natural Light Auburn box.

He stepped forward, boxing her in, blocking the door. She couldn't escape.

Dropping the box on the counter, she notched up her chin. "You're not supposed to be on this floor. I understand why you came up here with Kimmie, those were extenuating circumstances, but now you need to leave."

He shook his head, erased his question from the Magic Slate to write, I MADE THAT AGREEMENT WITH JANE BROWN.

Dread flooded her body. Turned her cheeks first cold and then hot. "How…" She cleared her throat. "…did you find out?"

I'M NOT A FOOL, he wrote. BUT YOU'VE MISTAKEN ME FOR ONE.

"I haven't. It's not like that." She shook her head, bit down on her bottom lip.

Glaring, he stalked closer.

She let out a tiny shriek, rocketed backward, ran into the wall. What now? Where to go?

Angrily, he lifted the top sheet of the Magic Slate, and in tight, angry script wrote, WHAT'S YOUR CON?

"No con." She shook her head vigorously.

His frown deepened.

"I swear it."

Who are you? he mouthed silently.

She could give him one of her other aliases. Stringing him along until she could get out of here.

And go where in the middle of the night?

Anywhere. It wasn't the first time they'd had to pull up stakes without notice.

But she was so tired of running. So tired of hiding. So tired of people calling her by false names. And she owed him an explanation. *What if you tell him and he goes to the police? What then?*

She needed to trust him. She had to start trusting someone, sometime. Hopefully, he'd believe her story.

And if he didn't?

He moved toward her again, his jaw granite.

She held up both palms. "Okay, okay. I'll tell you, but you've got to make me a promise."

His eyes narrowed.

"Please," she whispered.

There must have been something in her eyes that convinced him, because he backed up all the way to the door.

He folded his arms tightly over his chest and silently mouthed, *Talk.*

"Not here. The kids need to sleep. Let's go into the guest bedroom."

He gave a curt nod and led the way, Meredith followed, her dread mounting with each step. Would he believe her? Or would he call the police?

He toed open the guestroom door, flicked on the lights, and waited for her to enter ahead of him. She looked down at her University of New Mexico sweatshirt stained with auburn hair dye. How dumb to have held on to this sweatshirt. Giving away her roots. But it didn't really matter now. He already knew something was off about her.

How long had it been since she'd been in a bedroom alone with a man?

The curtain was open to the window facing the street, letting in the colorful spill of winking Christmas lights. He clicked the door closed behind them.

She gulped, spun to face him.

His face was flat, emotionless.

She took a deep breath. "My real name is Meredith Sommers. It used to be Meredith Sloane. When I was married."

He laid the Magic Slate on the dresser, folded his arms over his chest, his eyes flinty.

Just say it. Just get it out.

She opened her mouth, shut it, and then opened it again. "I lied when I told you Ben's father was dead. He's very much alive. I only wish he were dead."

God, she thought she might throw up. Talking about Sloane, thinking about him, always nauseated her. She closed her eyes briefly, licked her lips, and peeked at Hutch.

His features never changed, stayed hard-edged, stony.

"I'm sorry I lied to you." Her chin trembled, and she blinked hard to keep back the tears. She hated lying. Hated that it had been her life for the last five years. Lies had warped her, diminished her. But coming clean wasn't easy.

Meredith put a palm to her mouth, glanced down at her bare feet, and curled her toes into the rug as if anchoring herself to the earth.

It was shame that had tears on the verge of falling over her eyelids, and tumbling down her cheeks—shame for having been so stupid, for not having known better, for getting herself into a situation that would end up ruining her entire life.

She wrapped her arms around her waist, turned away from him to stare out the window, gathering her courage. Across the way, the red nose of the wire reindeer in Flynn and Jesse's yard blinked off and on. She could feel the cold air rolling off the window pane, smelled wood smoke in the air. Christmas. It was supposed to be a happy time, but it always made Meredith sad deep within the seat of her soul. She had no family to gather round the holiday tree with. It was only she and Ben.

Until this year. Until Twilight. Until Hutch and Kimmie.

When had she started thinking of them as family? She kneaded her brow with her fingertips. *I'm sorry, baby*, she mentally apologized to Ben. *For so many things.*

She heard Hutch shift behind her. He was growing impatient.

Meredith hauled in a deep breath, paused, blew it out, and without turning back to look at him, confessed, "There's something else you should know about me."

He came nearer. She could feel the tension in him, and see him in the glass. Their eyes met in the reflection.

"I'm wanted for the attempted murder of a police officer."

Chapter 12

Of all the things Hutch thought she might say, this confession wasn't even on the list. Uncertain that he'd heard her correctly, he cocked his head, stared into her urgent eyes.

She nodded, moistened her lips, and ran her open palms over the tops of her thighs.

He'd spent his life prepared for anything—first with his unpredictable mother, and then in the military—but she'd still taken him by surprise, and it took a moment for the information to infiltrate his stupefied brain. Jane was on the run for trying to kill a police officer.

Meredith. Her name was Meredith.

He liked the name and he liked her. Liked? Who was he kidding? What he was feeling was several notches above like.

She looked much more like a Meredith than a Jane—

regal, self-contained, a cut above the rest. He was glad, now, for his inability to speak because he had never called her by the wrong name. When she heard his voice for the first time, he wanted her real name to roll off his tongue. Meredith.

Getting ahead of yourself, Hutchinson. First, you gotta speak. Second, she has to be here in order to hear you say her name.

She sounded so lost that he reached out a hand to touch her, to reassure her, let her know that he did not judge her, to encourage her to keep going. But he hesitated, not wanting to scare her or upset her by breaking her rules.

Hey, the hard-ass devil on his shoulder argued, *she broke the rules first by lying about who she was. All bets are off.*

Acting on instinct and hoping it was the right move, Hutch gently took her by the shoulders and turned her around. Her eyes were forlorn, but her chin notched up defiantly. "The policeman I shot was my abusive ex-husband."

But she hadn't killed him? Too damn bad. Any man who would abuse a woman deserved his comeuppance, and Hutch was of a mind to finish the job for her.

"I suppose I should start at the beginning," she said, although she looked as if she'd rather have all her teeth pulled without novocaine.

He shook his head, letting her know that she owed him no explanation, but she raised an index finger and pressed it to his lips. "You need to know what you're dealing with. I should have told you before, but I didn't know how to go about it. And secrecy has been my protection for so long, I've forgotten how to trust."

Yet here she was, trusting him now. She didn't have to. She could have just packed up and walked away.

Clearing her throat, she told him about her parents, hot air balloonists who dragged their young daughter around the country on their nomadic lifestyle.

"We were gypsies, living in a small motor home. I was homeschooled. In spite of—or maybe because of— my unorthodox upbringing, I was a happy kid. Who knows?" A soft smile came over her lips as she told him about her parents and how loved they made her feel.

He was glad for her. He wished he could say the same thing.

"But even though I had food to eat and a warm bed to sleep in, I had white picket fence dreams." She gave a sardonic laugh as if it was the most ludicrous dream in the world.

Hutch peered deeply into her eyes, giving Ja—Meredith his spellbound attention.

The light that had flared in her eyes when she started talking about her parents winked out. "They were killed in a balloon accident when I was sixteen. I was on the chase crew, and I… I…" She paused, blinked hard. "… saw them go down."

Aww shit, baby no.

He thought about his own loss at sixteen, when he walked into the house just minutes before the school bus deposited Ashley at the door. Finding his mother's body, realizing she'd finally gone and made good on her threats. Snatching up the suicide note. *You drove me to this, Brian.* She'd been mad because he'd thrown her worthless, dope-smoking boyfriend out of the house the day before.

Feeling absolutely nothing, he'd crumpled up the note

and stuck it in his pocket. Calmly called 9–1–1, then went outside just in time to stop Ashley from walking into the house.

That night, his famous cool snapped and he went on a grief-fueled rampage, smashing every mailbox on the street with a baseball bat. Caitlyn's father, Judge Blackthorne, had caught him, but instead of turning him over to the police, he'd counseled him. Advised him to join the army as soon as he got out of high school. And the judge went with him to speak to the owners of the mailboxes while he apologized and promised restitution.

If it hadn't been for the judge—who later heard his case and granted him emancipated minor status so he could get Ashley out of the foster care system—Hutch knew his life would have taken a much darker turn.

He was glad he could not tell Meredith about all that. He'd put away the past a long time ago. Moved on with startling success considering where he'd come from. He'd dived headfirst into the military, used it to escape his suffering. But then an ambush on the other side of the world brought him full circle right back to where he started.

Irony. What a bitch.

Meredith wiped away the tears pooling underneath her eyes and took a deep breath. "I don't wallow in self-pity. I'm telling you all this so that you'll understand. At the cookie swap party they told me you lost your mother when you were sixteen. What a rotten thing for us to have in common."

He nodded and made a fishing gesture as if he was trying to land a one-ton marlin, illustrating struggle and resistance, and then he opened his palms, letting go.

"Exactly. You can't hold on to grief forever or it will drag you down. At some point you simply have to let go."

Yeah, here he was preaching to her in made-up sign language about letting things go and yet he was the one hanging on to grief, rage, and resentment over what he'd lost. He could sure dole out the advice, but he couldn't seem to take it.

But how could he fully let the past go until he'd done his duty and visited the families of his men?

It all came down to that. His inability to speak. What was a man without a voice?

"After my parents died, I went to live with my mother's mother. Gramma was the only close relative I had left and I finally got my wish to be rooted in one place. I was so excited to go to high school. But I'd been home-schooled for so long it was hard for me to fit in, and my mother had done such a great job teaching me, I was able to bypass my senior year. Instead, I went to massage school so I could put myself through nursing school. My parents didn't have anything but their balloons and our RV, and Gramma was on a fixed income. I couldn't expect her to pay for college."

What a smart, resilient kid she'd been. He wished he could have known her then.

"My first year in college, Gramma got cancer. She fought a hard battle for four years. She was determined to see me graduate." Sadness and regret settled on Meredith's face. "Gramma died two days before graduation."

He touched her upper arm.

She tilted her head and looked up at him. Her hair was starting to grow out a bit and the auburn color softened her skin. Did she have any idea how utterly gorgeous she was?

Shyly, she lifted her hand to the nape of her neck. "I've colored my hair so many times that I've forgotten what shade of brown my real color is."

Black, blond, brunette, redhead, Hutch didn't care what color her hair was. She could dye it lime green and she'd still be the most beautiful woman in the world in his eyes.

Meredith. Man, he wished he could talk so he could say her name over and over again.

"I'm hedging, aren't I?" She hugged herself, rubbed the palms of each hand over the opposite upper arm as if she were cold and trying to warm herself. But the temperature in the room was perfectly comfortable.

The chill she was feeling came from the inside. Hutch's jaw tightened. Already his hands were packing into fists, yearning to punch the son of a bitch who'd damaged her. He wasn't any more eager to hear her tale of domestic abuse than she was to tell it, but their relationship was at an impasse until she did. They both knew it.

"I'd never really dated, what with living on the road and then losing my parents, going to massage school and then college. Taking care of my grandmother when she got sick. There wasn't any time for a real social life. I had friends, sure, but not close ones because I didn't have time to go do all the normal things teenagers do."

He let her take the wandering path to her narrative destination. The secret she was about to reveal was buried deep and it would take some digging to get it all out.

"His name is…" Meredith paused, glanced over her

shoulder to the left, and then looked right as if expecting him to slip up behind her. "Vick Sloane."

Hutch hated him already.

"I met Sloane a month after graduation when I was doing an externship after college. He ended up in my trauma room after a prostitute bit him. Another nurse got the prostitute, who'd been badly beaten. The woman claimed Vick was the one who'd beaten her. He claimed it was her pimp. It was the word of a LAPD detective against a hooker. Guess who won? It should have been a warning, but I was so damn gullible. I fell for his mustachioed smile and vigorous lies."

She ducked her head, shuddered.

Tenderly, Hutch reached out to cup her chin, angled her face up to meet his eyes, and slowly shook his head. She had been young and open and trusting. She shouldn't feel ashamed or embarrassed for being innocent.

"I was twenty-two and a newly minted RN and he was thirty-three and a police detective. I was overwhelmed by his attention. No man had ever given me the full court press like that."

Hutch's heart was breaking for her. He wished he could go back in time, be the one who had met her when she was twenty-two. If he had, if they'd had each other, how different might both of their lives have been?

She turned away from him again, and still hugging herself, walked back to the window and stared out. For a long moment the only sound in the room was the sound of their simultaneous breathing. Doing yoga together had them breathing in synchronized rhythm. He smiled briefly at that. This wasn't the time to be thinking about what other rhythms they might be good at.

In a small voice she asked, "What is it about sociopaths? How do they know exactly who to pick on?"

He wished he could offer her an answer, but even if he could speak, he could not explain the motives behind black hearts.

"Sloane was charming."

Once upon a time, Hutch had been charming too. It was what women had loved most about him. He would cock his head, send the woman on his radar a secret smile, pin her with a laser gaze, and say something light and witty.

It always worked. He'd never struck out. Not once.

"He completely swept me off my feet." She shivered. "I still hate that phrase. That's the thing that bothered me the most when Ashley took off with that guy. She said he swept her off her feet."

Uneasiness had him scratching the backs of his knuckles, itchy as they healed up from when he'd punched the front door.

"He asked me to marry him after only three weeks of dating. I was so lonely without Gramma, still grieving for her, and Sloane looked to be everything I thought I wanted. Steady, stable, with a secure job. He promised me a house, babies, all of it."

Hutch hated to see her beating herself up like this, but he'd done the same thing over his mother and Ashley. Was still doing it over the loss of his teammates because he'd walked out as the lone survivor.

She moaned softly. "I fell for it hook, line, and sinker."

Hutch came up behind her, rubbed a palm over her back, and to his surprise she leaned against him.

"Sloane was a decorated cop. He took risks other

policemen wouldn't take. Of course that was part of his pathology, but no one saw it that way. People saw his arrogance as self-confidence. I did too. I thought he was strong and capable and in control. I didn't realize it was a cloak for meanness and cruelty."

She turned back to face him once more. The more she talked about Sloane, the more she withered—her shoulders rounded and drew forward, her eyes dulled, her voice wavered.

If that bastard were standing in front of him right now, Hutch would cheerfully bash his face in, numerous times, before he killed him. He imagined the fistfight. Tasted blood. Over the course of the last few months he'd lost his taste for blood, for war and violence, for discord and crisis that he used to thrive on, but for Sloane he'd happily make an exception.

"I loved being a nurse, but Sloane didn't want me to work. So I quit my job before the wedding. So dumb of me." She smacked her forehead with her palm. "So damn dumb. It was his first step in isolating me. And the minute he put that ring on my finger, and I was legally his, the craziness began."

A faraway look came into her eyes as if she were wishing she could reach back in time and rescue that young woman. She was getting to the hard part now. The part he didn't want to hear.

He could feel her knees trembling. He took her by the elbow and guided her toward the bed. She perched on the edge of the mattress, drew her knees to her chest, wrapped her arms around her knees, and sat rocking herself gently.

"Have you ever seen that movie *Sleeping with the Enemy*?"

As a kid, he had a major crush on Julia Roberts, so, yeah, he'd seen the movie. He nodded. Julia's character was married to a man so violent and controlling that nothing in the house could be an inch out of place or he'd abuse her. Life with him was so intolerable that the heroine faked her own death to get away from the sociopath. But he tracked her down anyway.

The movie had been damn chilling, because even then, when he'd seen the movie as a preteen, he'd recognized how easy it would be for his mother to have fallen under the influence of someone like that. He remembered wanting to get a gun and protect Julia from her insane husband.

"It was just like that," Meredith said, and proceeded to describe in detail the depth of his abuse and her dawning horror that she'd married a monster who was never going to let her go. "Except instead of faking my own death, I managed to find a great psychologist who helped me get away from him to the point of providing me fake credentials and hiding me in a safe house. Considering Sloane's career and the power and clout he had, she understood that I was a special case. Unfortunately, she paid for it with her life."

He arched an eyebrow.

Meredith told him how she believed Sloane had tampered with the brakes of her psychologist's car after he stormed into her office and she refused to tell him where Meredith was.

"I left Sloane three months after I married him and then I found out I was pregnant."

Hutch sank down on the mattress beside her, his impulse to comfort her, but then he worried she might think he wanted something more since they were sitting on a bed, so he didn't make another move.

"I was so happy when Ben was born," she said. "No matter who his father was, I swore my little boy was going to know only love, and you can see for yourself what a sweet child he is."

He nodded. Ben was a loving child. It wasn't just a mother's natural prejudice.

"I did everything I could to keep him safe. Moving from town to town, changing my name and appearance. Always looking over my shoulder. Holding my breath and waiting, just waiting for Sloane to find me again."

He rubbed a thumb over her knuckles. Her jigsaw smile broke his heart.

"So now you know why I was so trigger-happy with the pepper spray. You're about the same height and build as Sloane, and when you came out of the house, I saw him even though I knew it wasn't."

He wanted to tell her that was just fine. She could pepper-spray him every day if it made her feel safer.

She pulled her hands up inside her sleeves. "I couldn't be a nurse, Sloane would look for me in hospitals and clinics, so I took any unskilled labor jobs I could find. It's hard feeding a child and living in a safe place on minimum wage. I tried working two jobs, but then I was never home with Ben. Then I remembered that I'd never told Sloane that I was a licensed massage therapist."

He so admired her courage, respected her resilience and ingenuity. She'd managed to survive being stalked by a sociopath for five years with very little help from anyone. She was remarkable.

"Whenever I'd go to a new town, I'd tell a version of

my story to the spa owners, show them my real ID and massage license and tell them I was on the run from an abusive ex-husband and I need to keep my identity hidden for my own protection. Everyone understood and kept my vicious secret."

She'd suffered so much. Thinking about her pain was a samurai sword slicing clean through his shabby heart. How he wished he could have been there to protect her, to keep her safe.

Meredith drew in a deep breath and continued. "What I didn't tell them was that I was wanted for attempted murder in Colorado."

Restlessly, she plucked at a loose thread on the sleeve of her sweater. "When Ben was two years old, Sloane caught up to me in Fort Collins. His mistake was thinking I was still that naïve young woman he'd married. You should have seen his face when I pulled out the Colt and told him to get out of my house."

Wow. His entire body tensed as he imagined petite Meredith facing down a guy as big as he. He could just see her, Mama Bear fierce at the end of her rope, prepared to go down fighting.

"He didn't believe I would shoot him and he came right for me, assuming I'd crumble." A savage laugh burst from her lips. "You should have seen his face when I pulled the trigger and the bullet hit him dead in the center of his chest. I thought I'd killed him. I prayed I'd killed him. But I didn't wait to find out. I snatched up Ben and my purse. I put him in the car and drove away as fast as I could. It never occurred to me until I heard about it on the news that the son of a bitch was wearing a bulletproof vest. Of course," she finished, spongy regret in her voice, "the cops believed his version of events."

Violence. More violence. She'd had a life strewn with it.

His life had been littered too. He'd made a career of violence just like Meredith's ex-husband. Why had Sloane turned out one way and Hutch another? Was it genetics? Nurture? Life experiences? All three?

What made a man in a position of power go bad?

Had he been guilty of abusing his power? Lines could blur so easily. He thought of some of the sketchy situations he'd been in, some of the questionable on-the-spot decisions he'd been forced to make.

Yes, he convinced himself he was in the right. It was easy when you believed you were right. He was fighting on the side of the good guys, right? But nothing in life was ever like the old Westerns where the bad guys wore black hats and the good guys wore white.

How did a man square who he thought he was against the things he'd done? How did he reconcile his identity with his ideals?

When Hutch walked out of Walter Reed, he had no idea who he was anymore. His identity had fled with his voice. He was no longer part of The Unit. His teammates, his close friends and comrades-in-arms, were dead. They had been his family. His identity. Without them, he was adrift.

And he'd returned home to find Meredith and Ben and Kimmie, who were equally adrift and needed someone to plot their course. He rallied himself to fill the void, and the strangest thing had happened. He'd discovered not a new identity, but the very essence of who he really was.

He'd become a father figure. Someone people could depend on. All the good images of a father filtered through his head. The father he'd never had, but the example that had been set for him by the many kind men in Twilight, like Hondo Crouch.

It hit him like a sledgehammer how the men of the town had taken him under their wing. It was something he'd never really appreciated before. Judge Blackthorne had taken him fishing, taught him to love the river. Hondo had shown him how to build things. Flynn's father, Floyd MacGregor, had taught him how to cook. The men of Twilight had shaped him, kept him from going completely off the rails when he could have so easily ended up in prison for his tendency to get into fights protecting his mother and sister. They'd channeled his aggressions. Shown him a better way.

"So you see why I freaked out when you threw the Magic Slate? I know I was wrong to paint you with the same brush as Sloane, but I've been running scared for so long that I overreacted."

He shook his head. She'd done what she needed to do to feel safe.

"You've also probably guessed by now that I thought I saw Sloane in the town square and that's the reason I was packing. I'm probably wrong. It's not the first time I thought I saw Sloane when it wasn't him. I don't want to go, but I'm scared."

Christmas lights shone through the partially open curtain, blinking rhythmically as the preprogrammed pattern changed tempo. The shifting colors, from white to blue and back again, cast the room in an icy winter wonderland glow.

They sat side by side on the mattress, and he could

feel her body trembling through the box springs. Simultaneously, they turned their heads toward each other and their gazes wed.

"Hold me, Hutch," she whispered. "Please hold me."

Hutch drew her into his arms and he pressed her face against his chest and just held her like that for a long time. Feeling heartbreaking tenderness for her and an unspeakable rage at the bastard who'd reduced her to a life of running and hiding in the shadows.

After several minutes, she pulled away.

He stared at her and she stared right back, his throat swelling at the thought of what she'd suffered at the hands of her ex-husband until he feared he would choke on the bile of his anger.

"I've made so many mistakes," she whimpered.

He put his index finger against her lips. Shh. He'd made tons of mistakes himself.

Her lips parted and she leaned toward him.

God, he wanted to kiss her more than he wanted to breathe but he wasn't going to do it. He would not take advantage of this situation.

"Hutch." She moistened those sweet lips. "Would you mind if I kissed you?"

Mind? Excuse me while I do a few back flips.

He leaned in slightly, testing her intent, but giving her enough room to skitter away in case she had second thoughts. It was tough because he wanted to gobble her up, give her hot, passionate kisses that would leave them crazed for each other, but she'd been through too much for that.

"Don't hold back," she said, reading his mind. "I'm not a china doll. I'm a real live woman."

Yes, you are.

"I want to be kissed by a good man with a kind heart."

Oh baby, why did you have to say that? I'm pretty damn far from good.

Her pupils widened, darkened to midnight blue, the color of misty twilight. Tentatively, he dipped his head, kept his eyes trained on those beautiful lips. The most perfect lips in all the land. He felt as if he were in a fairy tale, a children's cartoon. He was the hulking ogre and she was the beautiful princess.

He stopped, waited for her to make the first move.

"I changed my mind," she said.

That's okay, that's okay. His muscles were corded so tight a cannonball would have bounced off them. Delta Force operators were nothing if not highly controlled. Too soon. It was too soon. He'd known that.

"I want you to kiss me."

That was a twist. He gave her a look that said, *Are you sure?*

"Certain," she confirmed.

He pressed his lips to hers so lightly it was more a mixing of breath than skin. A hundred fears and expectations coalesced into one quivering question in the anxious brushing of their cautious mouths.

Is this really what you want?

Hutch could see her heart hammering through her clothes, could hear his own pulse quicken pace as blood galloped through his ears.

He tumbled into those liquid eyes, sank right to the bottom and swam around. This was what he'd never known he'd spent his life searching for. He saw past all the hurt and sorrow and tragedy that had led her to

him and marveled at how she'd retained her inner goodness, hope, and beauty in the face of such dark forces.

She kissed him right back with all the passion that
had been building inside them both for the past few
weeks. Meredith was the one who took it deeper, her
saucy tongue teasing his teeth apart, and he loosened
his jaw, letting her all the way in.

This could get out of hand real quick, Hutchinson.

A soft moan seeped from her and she curled both
hands around his forearm, clung to him.

More. He had to have more. This taste was sweet,
but it was not nearly enough.

He tilted her head back, exposing that magnificent
creamy throat, and planted a hard kiss on the under-
side of her chin.

The furnace clicked on, sending warm air shoot-
ing through the ceiling vent, adding heat to the flame.

She swung herself into his lap and went exploring,
slipping a palm up underneath his T-shirt, skimming
hotly over his bare chest and unraveling him completely,
and for a moment he was operating on nothing but blind
masculine instinct, going for what he wanted.

Hutch kissed his way up the left side of her neck, to
her earlobe, where he nibbled lightly, as she wriggled
with delight. His tongue found the jagged scar behind
her ear and he did not have to ask, but she supplied the
answer anyway.

"Sloane broke a beer bottle over my head."

Talk about a mood killer, but he was glad she said
it. Glad she reminded him precisely why this was a bad
idea. Meredith was not in a good place emotionally. She
was using him as salve. He wasn't opposed to that in

principle, but she was too fragile for that whether she knew it or not.

He pulled back.

"Don't stop!" she protested, and captured his face between her hands. "Please. I need this. I need you."

God, he was only human. A mere mortal, and she was the sexiest thing that had ever straddled his lap. He didn't know if he possessed the strength of character to turn her away.

The sound of a tiny little fist knocking on the door drew both their heads up at once. From out in the hallway, Ben's little voice called, "Mommy, I feel hot and shivery all over."

Chapter 13

His kiss left her in ruins.

Meredith lay in the darkened bedroom, two sick kids tucked on either side of her, still wide awake and thinking of what had passed between her and Hutch in the guest bedroom.

From the look in his eyes, he'd been just as decimated as she. Knocked sideways by the sheer force of their hunger for each other. If Ben hadn't knocked on the door when he did...

She blew out a breath, and laid the back of her hand against her forehead. Although this chemistry had been building from that first day when she'd undressed him in the bathroom, Meredith never anticipated that kissing him would feel this damn good.

Clichés flew around in her head—mind-blowing, earth-shattering, lightning-that-lingered, but none of those trite, overused phrases began to describe this. She felt as if she had been born blind, and Hutch's kiss had restored her vision. There was a whole big world out there she never knew existed. Eyes wide open, and there was so much to see.

How could a kiss promise so much? Be both sweet and arousing? And why did it have to come from the most complicated man she'd ever met?

She traced her fingertips over her lips, remembering, closed her eyes, and sighed. She had asked him to kiss her and he'd obliged. It had been so long since someone had kissed her with true tenderness. So very long, and she'd sponged it right up.

And she'd told him everything. Stripped her soul bare. She'd held nothing back. He knew all her secrets and she didn't know his.

What was she doing? What was she thinking? She didn't have to tell him the truth. She could have just left. It would have been so much easier to leave.

This could go no farther. Nothing more could happen between them.

But oh those lips of his…

Meredith moved her hand from her forehead to her mouth, bit down lightly on the knuckle of her index finger. Mistake. Kissing him had been a mistake. Stirring instead of sating the sexual tension. Why did he have to be a world-class kisser? Madness. This was madness. Torturing herself over something she could not have. All right. He was a magnificent combination of admirable masculinity, sheer brute sexiness, and alarmingly disarming kindness. But they both needed saving and she was smart enough to know that two drowning swimmers would only pull each other down. He had to find

his own salvation and she couldn't be saved. Not until
Vick Sloane was six feet under.

Ben was her primary concern, her only concern.
His safety and happiness would forever come before
her own.

Her breath stilled in her body, a hushed quiet that
led her deeper into the landscape of her own mind. Air
stifled, pressure built, her lungs burned, aching with
certain knowledge that there could be no happily-ever-
after for her and Hutch, no matter how desperately she
wished it.

The next morning Meredith and Hutch took the children to see the pediatrician. Mild virus. Going around.
Bed rest. Plenty of fluids. Children's ibuprofen. Good
as new in three days.

Things looked rosier in daylight and Meredith was
glad she hadn't cut and run after what she perceived was
a Sloane sighting. Otherwise, she would have been on
the road when Ben's fever spiked. And that wasn't the
only reason she was thankful. Last night, sharing her
secret with Hutch, telling someone the full truth about
herself for the first time in five years, brought a sense
of liberation she had not expected.

Despite waking up several times to check on the sick
children, Meredith experienced the best sleep of her life.

Bright side of what had happened last night.

On the opposite end of the spectrum, things between
her and Hutch were tenser than ever. The sexual tension
that had been simmering between them for weeks had
erupted into a full, rolling boil in the span of an hour.
No putting that alchemy back in the genie bottle. And
yes, she knew she was mixing her clichéd metaphors.

The situation flummoxed her. She couldn't leave, not with a sick child. Didn't want to leave. And those sparks were undeniable. Sooner or later the forest was going to burn down. Did she really want to be in it when that happened?

To make things worse, the massage bookings took a dramatic dip the week leading up to Christmas, leaving Meredith with more time to spend around the house. Normally that would be a good thing, but with all the rules broken and the boundaries knocked down between her and Hutch, she worried how they would navigate so much togetherness without giving in to temptation.

The first three days went by fairly smoothly because the sick children kept her occupied. The only private conversation she had with Hutch was about the gifts Ashley had put on layaway for Kimmie at Walmart. Via Magic Slate, Hutch told her he'd take care of the layaway.

"Would you pick up my layaway for Ben while you're there?" she asked, reaching to get money from her purse.

Hutch shook his head, wrote: MY TREAT.

"No, I take care of my own child. You're not paying for my layaway." She thrust out both her jaw and the money at him. "Take it."

At first, she thought he was going to refuse it, but then an expression came over his face as if he'd just gotten a brilliant idea, and he accepted the money.

"Hmm, what are you up to?"

His insouciant shrug said, *You'll never guess.*

On the day before Christmas Eve, with the pediatrician's okay, they took the children to pick out the

Christmas tree. They roamed the graveled lot looking for the perfect one.

They passed a pine flocked in pink and Meredith felt a tugging at the bottom of her coat. "Mommy," Kimmie said. "Can we get this one?"

Meredith's chest iced up cold while her heart beat hot. Kimmie had called her Mommy again. *Ah, dammit, Ashley. Come home. It's Christmas and you're missing the most wonderful part of it.*

She clenched her jaw and looked up, her gaze catching Hutch's. He'd heard it too. Their original agreement had been for Meredith to stay through Christmas, but that had been with the assumption that Ashley would be home by then. What would happen to Hutch and Kimmie if she did not return?

"We're not having pink. Guys don't have pink trees, do they, Unca Hutch?" Ben asked.

"Well, I'm a girl and girls wike pink trees." Kimmie pouched out her lips in a forceful pout and folded her arms over her chest.

Ben shook his head vigorously. "No way, Jose."

Kimmie pressed her palms together in supplication and batted her big blue eyes at Hutch. "Please, Unca Hutch?"

"No," Ben said, and gave her a shove.

"Excuse me, young man," Meredith scolded. "We don't shove. You apologize to Kimmie. Right now."

Ben hung his head. "Sorry."

Kimmie lifted her nose in the air. "Hmph."

"Their first fight," Meredith said to Hutch, and laughed. "They'd been cooped up indoors too long." To Kimmie, she said, "We're not going to get a pink tree, but later we'll go get hot chocolate with pink marsh-mallows in it at Perks."

"Yay!" The kids applauded in unison, happy again.

If she let herself it would be so easy to imagine this as her life, the mother of two children and married to a brave man like Hutch who could keep her safe. A man she could trust with her darkest secrets. She never thought it possible that she could find a man like him.

But he wasn't hers, was he? She could never forget that a monster dogged her every step, and the second she let down her guard, he'd be upon her.

But how tempting the dream!

Hutch led the way to the back of the lot, but stopped after he'd taken a few steps and waited for them to catch up. The children darted between the trees, laughing and playing tag.

"Be careful of running on gravel," Meredith warned, just as her own boot caught on a loose rock and her knee buckled. Going down. Bracing herself for the fall, she squeezed her eyes closed, gritted her teeth.

But instead of hitting the pavement, a pair of strong masculine arms went around her. Hutch. Righting her, he kept his hand pressed to her back. Gently rubbing his palm in a circle in a wonderfully comforting gesture that said, *It's all right. I'm here. I've got your back.*

She peeked over her shoulder at him. Their eyes met. Over the loudspeakers, "Baby, It's Cold Outside" played.

They stood close to each other, neither one moving away. She was aware of his scent and the way his hair fell into a natural part on the right. She wondered what he was thinking. She wished he could talk and she wondered what his voice sounded like.

Meredith couldn't stop looking at him. Hutch. Brian, a tall force-of-man that would make any woman's knees buckle, naturally tanned skin, leather jacket, the scars on his neck and hands making him that much sexier. Declaring he was a man who had lived and survived.

He pointed to a tree. This one.

Oh yes. The reason they were here. Buying a Christmas tree.

The salesman helped him load it into his pickup truck. They'd brought both vehicles because of the car seats.

The children, still a little weak from their bout with the virus, lifted their arms up and begged to be carried. Hutch scooped up Kimmie, and Meredith tucked Ben onto her hip.

"You're getting too heavy for this," she said, sad for that fact, but happy she had this one last Christmas to be able to lug him around.

At Perks, they got a table near the window so they could look out and watch the town square decked out in Christmas pageantry. Couples strolled hand in hand to a Christmas music medley. Last-minute shoppers raced from store to store. Was it possible to fall in love with an entire town in less than three months? Apparently so, because Meredith had already given her heart away.

Caitlyn and Gideon Garza and their two boys walked into the coffee shop. They waved and came over. Caitlyn jiggled her two-year-old son, Levy, on her hip. Meredith smiled, remembering when Ben was that age. She'd always wanted at least three children, but Sloane had killed that dream forever. With the life she led, she could not have a long-term relationship, much less another child.

"So many exciting things happening." Caitlyn's eyes sparkled. "Have you heard the weather report? They're calling for snow for Christmas! In North Texas. Can you believe it?"

"Buckets of it," said their preteen, Danny.

"Snow, not ice," Gideon clarified. "For you out-of-towners." He grinned at Meredith. "In this neck of the woods, we mostly have ice storms instead of snow."

"Do you know how often we have snow on Christmas?" Caitlyn marveled, and then answered her own question. "Maybe three or four times in the history of North Texas weather keeping!"

"Don't get your hopes up too high," Gideon cautioned. "You know Texas weather. It can change in a blink."

The children wriggled and giggled over the possibility of snow. Ben made funny faces at Levy.

"Also, did you hear about the Secret Santa?" Caitlyn put Levy down so he could climb up on the chair with Ben.

"No." Meredith cocked her head, watched her son interacting with the younger boy. Ben was trying to explain to Levy what snow was.

"Well," Caitlyn said, more animated than Meredith had ever seen her. "Two days ago someone went to Walmart and paid for all the accounts that were on layaway. There are a lot of hardworking moms and dads in town who are going to have a great Christmas because of a generous soul."

"That's so kind," Meredith said as her gaze strayed to Hutch. "Do they have any idea who this person was?"

"Walmart promised anonymity to the Secret Santa, but someone used the pronoun 'he.' All the Fort Worth

TV stations sent a camera crew out here to cover the story. It's generating buzz, which for a tourist town is always a good thing."

"It was a man, huh?" Meredith locked eyes with Hutch. Two days ago he'd gone to Walmart to pick up the toys she and Ashley had put on layaway. "That must have cost someone a fortune."

"They're saying in the neighborhood of five thousand dollars," Caitlyn said.

Hutch's face gave away nothing. He looked innocent as all get-out. But his pupils darkened slightly and he couldn't hold her stare for long. He got up and waved for Caitlyn to take his seat. Then he and Gideon picked up a nearby table and butted it up to the table they were at so everyone could sit together.

"I like that new hair color on you," Caitlyn said to Meredith. "Thumbs up."

Meredith touched her head. She'd almost forgotten she colored it, and that sent a fret of fear running through her. She'd never stayed in a town after she'd changed her hair color. "Thanks."

Caitlyn leaned over to whisper in Meredith's ear. "The man is besotted with you."

Meredith startled. "What?"

She nodded in Hutch's direction. "He can't take his eyes off you."

He *was* staring at her. Heat swamped Meredith's body even as cold air came in with the latest customer, the cowbell over the door jangling merrily.

"Mommy," Kimmie said. "Your cheeks are the same color as the marshmallows in my cocoa."

Caitlyn raised an eyebrow, but said nothing.

The conversation shifted back to snow and the Secret Santa and the Angel Tree project Gideon and Hutch were working on together. Tomorrow, they would be delivering toys and Christmas dinners to needy families in the community.

It was fun. Sitting there laughing and chatting like a normal family with their friends. Drinking hot chocolate and eating slices of chocolate cream pie.

Meredith's gaze strayed across the square to the spot where she thought she'd seen Sloane. She touched her hair again, unable to tame her uneasiness.

Yes, spectators peeking in the window at them would think they were leading a picture-postcard life.

They would be wrong.

The snow started on Christmas Eve morning, and just as Danny predicted, buckets of fat, wet flakes fell from the sky, and just for a little while, Meredith allowed herself to believe in Christmas miracles. If it hardly ever snowed in North Central Texas on Christmas Eve or Christmas Day, this was truly special.

Maybe Ashley would come home in time for Christmas.

Both Meredith and Hutch had continued to try to contact Ashley at least once a day, with no luck, but after Kimmie got sick, Meredith had started texting her every few hours. Was the woman still in Acapulco with her boyfriend? If not, where was she and why hadn't she at least called?

She and Hutch discussed Ashley's disappearance more than they had in the beginning, but he still seemed confident she'd show up. Meredith couldn't tell the man what to do. He knew his sister and her mental disorder far better than she did. Plus, what would she have him do? He couldn't speak. He could fly off to Mexico in search of her, but then what? He might be a former Delta Force operator, but he was one man on his own. And they had no idea where Ashley was. She also knew he didn't want to go off and leave her and the kids. Especially after she'd told him about Sloane.

Hutch did ask Hondo to see if he could use law enforcement connections to help track Ashley down, but the only information Hondo was able to dig up was that American Airlines confirmed that Ashley had boarded the flight to Acapulco on a one-way ticket, and they had no record of her return. There had been no man on the flight named Eric, and Meredith wondered if she'd gotten the man's name wrong.

The information about the one-way ticket sealed the deal for Hutch. I DON'T THINK SHE'S PLANNING ON COMING BACK, he wrote on the Magic Slate after Hondo broke the news, and that broke Meredith's heart.

On Christmas Eve, Sarah Walker called. "Don't forget to make the kismet cookies. It's your only chance this year to dream of your one true love."

"Okay, okay. I give up. I'll bake the kismet cookies."

"And sleep with a cookie under your pillow tonight?"

"Yes, yes."

"You swear it?"

"If it means that much to you."

"We'll make a romantic of you yet." Sarah laughed. "Have a merry Christmas."

Hutch made a run to the grocery story to make sure they had plenty of supplies and stacked up the wood he'd split on the fireplace.

By evening, snow covered the ground two feet deep. Hutch stood at the sliding glass door, with the Magic

Slate, looking out at the deck while Meredith and the children baked cookies and scented the air with delicious smells. He turned to Meredith and showed her what he'd written. IT'S ONE FOR THE RECORD BOOKS.

He didn't use the Magic Slate as much now as he had when he'd first gotten home. They'd formed a language of their own with the looks they gave each other and the subtleties of body language. It created a special intimacy between them that went beyond sexual attraction and caused Meredith to long for things she shouldn't be longing for.

"Can I draw you a picture, Unca Hutch?" Ben asked.

Hutch handed the slate to him.

"I wanna draw him a picture first," Kimmie said, jumping off her chair and running over to grab the slate out of Ben's hands.

"Kids," Meredith chided. "It's Christmas Eve and Santa is watching."

"I had it first." Ben wrestled the slate back.

"Mine!" Kimmie snatched at the filmy gray top sheet and yanked.

The top sheet ripped clean off.

Ben's eyes widened. "You brokeded it!"

Kimmie burst into tears. "I sorrwee, Unca Hutch. I didn't mean to."

"It's okay," Meredith assured her. "We'll get Uncle Hutch another one. But it's getting late. Let's put out cookies and milk for Santa and feed for his reindeer, and then get ready for bed."

Hutch picked up the bottom of the Magic Slate, naked now without the covering top sheet, the impressions of everything he'd written buried deep within the black wax. For the briefest of seconds, a look of irreparable loss crossed Hutch's face. A look so hopeless it broke Meredith's heart.

The slate was completely replaceable and she knew he was not upset with the children. But his eyes told the story. The slate symbolized his voice—tattered, broken, useless—and he was no closer to recovery now than he'd been the first day he'd come home.

It was the most wonderful Christmas of Meredith's life.

Just the way she always imagined Christmas morning could be. When she was a child, her avant-garde parents and their friends would take a Christmas morning balloon ride as long as the weather permitted. In December they usually camped in Florida, California, or South Texas. Although once or twice they had Christmas in Albuquerque with Gramma, for the most part, she came to them for the holidays.

Ballooning might have been in Meredith's blood, but she never caught the fire of it. Going up in the balloon on Christmas morning was no different than going up in the balloon any other morning except that Dad would trim the basket with holly and Mom would bring along eggnog for the their picnic breakfast in the basket. Mom and Dad laughed gaily and sang Christmas songs, but that always made Meredith feel a little bit sad because she did not have a real home for Santa to visit. No chimney for him to come down.

The presents she received were usually small, and best suited for a transient lifestyle. When you went from campground to campground, festival to festival, you had to travel light. Not a lot of space for toys. Mom baked her treats, and from roadside stands she bought oranges and nuts to put in her stocking. Under the table tree in their RV, she found four presents every year. Her mother believed in the rule of four when it came to gift giving—something you want and something you need, something to wear and something to read. And for every new gift Meredith got, she had to give away something old.

Townie kids who came to the balloon festivals thought she had a cool life and wished their parents were like hers, but all she had ever wanted to be was normal. To fit in.

She dreamed of one day having a family of her own. Waking up on Christmas morning to the delighted smiles of her children as they opened miles and miles of presents they would never have to give away. She would make breakfast, pancakes and hot chocolate, and her husband would snap tons of pictures, and they'd go out in the snow—in her fantasy there was always snow on Christmas Day—and make snow castles. They would listen to Christmas music, and in the evening they would pile into the car and drive around looking at Christmas lights.

Last night she'd sheepishly taken one of the kismet cookies and slipped it under her pillow. Her head had no more than hit the pillow when she fell into a deep sleep.

And she dreamed! Boy, did she dream.

Of a handsome soldier with kind eyes. A big, kind man who didn't say a word, just took her into his arms and danced with her to "I'll Be Home for Christmas." Then he dipped her low and kissed her.

Meredith's eyes popped open before dawn, a deep

smile on her face and calmness inside her that she'd never felt before.

Hutch. She'd dreamed of Hutch.

Sarah would say that meant he was her One True Love. Her mother would say she'd found her True North. All Meredith knew was now she was a believer—in kismet cookies and hot air balloons, in long slow kisses on cold winter nights.

She believed in love. She believed in Hutch.

And pancakes.

The smell of pancakes wafting into the room had her throwing back the covers and leaping out of bed, vibrating from her head to her toes. She galloped downstairs to find Hutch and her giggling children gathered around the stove making Mickey Mouse pancakes as they had done on that first morning, and joy overflowed her heart.

The drapes covering the sliding glass door were open, letting in the mellow colors of encroaching morning and revealing silvery white snow. Silently, fresh flakes twirled in that sweet space between darkness and dawn. A white Christmas. Life didn't get any better than this.

If she died now, she would die happy.

When he saw her, Hutch smiled at her in a different way. His smile was fuller somehow, richer, holding nothing back. She'd opened herself up to him, and by doing so he'd opened more fully to her.

Her heart stumbled. He reached over and turned on the radio. "Jingle Bell Rock" bounced out. He held out a hand to her.

Never mind that she was in pajamas and her hair was

mussed and she had on no makeup. He looked at her as if she was the most gorgeous thing he'd ever seen.

She took his hand and he spun her around the room.

The kids jumped off their chairs and started dancing around beside them, kicking their legs and flailing their little arms. The room filled with so much Christmas cheer that tears misted her eyes.

And damn if Hutch wasn't tearing up too.

He gave her a pointed look and she thought that meant he was going to dip her. She prepared to be spun away and pulled back again before the big dip, but instead, Hutch lowered his head and kissed her, right in front of the children.

Deeply, passionately, sweetly, miraculously, putting every wonderful emotion in the world into that kiss. He didn't need to say words because his glorious kiss said everything. No man would ever need a voice if he could kiss like this. Everything he wanted to say was in that kiss.

I want you, I need you, I respect you. I desire you. I love you.

Love.

She wasn't imagining it. She could taste love on his lips and it was the flavor of Christmas. Kismet cookies and peppermint candy canes. Gingerbread and butter cream. It was the flavor of wishes coming true, of hopes actualized, of dreams realized.

In didn't matter how long this moment would last. For right now, right this minute, Meredith had everything she had ever wanted. A home. Children. A beautiful Christmas tree surrounded by presents. Meaningful music as the song changed to John Lennon and Yoko Ono singing "War Is Over."

Another year was over and what had she done? She had found her True North. Her mother would be so proud.

The children ate as quickly as they could, stuffing pancakes into the mouths so they could get breakfast over with and get to those presents. They delighted over the fact Santa had taken a bite out of the kismet cookies they'd left for him, and the reindeer food was gone, and there was a sooty boot print on the fireplace bricks. Clever Hutch.

"Can we open our packages now, Mommy, can we, huh, can we?" Ben asked, pancake syrup stuck on the corner of his mouth.

Kimmie was already out of her chair, spinning around the living room.

Meredith met Hutch's eye. He nodded. They abandoned their own half-eaten breakfast so the kids could get to their packages.

Wrapping paper flew. A flurry of foil. Ripping. Tearing. Shouts of delight. Squeals of joy. Hutch manned a video camera. Meredith took still shots with her camera phone. When Ashley got home, they'd have every second of it recorded for her.

Ashley.

She was the missing piece, the one thing that made the holiday incomplete.

If practicing yoga had taught Meredith anything, it was how to stop focusing on what was missing and appreciate what she had. Purposefully, she turned her mind from the distressing thought of Ashley's absence and focused on what was right in front of her.

"Thomas the Train!" Ben exclaimed. "Open the box, Unca Hutch. Open it now!"

Chuckling, Hutch took a multitool from his pocket and went to work on the box.

"Look, Mommy." Kimmie had put on a tiara and plastic glass slippers. "I Cinderella."

Mommy. Kimmie kept calling her Mommy.

"Yes, you are, sweetheart." Meredith smiled at her. "Yes, you are."

Hutch freed Thomas the Train from the box and Ben flung himself across it. Joy radiated from every pore of his body. This was what Christmas morning was all about, children's happy faces.

Oh, Ashley, you are so missing out. Choosing to spend Christmas with a man you don't even know over being here with your child.

She felt a nudge against her knee, looked up into Hutch's face, and realized she'd been woolgathering. He extended a small box wrapped in silver paper and topped with a bright red bow toward her.

The box was the size of a jeweler's box, and for one awful second, she thought, *It's an engagement ring.* Immediately, images of Sloane proposing to her only three weeks after they'd met sprang into her mind. The way she'd stupidly fallen for his slick charm, thrown herself into his arms, and exclaimed, "Yes, yes, I'll marry you."

Meredith turned to stone, stared at the pretty box sitting in Hutch's palm. "You shouldn't have gotten me anything. Christmas is for children."

What was she going to do if it was a piece of jewelry or worst of all, a ring? Surely he wouldn't do that to her, would he? Not after everything she'd told him.

Her stomach pitched. She liked him so very much, was even on the verge of falling in love with him, but Sloane had been a cruel teacher and she was an apt pupil. She no longer trusted herself when it came to matters of the heart.

Hutch crouched in front of her, watching her face expectantly. Was he about to go down on one knee?

No, no, no.

He put a hand on her knee, stared into her eyes, and sent the mental message, *What's wrong?*

She pasted a half smile on her face, pretended as if nothing was wrong. No point leapfrogging off onto a lily pad that wasn't there. She tugged on the ends of the bow and it gave easily, unfurling into one long ribbon that fell from her lap and dropped to the floor.

Her fingers felt stiff against the crisp foil. She tugged off the Scotch tape holding each end of the wrapping paper closed. It sprang open revealing a black box embossed in silver letters with the name of the company.

True North.

For one shocked second her heart literally stopped. She inhaled a sharp gasp and her heart started again, chugging like an overworked steam engine.

His hand tightened on her knee and he reached out two fingers to tip up her chin, urging her to meet his gaze. Concern filled his dark eyes. *What's wrong?*

"Nothing," she said, tracing the embossed letters with her fingers. True North. "Absolutely nothing."

Her mother had been a kooky free spirit who believed in the universe giving signs on which path to follow, and if you paid attention to the signs, they'd guide you to your destiny. Mom considered getting caught in the Albuquerque box with Meredith's dad as a sign they were meant to be. He was her True North.

Meredith had never been a believer in that sort of thing. It defied logic, science, and the laws of nature.

But here she was with a man she was swiftly growing to love, holding a box branded with the very words her mother used to describe her philosophy about life. *When you find the right mate, he will be your True North.*

If this wasn't a sign, then nothing was.

She'd never heard of a True North jewelry store. Nevertheless, she held her breath as she lifted the lid on the box.

There, nestled inside a Styrofoam base, was a key-chain-sized pink canister of pepper spray. There was a card underneath the canister that read: *To my Meredith. For when I'm not around to keep you safe.*

My Meredith.

She raised her head.

He knelt before her, shoulders back, chest forward, jaw relaxed in a beguiling posture that said, *I'm solid, have faith in me.*

She laughed, palmed the pepper spray. "Wicked sense of humor, Brian."

The left side of his mouth quirked up and he dropped a sly, you-ain't-seen-nothing-yet wink.

"Mommy," Ben said, picking at his seat to remove a pajama wedgie. "There's one package left with no name. Is it mine?"

"No, that package belongs to Hutch."

"Aww, man. I thought it was mine."

"Told ya it wasn't," Kimmie said.

"It's not yours neither."

Those two acted more and more like real brother and sister with every passing day. Their endearing squabbling brought a smile to her face. "Ben, why don't you hand Hutch his present?"

Hutch's grin hung crooked like a door half off its

hinge. Genuine. Beguiling. Irresistible. She liked that smile. She hitched up to it. Smiled back.

They sat watching each other for a long moment, grinning.

The radio played Pachelbel's Canon in D for Christmas. It was her favorite piece of classical music. Surely, in heaven they played Pachelbel. The beautiful sound stirred all of Meredith's long-buried hopes, and a tear rolled from her eye and slid down her cheek.

Tenderly, Hutch leaned forward, cupped her chin in his palm, and gently wiped the tear away with his big calloused thumb. Her bottom lip trembled. He knew just as much as she did how precious and fleeting this moment was. They breathed in a shared breath, held it, and then released it in tandem.

Kimmie waggled her tiara in time to the musical beat and clomped across the hardwood floor. Ben nudged Hutch in the ribs with his knee. "Aren'tcha gonna open it?"

Hutch removed the bow and stuck it on top of Ben's head.

"Hey!" Ben laughed and slapped both hands on the bow.

Kimmie giggled. "You look bootiful."

Hutch removed the wrapping paper.

"It's not much," Meredith apologized.

He tilted his head back and lasered her a look that let her know he didn't care what was in the box. The fact that she'd given it to him was enough.

"We made you fudge," Kimmie said in the overly loud whisper of a four-year-old.

Hutch opened the box, took out the fudge she and

the children had made for him, and offered everyone a piece.

"There's something else in there too," Meredith said.

He examined the box, pulled out the folded piece of paper she'd stuck underneath the fudge, a gift certificate for a free massage.

The glint in his eyes silvered. He refolded the certificate, slid it into the front pocket of his shirt, and patted it solidly over his heart as if it was the most priceless gift he'd ever received.

Chapter 14

Hutch cleaned up the wrapping paper mess in the living room while Meredith put a roast in the oven for Christmas dinner and they did the dishes together. The children begged to go outside and play in the snow, so all four of them bundled up.

They showed the children how to fall backward in the snow and make snow angels, and then they had a snowball fight. It was Meredith and the children against him. They shrieked and laughed as Hutch pretended to be the Abominable Snowman, and tossed the children into the snowbanks, only to have them come right back at him.

Wood smoke curled from chimneys. The smell of turkey floated in the air. Other families had been outside, and lawns were dotted with snowmen. To be different, they decided to build a snow fort rather than a snowman. When they were finished, the kids crawled inside the snow fort to play.

"I have to go check on the roast," Meredith told him. "Don't let them stay out too much longer. Not too long ago they both had a fever."

Hutch nodded and he watched her go, unable to tear his gaze from her magnificent butt. He touched his left front pocket, the gift card for a massage. By giving him that gift card, did the woman get that she was tossing gasoline on an open flame?

Meredith stopped when she reached the porch and turned back to catch him staring at her. A happy smile stretched across her face, aimed right at him.

Hutch's heart warmed in the dead center of his chest. If he could spend the rest of his life putting that smile on her face, he would consider it a life well spent. The warmth spread out, slipping into his bloodstream, circulating throughout his system until his entire body tingled.

He wanted her. Yearning swelled. Hope crested.

Ever cell in his body hummed her name—*Meredith, Meredith, Meredith*.

But he had nothing to offer her. He had some money put away and he'd get his government pension, but he had no job and he couldn't even speak. It killed him that he couldn't tell her with his own voice how much she meant to him.

He curled his gloved hands into fists.

She waved.

He waved back, feeling stripped naked and hung out to dry by his feelings. Too much. He wanted her too much. It wasn't healthy, this need.

She shivered, wrapped her arms around herself, nod-

ded toward the house, and gifted him with one last wide
Christmas smile before she went inside.

God, he was a lucky bastard, even if it was only for
this brief span of time. To have a woman like her smiling at him like that. As if he was something truly special. Some people went an entire lifetime without ever
brushing up against something so divine.

The kids giggled at him from the snow fort. Two little faces with red noses and cheeks beaming up at him.
He wanted to tell them they looked like Rudolph, but
he could not say the words. Instead, he motioned as if
he was drinking a cup of hot chocolate and rubbed his
hands together, pantomiming warming himself in front
of a roaring fire.

"No way, Jose," Ben shouted.

Both kids shook their heads and backed into the snow
fort so deeply that he could no longer see them.

Hutch got down on his knees in the snow, dug them
from the fort, and carried them inside, a laughing child
hanging from each arm.

Their faces could have passed for tomatoes, their
eyes sparkling as they chattered about the snow. Less
than a week ago, they'd both been sick with a fever, now
it was as if they'd never been sick at all. Kids were mi-
raculous. They healed so quickly.

Ben and Kimmie skipped toward Meredith, chant-
ing in unison, "Hot chocolate, hot chocolate, we want
hot chocolate."

"Where's your ski cap?" Meredith asked Ben.

Ben shrugged repeatedly and shuffled his feet all
loose-limbed and jerky, making it look as if he was afflicted with Saint Vitus' dance.

"You're always losing your winter clothes. I'm not

made of money, son," she chided gently. "Go back and look for it."

"Okay-dokey." Ben darted for the back door.

Meredith turned to Hutch. "Could you go with him? Sorry to be so skittish but ever since I thought I saw Sloane on the town square—"

Hutch understood. She hated letting the boy out of her sight, but she also recognized that he was growing up, she could not keep him tied to her apron strings. At this age, Hutch made a better guard dog for the boy. Plus he was better equipped to deal with Sloane if he did appear. Meredith seemed to have the idea the bastard she'd married was as untouchable as Lex Luthor.

He went out the back door, stepped off the deck, and rounded the side of the house into the front yard.

Ben was nowhere in sight.

Okay, kid, where are you? A fissure of panic wormed into his gut. Igloo cool. Nothing to freak out about. The boy had most likely gone across the street to visit the Calloways.

Behind Hutch lay the swollen Brazos River. The kid could have taken a header right off the deck and gone into the water. In his mind's eye he saw the boy's body swirling in the cold, murky waters. His palms slicked with sick heat. He staggered to the edge of the deck, his boots kicking up snow, and peered over the rail.

Nothing but rocks and trees and swift-moving water. Nah. The boy had not gone down there. He would not believe that. *Easy, easy. Don't get freaky-deaky.*

Dammit. He wished he could yell. Call Ben home. He returned to the front yard and scanned the street with warrior precision, taking note of everything, on the lookout for enemies.

From the north a white sedan toiled slowly up the street.

He felt a hole open up in his stomach, an eddy of tornadic whirls spinning there and sucking up all his insides. *Who goes there? Friend or foe?*

Where was the boy? Not in the sedan. If someone in the white sedan had kidnapped Ben, the vehicle would be moving away from the house, not toward it.

The white sedan edged closer. Hutch honed in on the only thing moving in the lonely, snow-strewn landscape and recognized Dotty Mae Densmore behind the wheel. What was the little old lady doing out in this weather? If he weren't focused on finding Ben, he would offer to drive the sedan home for her.

How could the child have vanished so quickly? He hadn't been a minute after him.

Hooyah. Snap to. Footprints. Look for footprints.

Footprints. Easy tracking.

In the aftermath of their snowball fight a flurry of footsteps furrowed the middle of the yard. A slurred mix of his big boot prints, Meredith's petite foot, and twin pairs of identically sized tiny impressions marked the path from the middle of the yard, to the snow fort and back to the house. But there were no other prints anywhere else in the yard. None going into the road, or to the neighbor's house on the left or to the ranch land yawning right beyond the white split-rail fence.

Unless something or someone had snatched him up from thin air, the child had to be in the snow fort.

Relief pushed his belly out, expelling pent-up air from his lungs. Hutch trod toward the snow fort. No rush now. He knew where the boy was.

The acrid taste disappeared from his mouth and the

release of tension left his muscles shaky. He'd never panicked in the heat of battle. That's why they'd called him Igloo. Calm. Cool. Collected. Level-headed and easygoing.

With his own life, he was fearless, but when it came to children…*his* children—because while Kimmie and Ben might not be his children biologically, he felt as responsible for them as if they were his own—it was a different story.

Hutch was not a poetic guy. He was not given to deep thought. But in that moment, in the snow, he had an epiphany. He loved those two kids.

Ben poked his face out of the snow fort, grinned impishly.

On the road, the sedan hit a slick patch and Dotty Mae's mouth opened in a wide O as her car fishtailed and she lost control.

Hutch's legs were running, but they felt as useless as paddlewheels churning a molasses sea. No matter how fast he moved, he wasn't going to reach Ben in time to stop disaster.

Invisible fingers closed around Hutch's throat, squeezing down, cutting off his breath. Too late. Too late. There was nothing he could do.

In an icy, vehicular ballet, the white sedan spun a full three-sixty, hit another slick spot, and flew across the road, heading straight for the snow fort. Through the windshield, Dotty Mae's eyes locked with his and something like hot-wet electricity shocked the dead center of his heart, blue lightning shearing a tree, killing it dead with one split-second strike. It charred the tip of his tongue and burned a smoldering path down his throat to his lungs.

No! No! His knees and his heart stumbled, collapsing into the snow.

The headlights of the sedan glinted off the tinkling Christmas lights lining the walkway, making them look to Hutch's eyes like muzzle flashes. Instantly, the snow melted into sand and he was no longer in Twilight, but back on the streets of Aliabad. It wasn't noon on Christmas Day, but just after dawn on Labor Day. They'd come up empty-handed. Their target in the wind. The Unit didn't fail often, but when it failed, it failed spectacularly.

In his flashback, Hutch saw now what he had not seen then because he had not wanted to believe what he was seeing. It wasn't his voice that had failed him in Abas Ghar.

It had been his eyes.

Hutch reached out a hand, opened his mouth, and in a hoarse, gruff voice he did not recognize as his own, shouted. "Ben! Get out of that fort now!"

Meredith had just settled the roast onto a serving platter and picked up a kitchen towel to wipe away a dribble of au jus on the kitchen counter when she heard a man yell Ben's name.

Her eyes widened. Who was that?

Next came a high-pitched scream, followed by a quiet thud, and then a prolonged honking noise as if someone were laying on a car horn.

She tossed aside the cup towel, rushed past Kimmie, who was in the living room playing with the LeapFrog computer Hutch had gotten her for Christmas, and ran to fling open the front door. She blinked, her brain trying to puzzle together what her eyes saw.

Dotty Mae's car was on their front lawn, the front tires obliterating the snow fort. Inside the car, the air bags deflated. The continuously honking horn drew neighbors from their houses. Jesse came running from across the street.

Hutch was on his knees in the middle of the yard, facing the road, his back to her, and he clutched Ben tightly in his arms. With his red ski cap perched jauntily on his head, Ben spied her and raised a hand. "Hi, Mom. I found my cap, and oh yeah, Hutch talkeded."

Neighbors thronged around the car. Dotty Mae was conscious and talking but no one wanted to move her or let her move herself. Ambulance sirens wailed, coming closer.

Dazed, Meredith stepped off the porch and walked toward Hutch and her son.

The ambulance arrived, lights flashing, the siren cutting off mid-scream as they pulled up beside the sedan. Two paramedics piled out, converged on Dotty Mae.

Still holding tight to Ben, Hutch got to his feet, turned.

She saw the story in his face. Ben had been in the snow fort when Dotty Mae's car had come careening toward it. "You spoke."

"Yeah," he said. His voice was scratchy, like the sound of a butter knife scraping the black off burnt toast. But the timbre, the weight of it was exactly how Meredith imagined his voice would sound—deep, resonant, peppered with a self-assured Texas drawl.

"To save Ben's life." It fully hit her then that her son had almost been killed. Her knees gave way and she crumpled.

But Hutch was there, setting Ben on the ground,

lifting her up. "Meredith," he murmured. "He's okay. You're okay. We're all okay."

Hutch put a hand to her back, holding her steady. He was her ballast. Her rock. He'd saved her son. "Breathe, Yoga Girl. Just breathe."

She pulled in a couple of deep breaths but had no patience for it. "Come here, you," she said, and scooped Ben into her arms, squeezing him hard.

"Mom!" He wriggled. "You're suffercating me."

Reluctantly, she let him go, looked up into Hutch's magnetic dark eyes. He'd saved her son. Hutch. Her True North. Love for him spilled from her, a cup overflowing, and she could no more hold it back than she could stop breathing.

Oh God, she was in so much trouble.

Unable to bear the exquisite pain of her feelings, she glanced away. Over at the sedan, the paramedics were trying to talk Dotty Mae into going to the hospital to get checked out, even though she kept insisting she was okay. "Take care of that little boy," she told them. "I almost plowed right into him."

One of the paramedics came toward Ben, but Hutch held up his palm. "The boy wasn't harmed."

His strong, commanding voice stopped the paramedic in his tracks. The man nodded. "Yes, sir."

Kimmie joined them on the lawn, wanting to know what had happened. The paramedics finally convinced Dotty Mae to go with them. Neighbors, including Flynn and Jesse, walked over to comment on luck and disasters averted and how maybe it was time for Dotty Mae to stop driving. They congratulated Hutch on getting his voice back. He nodded, looked uncomfortable by their atta-boy sentiments, and barely said a word. Someone offered to drive Dotty Mae's car over to her house. Someone else volunteered to go to the hospital to check up on her. A third person went off to call Dotty Mae's sons and let them know what had happened and probably chew them out for leaving their mother alone on Christmas Day.

Kimmie and Ben and some neighborhood children started a snowball fight. That lasted until a parent took a snowball to the back, and then people started rounding up their offspring and drifting back home to their holiday celebrations.

Flynn shifted a grinning Grace to her other hip and put a hand on Meredith's shoulder. "I know getting his voice back is a big moment for Hutch. Jesse and I discussed it, and we'd like to take the kids for the evening so you two can have a chance to really talk."

The other woman's generosity touched Meredith. She placed a palm over her chest. "That is so sweet of you, but it's Christmas, and I'm sure you have plans with your family."

"Actually, we do our family thing on Christmas Eve. Honestly, we wouldn't mind a bit. And we're right across the road if you get lonesome and want to come after them. Or..." Flynn leaned in and lowered her voice. "You can let them spend the night if Hutch really opens up to you and you guys need more adult alone time."

"We're not...it's not what..." Meredith started to deny and protest the depth of her relationship with Hutch, but to tell the truth, she did want a chance to explore the feelings he stirred in her. Nothing might come of it. "Are you sure?"

A knowing grin lit up Flynn's pretty face. "It'll be

fun. We'll watch movies, play games, and Grace will love having playmates."

Flynn was the children's teacher, after all, and Meredith had to start trusting someone sometime. But what if Sloane came for her? It was so like him to show up on Christmas Day to ruin everything. But if that were the case, wouldn't Ben be safer away from her? Torn, she slanted a look at Hutch, who was listening to Jesse suggest the same thing to him. He nodded.

"Your call," Flynn said. "We don't want to intrude, just thought you two might need to decompress."

Meredith swallowed back her hesitation, reached for the helping hand. *He'll be right across the street.* "Maybe for just a few hours. Thank you so much for offering."

"Great. Do you want to bring over some extra clothes in case you decide to let them stay the night?"

"I'll do that."

Flynn turned to Kimmie and Ben. "Kids, would you like to come over to my house? We're going to watch *How the Grinch Stole Christmas*, play Candy Land, make popcorn balls, and read Thomas the Train."

"And *The Magic Christmas Cookie*?" Kimmie asked.

"And *The Magic Christmas Cookie*," Flynn confirmed.

"Yay!" Kimmie clapped.

"Mommy." Ben looked at her. "Is it okay?"

"Sure it is."

Disbelief crossed his little face. "Really?"

She'd been holding the reins too tightly. She knew that, but it was so tough letting them go. "Really."

"Cool." He turned to Flynn. "Let's go."

Leaving Meredith shivering in the cold, until Hutch

put his arm around her shoulder and whispered, "That first step is a doozy, Mother Hen, but everything is going to be okay."

Flynn waited while Meredith gathered up clothes for the children. Hutch tidied up the kitchen, putting the roast in the fridge for later. Then they stood on the porch together and waved good-bye to the children until they disappeared into the Calloways' house.

"Looks like it's just you and me," Hutch said, and guided her inside.

He closed the front door, and it was all Meredith could do not to run across the street and tell Flynn that she'd changed her mind. She wanted her boy back.

But her situation had already stunted Ben's life. He had no family, no long-term friends. If she wanted Ben to have a prayer of growing up strong and self-confident, she had to start giving him some independence in bite-sized doses. Never mind that the thought made her hyperventilate.

The house was so empty without the children in it.

"You could change your mind," Hutch said in that midnight-deep voice that made her toes curl. "Do you want me to go get them?"

"Do you?" She sank her top teeth into her bottom lip. "Want to go get them?"

"I only want to please you."

The simplicity in that statement, the honesty in his eyes told her it was true. "I… I think we need time to-gether. To really talk."

"Yeah," he said huskily. He was standing with his back against the front door. She was in the foyer, a few feet away from him, and remembered that first day when she'd guided him inside his own home.

She raised a hand to her throat.

"Are you nervous?" he asked.

Of Hutch? No. Never. Slowly, she shook her head. "Are you?"

"Hell, yeah." He combed a hand through his hair, exhaled. "I gotta tell you, babe, I've never felt like this before. Brand-new territory."

"How's your throat?"

He gave a wry, self-effacing smile. "I'm rusty, but I can talk."

She gulped, shifted her gaze to his shirt pocket. "Do you want to redeem your gift? A massage might help you relax."

His lips pursed in amusement. "Meredith Sommers, do you realize what you're proposing?"

"I'm well aware of how responsive you are to touch," she said. "That first day we met—"

"I do apologize for the impromptu hard-on, but you *were* undressing me."

"And I'd just blasted you with pepper spray. How many men could get an erection under those circumstances?"

"What can I say? You are one red-hot woman."

She gave a little laugh, flattered by the hungry expression in his eyes, and pressed two fingers to her lips.

"I'm not kidding. Just talking about it is getting me charged up. You sure you really want to give me a massage because I—"

She rushed across the space between them to plant her mouth on his in a quick, hard kiss that had his eyes bugging. "I know you just started talking again, but hush."

He nodded vigorously.

Are you sure you're ready for this? You know exactly where this massage is going to lead. Yes. Precisely. "The massage table is in my bedroom closet. The one I use at work belongs to Hot Legs Spa. Just give me—"

"We don't need no stinkin' massage table." Hutch bent and scooped her into his arms.

"You're not sweeping me off my feet, are you? Because you know how I feel about that."

Immediately, he set her down.

"I was joking."

"I'm not. I don't want to do anything that reminds you of him."

She didn't meet his eyes, but she reached out to toy with the button on his shirt. "You're not like him in any way, but his influence has taken over my life."

He closed his hand over hers. "Meredith."

She caught her breath.

"Look at me."

Reluctantly, she raised her head. There was nothing in his eyes but kindness, patience, and love.

"You're not ready for this step."

"I am."

"We've only known each other a little over three weeks."

"Plenty of people make love on the first date, and while we've only known each other three weeks, we've been living together and it's been…amazing." She wasn't romanticizing their connection. They'd been great in the rough spots—their disagreements, taking care of the kids, the ups and downs of their emotional baggage, the communication barrier—working through everything and coming out on the other side better people for having gone through the struggles.

"Even when you threw me out of the house?"

"Yes." She pressed the flat of her palm against his chest. "Because we both learned something from that and we grew closer because of it."

He brushed his fingertips over her temple. "I want you. More than you can possibly know. But it has to feel right to both of us."

"It does feel right. Nothing has ever felt more right." She was scared that he wouldn't make love to her. "Doesn't it feel right to you?"

"I can't think of a more perfect way to celebrate Christmas Day than making love to you for the first time."

"Then take me upstairs." She jumped into his arms.

He caught her in his powerful embrace and she wrapped her legs around his waist, entwined her arms around his neck, and rested her head on his shoulders. Sunshine parted the thunderclouds of the last five years and she was home. Moored.

He carried her up the stairs and she could feel the steady, reliable lub-dub of his heart beating against her breasts.

This was so easy. Who knew that being with him would be this easy? Effortless as a bird gliding on the breeze.

She tilted her head back to get a good look at him. Those dark eyes, that strong chin and masculine nose, a neck marred with scars. Scars she didn't even notice anymore. Some people might think he looked scary. To Meredith he was the most handsome man in the world. How had his face become so familiar to her in such a short time? It felt as if they'd known each other all their lives.

He was so gentle with Kimmie, so kind to her son, infinitely patient with both children. She'd thought he was sexy from the very beginning, although she hadn't really allowed herself to think those kinds of thoughts, but the more she came to know him, her attraction took on added layers. What she felt for him was much more complicated than simple sexual chemistry, although there was plenty of that too.

She could not wait to be with him, to feel his body inside hers.

Hutch opened the door to her bedroom, crossed over the threshold, and then kicked it closed behind them. He set her down on the bed, stepped back to send an appreciative gaze traveling over her body, his hair curling around the tops of his ears in a totally disarming way. His face dissolved into a knowing grin that said, *I want to see you naked.*

"You are so beautiful," he murmured, his words catching on the last word, rusty, as he'd said.

She was feeling pretty rusty herself and her hands were shaking again. This was a big step. The first time since… No, she wasn't going to think about *him*. Wasn't going to let *him* ruin this cherished moment.

If she'd planned this, things would have gone much differently. She would have made a real seduction of it. Shaved her legs. Done a special job of applying her makeup. She would have brought some sexy lingerie instead of wearing cotton undies that didn't match her bra. She would have lighted candles and put on some mood music. Bought plenty of condoms.

Condoms. Oh no. Was that going to be a deal breaker?

He sauntered toward her.

Her heart rate jacked up. She held up a stop-sign palm. "Wait."

He froze to the spot and his eyes clouded. "Change of heart?"

"Protection." She said it like a smart modern woman. It had been so long since she'd felt sexy and in control. "You got any?"

The crooked smile overtaking his mouth was pure rascal. "Babe, they don't call Delta Force The Unit for nothing."

"Are you saying you're all a bunch of pricks?" she teased.

He burst out laughing. "What language, Ms. Sommers."

"You started it with the sexual innuendo."

"So I did." He stepped closer. "To answer your question." He whipped his wallet from his back pocket, opened it up, and a condom dropped into her lap.

Picking it up between two fingers, she said. "Do you think this will be enough?"

"Gotta box of them in my room."

Boldly, she reached out her right hand, hooked it around his back, and pulled him to her until the bulge in his jeans nestled against her zipper.

Smooth as silk, he reached for the top button on her shirt, but he fumbled a bit with his left hand. Beneath the shadow of dark stubble at his jaw, a muscle clenched. He was embarrassed about the missing finger.

She took his big hand in both of hers, bent her head, and kissed the scar where his index finger used to be.

"Meredith." He breathed her name. "This is the first time I've made love to a woman since this happened to me."

"Not as slick as you used to be, huh?" She was teasing him again, hoping to coax out another one of those rascally smiles.

He took her chin in his hand, tilted her face up, rested his forehead on hers, and looked deeply into her eyes. "None of that slickness with you, babe. Between us it's always going to be honest."

Bowled over by the intensity in his gaze, she reached for light and flirty. "I don't warrant razzle-dazzle?"

"I never said that." He growled, and with his forehead still pressed to hers, pushed her all the way back onto the bed.

She stared up at him, one leg hanging off the bed, the other wrapped around his waist as he straddled her, a knee dug into the mattress on either side of her. His rock-hard erection pressed against her crotch, his inscrutable eyes drilling into her.

For one terrified moment Meredith panicked. She rammed the heel of her palm into his chest and shoved him off.

Chapter 15

Hutch staggered back. After what she'd told him about her ex, he'd been afraid of this. Apparently, he wasn't the only one in the house with PTSD flashbacks.

"It's okay," he said before she ever spoke. "I get it."

She sat up shaking her head and wrapping her arms around herself. "I don't know why I did that. I want you. I want to be with you."

"We don't have to do this tonight. There's no rush."

"But I *want* to do it."

"We can't force this. You're ready when you're ready."

"Why not? It took the trauma of seeing Dotty Mae about to crash into the snow fort with Ben in it to force you to speak."

"That's different."

"Is it?"

"I don't want to make love to a woman who is just gritting her teeth to get it over with." Truthfully, as badly as he wanted her, part of him was still trying to process the fact that he had gotten his voice back. He was happy about that, yes, but was he using sex with Meredith to bury his feelings?

Hutch ran a palm along his jaw. He sure as hell wasn't ready to think about that, much less dissect it in a lengthy conversation.

"I want to try," she insisted.

"How about we just lie here side by side."

"I don't think that's enough for me."

"There's no rush, babe," he soothed. He wanted to touch her again, but was afraid he'd trigger something dark from her past again. "I'm not going anywhere."

She swallowed and scooted across the mattress.

He sank down beside her.

Simultaneously, they lay back on their pillows and stared up at the ceiling.

"I hate him," she said with so much fury that Hutch startled. "He took everything from me. Even this."

"No. He did not take this. He's not getting this," Hutch reassured her. "He's not getting us."

"I'm broken."

"No more so than me. It's fixable. We're fixable."

"I wish I could believe that."

"This morning I didn't think I was fixable and look at me now. For almost four months I couldn't speak a word and here I am suddenly chatty as a teenage girl."

She gave a soft laugh that thawed the doubt inside him. "You make me believe anything's possible."

"Where we're concerned, it is."

"You sound so certain."

"Only because of you."

"He's relentless," she warned. "Like a shark. He'll never let me go."

"I'll kill him."

"And go to prison for the rest of your life over a scumbag like Sloane? No."

"Babe, I'm Delta Force. He would disappear without a trace."

"Seriously, you could do that?" she asked, her voice infused with awe.

"If anyone ever tried to hurt you or Ben, I would."

"Killing isn't a good thing."

"No, it's not," he agreed. "But sometimes you have to defend yourself."

"I used to think every human life had worth. Until I met Sloane."

They lapsed into silence.

After a long time, she whispered, "He said I was a terrible lover."

"To hell with that bastard. You know he's a sociopath. Why are you letting him get inside your brain?"

"Because he's an expert at it."

"What about before you met him? What about the other men you were with?"

She hitched in a deep breath, cutting it into two clear, distinctive parts, inhaling first deep in her belly, and then hitching in more air to fully fill her lungs. "That's just it. I was never with anyone else. I was a virgin when I got married."

Aww, damn, babe, no. "So you've only had bad sex."

"Cruel sex," she clarified. "I don't know any other way."

"He forced you to do things. Hurt you."

She didn't answer.

"Thank you for sharing that with me," he said quietly, giving her no hint of the rage in his heart for the sadist who'd treated such an exquisite woman so horribly. Castration was too good for the bastard.

Hutch stretched out his arm between them, palm up, and waited to see if she would take his hand. She didn't hesitate. Her palm landed on top of his and he interlaced their fingers, chaining them together.

After a while she said, "Maybe we should take off our jeans. Get comfortable."

"Are you sure?"

"You don't have to keep asking me that."

"Yes I do."

"All right then, yes, I'm sure."

She let go of his hand—leaving him lonely—stood up with her back to him, and shyly eased off her jeans.

He probably shouldn't have been ogling, but he couldn't help himself. The soft gray light coming through the window cast her in a dusty glow. He watched her slip her pants down over her legs, and he sucked in his breath at the sight of her pink bikini panties. Not just because she was full-on the sexiest thing he'd ever seen, but because he was beginning to fear he could not live without her. He would find a way to convince her that she and Ben were safe here with him, that they were cherished and loved. That he would protect her with his dying breath.

She turned back to him. "Now this isn't fair. I'm half naked and you're still wearing your pants."

He didn't bother standing up, just arched his back and reached a hand to the snap of his jeans. He flicked it open with his thumb, slid down the zipper.

Her gaze tracked his movements as she moistened her lips.

"You gonna watch?"

"You watched me."

He laughed. "So I did."

"Here, I'll even help." She went to the foot of the bed, grabbed hold of the cuffs of his pants, yanked them off, and tossed them casually over her shoulder. "That's better," she said. "You comfortable?"

"As comfortable as a guy can be with a massive hard-on."

Her gaze flicked to his erection, but she quickly looked away. "I'm sorry."

"Don't apologize. I was merely stating a fact. I don't expect you to do anything about it."

"Oh." She sounded disappointed, and eased back down on the bed beside him.

This time, she was the one who extended her arm between them, palm up.

He didn't leave her hanging.

Kiss her. The words lit up his brain in neon red, but special ops training had honed his discipline to a razor-sharp edge. No matter how hot she was, he would not push things. Her pace was her pace and he would respect that. If he had to wait twenty years for her to be ready, then, by God, he'd wait twenty years.

"Thank you," she whispered. "For being so patient with me."

"Thank you for trusting me enough to be here with me," he said. "For not running away."

"I can't promise I'll stay. If Sloane comes for me, I'll have to go. I will not put you and Kimmie in jeopardy."

He started to argue, but her fear of her ex-husband

was palpable. He wasn't going to convince her that he could protect her simply by saying so. Actions spoke louder than words. Trite, yes, but losing his voice had shown him the power of that cliché.

Hutch turned on his side and pulled her into his arms, snuggling her against his body. He stroked her hair and told her the story of how he'd repaired and built on to the house with his own hands, imagining that one day he'd have a family of his own to fill it.

She told him about hot air ballooning. What it was like to rise into the sky at dawn, the air crisp and thin, the heated flames from the burners lifting the brightly colored balloons higher and higher until they caught the right current and floated in the vast silence of sky. Her voice took on a dreamy quality, as if she entered another land.

They talked for hours about things they'd been unable to say to each other before. Her voice filled with love when she spoke of Ben and how becoming a mother had changed everything. He told her about being there the day Kimmie was born. They discussed movies, books, gardening, health care, politics, religion, and travel. The only subjects they veered away from were Meredith's life with her ex, Hutch's experiences in The Unit, and Ashley's whereabouts; neither one of them wanted to sour their growing intimacy with dark discussions. Those were topics for another time.

To Hutch's happy surprise, they had a lot more in common than he imagined. They both loved sushi and crème brûlée, although not necessarily at the same meal. They agreed that Sunday afternoon was the saddest time of the week and that there was nothing more soothing than sitting on his deck at twilight watching the

Brazos River rolling by. They confessed to talking to themselves out loud when working through a problem. They discovered they'd both had imaginary playmates when they were four. His had been a Native American boy with the unlikely name of Horatio. Hers had been a kangaroo called Bouncy. They were both frugal, although she admitted with a laugh that her frugality was born of necessity.

Even their dislikes dovetailed. He hated waiting in line. She loved it, because it gave her a chance to read a few paragraphs of a book on her smart phone. She hated doing laundry, he found the mindless task Zen-like. He loved to paint houses, but disliked the prep work. She loved the prep, but grew bored with painting. She liked dark meat chicken. He liked breasts.

"Of course you do." She laughed.

He hugged her tighter, so glad to have found her. The loneliness of the kid who'd grown up without a father and a mentally unstable mother, the pain he hid behind a ready smile and his Igloo cool, stopped hurting.

Meredith. He rolled her name around in his head, a litany of all good things. Meredith.

"Hutch?" she whispered.

"Uh-huh?"

"Would you please kiss me again?"

"All right," he said, knowing it was going to kill him to simply kiss her and go no farther, but also knowing she needed time and space before taking their relationship deeper. "But just kissing, nothing else."

"Are you sure?"

"That's my line." He kissed the nape of her neck.

"See how annoying it is."

"You make a good point."

She turned over, looked at him. "Please."

"I've got to warn you, if you start getting too charged up, I'm leaving your bed."

"I'll be good," she vowed.

Yeah, but would she keep her promise? He pulled her into his arms and they kissed until their lips chapped; unhurried, dreamy kisses, intended to soothe, not kindle. But despite his restraint, the smooth, butterscotch flavor of her and the wet, sexy sound their lips made charged him up.

Need, desperate as a Hail Mary pass, coiled his body tight. He held his breath against the yearning building in his groin. Desire blasted from his pores in a sweat that smelled of testosterone. Her sweet taste lolled on his tongue, indolent and taunting. *C'mon, dontcha want more?*

Of course he did. He wanted all of her.

Meredith passed the line of scrimmage, trailing her fingers down his chest to his waist.

He manacled her wrist. "Hold on there, beautiful. You're out of bounds."

"Who says I'm playing by the rules?"

"Oh, that's funny." He chuckled, and imitating a female voice, he said in a prissy tone, "Rule #4. You don't touch me. I don't touch you. Ever."

She sat up, and laughing, gave his shoulder a slight shove. "I do not sound like that."

"Hey, it was your rule."

"And I said we could renegotiate at any time."

"Is that what we're doing?" He lowered his eyelids. "Renegotiating?"

"It is."

"So what are the new rules?"

"Touching is now allowed."

"That's too vague. I need specifics." He propped himself on his elbow and studied her. "I'm a detail-oriented kind of guy."

She drew her knees to her chest and slipped a palm under each socked foot. She wore a red and green plaid button-down flannel shirt, red socks with Santa's face printed on them, and her pink cotton bikini panties. She looked cute as hell.

"Can I touch here?" He reached up a finger to trace her collarbone.

She gulped. Nodded.

He tracked his hand down to the top of her cleavage. "Here?"

"Yes," she whispered.

"I see." He slid his hand over to a nipple that was beaded so hard he could see it through the material of her bra and shirt. "How about here?"

"Uh-huh." She whimpered.

His fingertips fanned out as he dragged them down her chest to her belly. "Is this okay?"

Goose bumps flared over her skin and she shivered.

"Are you cold?" he asked.

"No."

"You're trembling."

"Am I?"

"If you're not cold, you must be scared. If you're scared, we're not going any farther."

"Not scared." Her gaze caressed his face. "Excited."

"I'm trembling too," he confessed.

"You? You're unshakable. Everyone says so."

"Propaganda." He held up his hand for her to see. It quivered in the air.

"If you're scared," she mimicked him, "we're not going any farther."

"Not scared," he said. "Terrified."

"Are you? What about?"

"That you'll decide I'm not really the guy you want to be with."

"Hmm."

"What does that mean?"

"I imagined Delta Force operators would be much cockier than this."

"I used to be," he admitted. "Before."

"Before whatever happened to you in the Middle East?"

"No." He paused and leveled her an intense stare. "Before I found you."

Meredith did not glance away. In fact, she locked eyes with him. Her radiance shimmered like heat waves off the desert floor, so real it was almost touchable, and he caught a glimpse of heaven in her eyes. For a long moment they just stared into each other, barely breathing, not moving.

"With you," she said, "I feel normal for the first time."

"That's the nicest thing anyone has ever said to me."

"I lied," she said. "I am scared."

"I know. It worries me that you're afraid of me."

"I'm not scared about you." She paused. "Or about us."

"It's him," Hutch said coldly, flatly. "What he did to you."

"Not just that." She covered her head with her hands.

He stroked her hair. "Talk to me, Meredith."

She pressed her chin to her drawn knees, turned

her face away from him. "Sex comes easily to some women."

"It can come easily to you if you let it. Most natural thing in the world."

"My body knows that. My mind? Other story entirely."

"What are you so afraid of?"

"That I'll disappoint you." She said it so softly that he could barely hear her.

"Look at me," he commanded.

Reluctantly, she drew her head up.

"Meredith, you could never disappoint me."

"You say that now…"

"Oh, babe. I want you. If our first time isn't so hot, we keep trying until we're perfect."

"What if…what if it can never be any good between us no matter how much we practice?"

"You're overanalyzing. Relax. Just let go and let it happen. Or not. Remember, we don't have to take this step. No pressure at all."

"I want to take this step. I want you to make love to me."

"But?"

She covered her head with her hands and mumbled. "I equate sex with pain."

The hot taste of anger filled his mouth, and his hatred for the monster who had treated her so terribly jerked his stomach up into his throat.

"I'm afraid he ruined me forever." She lifted her head. A tear slid down her cheek.

"Babe, oh babe." All anger fled and the only thing he felt was deep sorrow and sympathy for her. "It's okay, it's okay."

He drew her into his arms and rocked her as tenderly as if she were Kimmie. She rested her head against his chest and cried silently, her shoulders moving up and down, her tears soaking his shirt.

Finally, she pulled away and swiped at her face with the back of her sleeve. "This isn't going very well, is it?"

"It's going fine."

"How many girls have cried on your shoulder before you made love to them?"

"You're my first," he admitted. "But hey, that makes you special. Usually they cry after."

"With relief that it's over?" she teased, smiling past the tears.

"With joyous rapture."

"Hmm, I'd like to try that sometime."

"We'll get there."

"I want to do something special for you. How about we redeem that gift card for your free backrub now?"

He was going to tell her he didn't give a damn about a backrub, but maybe giving him one would give her a sense of control.

"Sure." His voice went up slightly for no good reason.

"Still rusty?" she asked.

"As a door hinge." That was the thing. He hadn't had time to process the return of his voice. He was glad, and it was a monumental boulder scaled on his trail to recovery, but that meant it was time to start his pilgrimage to see the families of the teammates. That was not going to be easy. A lot of dark stuff was going to pop to the surface like a bobber on a pole after a hooked fish got away, and it meant leaving Meredith and Ben and Kimmie behind.

How could he leave when they still needed him so much, but how could he not go when completing his mission was the only way for him to fully heal?

"Give me a few minutes to get the room ready," she said.

"You want me to leave?"

"Please. But come back. Definitely come back."

Hutch left the room and considered not returning. Taking a step back was the right thing to do, the smart thing to do. So why couldn't he do it?

Chapter 16

Meredith was so very happy to see Hutch poke his head around the door. She'd freaked out on him and he hadn't run away. The man was either a keeper or a glutton for punishment. He'd been beyond patient with her.

"You ready?" he asked.

Gingerbread candles flickered on the dresser. The lights were off. The table was set up, and the massage oil warmed.

"Come…" she squeaked. She couldn't blame a rusty voice for the changes in her pitch. It was pure nerves. She cleared her throat, tried again. "Come in."

He strutted into the room, cock-of-the-walk, with nothing but a towel around his waist. He took one look at her face and said, "You're not ready for this."

"I'm always ready to give a massage."

"That's not what I'm talking about and you know it."

She ignored that. Patted the table. "Up here."

His eyes narrowed to her neck.

She reached up to finger the simple gold chain that had once belonged to her mother.

His gaze dropped to her body. "You put your jeans back on."

"I got cold."

"You have me at a disadvantage."

"That wasn't my intention."

"I've never had a professional massage."

"Really?"

"I'm a virgin," he said, his voice all heat, silk, and chocolate now, any signs of rust gone. "Be gentle."

"You're mocking me."

"No." His teasing tone vanished. "I didn't mean to sound that way."

"Table," she said, but she couldn't keep looking into those dark enigmatic eyes. "Facedown."

He climbed up on the table, and once he was settled with the towel still draped around his waist, Meredith poured a quarter-sized dollop of jasmine-scented massage oil into her palm. She ran her hands over his hard body, her fingers exploring his tight muscles. Everywhere she touched him, her own body lit up in the same spot.

"You're the Secret Santa who paid off everyone's layaway at Wal-Mart, aren't you?"

"It's called Secret Santa for a reason," he said. "Santa remains a secret."

"I know it was you."

He didn't say anything, but she felt his muscles tighten.

"It was very nice of you," she went on.

He shrugged as if it were no big deal. "When I was helping with the Angel Tree drive, it occurred to me that there were a lot of single parents and young families out there that weren't poor enough to receive help from the Angel Tree, but were still struggling to make ends meet. Paying off a few layaways at Wal-Mart was the least I could do."

"It was no small thing."

"In the grand scheme of things, yes it was. Please don't tell anyone."

"Your secret is safe with me. You're a good man, Brian Hutchinson."

His muscles grew even tauter. "I'm no hero."

"You're so wrong about that."

"I had a job to do and I did it. That doesn't make me a hero."

She fisted her hand, dug it into a big knot beneath his shoulder blades. Talking about this was tensing him up, not relaxing him.

"There," he said. "You've hit the spot."

She worked the hard muscle, concentrating on loosening him up. No matter what he said, she knew he was a good man. Only a good man would be plagued with guilt over the things his job as a soldier forced him to do. In spite of his absurdly masculine body and strategic mind, there was an inner gentleness to this big man.

Meredith had always been attracted to über-alpha guys because they made her feel safe and secure, but after Sloane, she'd come to fear strong men. If an alpha man had a cruel and vindictive nature, he could just as easily turn his strength against you as protect you with it. But a truly strong man would never hurt a woman. Hutch possessed real strength. Not just the external strength that came from granite muscles and carrying a gun. Hutch had strength of character and strength of mind as well.

"Why did you become a soldier?" she asked, kneading her knuckles along his spine.

He didn't answer right away. His breathing was slow and deep, and just when she thought he'd fallen asleep, he said, "You want the practical reasons or the lofty ideals of a goofy teen or the darker reasons I don't like to think about?"

"All three."

"I really couldn't think of another way to make money and my friend Gideon had just joined up. I thought it would be fun." He laughed at that.

"What were your lofty ideals about military service?"

"I felt a personal obligation to make things right. Someone has to protect our country. If not me, then who?"

"That's a big burden to carry around." She ran her hand over his scapula. "While these shoulders are broad, they weren't meant to carry the weight of the world."

"What I learned is that the world is not either black or white like I thought. No clear-cut path to the truth. After all, a mother with borderline personality disorder raised me, and that black and white lens is how people with BPD see the world."

"Going to other places, being around other cultures, showed you other ways of being."

"Yeah. I learned that not only are there hundreds of shades of gray, but that black isn't really black. It's a mix of all colors—red, yellow, green, blue, orange. And that white, not black, is the absence of color. It's all in the way we perceive things. And because of that, good people can justify doing bad things, and bad people can sometimes do good things, until you can no longer label people as bad or good."

"Wow. That's insightful, brawny, and brainy too. You're the whole package, Brian Hutchinson."

"Don't go putting me on a pedestal, Meredith." His voice rumbled through his chest. "My feet are made of clay."

Her pulse skipped. Not because he scared her, but because his compassion touched her so deeply. "What is the dark reason you joined the army?"

He paused, took a deep breath.

"It's okay if you don't want to talk about it."

"No, it's okay. Maybe talking will help me work through it."

"I don't want to pressure you to discuss something you're not ready to discuss."

He cleared his throat. "Ashley was the reason I joined the army. I couldn't control her anymore. She was only fourteen and slipping out at night to meet guys. I was working two jobs to make ends meet and I couldn't keep an eye on her twenty-four/seven. I could scare off the guys, but I couldn't scare Ashley."

"That's because she knew what a real softie you are inside."

Regret and shame tinged his voice. "Honestly, I wanted some relief from being her parent. I know that makes me a coward—"

"It does not," she said sharply. "It makes you human. You already did so much for her. You couldn't surrender your entire life over to her."

"I tried," he said. "But it didn't work. The more I did

for her, the more she took advantage of me. When I tried to lay down the law, she called her biological father and asked if she could come live with him. The guy was an alcoholic, but he'd finally gotten into recovery and joined AA. I guess he was working step nine and feeling guilty for having abandoned my mother and Ashley and he was trying to make amends."

"You two are half siblings?"

"Yeah. So once Ashley went to live with him, I was free to pursue my own career. I was so relieved to be free…" Beneath her fingers, his muscles turned to marble slabs.

"Don't beat yourself up for feeling relieved. It's easy for caretakers to get burned out. We keep taking on more and more responsibility and beating ourselves up for being selfish if we take time for ourselves, but the truth is, if we don't take care of ourselves, we really can't take care of others."

"You're talking about your grandmother."

"Yes," she whispered. "I know how that guilt feels. I'd been at my grandmother's bedside every single day for the last six months of her life and the one day, just this one day, a friend comes over and insists I get out of the house. I was at the park sitting on a bench with my friend, warming my face in the sun when the hospice nurse calls to say Gramma passed away without me."

"Aw, babe." Hutch sat up, swinging his legs over the edge of the massage table and tugging her into his arms.

"I'm okay," she said. "It's okay."

"I know." He kissed her forehead.

She closed her eyes and sank against him.

He kissed her eyelids, first one and then the other. Kissed the tip of her nose. Softly claimed her mouth.

They kissed for a long moment and finally, Meredith broke the kiss. "I can't take any more of this."

His eyes gleamed feral in the candlelight. "Me either."

"I need you, Hutch," she said fiercely.

He gave her a poignant smile that cracked her heart wide open. "You've been doing just fine on your own for five years. More than fine. You've survived, thrived in spite of the awful things you've been through. You're a strong woman, Meredith. You don't need anybody."

"That's where you're wrong." She was surprised to realize she was ready to fully trust, one hundred percent. And she did need him badly. She'd tried not to fall for him, had set up ground rules to keep her heart safe. The last thing she had wanted was to be with a man.

But Hutch wasn't just any man, and over the course of the last few weeks, he'd chipped away at the resistance she'd put up, until that wall was so full of holes her heart was leaking out.

"Let me rephrase," she said. "I *want* you."

His eyes simmered with sadness; the smile that tugged at his lips was soft and gentle. He'd changed from an embittered, wounded warrior to a man well on his way to a full recovery, and Meredith knew she was seeing the man he'd been before he was wounded, before pain and loss and anger had twisted him up inside.

"I want you too," he said.

"I can't promise you any more than right now. The future is not mine to give."

"I don't need anything else," he said.

She reached up to cup his face, the stubble of his heavy beard rough against her palm. She kissed him lightly. "I am ready for this. I'm ready for you."

"I'm not convinced."

"Does this change your mind?" She slipped her arms around his neck and kissed him with every ounce of passion she had inside her.

In answer, he pulled her up onto the massage table beside him and they were kissing like mad people. His hot mouth took command of her, fully in control.

But surprisingly, that did not scare her one bit. She trusted him and did not fear letting him take the lead.

Before this, he'd only kissed her tenderly, sweetly, taking great care to make sure she was comfortable, but now his kisses were wild and fiery, guiding her toward unknown terrain.

His fingers undressed her as his lips did their magic, his hand at the buttons of her shirt, slipping it over her shoulders, and then at the hook of her bra.

He tipped his head up to look at her, his long black lashes softening the hard angles of his cheekbones, his dark chocolate eyes searching hers. He looked so vulnerable and endearing in that moment that she touched three fingers to her lips. He might be strong and in control, but her love had the power to shatter him into a million pieces, and that knowledge shook Meredith to the core.

He trusted her too! Her heart liquefied in her chest.

Hutch dipped his head and tenderly sucked her nipples, first one and then the other until she squirmed with need. He stopped and straightened, knowing just how far and how fast to push things.

While his eyes stayed fixed on her, watching every emotion that flitted across her face, and gauging her reaction before he moved on, Hutch's fingers plucked at the snap of her jeans. The snap popped open. Millimeter by excruciating millimeter, he eased down the zipper. Leisurely, he hooked a thumb in the waistband of her jeans at each hipbone and peeled the pants down her legs, his palms skimming the backs of her thighs as he went.

Awed, she stared down at the top of his head. "That's a cool trick."

"I've learned a few things over the years."

"How many women have you undressed?"

"Let's not get into specifics. Just know that none of those women could hold a candle to you."

"You're making me blush."

He stared into her. "It's not a line, Meredith. I've never felt like this with anyone else."

"Not even the girl you almost married?"

He winced. "Gossip. Gotta love small-town life. But no, not even with Celia."

"How come you asked her to marry you if she didn't make you feel like this?"

"Because until you I didn't know it was possible to feel like this."

"Me either," she whispered.

He positioned her until they balanced sitting face-to-face in the middle of the massage table, totally naked. His legs were around her waist. Hers locked around his. The flagpole of his erection jutting up between them.

They couldn't get enough of staring into each other. His intense eyes rippled with unspoken emotion.

Oh, the things that man could do with his hands. His skillful hands seemed to be everywhere at once—on her lips, on her chin, on her belly and her shins. And then he eased her onto her back and straddled her.

He paused. "You okay?"

Mutely, she nodded.

He lowered his head and began to explore her body with his tongue.

The fact that she was so willingly, so eagerly allowing him full access to her body, without a shred of fear or panic, was earth-shattering. She'd never dreamed she could get here. So open. So willing to trust him.

Slowly, sweetly he loved her with his tongue, in a way she'd never been loved before.

He kissed languid circles of heat and she was hypnotized. Her skin was incredibly sensitive, her body tingling and tender.

And then she broke in a wave of sensation unlike anything she'd ever felt. It rippled through her muscles, claimed her, leaving her trembling and gasping in his arms.

"What," she gasped when she was finally able to catch her breath. "What was that? What just happened?"

Hutch's chuckle was rich and deep. "Babe, unless I miss my guess, I'd say you just had an orgasm."

Hutch carried her to bed and they lay there holding each other. Nothing had ever prepared him for this feeling. This pure love. He'd told Meredith that it didn't matter if she couldn't give him anything more than right now, but it wasn't true. He wanted to keep her with him forever. He'd never known he could feel love like this. Didn't know such a state existed.

His eyes stung at the intensity of his feelings. She felt so delicate in his hands. He wanted to cup his palms around her like a fragile china teacup and hold her safe from the ugliness of the world.

"I had no idea," she whispered, her lips rasping

against the stubble of his beard, "that it was possible for me to ever have this, feel this. You are…this is… amazing."

Her words of awe flooded him with an abiding desire to heal, left his throat hurting as he tightened his arms around her, held her protectively, and felt her breath fan the hair along his neck.

Hutch combed his fingers through her short curls, and she murmured with pleasure. He massaged her scalp with slow, rhythmic motions…scratching lightly, kneading, caressing. Each stroke stirred her scent, the sweet, feminine aroma imbedding deep within his memory, forever branding her fragrance in his brain. Her hair was so soft, thick, and fine. It had grown out about a half an inch since he'd met her and he brushed his fingers up the nape of her neck, pushing it up and smoothing it back down, then tickling behind her left ear, his heart breaking as he etched along the jagged scar.

She shivered and whimpered in the back of her throat.

Until he was doing it, Hutch didn't realize he'd been longing his whole life for an intimacy like this, so much passing between them in a simple touch, a light sweeping of their lips. He'd become a hull of a man, shelled out by life on the edge, cold as winter soil. But she was springtime, breathing warmth and freshness into his bones, coaxing his heart to beat with budding hope. She filled him, made him whole, healed the cracks in his soul.

Punch-drunk with love for her, Hutch lifted his head and captured her mouth with such a rush of gratitude, the force of it left him breathless. He wanted to say the words, to tell her he loved her, but he was too afraid of scaring her off, so he simply showed her how he felt, pumping every last morsel of his emotions into that kiss.

Swiftly, his thankfulness morphed into the richness of new-blooming romance. He rolled her over onto her back and gently pressed her into the mattress, his eager hand traveling leisurely over the curve of her neck and down her shoulder, while his mouth drank in the nectar of her luxurious lips. He splayed his palm over her cheek, spreading his fingers over her face, his thumb hooked underneath her chin. His body ached to join with hers, but he did not want things to go that fast.

"Do you know how long I've been dreaming of this?" he crooned.

Her lashes fluttered. "Tell me."

"Since the day you pepper-sprayed me."

"That was fast."

"One look. One look was all it took." Had he said too much? Was he scaring her away by admitting how quickly he'd fallen for her?

Her hands flattened against his chest and he feared she was going to push him away, but instead she pushed her palms around his torso until they encircled his back, and she pulled him down flush against her body.

"Make love to me, Hutch," she begged. "Make love to me now."

He fumbled on the bedside table for the condom. Dropped it twice before he got it unwrapped and rolled into place. He stopped to kiss her once more, taking her willing mouth, touching his tongue to hers.

She thrust her pelvis up, dropped her legs open, and she was so warm, wet, and welcoming that he simply slipped right in. The breath left her body in a delighted gasp and she brought her legs up to lock them tightly around his waist. He shifted his hips, found a cozier fit, improved by the sway and wriggle of their bodies that expanded their joining into much more than just physical merger. Heaven. Sheer heaven. Their union stirring more than the blaze of blood and thump of hearts, stirring too the assurance that they were meant to be together.

He hovered about her, supporting his weight on his elbows, fearful of hurting or scaring her.

"Meredith," he whispered. "I never knew I could be so lucky."

In answer, she raised her hips higher, egging him on. Urging him closer. Deeper.

For several brilliant minutes, they satisfied themselves with a steady rhythm that wove them ever more tightly to each other. The candle flickered, throwing long shadows against the wall.

Finally, Hutch could stand it no longer and he looked down into her precious face to find the same ravenous expression in her eyes that was clutching at his throat. They gawped—reinvented—clung to each and rocketed to the ultimate physical expression of love.

Space hung suspended, and after a time, Hutch hauled them back safely to the shores of the bedroom.

Or at least he thought they were safe until he realized Meredith was softly sobbing.

His gut clutched. "What is it, babe? Did I hurt you?"

"No," she whispered.

Alarm twisted him up and sweat broke out on his upper lip. "Why are you crying?"

"Because…"

"Because what?" He lifted up, peered into her face, and brushed her temple with his finger.

Her eyes shimmered through the fine mist of tears. "Because you were right."

Confused, he rubbed his palm over his forehead. "Right about what?"

"The rapturous joy. Oh, Hutch, I've never in my life been this happy."

Chapter 17

At three in the morning, Meredith and Hutch sat at the kitchen table eating cold roast beef sandwiches and smiling at each other.

"Wait," he said.

"What?"

"Hold still."

She swallowed the bite in her mouth and wiped at her face. "What is it? A smudge of mayo?"

"This…" He leaned over and kissed her.

"Oh, you," she said, feeling as lighthearted as a girl, and kissed him back.

"I'm happy," he said.

"Me too."

He grinned as if he'd just found a million dollars lying in the road with no one around to claim ownership. "I think practicing yoga with you these last few weeks really enhanced what happened between us."

"Oh?" She lowered her eyelashes and sent him a naughty look. "If you think that was something, just wait until we start practicing Tantric yoga together."

His body perked up and his eyes glistened. "I like the sound of that. What is Tantric yoga exactly?"

"Personally," she said, "I've never experienced it, but it's using yoga to connect with your partner on a deeper level, both mentally, spiritually, and physically."

"I heard it had something to do with hour-long orgasms."

She made a purring noise. "That too. In Tantric philosophy, sex is considered the greatest source of energy in the universe."

"Can't argue with that."

"Practitioners of Tantric yoga believe that orgasm is a cosmic and divine experience."

"My, my, my," Hutch murmured, leaning in closer. "In light of that definition, as far as I'm concerned, we've already committed Tantric yoga."

"Ah." She tilted her head. "But we could take it so much deeper."

"Wow." He exhaled loudly. "I'm not sure I have the stamina for that."

She crinkled her nose, put her hand on his thigh. Instantly, he was hard again. "Don't underestimate yourself. You rally pretty quickly. I'm certain you can handle me."

"Now who is underestimating herself?"

"Hutch," she said. "You make me feel powerful."

"You *are* powerful." His eyebrows dipped as he

scowled darkly and pressed his forehead to hers. The heat from his stare pierced straight through her.

"Not nearly powerful enough," she whispered, the persistent shadow of her past gathering pleats of anxiety around her like thunderclouds marshaling before a storm.

Abruptly, Hutch pushed back his chair, got to his feet, and stalked to the sliding glass door. He tugged open the drapes, stared out the window at the moonlight glittering off the Brazos River.

"Hutch?"

He didn't answer her.

Concerned, Meredith stood up and moved to him. She slipped her arms around his waist, and locked her fingers together over his taut belly.

He placed a palm over her hands, rubbed the backs of her knuckles, but said nothing. She pressed her ear against his back, listening to the steady, forceful, *thump-thump* of his heartbeat.

"What is it?" she asked, trying to ignore the fear plucking at the hairs along the nape of her neck.

"I hate this."

She shrugged, even though he could not see her. His body was as tight as an overtuned guitar, the stretched strings ready to snap under the pressure. "I hate it too, but what can I do?"

"You can stop running. Stay here with me. Trust me to keep you safe."

"Hutch." She could barely force his name past the constriction in her throat. "It's not that simple."

"It is that simple," he said. "All you have to do is take a stand and fight. As long as you allow fear to drive you, Meredith, you will never be free."

"I already know I won't be free until Sloane is dead."

"I could kill him for you."

"I know," she said. "I know you would do it and you have the ability to dispatch him without leaving a trace. You could get away with it."

He turned toward her, pulled her into his embrace, pressed his mouth to her ear, and whispered, "Then tell me where to find him."

"My burden to carry, not yours."

"Heartbeat. Say the word and it's a heartbeat away."

Her skin prickled at the thought of having Sloane eradicated from the earth. How easy it would be to say yes. She shook her head, looking up into his precious eyes. "I can't allow you to be the instrument of my revenge."

"Meredith, all I want to do is keep you safe."

She flattened her palm against the left side of his chest. "There are enough stains on your soul."

He flinched.

She knew his job had required him to do things she could not even imagine and that he was still dealing with the fallout from that.

"We could fight him legally."

"I'm wanted for attempted murder. I can't go to the police. I'll be arrested and that will leave Ben without a mother, and that's a risk I simply cannot take. As wonderful as it's been here with you, as good as we are together, I'm sorry, but my son must come first."

"And that's one of the things I love most about you," he said. "You put your son's needs ahead of your own."

"Don't all mothers?"

A faraway look came into his eyes. "No."

She rubbed his upper arm. "Let's just enjoy what we have now."

"What if you just stayed and if he catches up to you, we deal with it when the time comes."

A bitter laugh escaped her lips.

"What?" he asked.

"For a man who's seen the darker side of life, that's a naïve statement. He's relentless. He will never stop searching for me. Until you've been through something like that you have no idea…"

He put a hand to the nape of her neck, pressed her close to his chest. "I feel so helpless. No matter what I do, I'm doomed to lose you."

She sank into the hollow of his arms. "Many people don't even get this little spot of happiness, Hutch. Let's try to make the most of the time we have together."

"There has to be another way."

"There's not. I've had five years to think about it."

"For all you know, the guy has moved on to stalking some other poor woman and you're in the clear. He could be incarcerated. Or he could be dead and you're still roaming around the country trying to escape a monster that's no longer chasing you."

"You might be right, but I have no way of knowing any of that."

"Got a proposal for you," he ventured. "Please, don't reject it out of hand."

She tipped back her head and studied his face. He looked so earnest. "I'm listening."

"Sheriff Crouch is a Vietnam vet and a good friend. He's been a father figure to me over the years. With your permission, I'd like to tell him about your history and ask him to look into your ex-husband, see what he can dig up."

Her body frosted up at the same time hope sent her heart catapulting into her throat. "I'm a fugitive from the law, Hutch. He will arrest me."

He turned her face up so she could see his steadfast certainty. "He won't."

"How can you be so sure?"

"I know him."

"I don't."

"But you know me, right?"

"Yes."

"And you trust me."

"You're the *only* one I trust."

"And I trust Hondo," he said. "Can you put your faith in my opinion?"

She gulped. "What you're asking me is huge."

"I know."

"If you're wrong about Hondo, you still lose me and I will not only lose everything, but Sloane will get his hands on Ben. I cannot let that happen."

He barely reacted, but a muscle in his jaw ticked. She could see it jerk beneath his dark beard stubble. He closed his eyes, took a deep breath, slowly opened them. "I know."

"And it's a risk you're willing to take?"

"Hondo is not going to arrest you," he said patiently.

"You believe that one hundred percent?"

He captured her chin between his thumb and finger, peered into her eyes as if trying to burrow into her brain and rearrange her thinking. "We've got to try, Meredith, for Ben's sake as much as ours. Growing up on the run is going to have an effect him."

"I know that," she whispered. Not being able to give her son a stable home was her deepest regret.

"Look, you were going to leave after Christmas anyway, right?"

She nodded.

"So this time, instead of running off blind, I feel Hondo out. If I sense he won't react the way I expect him to, I'll text you and you can take off with Ben. Once you get to where you're going, I'll load up your stuff and bring it to you."

"I don't know."

"How would it be any different than you just leaving?"

"Because law enforcement would know where I was."

Emotions shifted across his face—concern, yearning love. No faking it, there was love in this man's eyes. Love for her. "It's your call, but I want you to understand that I will always protect you. No matter what, I will always have your back until I take my last breath."

It came down to how much she trusted Hutch. They both knew it. This was a test of their relationship. Could she put aside her fears and place her faith into those big strong hands, or was she going to allow Sloane to ruin this too?

"All right," she whispered. "Go talk to Sheriff Crouch."

Just as Hutch forecasted, Hondo believed Meredith's story, reinforcing her faith in both men. But part of her still worried. If Hondo spoke directly to Sloane, her ex could easily persuade the sheriff that she was not only mentally unstable, but dangerous. He'd done it many times before. Dr. Lily was the only one who'd seen through his serpentine charm.

Meredith called the hospital to check on Dotty Mae and learned she'd already been released with a clean bill of health. Her only issue was distress over having almost run over Ben. Meredith walked over to the elderly woman's home, bringing her a fruit basket and taking the children with her so Dotty Mae could see that Ben was all right.

Two days after Christmas, Sheriff Crouch arrived on the front porch. Hutch went to answer the door, while Meredith sent the kids up to her room to play. Breath held and heart thumping, she waited at the foot of the stairs, out of sight from the front door. It was all she could do not to grab Ben up, race to the minivan in the garage, and flee town.

"Is this a good time?" Hondo asked.

Hutch must have nodded or waved him inside, because she heard the floorboards creak and the shuffle of footsteps and then there they were in the living room.

The sheriff caught sight of her, and removed his cowboy hat. He wore a gun on his hip and she couldn't seem to stop staring at it. "Ms. Sommers," he said. "Are you all right?"

She put a hand to her cheek, realized her face was ice cold. Was her skin as pale as it felt? She started to speak, but she'd been pressing her lips together so tightly that they were momentarily stuck together. She forced them apart. "I'm all right."

Hondo looked to Hutch, then back to Meredith. "We should sit down."

The chill that had begun in her face moved down her body, icing her neck, flowing over her collarbone, embedding deep inside her lungs and her heart until all her organs were cold as a winter grave. Her knees bobbled. Oh God, was Hondo here to arrest her?

If Hutch hadn't taken her by the elbow and eased her onto the sofa, she would have toppled over. He sat down beside her, hitched his arm around her waist, held her safe and secure.

Hondo took the recliner, and for a moment, he didn't say anything, just studied Meredith with inscrutable eyes. The sheriff was a strong-jawed, muscular man who looked a decade younger than his sixty-something years. The lines on his face, the scars on his hands, said he'd been in some dark places himself. And Hutch had told her about Hondo's struggle with heroin addiction. How he had not only triumphed over that battle, but he'd also married his childhood sweetheart later in life and got elected sheriff of his hometown, finally finding lasting joy and happiness in his golden years.

Inspiring.

But Meredith was in no mood to be inspired. She was too keyed up, too nervous about what he had to say.

Hondo leaned forward, rested his elbows on his knees, and toyed with the brim of his cowboy hat, his gun sandwiched between his thigh and the arm of the recliner. "I'm afraid I've got some tragic news."

Instantly, her hand flew to her throat. Oh dear God, Sloane had killed someone else she knew or had cared for.

Hutch tightened his hold on her, bracing her and keeping her from flying off into a million little pieces.

She gripped hold of Hutch's left knee, gritted her teeth against the terror closing off her airway. Who? Who could Sloane have murdered?

She thought of the few distant relatives she had left—a great-aunt in Memphis, a cousin in Montana, another who lived in Germany. She thought of the people she'd met over the past few years, those who had befriended her—a store clerk, a yoga instructor, a mail carrier. Which one of them had lost their life because of her? Why was Hondo torturing her like this? Just say it!

Hondo cleared his throat. "I'm afraid your ex-husband has lost his life."

What? She blinked, unable to process what the sheriff had just said. Lost his life? As if he'd misplaced it. What did that mean?

"Ms. Sommers?" Looking concerned, Hondo got to his feet, came toward her.

"Meredith?" Gently, Hutch, stroked her hand. "Did you hear what Hondo said?"

She shook her head. Sloane dead? No. He was invincible. He wasn't dead. He was just playing possum. She knew better than that. He was a trickster, a con artist, the devil himself. Satan didn't die.

"When?" Her voice cracked.

"November fifth."

Sloane had been dead for almost two months? She could not have seen him in the Twilight town square. How had her instincts been so wrong? Her ability to sense his presence was the only thing that had kept her alive this long. Maybe she was shell-shocked. Seeing danger and disaster in even the most innocent things. After all, she'd shot Hutch with pepper spray even after she'd known that he was not Sloane.

"How?" she asked.

Hutch was gently stroking her back, but she could barely feel his hand. Could barely feel anything.

"Your ex-husband was on the run from law enforcement," Hondo said.

"Huh?" She shook her head, blinked again, and glanced around as if she could find meaning from the living room furniture. "What do you mean?"

"LAPD internal affairs was investigating Sloane over numerous incidents of misconduct, planting evidence, abusing detainees, even a suspected murder rap. They dug up enough evidence to put him away for the rest of his life. He was arrested but escaped custody, and a manhunt ensued."

"How did he die?" Meredith still couldn't believe it. She felt like Julia Roberts in *Sleeping with the Enemy* when the character thought her stalker ex was dead and he reached out to grab her again.

"Sloane committed suicide by running his car into a parked oil tanker truck. Luckily, no one else was hurt or killed in the crash."

She jumped as if she'd been grabbed.

Hutch dropped his hand as if sensing she was too distressed by the news for touch.

Nausea churned in her stomach, *Don't be sick, don't be sick*. Fighting off the urge to vomit, Meredith put a palm to her mouth, and closed her eyes.

"It's over," Hutch murmured. "He's gone. He'll never bother you and Ben again."

"A tank…" She had to stop, clear her throat, start over. "If he ran into a tanker truck, I'm assuming there was an explosion."

Hondo nodded. He came over to crouch in front of her, his kindly face furrowed with concern for her. "His body was badly burned."

"But they were still able to identify him with dental records, right?" she said, the nausea waiting in the wings, threatening to overtake her.

"Unfortunately, the high heat of the fuel incinerated him."

"So there was no positive identification that it was his body in that car," she said.

"They did find some bone fragments that are awaiting DNA confirmation, but they are ninety-nine percent sure it was Vick Sloane's body in that car."

"But there is at one percent chance they are wrong," she said.

Hondo glanced helplessly at Hutch. She knew what the sheriff was thinking. She had been so traumatized by Sloane that she was irrational, and there was probably some truth to that. "Yes, there is that one percent chance someone else was in that car besides your ex-husband."

"Then I can't truly relax until those DNA tests come back." She met Hutch's eyes. There was no judgment there. Nor did he look like he was simply humoring her.

"Are you sure? DNA test are only 99.99 percent positive," Hondo asked gently.

Meredith could tell the sheriff was not being sarcastic, simply pointing out her skewed thinking. When would proof ever be enough? At some point, she was going to have to take a leap of faith and assume it was true, that Sloane was indeed dead. Until she could do that, she could never fully move on with her life. She had to stop jumping at shadows. If she clung to the belief that Sloane was still alive she could never build a life with Hutch.

Letting go of her fear was a brave first step. She didn't yet feel it in her heart, but maybe she could fake it, and eventually, her heart would catch up with her brain.

She moistened her lips, raised her head, and squared her shoulders. "What's the next step?"

"It's time to get a lawyer," Hondo said. "And make your arrest warrant disappear."

Chapter 18

It took a day or two for the news of her ex-husband's death to fully sink in, but almost immediately after Hondo left, Hutch noticed a change in Meredith. She started talking about the long-term future, something she'd never done before, and on Monday she made an appointment to speak to a lawyer after the New Year.

Gideon and Caitlyn had invited them to a New Year's Eve celebration, and the ensuing days leading up to the party were filled with relief and lighthearted joy. He and Meredith didn't want to confuse the children, so they did not share a bed in front of them, but at night after Kimmie and Ben were asleep, they rendezvoused in the spare bedroom upstairs and then returned to their own beds just before dawn.

During those heady days and nights, Hutch experienced the kind of happiness he'd never even dreamed was possible. They didn't get much sleep, but in spite of it, they seemed to have boundless energy and insatiable appetites for each other. He reveled in the way their bodies fit together so perfectly, and how his heart caught fire every time she gave him one of her slow, welcoming smiles.

He loved rolling over in his sleep, finding her there, tucking her into the curve of his arms, and smelling the sweet scent of her hair. To awaken before she did and lie there a long moment, studying her in the predawn light and wondering how he'd gotten so lucky. He delighted in her buttery lips and in knowing he could kiss them anytime he wanted. He kissed her when she headed off to work, usually in the pantry so the children couldn't see what they were up to.

He spent the days cleaning the house, cooking dinner, considering what new career to pursue, worrying about Ashley and Kimmie's future, all the while anxiously awaiting Meredith's return. He thrilled watching her read to the children at bedtime, and his heart gave a thump every time she looked up and caught him standing in the doorway. In the evenings, they played with the children together. One night building a tent out of blankets and camping out in the living room. Another night, pretending it was Old West days, the kids were wagon train scouts, and he and Meredith were the horses, prancing around the house with a laughing Kimmie and Ben on their backs.

Hutch couldn't get enough of wrapping his arm around her waist and pulling her into his arms. Or giving her a taste from the fork or spoon of whatever he was cooking for dinner that night. Her sweet moans of *mmm* made him feel both sexual and appreciated.

He took her shopping to buy a new dress to wear to the party, and when she came skipping from the dressing room looking like a goddess in a golden sheath dress and high heels, his pulse took off like a Lamborghini. He'd never seen her dressed to the nines and he was bowled over anew at how completely beautiful she was.

They kept practicing yoga outside the bedroom, and inside the bedroom she taught him a few Tantric tricks that made him last far longer than he'd ever thought possible. With Meredith by his side, even mundane things like going to the grocery store and running errands were fun. He lived to do things for her—gas up her minivan, massage her feet after she'd had a long day, open the door for her, put a towel in the dryer to warm for her and slip it into the bathroom while she showered. Meredith was so sweet and feminine, so patient and kind. He couldn't get enough of her.

For those short few days leading up to January 1, Hutch's life was total bliss.

New Year's Eve arrived and they loaded the children into the car just after seven. Caitlyn and Gideon lived on a ranch south of Twilight, and they had hired babysitters to watch the children upstairs while the adults welcomed the New Year downstairs. Their hosts had decorated their rec room with New Year's banners and set up a makeshift stage for the four-piece country-and-western band they'd hired for the event. They'd also arranged for overnight accommodations or designated drivers for guests who enjoyed too much holiday merriment.

All during the party, Hutch couldn't stop looking at Meredith in that golden dress. The word "bombshell" didn't do her justice. She could have stepped off the red carpet of a 1940s movie premiere.

Neither of them had champagne. Meredith rarely drank because she'd needed to stay alert at all times, and Hutch had given up alcohol with his PTSD diagnosis. Instead, they danced the night away.

The other guests watched them dancing together, smiling and winking, whispering happily to one another behind their collective palms. He expected nothing less than his friends and neighbors to revel in his newfound joy. After all, Twilight was a town of romantics.

And hell, with the way Meredith made him feel, Hutch was becoming a full-fledged romantic himself.

Just before midnight, the band started playing, "For He's a Jolly Good Fellow." Gideon went up on stage to grab the microphone, his eyes on Hutch.

Uh-oh. What was his buddy to up?

The band stopped playing.

"Igloo," Gideon said, "this isn't just a New Year's Eve party. This is your official welcome home party."

The band launched back into the song and everyone joined in, guests migrating into the rec room from other parts of the house to declare him a jolly good fellow.

After the music died down again, Gideon raised a hand. "You've worked hard to heal and it's paid off. You've regained your voice."

A cheer went up from the group.

"We're so proud of you," Gideon continued. "And how far you've come down a long, hard road."

People came over to pound him on the back, shake his hand, express their appreciation. The glow from their praise was nice, but what lit Hutch's heart was when Meredith slipped her arm around his waist and rested her head against his shoulder.

Gideon tapped the microphone to get everyone's attention again. "We're not done yet, folks. Hutch, to thank you for your service to our country, my brother, we want to help you on your road to recovery."

He looked down at Meredith. "Did you know about this?"

Her eyes crinkled with a happy smile and she nodded. "These people love you so much."

Gideon motioned him forward. "We know there is a sacred mission you need to undertake in order to complete your healing and bring closure to the life you've left behind. We passed around the hat and scraped together enough money to pay for your trip."

Floored by their generosity, he ducked his head, pausing to take a deep breath before looking up again. His chest ached in a good way and the tops of his ears tingled. It was a Christmas morning kind of tingle, full of anticipation and appreciation.

"The military teaches us that we're all teammates," Gideon went on. "Therefore, Nate, Hondo, and I couldn't let you embark on your sojourn alone. We're all going with you."

Hutch tapped a loose fist against the side of his chest and a sweetly strange sense of being at the center of the universe swept over him.

"And in case you're looking for something to do when you come home," Gideon said, "Nate and I want to offer you a job at our security firm."

Aw hell, aw damn. What had he done to deserve such great friends?

"Speech!" someone yelled, and then the whole room picked up the chant. "Speech, speech, speech."

Once upon a time Hutch would have glibly jumped up onto the stage, taken the microphone with a cocky bow, and proceeded to crack a joke or two, shrugging off the accolades. That had been his old style.

If they'd sprung this on him right after his return to Twilight in the wake of his forced discharge from the army, he would have gotten upset and stalked out, too enmeshed in anger and grief to gracefully accept the honor.

But tonight, with Meredith standing in the crowd looking at him with adoring eyes, he was deeply humbled by their moving tribute.

Feeling as graceful as an ox, he lumbered up onto the stage and accepted the microphone Gideon passed over to him.

Caitlyn and Flynn handed out flutes of champagne and sparkling cider.

Everyone in the room saluted him, eyes misted with tears. And damn if there wasn't a lump the size of Texas stuck in his throat, but he wasn't going to let that stop him from expressing his gratitude.

"Thank you," Hutch said. "Thank you all so much for being my friends and putting up with me when I was less than hospitable, but I would not be able to stand here before you today if it weren't for one special woman who was able to see past my pain and fear and challenge me to readjust my thinking."

Heads swiveled to stare at Meredith.

Hutch peered into her eyes and held out his hand. "Babe, you brought me back to life when I thought I was long past dead. Without you, I'm nothing. Please come up here with me. This is your victory too."

Amid eardrum-busting applause, Meredith blushed prettily and came to take her place at his side.

Then just as the clock struck midnight, their friends toasted them as Hutch spun her into his arms and dipped her in a long, deep kiss that had everyone cheering.

On January 2, in the misty light of a platinum dawn, Hutch stood on the front porch in his Special Forces dress uniform, saying good-bye to Meredith. The children didn't return to school until Monday and they were still sound asleep. His truck engine was running, heating up the cab. After this, he'd pick up Gideon, Nate, and Hondo, and they'd drive to the airport together. They would leave his truck in long term parking at DFW. The plan was to fly into the major airports and then rent a car in each city so that they could drive to the homes of the families they intended on visiting.

She pressed a palm to his collar, ironing out imaginary wrinkles.

"I'm never going to wear this uniform again after this trip," he said. "I'm done with killing."

"I thought Delta Force didn't wear uniforms."

"They don't, but the uniform represents the life of a soldier and that life is behind me. This is the last time. I'm closing the door of that chapter of my life, so I can start over healthy and peaceful." He didn't add, *With you.* He wanted to so badly, but it was too soon. She needed time to fully trust him and the relationship they were building.

"From resentful wounded warrior to accepting, loving father." She smiled a soft smile. "You've made quite the journey in a short amount of time, Brian Hutchinson. I'm so proud of you."

"I'm not the only one who's changed." He held her close, pressed his forehead to hers, and looked intently into her eyes. "I don't want to go."

"You have to. Your transformation won't be complete without this step."

"I know."

"The sooner you go, the sooner you'll be home."

"This is killing me."

"Me too."

They held each other tightly as if he was headed off to war. "I hate leaving you alone."

"I'll be fine. Now that I don't have to worry about Sloane..." She shivered.

Hutch knew she still had her doubts about her ex-husband's death. Sometimes, she'd wake up in the middle of the night, thick in the throes of a nightmare, and he'd pull her snug against him, kiss her face, and tell her repeatedly that she was safe. He knew the effects of the abuse she'd suffered would linger for a long time to come. Just as he still battled his own demons. But each day, they were getting better, growing stronger because they had each other to lean on.

"He can never hurt you again," Hutch said.

"I can't seem to shake the feeling that he's just around the corner waiting to spring. Please be patient with me."

"Always." He kissed her forehead. "Infinitely."

"After you get back we'll go see the lawyer," she said. "And discuss what to do about Ashley."

"Yeah." He cradled her hips in his palms. "We've got a lot to talk about when I get back."

"Until then, just do what you have to do to get some closure."

"Listen to me, babe. I know you're used to being independent, and I admire that about you, but you've got to promise me that if anything comes up, you'll go to Jesse and Flynn for help. Wrangling those two little ones by yourself isn't going to be easy."

"I'll be fine."

He captured her chin, tilted her face up. "Promise me, Meredith, that you won't try to go it alone."

"I promise," she murmured.

God, he hated going off and leaving her just when they were really starting to bond. He made sure his smile reached his eyes, gave her a teasing wink to ease up on the seriousness. She'd had enough doom and gloom to last her a lifetime, and he was determined to be her True North, as she called it. Right now, she needed his strength. "You know your nose will grow if you lie."

"I swear, I'll ask for help."

"Okay, because I don't want to come back and find you've got a schnozzle as long as an anteater's snout."

She laughed past the mist dusting her lashes, and that was what he was going for because he could see she had been on the verge of tears.

"Aw babe," he gathered her closer, pressing her lithe body against his hard muscles. "It's going to be all right. I'll be back before you know it."

"Not if you don't ever leave," she said, and gave him a little shove. "Go on now. Your buddies will be wondering where you're at."

"They've all got women they're saying good-bye to.

I image we're not the only ones standing on a porch in the cold."

He gave her one long, hard, final kiss, and let her go, his lips tingling from the pressure and hot taste of her. "I'll call you from the road."

Then before he could change his mind, Hutch rushed to the truck and drove away. The image of Meredith forlornly hugging the porch post burned into his brain.

On the spot, Hutch vowed that once he returned from this trip, he was never, ever going to leave her again.

Meredith went back to work on Monday, the same day the children returned to school. She and Hutch talked every day on the phone. He had five families to visit. Five hometown main streets to drive. From the farmlands of York, Pennsylvania, to the manicured lawns of Galena, Illinois, to the cornfields of Crawford, Nebraska, to the mountains of Park City, Utah, and along the waterways of Seattle, Meredith and the children followed his journey on the map.

He kept their conversations light, asking her about her day and how the children were doing. He talked about the meals they'd had on the road and the beauty of the places they passed through, but he never mentioned the details of the serious task he was about. But she could hear the weariness in his voice, and once he wondered if he was doing more harm than good by stirring up the families' memories.

She was so happy that he had Hondo, Gideon, and Nate with him. Only they could truly understand what he was going through. So she did her best to cheer him up, telling funny things the kids had done, planning the places they'd visit together when he returned, asking his advice on how to best cook the crappie Jesse had brought them after a banner fishing expedition.

Late Thursday evening, Hutch reached his last destination in Seattle. They would be there until Sunday. The family of the slain Delta Force operator had arranged a memorial service for Saturday morning to coincide with Hutch's visit.

Just two more full days, she told herself. Two more days and he'd be back home. How she missed him!

After she arrived at the spa on Friday, she realized she'd left her cell phone on the charger at home and she couldn't risk going without it. What if the children got sick or Hutch wanted to hear her voice or by some miracle, Ashley called? Her client hadn't yet arrived, so she asked the receptionist to seat the woman in the meditation room with a beverage, apologize for the delay, and offer her a fifteen percent discount.

Her mind on Hutch's homecoming and the sexy little nightie she'd picked up the previous day at one of boutiques on the square, she zoomed back to the house. She blushed thinking about the look that would come into his eyes when he saw her in it. The man made her feel so sexy!

She hopped out of the minivan and hurried into the house, but the minute the door snapped shut behind her, a strange prickling, like a spider crawling, went up the back of her neck. She had no explanation for the feeling, but it was the same kind of terror that had struck her when Sloane tracked her down in Colorado.

The house was utterly quiet. She could hear nothing but the hum of the refrigerator and the soft ticking of the kitchen clock. Her shoulders turned to rocks and she craned her neck trying to peer around the foyer wall and into the living room.

Nothing.

She jammed her hands into her armpits and took a tentative step forward. A floorboard creaked loudly. Meredith leaped.

Jumping at shadows. This was ridiculous. No one was in the house.

That's what her mind told her, but her gut was saying something else entirely.

Warning! Danger!

Ninety-nine percent. Hondo had been ninety-nine percent sure Sloane was dead. There were only one percent odds that the monster from her nightmares had tracked her to Twilight. That he'd been in her house.

You're being ridiculous, she scolded herself. *Get your cell phone and go back to work.*

She eased into the living room, looked right and then left, darting her gaze up the staircase. Nothing was out of place. Not a throw pillow. Not the remote control. Not even the rag doll Kimmie had left propped against the recliner. The room was just as they'd left it this morning.

Still, she didn't dare draw in a breath of relief. For five years, her internal alarm system had kept her alive. It was hard to switch it off.

She went into the kitchen, got her phone from the charger, and checked both the sliding glass door and the door leading into the garage. Both securely locked.

No reason not to go on back to work, a client was waiting, but she couldn't ignore the creepy-crawling sensation tickling every hair on her skin. She searched the rest of the house, looking under beds and in closets—Kimmie's room, Hutch's room that was still quasi

Ashley's, and the guest bedroom upstairs that had turned into their midnight rendezvous love nest.

In spite of her fears, she smiled in that room.

It was in her bedroom that her heart stood still.

When she opened the door the whisper of aroma drifted out—motorcycle oil, cigar tobacco, and the fetid odor of hing, a smelly spice indigenous to India that Sloane had loved.

Instantly, cold chills broke out over her body, her palms went clammy, and her leg muscles cramped. She couldn't breathe. Didn't want to breathe in that horrific smell.

Run! Get out, now!

But before she could move, the past bulldogged up, smashing her hard in the face, and she was trapped in the talons of a full-blown flashback.

He had her by the hair of her head, long brown hair back then, dragging her across the living room rug, the rough jute burning her elbows and knees as she tried to twist away from him. But she didn't care about the abrasions. They were nothing. What terrified her to the bottom depths of her soul was the cage that he was dragging her toward.

"No," she howled, begged. "Pleased don't put me in the cage!"

"Stop fighting," he said calmly. "You know what happens when you fight."

Yes, she knew, but the menace of that cage was stronger than his threat. She clawed at his hands, digging in with her nails, ripping off hunks of his flesh in a satisfying scrape.

He punched her in the face so hard she literally saw stars—bright bursts of white and yellow lights burned her retina. The pain was so intense, she couldn't think, couldn't move, could barely even feel herself being stuffed into the large wire dog crate.

"You behave like a bitch. You get treated like one." He slammed the door closed, clicked the lock, pulled the black canvas cover down over the crate, dousing her in darkness.

"Please," she whimpered. "Please let me out. I'll be good. I promise."

"You should have thought about that before you served me burnt toast."

"How long?" she blubbered pathetically. "How long this time?"

"If you're completely silent, for a week. But every time you speak, I'll add another day."

She stuffed her fist into her mouth, bit down on her knuckles to keep from crying out. She had to pee, but she wasn't going to ask him. She knew what he would tell her. *Pee on yourself like a dog, bitch.* And then he would beat her for stinking like pee.

That was the day she realized that if she didn't find a way to escape she was going to murder him.

Meredith blinked, hauled in a deep breath, and she was back in her bedroom at Hutch's house. The smell was gone from the room. Had it ever been there? She sank to the floor. Oh God, she thought she'd gotten past this. The scent had been nothing but an olfactory hallucination. She knew that, but she couldn't help feeling that Sloane had been in this room.

With a trembling hand, she lifted the bed skirt and peered under her bed. The lockbox containing the Colt Defender was still there. She felt along the bottom of the bedside table, brushed her fingers against the key taped there, and exhaled in relief.

She was okay. Sloane hadn't been in the house. He was dead.

But just how long was it going to take before it fully sank in that she was finally free of the monster who'd almost destroyed her?

Chapter 19

At 0800 hours on Saturday morning, Hutch peered from the window of his hotel room in downtown Seattle at the street below and pressed the palm of his left hand on the fogged windowpane, leaving the imprint of three fingers, not four.

It was okay. He was learning to live with things missing. Life was never tied up in a neat, shiny Christmas bow. It ebbed and flowed. But Meredith and the kids kept him bolted together. They'd changed his life in so many ways, all of them good.

On the streets below, angry war protesters carried picket signs. "Get Out of Afghanistan."

"War Is Sanctioned Murder."

"Special Ops = U.S. Death Squads."

"Good Riddance to Killer Keller."

That last one torqued him. He clenched his jaw. Michael Keller had been Hutch's best friend.

Misguided rabble-rousers. Protesting something they knew nothing about. Didn't they understand that if it weren't for soldiers, they wouldn't enjoy the freedom of picketing? Mike would have laughed it off, but it sure as hell wasn't fair that protesters were spoiling the memorial for Mike's family.

Somehow, word of the service had gotten out. Delta Force operations were highly secret and there had been no official acknowledgment of the loss of Hutch's team or that he'd been the sole survivor. Nothing in the media.

But no matter how hard the Pentagon tried to keep a lid on Delta Force, people were people, and eventually someone leaked information.

The bitterness that had dogged him after the ambush resurfaced, but he pushed it down, pushed it away. If being with Meredith had taught him nothing else, it was that letting go of resentment was the only way he could find happiness again. She'd been through so much herself, and yet, in spite of it, she was a happy person.

Just thinking of her brought a smile to his lips. Soon. Very soon he'd be home, and his journey would be behind him. He would have kept the promise he'd made to himself, even at the sacrifice of leaving Meredith and the children behind.

It had been the most difficult thing he'd ever done. Going from house to house, grief to grief, sharing in each family's personal anguish. He couldn't begin to express his appreciation to Gideon, Hondo, and Nate for coming along to support him. They were truly the best friends any man could ask for.

The door clicked as a key card was slid home, and

Gideon came into the room. Hutch turned from the window.

"Assholes," Gideon said.

Hutch shook his head. "Holding a grudge doesn't solve anything."

"Yeah, maybe not, but not everyone is as enlightened as you. Hondo talked to law enforcement. The police said there had been death threats and have advised the family to halt the memorial, but the Kellers refused. Their son spent his life fighting against terrorism and they're not about to allow a few rabble-rousers to terrorize them."

Hutch lifted his eyebrows. "Death threats against whom?"

Gideon's face didn't change, but he widened his stance, touched his hip where his holster usually sat as if he felt naked without his duty weapon. "You. Me. Us. Any soldier."

Hutch shrugged. "Washington is a blue state. They have different ideas about things. That's what America is about. Being able to freely voice your opinion."

"Hypocritical if you ask me. Protesting war, but issuing death threats."

"Means someone is human. We're all hypocrites at one time or another."

"You're in a forgiving mood."

"People get hurt, lash out. They're not always rational. Who among us can say we haven't done something stupid we later regretted?"

"Not me for damn sure." Gideon ran a hand over his head. "Either way, you've got built-in bodyguards, because I know you're still going to attend the memorial. Nate, Hondo, and I will be right there with you."

"I know. I can't tell you how much I appreciate you guys."

Gideon came over and gave him a quick, one-armed, masculine hug. "All I've got to say is protect yourself, buddy. I don't want to lose you."

"I don't want to lose me either." Hutch smiled. "I've got a whole lot to live for."

"Meredith." Gideon bobbed his head. "She's a good woman. I'm glad you two found each other."

"So am I," Hutch said, his voice choked with emotion. "I feel about her like you feel about Caitlyn."

"Then you better put a ring on her finger." Gideon grinned like a kid. "Before someone else snaps her up."

"I don't think she's ready for that yet."

"Are you?"

Without hesitating for a second, Hutch said, "Yes."

Gideon punched him lightly on the upper arm. "C'mon, let's get rolling, so we can get back home to the women we love."

In spite of the protesters, the memorial service was a moving tribute to Mike Keller. A barrage of uniformed officers, armed with pepper spray and riot gear, kept the picketers at bay behind sawhorse barricades.

When Hutch saw the pepper spray, he thought of Meredith and suppressed a smile. Mike would have laughed his ass off over the pepper-spray incident and told Hutch that he'd found a keeper.

The Kellers invited Hutch and his friends back to their house for a catered lunch, but he couldn't bear the thought of listening to stories and staring at pictures of Mike when he was young and happy. His parents accepted that, but they did insist that Hutch ride in the limo with them, and when they dropped him off at their hotel, they hugged him and told him that he was welcome in their home anytime and made him promise to keep in touch.

But it was a promise he couldn't keep. He said goodbye knowing he would never see them again. They'd buried the past. Mike was the only thing they had in common. Contact with them again would only bring up their terrible loss.

At 1100 hours he, Gideon, Hondo, and Nate had just stepped into the lobby when Hutch's cell phone rang. He pulled it from his pocket, checked the caller ID.

Meredith.

Just when he'd been thinking of her, she was thinking of him. He grinned because he was always thinking of her.

He answered the phone. "Hey, babe."

"Hutch." Meredith sounded strained.

His body immediately reacted to the alarm in her voice, muscles tensing, shoulders snapping to attention, eyes narrowing. "What is it?"

"I don't want to alarm you unduly," she said. "And I realize my past has made me a worrywart, but…"

He waved to his buddies to go on up to their room without him and maneuvered over to a quiet alcove of the lobby. "Talk to me."

"Ashley picked Kimmie up from school today and Flynn said she's lost ten pounds and looks like she's been crying a lot. I don't know anything about your sister's mental illness. Maybe this is symptomatic of some kind of psychiatric episode. Or maybe that guy she took off with got her into drugs. I'm very concerned." Meredith was talking fast, her anxiety almost palpable.

Hutch's gut flip-flopped. "Where is she now?"

"That's the thing. I don't know. When Flynn called, I rescheduled the rest of my appointments for the day and went home to check on her, but she wasn't there. I tried calling and texting her, but she won't pick up. Who knows? Maybe she doesn't have her phone anymore." Finally, Meredith took a deep breath.

"When did she pick Kimmie up?"

"About an hour ago."

"I'll catch the next flight out."

"That'll cost you a lot of money."

"I don't care. I'll be there."

"Are you sure?"

"Absolutely."

"Really, you could probably wait until your flight tomorrow. I just had to let you know what's going on. I'm a bit of a mess, I confess, but I'll do some yoga and get myself together."

"This can't wait and I don't want to leave you there to deal with this alone. It sounds like Ashley is in crisis. It's happened many times before. Most likely the jackass she ran off with dumped her or did something that caused her idolization of him to turn into pure hatred. It's the black and white flip of borderline personality disorder. I'm afraid she's using Kimmie as her emotional crutch."

"Oh dear."

"Especially since she hasn't come home. My mother used to do stuff like this all the time. After she broke up with a guy, she'd pull us out of school and tell us we were going on vacation. Ashley loved it, but I always resented it. I wanted to be in school."

"That must have been so hard for you."

"Mom would take off without any kind of planning. Sometimes she wouldn't have two quarters to rub together and when we ran out of gas, she'd go up to some guy at a gas pump, give him a sad sob story, and the sap would usually buy gas and give her money to feed us with. One year we got all the way to Florida that way. She said she was taking us to Disney World, but she didn't have money to pay for tickets."

"So your sister is repeating your mother's pattern."

"Yeah, it's bad enough that she disappeared for a month, but now she's back sucking her child into her emotional drama." Hutch gritted his teeth. "I'm not going to allow her to put Kimmie through this crap."

"That little girl is lucky to have you as her champion."

"I just wish I wasn't so far away."

"You'll be here soon. Flynn volunteered to keep Ben until we get this sorted out and now that you're coming home, I think I'll take her up on it."

He could hear the relief in her voice. "I'll grab my bags and head to the airport right now. I'll call you when I get to DFW. If I can get a flight out within the next hour, I should be touching down somewhere between eighteen hundred and nineteen hundred hours."

"What time is that?"

"Between six and seven."

"*If* you get a flight out."

"Let's think positive."

"Good luck."

"If Ashley comes home, send me a text."

"I will."

"And Meredith?" Hutch realized she might not be ready to hear what he was about to say, but he had to tell her. He'd been feeling it for a long time now and she needed to know. Yes, it was probably too soon to say the words, he was taking a risk, but hopefully it wouldn't freak her out.

"Yes?"

"I love you."

The second his plane touched the runway at DFW airport, Hutch turned on his cell phone.

He'd wrangled the last seat when he'd put his left hand, minus his index finger, on the ticket agent's hand. He was also still wearing the Special Forces dress uniform he'd worn to Mike's memorial service.

Gideon, Hondo, and Nate decided to wait until their scheduled flight the following morning. This was a family matter, after all, and they didn't want to intrude.

On the one hand, Hutch missed his buddies. His pilgrimage had been so much easier as part of a team. But on the other hand, Hutch was glad he was alone. He needed time to plan how best to approach Ashley. He had to handle her with kid gloves. It all depended on what kind of state she was in. Reading her moods—which could turn on a dime—was crucial to his success.

He hoped she would answer the phone when he called. Hoped she was still in Twilight or at least somewhere in the surrounding area. She had an eight-hour head start. Depending on how fast she drove and how many stops she made, she could be in New Mexico, Oklahoma, Arkansas, or the Texas Gulf Coast by now.

Just as he was about to text Meredith that he was on the ground, his cell phone rang.

It was Ashley's number.

Relief was a tidal wave. If she was calling him, he

was no longer on her shit list. Thank God for small miracles.

He answered in a light voice as if he didn't know she'd been in Mexico for the last month and had just jerked Kimmie out of school. "Hey, Ashes. What up?"

"Unca Hutch," wobbled a high-pitched little-girl voice.

Kimmie.

The sound of his niece's voice, clearly near tears, was a fist to his gut, and the passengers on his flight ceased to exist. "Honey, are you all right?"

"Unca Hutch." Her voice quavered.

He could almost see her little chin trembling the way it did when she skinned her knee or got some other kind of kid injury. "I'm here, sweetheart, I'm here. Where are you?"

"I dunno," she whispered.

He could almost see her tiny shoulders lift in a half-hearted shrug. "Can you describe the place you're at?"

"It's a room."

"What kind of room?"

"There's two beds in it."

A motel room? "What else is in the room?"

"A desk and a chair and a dresser and a TV and a little table in 'tween the two beds."

"Is the room part of someone's house?"

"No."

So it was not one of the many B&Bs in Twilight. It had to be a motel room. In the background, Hutch thought he heard a man murmur something. Alarm burned up his nerve endings. "Kimmie, who's there with you?"

"Mommy."

"Who else?" He clenched his left hand into a fist, and from his peripheral vision saw the tattooed musician type seated next to him staring at his missing finger.

"Nobody."

"It's okay to tell me the truth," he said. "Is there someone with Mommy?"

"No."

Maybe it had been the television he'd heard or someone outside the motel room. A long moment passed.

"Kimmie?" he prompted, drawing heavily on his old Igloo cool to keep from sounding as panicked as he felt. The last time he'd felt like this was when Ben had been in the snow fort with Dotty Mae's car bearing down on the boy. But he had seen that collision coming. There had been time to call out a warning. Here, he was completely in the dark. "Honey, are you still there?"

"Uh-huh."

"Can I talk to Mommy?"

"She can't come to phone right now."

"Why not?"

The flight attendant opened the door and the passengers sprang to their feet. Hutch had a window seat and even though every instinct in his body was screaming at him to get off the plane and get to Kimmie, his mission was better served by sitting still for the moment and keeping his niece talking.

"She's in the baffroom."

He exhaled. "You called me all on your own?"

"Your pitcher is on Mommy's phone, so I pusheded it."

"That's a good girl. You can call me any time you want." He strained his ears, listening for background noises. His mind was going to unspeakable places he didn't want them to go, but he knew too much of the dark side of the world to assume the best. He didn't hear anything. No man's voice. No TV noises either.

"Unca Hutch."

"What is it sweetheart?"

"Can you come get me?"

"I'll be there as soon as I can, but I need to know where you are. Did you and Mommy drive a long way after she picked you up from school?"

"No."

"And it's just you and Mommy?"

She hesitated again. Why? "Uh-huh."

Her voice was tense and he was skilled at knowing when someone was lying. Trouble was, four-year-old children had trouble telling fantasy from reality. How the hell was he going to find her? He could drive to every motel in town, but that would take too long.

"Okay. Listen to me, honey. They've been teaching you how to read in school, right?"

"I know my alfybet."

"Good girl."

"Wanna hear? A, B, C, D, E, F—"

"That's very good, but for right now, I want you to look around that room and see if you can find something with the name of the motel on it. Is there a drawer in that desk you were telling me about?"

"Uh-huh."

"Can you go over there and see if you can open the drawer?"

"Uh-huh."

"I want you to look inside the drawer and see if there's any paper or a pen in it."

"'Kay."

She must have put the phone down, because he could no longer hear her soft little breathing. His gut squeezed. He punched up the volume on his cell, heard a drawer creak open. Then the sound of little feet padding across carpet.

"I gotta piece of paper," she said, breathless.

"Good job. Is your mommy still in the bathroom?"

"Uh-huh."

"Are there letters on the top of the paper?"

"Uh-huh."

"Can you use your alphabet skills and read those letters to me?"

"'Kay."

He waited. She didn't say anything. Was he expecting too much of her? Most of the passengers had filed from the plane. He tucked the phone under his chin and stood up to retrieve his bag.

"Kimmie?" he asked, fearful that the connection had been lost.

"T," she said.

He exhaled.

"Good job. Keep going."

"W."

"Is the next letter an I?" he guessed, unable to wait through the agony of her painstakingly spelling out "Twilight."

"Uh-huh."

"Is the next one an L?"

"Uh-huh."

"What's the letter after that?" He hadn't felt this much tension in his Delta Force missions. Igloo. Be cool. He guided her through the rest of the word. "What's the next letter after the T?"

There were three motels in town with Twilight in their name. Twilight Inn, Twilight Arms, and Twilight Sands.

Kimmie made a hissing noise.

"What's that, honey?"

"It's the letter that hisses like a snake," she said. "Sometimes I forget."

"An S."

"Yes."

She was at Twilight Sands. Sweat beaded his brow as he raced down the Jetway, dodging around slow-moving people, his heart pounding. "I know where you are, sweetheart. Hang on. I'll be there as soon as I can."

Chapter 20

Driving the distance from DFW airport to Twilight, making the trip that should have taken over an hour in under forty minutes, Hutch pulled into the Twilight Sands Motel.

Mist was rolling in off the lake, deepening the evening darkness to midnight black. He cruised the parking lot, his headlights glaring against the fog, sweeping over the backs of vehicles and the thick privacy hedge of Ashe Juniper shielding the north side of the motel from the highway. At the end of the lot his headlights hit the rear of Ashley's compact powder blue Chevy parked in front of room 127 or 227, depending on whether she was on the first floor or the second. He could go ask the desk clerk, but he didn't want to waste any more time, and he pulled in near the Chevy.

Easy.

His sister responded best to gentleness, especially after she pulled a bonehead move and her self-esteem was in the gutter.

What he couldn't figure out was why she'd come to a motel instead of going home. Then again, he'd never been able to understand the way her mind worked. Things he considered irrational made perfect sense to her.

Instinct had him unlocking the glove compartment and reaching for his gun. Twelve years as a soldier and he felt naked without a weapon, but he'd stopped carrying it on his person because of Meredith and the children.

His hand wrapped around the grip, but he hesitated. Weapons in a domestic situation were rarely a good idea. He moistened his lip. The male voice he thought he'd heard on the phone still bothered him. What if Ashley's Acapulco bed buddy was in there with them? His mind flashed to a time before Ashley had Kimmie, when she was in crisis and got her hands on his gun. She'd threatened to shoot them both.

He let go of the weapon, closed the glove compartment, and got out of the car. A quick scan of the area revealed routine motel activity—someone at the ice machine, a maintenance worker hustling back to the office with a red toolbox under his arm, an elderly woman bundled in a heavy coat against the January wind coming off Lake Twilight, while her leashed Maltese took a leak under the glow of a streetlamp.

But routine could be a guise for nefarious activity. He had lingered at ice machines, posed as a maintenance worker, and walked dogs that weren't his to hunt down targets. And the dark, foggy night provided great cover.

Debating whether to call Ashley, he lifted the collar of his leather jacket and stuffed his hands into his pockets, waiting until everyone disappeared from the area before walking up and rapping on the door of room 127, even though no lights were on inside. If no one was there, then she was most likely in 227.

He raised his hand, but before he could knock, the door opened inward. The room was completely dark. Suddenly he realized just how vulnerable he was. How had he let himself get into this situation?

His instinct cried out for him to crouch and go for his gun.

From inside the room, a man's voice called out, "C'mon in, Hutch, we've been waiting for you."

The hairs on the back of Hutch's neck stood up. Who was this guy? Could he be the man Ashley had gone to Mexico with? Or was it someone else? What in the hell was going on here?

A flashlight switched on and he found himself staring into Kimmie's terrified little face.

Wrapped around her throat was a hairy-knuckled masculine hand, and pressed against her temple was the barrel of a 659 Smith & Wesson fitted with a silencer.

I love you.

The last words Hutch has spoken to her circled Meredith's head.

I love you.

She'd known he was falling in love with her and she was falling in love with him, but hearing him say it out loud changed things. If it had been anyone else saying the words so soon after meeting each other, she would have been terrified; maybe she should have been terrified, but she wasn't.

The only thing she wanted was for Hutch to come home so she could tell him to his face. He'd shown her so much love and kindness that she was no longer afraid of moving fast. When you found your True North, you knew it was right.

She trusted him with her life and the life of her son and that was huge.

He'd sent one terse text at four-fifteen p.m. On ground. She hadn't texted him back because he was driving, and later, she hadn't wanted to interrupt his meeting with Ashley.

But it was seven o'clock. She paced the living room floor, wondering what was going down between him and his sister. Worried if Kimmie was okay. She'd sent Ben over to Flynn and Jesse's until Hutch came home with Kimmie, but now she wondered if that was a mistake. She had nothing to keep her occupied. She tried doing yoga, but she was too agitated to settle.

Her gut told her something wasn't right. Hutch should have called, reassured her. What if Ashley had harmed Kimmie in some way?

Finally, unable to stand the tension any longer, she texted him: Everything okay?

She waited five minutes. Ten. Fifteen.

He never replied.

Hutch sat in a straight-back chair situated between the two queen-sized beds while Ashley, sobbing how sorry she was and begging his forgiveness, handcuffed his hands behind him as the man with the gun directed her. The cold handcuffs clicked tight around his wrists.

The gunman had made him empty the contents of his front pockets on the dresser. His wallet lay there and his cell phone.

Out of reach.

After Hutch had stepped over the threshold, the man, still firmly pressing the gun to Kimmie's head, commanded Ashley to chain latch the door and turn on the light. His niece clung to the flashlight in her hands like it was a lifeline.

"Sit down," he'd threatened. "Or I'll shoot the girl."

Kimmie's chin trembled, and seeing the terror in her eyes killed Hutch's soul. What kind of monster was this man?

A very dangerous one.

Frustration mixed with fury, but Hutch did as the man commanded, sitting down in the chair. Dammit, why hadn't he brought his gun? He would have taken the bastard out with one clean shot through the forehead and never blinked.

In front of Kimmie?

Using Kimmie as a shield, the dirtbag maneuvered around the end of the bed, moving between Hutch and the door.

Once Hutch was cuffed to the chair, the man, who looked like he could have come from a cattle call audition for the role of good-looking, smarmy cop, removed the gun from Kimmie's head and used it to motion Ashley away from Hutch.

The creep was as tall as Hutch, and almost as muscular. A bushy, 1970s porn star mustache saddled his upper lip, and even indoors at night, he wore mirrored aviator sunglasses. "We've been waiting for you."

"Burt Reynolds called," Hutch said dryly, trying to

give no indication how panicked he was to see his four-year-old niece in this ogre's clutches. "He wants his look back."

The gunman raised a wry eyebrow. "Really? That's the best you can do? A line as dusty as a library book on how to program your VCR."

"Sorry, I've had a long flight. Best I can do on short notice."

"Aww, you havin' a rough day, Captain Hutchinson." The man clicked his tongue. "Or should I called you Igloo?"

The asshole knew who he was. Ashley cowered near the door. She was painfully thin, her hair dirty, her clothes bedraggled, her skin marked with blemishes.

"Oh yeah, Captain, don't give me those surprised eyebrows. I've done my homework. I know exactly who my wife is screwing. But where are my manners? I haven't properly introduced myself. LAPD Detective Vick Sloane."

This maniac was Meredith's ex-husband? No wonder she'd been so terrified of him, and little wonder she'd been unable to let go of the idea that he wasn't dead. She'd been right to worry. He just wished he'd listened to her.

"And for the record it is Vick, not Victor. Don't ever call me Victor. It pisses me off when people call me Victor."

"No kidding?" He said it like he was ordering coffee at Starbucks. Multitudinous emotions ripped through Hutch—anger, outrage, grief, regret, sorrow, defeat, remorse, disgust, disbelief—but he couldn't indulge any of them. Not if he wanted to get Kimmie and Ashley out of here alive. "The LAPD labeled you a wanted fugitive."

"Those boneheads? They couldn't find their ass with both hands. And look how easy it was to shake them." Sloane snorted.

"We thought you were dead. In fact, Meredith and I celebrated when we got the news."

Jealous fury crossed Sloane's face, but he quickly tamed it. "Premature of you. The news of my demise has been greatly exaggerated."

"Whose body was in the car you ran into the oil tanker truck?" Hutch asked, trying to keep Sloane talking, stalling for time.

"Don't worry yourself over it." Sloane waved the gun. "Some inconsequential homeless guy."

Hutch fixed his gaze on Kimmie, tried to send her a message with his eyes that everything was going to be all right. That he would get her out of this. Briefly, he flicked a glance over at Ashley. She seemed hypnotized or drugged. It tore him up to think what she must have suffered at the hands of this savage.

"You lured my sister to Mexico just to get even with your ex-wife?"

This time, Sloane could not contain his fury. "You know what she did?" he yelled, spittle flying from his lips. "She took my son away from me. I didn't even know she was pregnant, until I tracked her down in Colorado and the bitch shot me. Now that"—he shook the gun at Hutch for emphasis—"was cold-blooded. You don't treat a man like that. She has to pay for that."

If only Ashley would snap out of it. He could lunge for Sloane, chair and all, giving her and Kimmie time to get out the door, but not with his sister so dazed. *Snap out of it, Ashes.*

"She shot me. You know that? If I hadn't been wearing Kevlar she would be in prison for murder."

"Too bad she didn't kill you."

"Now you're just getting nasty." Sloane yanked Kimmie up tight against him. "Do I need to remind you I can get nasty too?"

Ashley whimpered, covered her head with her arms, and sluggishly swayed closer to the door. Could she be picking up on the mental telepathy he was desperately sending her?

Sloane never even looked around at Ashley. He was too busy ranting against Meredith. "The bitch is wily, I'll give her that. It took me two and a half years to track her down. Of course, faking my own death helped so I could go after her full-time."

Kimmie was a stone statue in Sloane's embrace. Her little hands seemed petrified around that flashlight. It was big and heavy. How was she still holding it up? Had the child gone into shock?

"Imagine my delight," Sloane went on, "when I found her living with a stupid, gullible young woman just begging to fall in love."

Ashley whimpered again.

"Shut up, cow," Sloane said, but he never took his eyes off Hutch or let go of Kimmie. He wasn't that stupid. He knew Hutch was waiting for any kind of opening to charge him.

"You used my sister to get at Meredith." The room was so hot. Sweat trickled down his chest. He wished he didn't have the heavy overcoat on.

Sloane smiled like a shark with dolphin flesh in his

teeth. "Guilty as charged. I do like a good psychological game of cat and mouse, except you showed up and put a kink in the plans. But that turned into my favor too. I got to spend time getting to know your little sister." Sloane licked his lips in a lewd gesture, gigging him.

Hutch iced up inside. Igloo cool. Quelling the overriding urge to murder the bastard. He needed complete control over his emotions in order to get Ashley and Kimmie out of this. He kept his face expressionless and his eyes vacant.

"And something magical happened. My dear wife fell in love with you, putting a whole new weapon in my hands. Imagine the pain she'll feel when she learns I killed her lover boy." He went on in excruciating detail what he intended on doing to Meredith, his lip curling up in sadistic pleasure. "And then I'm going to make her scream for mercy but give her none."

Hutch's rage was a living thing, a beast inside him, carving up his organs with thick, sharp claws, desperate to leap from his chest and kill Vick Sloane.

From where she stood behind Sloane, Ashley moved in excruciatingly slow motion, reaching up to ease the chain lock off the door. Good girl. Hutch glanced away from her for fear of drawing Sloane's attention to his sister.

"Am I making you mad?" Sloane leered and leaned forward. "You want to kill me, don't you?"

You're not a catfish. Don't snap at the bait.

Hutch's calmness infuriated Sloane. "Did you hear me, soldier boy?"

Great. He'd rattled the bastard.

Quickly, he flicked his gaze to Kimmie to see how she was holding up. Sloane had one elbow hooked around her neck and he kept alternating pressing the gun to her temple and brandishing it at Hutch. Sloane was going to pay for this. Big-time.

His niece's lip quivered uncontrollably. Her eyes stared, empty, unseeing. She'd drawn deep into herself to escape her environment. Poor kid. He wished he could wrap his arms around her and promise her that everything was going to be okay.

But it wasn't going to be okay, was it?

Her chubby little hands were still clutched around the flashlight, but gravity pulled it lower and lower until she was barely holding on to the stub.

"Listen to me," Sloane roared.

Kimmie startled, lost her grip, and the heavy Maglite dropped directly onto Sloane's instep.

He yelped and let go of Kimmie.

As if equipped with springs on their feet, simultaneously Hutch and Ashley bounced. He leaped up, still handcuffed to the chair, but he did not have clear access to Sloane. He'd have to go either over the bed or around it.

Ashley, however, had a straight path. She yanked the door open and then jumped on Sloane's back. "Run, Kimmie," she yelled. "Run and hide!"

The little girl darted out into the damp misty night, the door shutting automatically behind her with a sharp click.

Ashley sank her teeth into Sloane's ear, shook her head like a rat terrier with a rodent in its jaws. Encumbered by the chair, Hutch was too slow to help her. As he rounded the end of the bed, Sloane bucked her from his back, spun around and cuffed her hard in the temple with his gun.

She dropped to the floor, slack and unmoving.

Hutch lunged, but Sloane two-stepped backward as he pointed the gun at Ashley's inert body. "Sit the fuck back down, hero. Or I'll blow her… Well, you can finish the cliché."

Furious, Hutch gnashed his teeth. If he weren't handcuffed to the chair, he'd break Sloane's spine in two pieces.

"Sit!"

Fuming, Hutch sat.

At least Kimmie had gotten out alive. Someone would find her and bring the police. But would they arrive in time?

Was Ashley still alive?

He shifted his gaze to his sister. Yes, she was breathing but unconscious, a large red whelp blooming at her temple. His heart belly-flopped. She'd been so brave, sacrificing herself for her daughter, attempting to make amends. He had so many regrets and he knew she did too. Sorrow yellowed his outrage, but he could indulge neither.

"Scoot back," Sloane said.

Grudgingly, Hutch scooted.

"Farther."

He glowered, didn't move.

"Really? You want to see your sister's brain splattered all over the walls?"

Gritting his teeth, Hutch backed up all the way to the wall.

"Much better," Sloane said. "Now you see, I had a couple of scenarios rolling around in my head. There was Plan A…"

Sloane paused as if waiting for a drum roll.

Hutch grunted.

"In which I lure you here by having the kid call you. Check. That part went down smooth as greasy snot. Part two of that plan was to use your phone to send a text to my dear wife and get her to bring my son over here." He spit out the word "wife" as if it was a rancid peanut in his bowl of mixed nuts.

"Ex-wife," Hutch corrected, struggling to keep his tone neutral.

"You know what's coming, right?" Sloane's sadistic pleasure vibrated through everything he did, his words, his face, his body language. He was enjoying this immensely. "You've gotta know how it's bound to end."

Hutch didn't give him the satisfaction of a reply.

Sloane cocked his head. "What's that? You don't want to know the ending?"

Think. Think. He's giving you enough time to come up with something.

"Oops. Sorry. Spoiler alert. Cover your ears if you don't want to hear, but wait, you can't, can you? You're all tied up. And here I thought Delta Force was supposed to be badass."

Hutch knew how to get out of handcuffs. That was no biggie with the comb he carried in his back pocket, but he didn't have time. Sloane could put a bullet in him before he could get his fingers into his pocket.

"So anyway, in Plan A, I make you watch while I kill your sister and your niece. Then I shoot you and the boy and make Meredith watch. Then I play with her for while, and then I kill her too and plant the gun in your hand. I was a police detective, remember? I know how to make it look like a murder-suicide."

"You're going to kill your own son?"

Sloane shrugged. "Eh, easy come, easy go."

Hutch gulped. This man was a certifiable psychopath.

"But alas, the kid just got away and exploded Plan A, so that leaves me with Plan B." Sloane paused again. "Don't you want to know what Plan B is?"

Do not react.

"No? Okay. I get it. When you reach the gates of hell you want to be able to tell Satan you never saw it coming. Good for you."

Sloane pointed the Smith & Wesson at Hutch and fired two rounds into his chest.

Chapter 21

Meredith's phone dinged. Stopping her in mid-pace. She raced over to scoop it up off the coffee table, read the text.

On the way home. ETA 10 min.

She let out a heavy sigh, sagged onto the couch; ankles crossed, and resisted the urge to text back asking about Ashley and Kimmie. He was driving and she didn't want to distract him.

Hmm, should she go get Ben so he could be here when Kimmie arrived? No. What if Kimmie wasn't with him? They'd need time alone to talk out what had happened.

After ten minutes, she roused herself from the couch and went to the foyer to peer out of the long, narrow glass window that gave her a view of the street. Her heart thumped and her palms went sweaty. She wiped her hands against the seat of her jeans and started pacing again, her body twisted tight as the strings on an overly tuned guitar.

Hutch's truck pulled into the driveway and he got out. Head down, he sprinted toward the house.

An instant smile broke across her face and she flung the door open. "I thought you would never get home."

"Miss me?" he asked, and raised his head.

Meredith's eyes flew open wide. Oh God, no! Not Hutch. It was the monster from her worst nightmares. How? How?

Sloane leered at her and shoved his way over the threshold.

Gun, screamed her primal instinct. *Get to the gun.*

She spun around, felt the whoosh of air behind her as he grabbed for hair that was no longer there. The bastard loved dragging her around by the hair.

Gun, gun, gun.

How was she going to get the box unlocked and the gun loaded before he was upon her?

Just move. The gun is your only chance!

She scrambled up the stairs, hearing the heavy thud of his footsteps behind her.

"You think that's a good idea?" he called. "There's no way out from the second floor unless you want to jump out the window."

Panic-induced adrenaline spurred her legs faster, sprinting at top speed, even though it felt to her as if she was barely moving. Nightmare. This was her worst nightmare come to life.

"You can run, but you can't hide," he shouted gaily.

*Just wait until I get my hands on that gun. I'll blast
you to kingdom come, you bastard.*

"Aw, you're not happy to see me?"

She reached the landing, didn't dare look back to see
how close behind her he was. She was done running. No
more. If Sloane killed her, he killed her. Hutch would
take care of Ben. She trusted that completely. Leaving
her son would be the hardest thing she'd ever done, but
she simply could not continue to live in terror. Either
Sloane was going to die or she was.

One way or the other, it all ended here.

Now.

Today.

She darted into the bedroom, turned the flimsy lock
she knew wouldn't hold him for long, but it might buy
her enough precious seconds to load the gun.

Meredith dived under the bed. The box, the box,
where was the lockbox?

Her mind whirled so fast, her emotions so agitated
that she couldn't see what was right in front of her.

The gray metal lockbox.

It was there.

She grabbed the handle, dragged it from underneath
the bed.

Sloane was twisting the door handle. "C'mon, really? You're going to make me kick the door down?"

Hand trembling, she quickly ran it underneath the
table in search of the key taped there. Found it, ripped
it free, and fumbled the key.

Sloane battered the door. Kicking it. *Bam. Bam.
Bam.* "I'm comin' for you. Nowhere to run."

Her breath came in short, quick pants. *Don't hyperventilate! It's you or him.*

Finally, she sank the key home, turned the lock, yanked open the box.

Empty. The box was empty.

The door imploded, wood splintered, hitting her face and there was Sloane grinning manically like Jack Nicholson in *The Shining*.

"Looking for this?" he asked, pointing the .40-caliber Colt Defender at her head.

Oh God. She felt the color drain from her face as her entire body went icy cold. Her heart hammered. Her head spun. No hope. No hope left. She was a dead woman.

In desperation, she flung the empty lockbox at him. He deflected it with his shoulder.

She lunged for the window.

He moved like a panther, caught her, fisted the back of her shirt in his hand, and dragged her backward.

A scream shot from her mouth.

"Don't worry, I'm not going to shoot you," he said. "I've got something much slower and more painful in store."

Meredith snatched at the bedpost, trying to hold on, trying to think, bur her brain was as numb as her body.

Sloane grabbed her by the hair of her head, but because her hair was so short, his fingers slipped.

She kicked ferociously, blindly. Jerking away from him.

Temporarily, he lost his balance, giving her the edge she needed to vault over the splintered piece of door and sprint out into the hall.

"Oh no, you don't," Sloane roared, and tore after her.

She hit the stairs, but in her haste, she misstepped. Down. She knew she was going down. She put out her hands to the wall to keep from falling, but momentum dragged her forward and she somersaulted to the bottom of the stairs.

Before she could right herself, Sloane was standing over her, grinning at her with his Chiclet teeth.

Fear squeezed every last bit of air from her lungs. "Hutch," she cried out. "Hutch, where are you?"

"Aww, isn't that sweet?" Sloane loomed down. "Calling for lover boy."

She tried to scamper to her feet, but he had one leg on either side of her.

"I hate to be the one to break it to you…" He crouched down. "No wait, I love being the one to break it to you. Your Prince Charming isn't coming to save you."

She kicked, bicycling her legs, determined to impair him any way she could.

He grabbed her left heel, flipped her over onto her belly, and started tugging her across the floor. "Wanna know why he's not coming for you?"

She slammed her right foot into his shin. "Go to hell."

He didn't even wince. "I did a bad thing. You are not going to be happy with me."

She clutched at whatever she could get hold of to slow his progress—the leg of the coffee table, the rug, one of Ben's LEGOs that she threw over her shoulder at him. Thank God, she had not gone over to pick her son up from Flynn.

"You see, I put a couple of bullets into lover boy's chest. I'm afraid you're never gonna see him again."

No. Hutch could not be dead. Sloane had a black belt in lying. "I don't believe you."

"That's your prerogative. But I've got his truck and his cell phone. Who do you think texted you?"

Oh God, no. Hutch could not be dead. Sloane could not have won. He could not have bested a Delta Force operator. Bile rose in her throat. She was going to vomit.

Do not throw up.

They were in the kitchen now. The tile was cold against her stomach. She was knocking down chairs, kicking hard, still trying to get away, but he was impervious.

Where was he taking her?

Fight, fight. Go out fighting.

She kicked with every last bit of strength she had left in her body and finally connected with his groin.

"Bitch!" he roared, and dropped her leg.

She went onto all fours, crawling frantically for the back door, and managed to wrench it open, letting in a blast of wet, frigid air before he clutched her shoulders and threw her onto her back. His face was livid, a purple vein throbbing at his temple.

She smashed the heel of her palm into his nose.

He yelped, cursed her, wrapped both hands around her neck, and pressed his thumbs hard into her throat.

An instant headache burst through her brain and bright stars before her eyes. She couldn't breathe. His fingers closed tighter, closing off her airway, strangling the life from her body.

No. Please God, no. She wanted to live for her son.

But it was all slipping away.

In the fog of waning consciousness, she thought she heard the front door slam open. Was it Hutch? Had he come for her at last? Or was it an auditory hallucination? The last winking out of awareness?

A woman screeched. Not her. She couldn't force any air through her throat past Sloane's pythonlike grip.

"You killed my brother," the woman cried out. Ashley. It was Ashley. "Now get your hands off my friend and prepare to die, you sick, twisted psycho."

Pain stabbed Hutch's chest. Every breath he took was like getting bashed in the lungs with a hammer. Yeah, it hurt, but if it hadn't been for those death threats at Mike's memorial service, if Gideon hadn't insisted they protect themselves with ballistic vests, if Meredith's urgent call hadn't sent him straight to the airport without changing clothes, if it hadn't been for his overcoat hiding evidence of the vest from Sloane, he would be dead.

He pressed the accelerator of Ashley's car all the way to the floorboard and bulleted through the dark, misty night, desperate to get to Meredith. He had been knocked out for less than five minutes, but he'd already wasted crucial time hot-wiring Ashley's car. He had no idea what Sloane had done with his sister, or where Kimmie might be hiding, but for the moment, Meredith's safety was paramount. He assumed Sloane had commandeered his truck to use as a ruse to get Meredith to open the door.

Gnashing his teeth, Hutch whipped the steering wheel, guiding the car around the bend leading into his housing division. He didn't have his phone to call for backup. He had to get to Meredith and Ben now!

Almost there. Almost there.

Habit had him reaching into the glove compartment to arm himself, but knowledge hit him. This wasn't his vehicle.

And he didn't have a gun.

* * *

Dimly, Meredith heard a handgun pop, felt the tightening of the band around her neck loosen all at once. A second gunshot reverberated in the close confines.

She coughed, blinked, sat up. Saw Ashley crumple into the doorway, the hand at her throat soaked with blood. The acrid smell of gunpowder burned the air Meredith struggled to suck into her lungs.

Sloane lay a few feet away clutching a kneecap that was no longer there, screaming in a high keen like a wounded animal.

In an instant, her oxygen-deprived, adrenaline-soaked mind read the situation. Sloane had shot Ashley first, but she'd managed to fire off a shot.

Every impulse in her body screamed at her to get away while she had the chance, but she couldn't leave Ashley. Hutch would want her to save his sister. He could no longer do it himself.

On hands and knees, Meredith crawled through Sloane's blood to get to her friend.

"Ashley," Meredith cried, forcing her name past her raw, aching throat.

Ashley's eyes stared vacant, unseeing. Her throat was gone. There was nothing Meredith could do for her. Grief ripped through her. First Hutch. Now Ashley. Sloane had to pay for this.

"Bitch," Sloane cried, and came for her.

Where was Ashley's gun? She scanned the area but didn't see it. Was the gun under Ashley's body?

Forget about the gun. Get out of here while he's incapacitated.

She leaped to her feet, lunging for the back door, but

Sloane was quicker and manacled his hand around her ankle, yanking her down on top of him.

He was wounded. She could beat him.

They grappled.

She punched him.

He punched her.

Blood was everywhere. Ashley's blood, his blood, her blood.

She kicked his shattered leg. He grunted in pain, but he held on tight. Nothing seemed to stop him. He rolled her over, away from Ashley's body and toward the back door.

The motion-sensitive porch light had come on, bathing the deck in a soft yellow glow.

Meredith raised her head, less than a foot to freedom.

That's when she saw it.

Her Colt Defender.

Somehow in Sloane's shootout with Ashley, the gun had landed on the track of the open sliding glass door. That's why he was rolling her toward the door, so he could get his hands on the gun.

She gave a primal war cry, aimed another kick at his knee, but he moved at the same time and she missed. He locked an arm around her throat.

No. She wasn't going to let him choke her again. She had the advantage now.

Aggressively, she jabbed her elbow into his gut, simultaneously pushing herself to her feet, only to slip in blood and almost go down again.

She latched on to the bar and regained her balance, only to look down and see that he was holding the gun.

Sloane stared her right in the eyes, racked the gun, and growled, "You're dead, bitch."

Chapter 22

Hutch pulled into the driveway and heard a woman scream.

Sweat broke out over his body and his pulse thundered. He jumped from the car, crossed the yard in two long-legged strides, and scaled the front steps.

The front door yawned open.

Hutch raced inside, not knowing what terrible thing he would find. In the entryway leading into the kitchen, he spied a woman's body engulfed by a widening pool of blood.

Meredith!

Except this woman had long blond hair. Not Meredith, no, but his baby sister, Ashley.

Hutch dropped to his knees, gathered her to his chest. Her head lolled back lifelessly over his arm. The warmth had already left her body. His troubled little sister had been murdered. Ashley was dead, but maybe, maybe there was a chance Meredith was still alive.

Forcefully detaching himself from his grief, he gently eased Ashley's body down to floor. That's when his knuckle brushed against cold steel.

His gun.

He picked it up. The gun was loaded. He followed the swath of blood to the open back door where the crimson trail led to the deck. Bracing for what he might find, he reached along the wall, found the switch to the outdoor flood lamps, and flipped them on.

Propped up against the rear of the deck, Sloane sat bleeding from his left knee, a belt cinched as a tourniquet against his upper thigh.

Hutch stepped from the house, gun aimed at the scumbag's head. "Where is she?" he demanded.

Sloane looked mildly surprised. "You're not dead."

"Next time you shoot a man in the chest, make sure he's not wearing Kevlar. Now tell me where Meredith is."

"Do it," Sloane taunted, ignoring Hutch's request. His face was the color of ashes. "Go ahead. Shoot me."

Tensed, alert, Hutch approached, racked the gun. "Where is she?"

"Kill me," Sloane roared.

"Tell me where Meredith is first."

"Fine, then I'll kill you." Sloane's hand quivered as he reached for the Colt Defender on the deck beside him, and raised it.

It was Meredith's gun. If he had Meredith's gun that meant…

Hutch shook his head, unable to follow that train of

thought. Deep fear clasped him in a horrific hug. "What did you do with Meredith?"

In the distance, sirens wailed. Someone had called the police.

"Now's the time to do it," Sloane coaxed, sweet tongued as the devil. "You can kill me and say it was self-defense. Everyone will believe you. I'm the rogue cop and you're the Goody Two-shoes."

Delta Force had taught him that the worst thing an operator could do was underestimate an opponent. He knew from Meredith's story of her marriage just how cunning and cold-blooded the man was. Sloane had a gun on him. Hutch was within his rights to blast him into the next dimension.

Sloane had lost a lot of blood and his hand was trembling so hard, the barrel bobbed. In his weakened condition, the weight of the weapon was too much for him. His hand flopped into his lap and he dropped the gun into a puddle of blood. It skidded slickly, fell over the side of the deck, and hit the water below with a splash.

"Looks like you're unarmed," Hutch said coolly. He would not give in to the fear. If Meredith was still alive, she was counting on him to keep a cool head.

"You want to do it," Sloane rasped. "Go ahead."

It would be so easy to pull the trigger, and satisfy the urge for revenge pushing up through him, to dispatch the son of a bitch straight to hell. This vile monster had terrorized Meredith for years, killed Ashley, and left Kimmie motherless. He deserved to die.

He closed one eye and stared down the sight, targeting the center of Sloane's forehead. Before the ambush in Afghanistan, he wouldn't have hesitated to pull the trigger. Sloane was garbage and he needed taking out.

But Hutch had had enough of killing. He would do it to protect those he loved, but Sloane was unarmed. Defenseless. Killing him under these circumstances would be murder, no matter how much the bastard deserved it.

"You've got people snowed with all your high-and-mighty, honorable-warrior crap. But I know the truth." Sloane still had the energy and audacity to wink. "Inside, you're just like me. You know there's no problem that can't be solved with a well-placed bullet."

Anxiety wrapped Hutch in a cloying fist. Sloane was stalling. Trying to keep him away from Meredith. That meant she was still alive. But for how long? No telling what kind of condition she was in.

He stalked closer.

Sloane tipped back his chin, sneered up at him. "You're exactly like me. A killer through and through."

Don't let him get to you. The bastard wanted him to lose control. That's the only thing the son of a bitch cared about. Control.

Hutch pressed the muzzle flush against Sloane's forehead. "Where is she?"

"You know she can't swim, right?" Sloane's voice was getting fainter.

"She's in the river?"

Sloane barely moved a shoulder.

God, that was it. She was in the frigid January water and she didn't know how to swim. His gut listed like a sailboat in a hurricane. How long had she been there?

The sirens were screaming closer, almost here. Meredith was in the water, needing him.

"Final chance," Sloane said, egging Hutch into doing the dirty work so he didn't have to spend the rest of his life in prison. He was no longer a threat. "Do what you do best. Kill."

"Fuck you, Victor," Hutch said, and fired his gun.

Hutch found her clinging to a piece of driftwood a few feet downriver. She was barely conscious, her face battered and swollen, trembling from shock and the cold. She was weak, but she was alive. He scooped her into his arms, treaded water to shore. He didn't even pause to catch his breath, just climbed from the water—both of them soaked to the skin—and carried her up the muddy embankment to the steps that led to his deck.

"You're alive," she whispered.

"I am."

"You came for me."

"I will always come for you," he promised.

She burrowed against him. In spite of everything they'd been through, it was a touching moment that choked him up.

He topped the stairs, walked onto the deck.

"Look away," he told her as they passed Sloane.

But she did not. "He's dead!"

Startled by her declaration, Hutch glanced over.

Sloane had fallen onto his side, and the belt that had been around his thigh was now thrown on the other side of the deck. His eyes were glassy, sightless.

"Oh Hutch," she said. "You killed him."

He looked down into Meredith's face and he saw relief mixed with sorrow, admiration, and disappointment.

"I'm so sorry." Tears rolled down her cheeks. "Because of me, you had to kill again."

Before he could tell her what had happened, she lost consciousness, just as half a dozen sheriffs' deputies converged upon them.

Meredith woke in her bed to find Hutch asleep in the chair beside her. Every bone in her body ached, but she couldn't stop smiling. At last she was finally free of Sloane and it was all because of Hutch.

She turned over onto her back, and immediately, Hutch was awake.

"What is it?" he asked, anxiety cracking his voice. "Are you all right?"

"You really are alive." She reached out to touch his dear face. "I didn't dream it."

"I'm alive," he confirmed gruffly, scooting his chair closer, and took her hand.

"But Sloane said he shot you."

"He did." Hutch unbuttoned his shirt, revealing a chest mottled black and blue.

"Ouch! What happened?"

"Kevlar."

"I'm grateful as can be, but why were you wearing a bulletproof vest?"

He told her about the death threats targeting his friend's memorial service and Gideon's insistence that they protect themselves.

"I'm going to kiss Gideon the next time I see him," Meredith said.

"No you're not." He laughed. "From now on, Meredith Sommers, all your kisses belong to me."

"And Ben."

"And Ben," he agreed.

"Kimmie too."

His face tightened at the mention of his niece's name and he swallowed. "We're a pair, both of us bruised from head to toe. I wanted to take you to the hospital, but you refused to go. Do you remember that?"

She shook her head.

"My doctor made a house call. Checked you out. Other than scrapes and bruises, you're all right physically."

She moistened her lips.

"You'll have to give a statement to the police."

"I know."

They looked at each other, both of them knowing how fortunate they'd been to escape with their lives. It could have ended so differently. It had ended different for Ashley.

Meredith reached out to stroke Hutch's arm. "I'm so sorry about Ashley. She saved my life." She told him about how brave his sister had been, rushing in to defend her and avenge Hutch. "If Ashley hadn't shot Sloane, he would have killed me. Your sister is dead because of me."

Anguish darkened his eyes, matching the torment in her own heart. "It wasn't your fault, Meredith. Sloane is the one to blame for all this."

"I can't help feeling responsible. I brought him into your lives, because of me—"

He laid a finger over her lips. "Shh. Let it go."

She pressed her lips together, allowed sorrow and regret to wash over her and then roll away. "Sloane was the one who lured Ashley to Mexico, wasn't he?"

Hutch nodded and told her what he and law enforcement had been able to piece together. After Sloane had shot Hutch and left him in the motel room for dead, he'd zip-tied a groggy Ashley's hands together and stuffed her into the backseat of the Hutch's truck. A long time ago, Hutch had taught Ashley how to get out of zip ties and he imagined she'd broken out of the makeshift cuffs, found the handgun she knew he kept locked in his glove compartment, and dashed into his house to save Meredith and Ben.

A lump came to Meredith's throat and silent tears shook her body.

He reached out and took her hand, waited for the tears to pass.

"Wait a minute," she said after a while, wiping her face with the tissue he handed her from the box on the bedside table. "Where's Kimmie? Is she all right?"

"She's fine and with Ben at Flynn and Jesse's. An attendant found Kimmie hiding in the juniper bushes in the motel parking lot and called the police. In fact, the whole neighborhood called the police after they heard the gunfire. Twenty-seven calls in all."

"We still have to tell Kimmie about her mother."

"It won't be easy," he said, "but we'll get through it. Our love will get us through it."

"I do love you," she said. "I didn't tell you that when you called because I was afraid of saying the words out loud, but I love you, Brian Hutchinson."

"I know."

"I wished that you hadn't been forced to kill Sloane."

He tilted her chin up, looked into her eyes. "I didn't kill him."

"You didn't?"

"I was going to kill. God knows, I wanted to kill him, but I'm not a cold-blooded murderer. He was weak, defenseless. If I killed him in the condition he was, I would have been no better than he was."

She frowned. "But I heard a shot."

"I'd cocked the gun, and I had so much adrenaline and emotion charging through me, I had to discharge it somehow, so I shot into a tree. In the end, Sloane killed himself by taking the tourniquet off his leg. The coroner said he wouldn't have bled out if he hadn't taken the tourniquet off."

"The coward." She shivered. "But I'm proud of you for not killing him. I don't know if I could have been that kind."

"Neither did I," he said.

She started crying again, thinking of all they'd both lost. "It's so sad."

Hutch climbed into the bed with her, gathering her close. Trembling, she rested her head against his broad, strong chest, and slipped her arms around his waist. He tightened his grip on her, pressing her closer until there was no more space between them.

"I was so scared," she whispered.

"He's gone, sweetheart. He'll never threaten us again."

"It's going to take a while for it to fully sink in. To adjust."

"That's okay. We'll do it together. We'll go to therapy, you, me, Kimmie, Ben." He paused. "I want us to be a real family, and not just for the kids."

"Are you asking me to marry you?"

He took her by the shoulders, moved back so he could peer into her eyes. He looked worried, scared. "Would you say yes if I did?"

Her heart fluttered. "I've been through a lot, Hutch."

"I know. So have I."

"Marriage to me…" She shook her head.

"It wasn't marriage at fault. Sloane was a sociopath."

"I know."

"Are you afraid that I'll—"

"God, no," she rushed to assure him. "I have no doubts about you."

"Then what is it?"

"I'm worried that I'm too damaged to be—"

"Shh, everyone is damaged in some way or another. The trick is not to let it ruin your life. If you allow what Sloane did to you to stop you from taking a chance on us, on love, then he wins."

He was right. She knew he was right.

"Marry me, Meredith. It doesn't have to be right away. We can take all the time we need. But tell me that you'll marry me. Let's put together a family. Let's build a life. We'll sell this house. It's full of too many bad memories. Buy a place together."

"Here in Twilight?"

"Anywhere you want."

"I want it to be Twilight. I love it here, Hutch."

"And I love you."

It might be scary, but she was going to choose happiness. She was going to choose healing. She was going to choose love. She was going to choose Hutch.

"Yes," she said. "Yes to everything. Yes to it all."

He let out a long exhale, smiled deeply. "You and Kimmie and Ben, you healed me. You made me whole."

Happiness swelled against her chest as she looked up into kind eyes that quickly turned lusty as they zeroed in on her lips.

He kissed her hard and she lifted her arms to encircle

his neck to deepen the kiss. He pressed a firm, broad palm against the small of her back, his mouth hot and urgent. She was just as frantic, darting out her tongue, egging him on.

Abruptly, he broke the kiss, leaving her whimpering in protest. *No! Don't take it away.* "Are you really up for this? You're hurt."

"So are you. Love is the best medicine. You're what I need right now. Any and everything else can wait."

"Meredith," he murmured, kissing her again and again.

His self-control was shot, but so was hers. In nothing flat, she was naked on her back, Hutch straddling her, his knees buried into the mattress. "We'll go easy."

She parted her legs and he lowered himself between them, made a hungry noise of masculine approval in the back of his throat. He stroked both sides of her face with his thumbs and peered deeply into her eyes.

Hutch's trembling hands threaded through her hair and he captured her mouth with exalted kisses. He moved inside her, slowly at first, but then urgency swept through them and he quickened the tempo.

She lifted her hips, urging him on, letting him know he didn't have to treat her like fine china. She could handle herself. She wanted the full brunt of him.

Life.

That's what he offered.

Full and robust. Life. She'd been living in the shadows for so long, she was ready to come out into the light and enjoy herself. Enjoy him.

His rhythm rose, claiming her with a thrusting sureness. She surrendered to him, mind, body, and soul. She was no longer afraid. This was where she was meant to be.

He pressed his mouth to her ear, whispered, "I love you, Meredith. I love you beyond measure. Love you beyond the earth and the moon and the stars. Love you until the last breath leaves my body. Love you now, forever, for always. You are my goddess, my queen, my everything. You've rescued me. Saved me from myself. And I want to spend the rest of my days honoring you."

"Hutch," she cried, and grasped him around the waist, pulling him in as deep as he would go, holding on as hard as she could while she tightened her body around him.

His entire body tensed and he breathed her name in a heated gasp, and a shudder rolled through him that matched the one quaking through her. They tumbled, reaching the peak at the same time in a thundering rush, and then lay exhausted and entwined, panting for air, basking in the earthy ebb.

Wet tears dropped onto her face from above, mingling with the tears seeping from her eyes.

"You're crying," she whispered, and touched his face.

"With rapturous joy," he assured her.

They kissed tenderly and held each other for a long, long time.

"I had no idea it could be like that," she whispered. "I never felt anything like this. Have you?"

He dried her eyes and she dried his and they looked into each other past a thousand lifetimes and into a future filled with possibilities.

"Only with you, my love," he assured her. "Only with you."

* * *

A week later, it seemed as if the entire town turned out for Ashley's memorial service. No seats remained inside the church, and overflow mourners lined the sidewalks outside. TV reporters had been roaming the streets for days, interviewing anyone who would talk to them.

Everyone wanted to know about the brave young woman who'd given up her own life to save those she loved. The story had made the national news and piqued the interest of a cable network that specialized in crime shows, leaving Hutch and Meredith to mull over the decision whether to allow their story to be dramatized. On the one hand, taking advantage of what had happened felt a bit like exploitation, but on the other hand, if the program could prevent even one person from going through what Meredith had been through, maybe it was worth considering. Not to mention that the money the network was offering could start a college fund for Kimmie.

A sad smile briefly lifted Hutch's lips. His sister would have loved the attention. In death, she'd gained the kind of respect and adoration she'd longed for in life.

Flynn and Jesse kept Kimmie and Ben during the memorial, but on the advice of a children's grief counselor, they brought them to the graveside services, where Ashley was laid to rest in the family plot. Kimmie was subdued, but she did not cry, and when it was over, she slipped her little hand in Hutch's and said, "Can we go get hot chocolate now?" He wondered how much of it she really understood.

The days that passed were muted and fuzzy and filled with legal obligations. They put the house up for sale and contacted a lawyer about getting the warrant that was out on Meredith dropped. The community rallied around them—bringing casseroles, watching the children for them when they had appointments to keep, offering sympathetic shoulders to cry on.

It was a bittersweet time, of deep sorrow mixed with the heady joy of falling deeply in love. Regretful that Hutch could not save his sister, but honored to be able to care for her daughter.

If the last few months had taught him anything it was this: that he couldn't save someone else, he could only save himself. It all came down to choices. The daily decisions, both small and large, that marked the passing of a life. If he wanted to live in peace, then he had to choose the peaceful path. It was as simple and as complicated as that.

A month later, he got a call from the mortuary saying that the angel headstone carved in Ashley's likeness that he'd commissioned had come in, and they planned a pilgrimage to the cemetery with the children for the following day.

That night, for the first time, Hutch dreamed of his mother and his sister together. It was spring and they were sitting on the dock in Adirondack chairs overlooking the river. Pink mimosas were in bloom and the sweet smell of fresh buds filled the air. Fluffy white clouds bumped across a powder blue sky like carousel horses. They wore flowy white dresses and wildflower garlands in their hair, looking as if they'd stepped from a Monet, soft and blurry and beautiful. They were laughing and talking and sipping peach lemonade.

Hutch stood across the river from them. He waved a hand, but they did not see him. He opened his mouth to call out to them, but shut it closed without uttering a word. They were beyond him.

The clouds parted and the sun came out. Simultaneously, they lifted their smiling faces to the sun, and he woke with the certainty that they were both finally at peace.

The next morning, there was lightness to him that had never been there before, as if someone had attached balloons filled with helium to his heart. He told Meredith of his dream and her eyes widened.

"I had the same dream," she whispered. "Right down to the lemonade, and I never even knew your mother."

Goose bumps went over his body. He had no explanation for them dreaming the same dream, nor did he want it explained. The fact that it had happened was significant enough.

They made pancakes in quiet reverence, and afterward, packed the children in the car for the trip to the cemetery.

Immediately, Kimmie was drawn to the angel statue atop Ashley's headstone. She crawled up to trace her plump little fingers over the angel's face. "Mommy," she whispered.

Meredith darted a concerned look at Hutch. *Should we intervene?*

He shook his head and marveled at how well they communicated without words—a look, a gesture, a touch, and each knew what the other was thinking.

"Mommy's in heaven." Kimmie breathed. "She's an angel."

Meredith placed a hand to her mouth, and tears brimmed her eyes.

"Mommy saveded me from that bad man, but then she had to go away."

Hutch crouched beside his niece, put his hand to her back. He wanted to comfort her, reassure her, but he didn't know what was the right thing to say.

"Heaven is in the sky." Kimmie cocked her head with awe in her eyes as if she'd figured the whole thing out.

In that moment a sunbeam of light broke through the overcast winter sky, and Kimmie's face dissolved into a beautiful smile. She tilted her face up to catch the sun and waved gaily at the sky. "Mommy is in heaven lookin' down on me."

Tears streamed from Meredith's eyes and she quickly turned away.

Hutch gathered his niece into his arms and hugged her tightly. "That's right, sweetheart. Your mama is in heaven looking out for you and she loves you very, very much."

Kimmie's chubby palms patted his cheeks. "Don't cwy, Unca Hutch. It's gonna be okay. I pwomise."

Epilogue

Twilight, Texas
Christmas Eve, one year later

Today, Hutch loved family therapy almost as much as he loved his family.

He sat on the hard wooden bench seat, watching the clock and counting off the seconds until the judge entered the courtroom. Normally, Judge Blackthorne wouldn't be hearing cases today, but after Hutch had done some tall talking, the judge had agreed. Hutch wore a wool suit. It was itchy, but he didn't care, didn't fidget. Both arms were slung over the back of the seat. Dressed in their Sunday best, Meredith sat to his right, Kimmie and Ben to his left.

The diamond wedding ring he'd placed on Meredith's finger a year to the day after his team was ambushed in

Afghanistan glistened in the light. She'd insisted on getting married that day. Something good to memorialize what he'd lost. He still couldn't believe she was his wife.

He'd worked for Gideon for a few months, but decided security work simply wasn't for him, and he took a job as a carpenter and loved it. They sold the house on the river and moved to town in a quaint Victorian just off the square, remodeling it in their spare time. Meredith had just completed a refresher course in nursing and she was excited about starting her new job working in the newborn nursery at Twilight General in January.

From the moment he'd used the Magic Slate to tell Meredith that he needed her, they'd been a team, both made stronger and bonded by their shared goal of caring for the children. Somewhere along the way that bond had turned into something deeper, richer, more textured and complicated.

Because of her, he'd become a better man. The road had not been easy and he knew there would be more ups and downs for them, but there wasn't another soul on earth he'd rather take the journey with than Meredith.

She was the other half of him. The part he'd never really known was missing until he found her. And they were just at the beginning. An entire future stretched before them and he couldn't wait to get started.

Meredith squeezed his hand, and he could feel the excitement pumping through her.

A big grin was welded to his face. Hutch could not stop smiling. All the love these three people pumped into him left his heart feeling as full as the stuffed turkey waiting for them at home.

Their lawyer sat in the row in front of them, along with the children's social worker and the family therapist they'd been seeing. She was there to vouch for them and bear witness to them officially becoming a family.

The side door opened and a robed Judge Blackthorne emerged from his chambers.

"All rise," instructed the bailiff, and everyone got to their feet.

The judge listened while the lawyer presented the case. He looked over the paperwork. Talked to the children, the social worker, and their therapist. Then he called Hutch and Meredith before them.

"Presiding over adoptions is the highlight of my job," he said. He proceeded to pronounce that Ben and Kimmie were now legally Hutch's son and daughter, and Meredith had legally adopted Kimmie.

After hugs and smiles and kisses and photographs, they linked hands and walked out onto the prettiest town square in Texas.

They had all been through so many trials and so much sorrow, but as Hutch looked at his dear family, he knew that he was living a blessed and wonderful life.

* * * * *